S0-ARN-741

Mankind
is the
endangered
species.

*continued . . .*

*For Sherry —*
*MERRY CHRISTMAS!*
*Enjoy!!*

# INVASIVE
# SPECIES

✦

*all my best,*

**JOSEPH WALLACE**

*Joseph Wallace*

**B**
BERKLEY BOOKS, NEW YORK

**THE BERKLEY PUBLISHING GROUP**
**Published by the Penguin Group**
**Penguin Group (USA) LLC**
**375 Hudson Street, New York, New York 10014**

USA • Canada • UK • Ireland • Australia • New Zealand • India • South Africa • China

penguin.com

A Penguin Random House Company

INVASIVE SPECIES

A Berkley Book / published by arrangement with the author

For information, address: The Berkley Publishing Group,
a division of Penguin Group (USA) LLC,
375 Hudson Street, New York, New York 10014.

ISBN: 978-0-425-26949-7

PUBLISHING HISTORY
Berkley premium edition / December 2013

PRINTED IN THE UNITED STATES OF AMERICA

10  9  8  7  6  5  4  3  2

Cover photos by Shutterstock/Getty Images.
Cover design by George Long.
Interior text design by Kelly Lipovich.

# AUTHOR'S NOTE

When do you start writing a novel?

For me, that's a complicated question. My novels usually begin with a combination treasure hunt/rummage sale: I am always accumulating offbeat facts, long-lost stories, and memorable details, usually with absolutely no idea when—or if—I'll be able to use them in a book. Then one day, out of the blue, a story comes together in my mind, and I'm able to say, "Now, *that's* why I kept those knickknacks around!"

I remember the most important inspiration for *Invasive Species*. It was a riveting essay whose title and author escape me (maybe one of you out there can help), detailing the author's move from the familiar northeast to a Texas farm filled with snakes and lizards and other wildlife unlike any he'd ever seen before.

The vignette I remember most vividly involved a wasp: a two-inch-long tarantula hawk, named for the spiders it would paralyze to feed its young.

The author was lying on a deck chair, watching the enormous wasp drag its paralyzed prey toward its lair.

Three times, the author poked at the wasp with a stick, wanting to see if the tarantula, left alone, would revive.

The first two times, the wasp rose in the air and circled around before returning to its prey. The third time, however, it made a beeline straight to a spot three inches in front of the author's face. Lying back in his chair, he was helpless. If the hawk had wanted to unleash its excruciating sting or bite, he couldn't have stopped it.

Instead the wasp just hovered there, staring into his eyes. The message was clear: I'm giving you another chance. You do that one more time, though, and you're dead meat.

Then it flew back to resume its task. And the author, his heart pounding, left it alone.

Interspecies communication between two apex predators at its clearest: a smart, agile, venomous predator telling a human what was what, and the helpless human understanding—and heeding—the warning.

*That* was where *Invasive Species* began.

# ACKNOWLEDGMENTS

You can't develop a long-remembered vignette into a novel without a ton of help. As always, my deepest gratitude goes to my wife, Sharon AvRutick, for many years now my first and most trusted reader. You would not believe how messy my books are before she sees them for the first time.

My children, Shana and Jacob, put up with my tendency to describe over dinner various fascinating, oft-disgusting things about bugs. Then again, they're used to me by now.

I'm grateful to my fellow members of the Marmaduke Writing Factory for gathering, renting the basement floor of a local historic house, and giving me access to the windowless conference room ("The Cave") where this novel was written. It's the best "writers' retreat" I've ever attended.

When you spend most of your time alone in a cave, though, you come to crave human company. Thank goodness for the existence of the Black Cow Coffee Company in Pleasantville and its manager and baristas, including Linton, Emily, Michelle, Danielle, Jianna, Mike, Natalie, Emma, Austin, and Steven. I'm grateful to all of them for putting up with me after my solitary stints writing about the end of the world.

Thanks also to my high school writing students, who always inspire me: Cary, Becca, Violet, and Benji. Special gratitude to Emmalisa Stangarone, who began the year as my writing student and (while also finding time to sing, act, study, and apply to college) ended it as my research assistant. You'll see the results of her investigations into various topics—ranging from terrifying emerging diseases to bizarre cargo cults—in my forthcoming follow-up to *Invasive Species*, currently called *The Slavemakers*.

You can see Emmalisa herself in the book trailer for *Invasive Species*, which can be found at josephwallace.com.

What would I do in these uncertain times without Deborah Schneider, my literary agent? For years now, she's been my sherpa through an ever-shifting publishing environment, putting up with my moods and the fact that I don't ever seem to write the same kind of book twice. My lifetime dream was to publish a novel; if not for Deborah, I doubt it would ever have happened.

I'm so glad that *Invasive Species* landed with Berkley. It's been a pleasure to work with my editor, Natalee Rosenstein, her assistant, Robin Barletta, and the rest of the team. Every journey to publication should be like this one.

If you're interested in learning more about me and *Invasive Species*, check my website (josephwallace.com), my writing group's blog (marmadukewritingfactory.com), and my YouTube channel. You can also follow me on Twitter @Joe_Wallace and find me on Facebook at facebook.com/joewallacewriter. Hope to see you!

# ONE

*Casamance Region, Senegal, West Africa*

**THE SINGLE-PROP BUSH** plane sliced through the base of a towering cumulus cloud and emerged into the brilliant tropical sunshine. Sitting in the shotgun seat, Trey Gilliard took in the explosion of colors: golden light turning the base of the clouds silver, a sky of the deepest purplish blue, and below, the vast, rumpled green expanse of rain forest.

Malcolm Granger's voice came over Trey's headset. "Looks like broccoli."

Trey had heard this before. They'd sat side by side in this two-seater Piper PA-18 many times over the years, Malcolm fighting through wind shear and thunderstorms and clear-air turbulence and air currents that could slam you into the ground like a fist, all to help Trey find what he'd come to see.

"I effing hate broccoli," Malcolm said.

Trey had heard this, too.

"Lower," he said.

He saw Malcolm frown and glance over, his mirrored shades catching the sunlight. But Trey knew he wouldn't have to ask twice. This was what it was like, being Trey's pilot. You did what he said or you flew with him once, kissed the ground when you landed, and never let him near your airplane again.

Malcolm was one of the few pilots who'd come back. In fact, if Trey called, he'd cancel whatever else he had on his schedule and haul this little Piper—or one of the other bush planes he owned—over to whatever forest, desert, or mountainside Trey had staked out.

"What's the fun in life," Malcolm told anyone who asked, "if you don't try to end it every once in a while?"

The sound of the engine changed, grew rougher, as the plane slowed and dipped toward the forest canopy. From above, the carpet of leaves seemed as soft as a huge bedspread, but this was a fiction. Guide your plane into it, and you'd find out soon enough exactly how soft it was.

People in Trey's line of work—and there were a few—had found out. He didn't need to learn it for himself.

Still . . .

"Lower," he said.

Trey was his own boss. He chose when to work, where to work, what he wanted to do.

He knew how lucky he was to be able to live this way, since no one in their right mind would hire him full-time. There were only a few people left on earth who, like Malcolm, could put up with him.

Over the years, though, a few organizations had figured out a way to use what he offered: an aggressive intelligence untethered to common sense; a willingness to take whatever chances were necessary to achieve his goals;

and the ability, above all, to plunge into the wilderness, see everything there was to see, and report back on what he'd found.

Turn the wheel of Trey's personality just one or two degrees, and he might have ended up a mercenary, a soldier for hire. He'd met enough of them on his travels and could see the similarities—foremost, a disdain for staying in one place, for following the rules, and for most of humanity.

The difference was small, but crucial: Mercenaries liked to kill, and Trey didn't.

Instead he preferred to save. To preserve. Which was why he was here now, in this remote region of Senegal, just beyond the line where the savanna ended and the rain forest began.

To see what was here. To see what was worth saving.

The organization paying his bills this time was called the International Conservation Trust. ICT. When they could tolerate working with him, they'd send him to some remote region and gladly forget about him for a while.

He'd disappear into the wilderness, and when he emerged weeks later, gaunt, dirty, sometimes ridden with parasites or feverish from disease, he'd report on what he'd found. What birds were new to science. What endangered mammals were making their last stand. What bizarre eyeless salamanders writhed through pitch-black caves. What plants, whose blooms or seeds might give birth to medicines that could cure cancer, clambered for the light in untracked swamps.

In an age of massive destruction, Trey told them where they should spend their precious resources.

Then off he'd head to another wilderness.

Staying sane, barely, only because he could spend most of his time where no one else would go.

"What do you see?" he asked.

He heard Malcolm laugh. They were fifty feet, no more, above the canopy. The plane bucked and slewed in the warm currents rising from the breathing leaves.

"Trees, Thomas," Malcolm said. "One fuckin' tree after another."

Malcolm was the only person who called Trey "Thomas." Though it was his name: Thomas Hunter Gilliard III.

Trey.

Malcolm pointed with his chin. Trey nodded. He'd seen it, too: a small troop of colobus monkeys, their thick fur red and black against the green. Six of them perched in the canopy's branches, looking up at the plane roaring past them.

Before Trey would disappear into the forest, he and Malcolm would undertake this kind of survey from the air. ICT called them Emergency Assessments, and what they did was allow Trey to identify the least damaged areas. Only then would he return on foot and begin to inventory what was there.

He and Malcolm had been flying a grid here in the Casamance forests for five days. So far Trey had been disappointed. The forests seemed tainted to him, impure. Sure, there were giant kapok trees, monkeys, beautiful birds, an abundance of butterflies down there. But also fresh clearings made by human hands, smoldering fires, and other signs that the forest was being plundered for wood or cleared for farms and pastures.

Maybe he'd come too late. He should have been here five years ago.

He lifted his gaze and felt himself grow still inside. "The hell is that?"

Even over the headset, Malcolm heard the change in Trey's tone. Following the direction of his gaze, he turned the plane to the west. The sound of his low whistle reached Trey's ears.

Perhaps two miles ahead of them, a large expanse of forest was dying. Bare trees looked like contorted skeletons, their branches pointing to the sky like accusing bony fingers. The leaves that remained were yellowing, sickly. As Trey watched, a gust of wind whirled some of them into a dust devil, leaving another bare branch behind.

"Ugly," Malcolm said.

Trey was silent.

"I'll take us north and back east," Malcolm said.

"No." Trey took a breath. "Maintain course."

"But—"

Trey knew. The dying forest lay beyond the boundaries agreed to by ICT and the Senegalese government. It was outside the grid. Trey and Malcolm didn't have permission to fly over.

"Maintain course," Trey said again.

Malcolm kept the Piper flying west. The dying patch of forest, miles in extent, drew closer.

Trey leaned forward, his gaze unwavering. Trying to see, to understand. Was there any kind of industry here? Had some oil pipeline burst, some mining-operation tailings lake overflowed?

Trey couldn't understand how. He could detect no

roads leading from the edge of the inhabited land, five miles to the north, to this stricken forest.

Maybe when they were closer . . .

But they never got the chance. Trey caught a glimpse of a sudden dark form rising from the canopy directly in front of the Piper. The computer in his brain, the part that identified and categorized everything he saw, said: *Bird. Raptor. Black kite. Second-year male.*

Then it struck the plane's propeller and became nothing but chunks of meat and a burst of feathers. A dark penumbra that wreathed the windows for an instant before being whipped away.

The plane's engine coughed, choked. Died.

They flew, glided, in silence. The single propeller on the Piper's nose did not move.

Malcolm, his left hand fighting the yoke, his right reaching for the ignition, said, "Shit." Trey didn't need the headset to hear him.

The plane dipped toward the canopy. Trey braced himself for the impact.

*I'll live*, he thought.

*I'm not done yet.*

They were maybe twenty feet from the topmost limbs when the engine fired. The propeller spun, slowed, then sped into a blur. Malcolm pulled back on the throttle and the plane's nose rose. Just a little.

They hit an air pocket and dropped ten feet. Trey could see butterflies spinning amid the branches below. A tiny pool of water trapped in a bromeliad plant winked in a beam of sunlight.

Malcolm pulled back harder. Again they rose, the engine coughing and groaning. The plane swung north.

Trey lifted his gaze and saw, a mile or so ahead, the edge of the forest, the almost surgical line where the jungle came to an end and the savanna began.

The savanna. Flat land. Fields and pastures and roads, any of which could be used as a landing strip if you really needed one.

Trey knew that the pilot's thoughts were traveling the same track. Malcolm pulled back on the yoke one more time. The Piper fought its way upward, until the rumpled forest was a thousand feet below. Trey could see the yellow grasslands, the gleaming silver stripe of the Gambia River, the blue Atlantic.

The engine died again.

"Hang on," Malcolm said.

The plane glided on the hot, rising air, losing altitude faster and faster even as they came closer to the savanna and possible salvation. Trey looked down and saw the forest reaching for them as they fell. He could see the muscles on Malcolm's arms knot as he struggled with the yoke.

Their destination lay just ahead: a flat grassy field across the Massou-Djibo Road, which ran along the forest's edge. Trey's brain calculated distances and speed, and he knew they wouldn't make it. They were going to hit the trees.

But they didn't. Trey hadn't calculated for Malcolm's cussedness, or his understanding of his little bush plane. Through sheer willpower and physical strength, the pilot wrestled the dead plane over the last line of forest. Vines whipped the wings as they went past, and then suddenly they were a hundred feet over level, treeless ground. The dirt road sketched a red-earth line through the grassland below.

"Hang on," Malcolm said again. The Piper glided, the blurred ground racing just below them. A moment later they made contact, rose a few feet, and then touched down for good and were bumping across the field. Stones kicked up by the tires rattled off the fuselage.

Malcolm brought the plane to a halt. After a few moments' silence, Trey pulled off his headset. "Thanks."

Malcolm shrugged and stretched his arms. "No worries."

Then, scanning the empty landscape around them, he sighed. "Guess we'll have to walk out," he said.

Trey unsnapped his harness, swung open the door beside him. Hot air wafted in, along with the sound of crickets and the staccato call of a red-eyed dove.

"Won't be the first time," he said.

Malcolm laughed. "Or the last."


**THEY STOOD ON** the road. There was no sign of cars, or people, in any direction. A single cow stared at them from a nearby pasture. Clouds were piling up to the west, foretelling storms that afternoon. There were storms in the Casamance every afternoon.

"Gonna get wet," Malcolm said. Then he rolled his eyes. "Yeah, I know: Won't be the first time."

"Let's go," Trey said.

They set off, maintaining an easy pace that still ate up the distance. Both of them were tall, but after that the similarities ended. Trey, an American, was dark, olive complexioned, with deep-set eyes and a strong nose and chin. People said they could never tell what he was thinking, which was fine with him.

Malcolm, who'd grown up in Cape Tribulation, Australia, was more solidly built, with a broad, flat face and blue eyes. If he ever traded this life for a desk job, he'd be fat in a month. His unkempt blond hair was thinning, and his face and freckled arms were always either pink, sunburned, or peeling.

Trey was thirty-six. He'd never asked Malcolm's age, but guessed about fifty.

As if intuiting Trey's thoughts, Malcolm said, "This is where I s'pose I should say that I'm getting too old for this crap."

Trey didn't even dignify that with a response.


**THEY'D WALKED FOR** about a half hour when Trey stopped still in the middle of the deserted road. He leaned his head back, let his eyes scan the sky until they focused on a martial eagle circling, a black cross against the blue sky high above.

Malcolm had seen this behavior before. He wanted to get back to civilization so he could collect his tools and a vehicle, come back, and rescue his plane, but he knew there was no point in interrupting Trey's train of thought.

As they stood there in silence, thunder rumbled in the distance.

Finally Trey allowed his gaze to drop. "Malcolm," he said.

"Yeah?"

"Back then, right before we hit that kite, did you smell something?"

Malcolm blinked. This wasn't what he'd expected. "Did I what?"

"There was an odor rising from that dying forest, something I've never encountered before. Didn't you notice it?"

After a pause, Malcolm shook his head. "Sorry, but if I did, the memory's been wiped clean by the almost-dying stuff that happened afterward."

Trey frowned. Before he could speak, they heard the sound of an engine. Perhaps a mile up the road, a pickup truck was heading toward them. A plume of reddish dust rose in its wake and the sun reflected off its black metal cab. They were about to be rescued.

Trey said, "What's killing that forest?"

Malcolm had no answer.

But it didn't really matter. When Trey got like this, he wasn't really talking to you. He was talking to himself, and you just happened to be in the vicinity.

# TWO

*Mpack, Senegal*

**IF YOU SPENT** most of your life in the wilderness, you learned to be a light sleeper.

Or maybe it was the other way around. Maybe only people who could awaken instantly chose to spend so much time alone in places inhabited by poisonous snakes, scorpions, and spiders, not to mention bigger creatures with sharp teeth and irritable dispositions.

Trey came alert in his one-room stone hut. For the briefest instant—as always—he was surprised to find that he was under a roof, not canvas, the forest canopy, or the sky. Then he was off his cot and getting dressed even as he registered what had woken him.

The sound of a man shouting, followed by a high and keening cry, a woman's voice, quickly cut off.

By the time Trey was out the door, into the damp morning air, there was little to see. A few young boys, already in their uniforms, were kicking a soccer ball around the town square as they waited for school. The doors to all the houses around the square were closed, which was unusual even at this early hour.

Trey knew these schoolboys. He'd caught their attention—and earned their laughter and catcalls—on the town's soccer field as soon as he'd arrived. And some real respect when he'd started to learn Kriol, their local lingua franca, right away.

Since then, they'd usually come running whenever they saw him, asking endless questions about America or showing him the latest lizard, frog, or insect they'd caught.

But now, as he walked into the square, they looked away, refusing to meet his eye. If anything, they seemed a little afraid.

This was interesting. Trey walked up to them, focusing on Moussa, the boy he knew was their leader.

Tall, thin, the most athletic of the group, Moussa held his ground as Trey approached. The other boys scattered, though all stayed within earshot. There was a hum of tension around them that Trey hadn't seen before.

"What was that shouting about?" he asked Moussa.

The boy said nothing, but Trey had expected no different. The unspoken answer, from several of the others, was just as clear as words would have been. They all looked at the medical clinic on the opposite side of the square.

The Diouf Health Center, a compact building of red stone erected within the past decade. A gift from the French government, complete with state-of-the-art scanning and surgical technology, as penance for two centuries of colonization and slavery.

Moussa followed Trey's gaze. "You cannot go in there," he said.

That was never the right thing to tell Trey.

**THERE WAS A** trail of blood, drying black in the warming sun, leading across the square toward the clinic.

As he approached, Trey saw a young man carrying a Kalashnikov rifle step out the front door. Dressed in a ragged camo uniform, complete with the square cap Senegalese soldiers all wore, he looked confused, shaken. Trey wondered if he'd been told to guard the entrance but wasn't sure exactly how. Was he supposed to shoot anyone who came in for Band-Aids or aspirin?

The blood trail led up three stone steps, between the soldier's feet, and under the closed door. Trey walked up the steps and said to the soldier, "Pardon me."

"It is closed," the soldier said. He was eighteen, maybe, with a child's smooth cheeks and no authority but what his gun gave him.

"Look," Trey said, pointing at the sign hanging beside the red wooden door. It read, *Toujours Ouvert.* Always Open.

The man stared at the sign without apparent comprehension. It was quite possible he only knew how to read Diol or one of the other local dialects, if he could read at all. When his gaze returned to Trey's face, Trey said, "Seydou Honso wants to see me."

The guard frowned. While he was pondering his response, Trey walked around him, opened the door, and stepped through into the waiting room.

The room was empty and dark inside. Someone had turned off the bright fluorescent lights that usually made everyone, pink skinned or brown, look jaundiced. The only light came from the blue-green glow of a computer monitor.

Trey took in a breath. The clinic was suffused with the smell of blood. And something else, too, a bitter, acidic odor.

A smell Trey had encountered once before.

The door leading into the examination room hung open, and through it Trey could see a single light burning. Four figures stood there, little more than backlit shadows clustered around the steel examination table.

There was something on the table. The light was focused on it, so Trey could see what it was.

As he made to step closer, two of the figures moved toward him. They came through the door, which they closed behind them.

Even in the shadowy light, Trey knew who they were. Seydou Honso, the physician who ran the clinic—and, according to legend, all of Mpack—and his daughter, Mariama.

Seydou was about sixty-five, with a face so lined and furrowed that it was easy to miss how clear his eyes were, how sharp his gaze. The people at the International Conservation Trust had urged Trey to stay on his good side or risk finding that no one in town, in the Casamance, would help him.

They'd also warned Trey to avoid Mariama Honso like the plague. Slightly built, with a square, determined face and the same piercing gaze as her father, she was no more than thirty. She had already made a name for herself in Senegal. Several names: Activist. Troublemaker. Agitator. She'd spent more than one stint in jail for speaking out against the government's treatment of the people of the Casamance.

Heeding ICT's warning as much as needed most, Trey had invited Mariama out for a drink the day he'd arrived. They'd gotten to know each other a little, and so far the world hadn't ended.

Now the two of them were looking at Trey, as if trying to figure out what he knew, what he'd guessed. How smart he was.

"You must leave," Seydou Honso said in French. "Now."

Trey didn't move. "What is that smell?" he said.

The old man's hands twitched at his sides. His daughter's chin lifted.

"I've smelled it before, you know," Trey said.

Neither spoke.

"Over a stretch of dying rain forest five miles south of the Massou-Djibo Road."

Trey never forgot the reaction this last statement provoked. Seydou Honso's face clenched, his eyes nearly disappearing behind the bunched ridges of his wrinkles. But Mariama's seemed to light up, her eyes gleaming even in the dimness.

"Papa," she said, "we have to—"

"No." The word rang out in the silent room. An instant later, Trey heard the front door open. Footsteps. The end of a rifle poking into his back.

Trey's arm rose to knock the gun away. Then, just barely, he restrained himself and allowed the soldier to push him toward the door.

Mariama's voice came from behind him. "Papa, listen—"

"No," said Seydou Honso again.

SOMETHING TREY HAD learned during his long solitary years in the world's last wild places: Pay attention to anything that doesn't fit. It's usually what's most important.

So as he crossed the square, the young soldier standing on the steps behind him, gun at the ready, he thought about what he'd glimpsed in the examination room.

The four figures: Seydou and Mariama Honso and two soldiers, both as young as the one who'd been guarding the door. The soldiers' faces, Trey had seen, had been filled with fear, even horror as they gazed down at what lay on the steel table.

Trey could understand why. They were looking at another soldier in uniform, lying on his back. Even at a distance, Trey had seen he was dead. His unmarked face had been frozen in its last expression of shock and horror, his eyes wide, his mouth pulled back to expose clenched teeth.

His face might have been untouched, but his midsection—everything from his waist to the middle of his rib cage—was an unrecognizable mass of shredded fabric and meat, glistening with black blood and bits of white bone.

As the Honsos came through the door and blocked his view, Trey had noticed one more thing: The fabric, and some of the man's flesh, was scorched. He'd been shot at closer than point-blank range. Someone had jammed a gun, something powerful like a Kalashnikov, into his belly and fired a burst from it.

Maybe the dead soldier had done it himself.

**MOUSSA WAS CROUCHED** in the center of the square, examining the splatter pattern of dried blood. Already tiny black ants and a beetle the color of an emerald had come to feast on it.

The boy stood when he saw Trey. "Phone," he said.

Trey thought about this. Mpack had no cell-phone service. The only public telephone was located in a concrete shack at the far end of the square, a building people called "the office," because it contained a desk, a chair, and that phone.

Who was calling? It was unlikely to be Malcolm Granger, who was fully occupied repairing the Piper. Anyway, Malcolm hated telephones as much as Trey did. If he needed to say something, he just showed up and said it.

Someone from New York, the closest thing Trey had to a home base? Equally unlikely. He had no family there, and not many friends, few of whom had any idea where in the world he was at any given time.

His brother, Christopher? No. Since Christopher had settled in Queensland, Australia, two decades earlier, he and Trey had spoken only once or twice a year. After their parents died, there hadn't seemed much reason to stay in touch.

Trey sighed, thanked Moussa, and walked toward the office, knowing before he picked up the receiver whose voice he'd hear and what she'd have to say.

He'd heard it all before.

\*   \*   \*

**"WE'RE PULLING YOU** out," Cristina Kendall, his boss at ICT, said.

What Trey had expected. "No," he said. "I'm not done here."

"This is not a request." Cristina was calling from Dakar, the capital city, but she sounded like she was right there in the room lecturing him. "We got the order today," she went on. "You're not welcome in the Casamance, in Senegal, effective immediately."

Trey was silent.

Her sigh came clearly over the line. "So," she said, "who'd you piss off this time?"

He didn't reply. Some strange, clanging music rang down the line.

When Cristina spoke again, her tone had hardened. "Trey, it's—what, about a seven-hour drive from Mpack to Dakar?"

After a moment, he said, "Yeah."

"Well, throw your stuff in your car and start driving. I've told our staff to expect you by evening."

Trey was quiet.

"You hearing me?"

He said, "Yeah."

"Listen," she said, her voice now little more than a venomous whisper. "You're dancing on very thin ice this time, Trey. One of these days you're going to fall through, and no one's going to care enough to pull you out. Got that?"

Trey hung up the phone.

# THREE

CRISTINA KENDALL HAD ordered Trey to return immediately to Dakar. Instead he drove his Land Rover three hours in the wrong direction.

First south from Mpack, then west back along the rutted red-dirt Massou-Djibo Road. He passed the field where he and Malcolm had landed—the plane had been hauled off to Ziguinchor—and seen that it was now populated with cows that, had they been there last time, might have defeated even Malcolm's ingenuity.

On past this landmark another twenty miles before finally reaching the junction of another dirt road. Nearly hidden behind the underbrush that grew at the forest edge, this one took him south again, into the rain forest itself.

Or maybe "road" was too generous a term. It was more like a wide path, a half-imagined thread winding this way and that between the forest's buttressed trees. Trey fought the wheel over ruts and exposed roots, past vines and branches that shrieked as they scraped the car's body, through patches of mud that grasped at the tires.

All the while, as he left the forest's edge behind and approached its heart, the trees around him gained in height and breadth. The canopy rose until it formed a roof 150 feet above him, leaving the forest floor as dark as if night had fallen. Only his headlights and an occasional stray beam of sunshine illuminated his way.

The road petered out for good at the base of a giant kapok tree. Trey turned the ignition key and sat there for a moment, listening to the engine making snapping sounds as it cooled. Then he took a breath, opened the car door, got out, and started walking.

**HE DIDN'T WORRY** about getting lost. Trey had been born with an unerring sense of direction, as if there were some metal inside of him that could always sense the magnetic pole. He knew from the moment he set forth where his destination was, and how long it would take him to reach it.

Just as he was always aware of the world around him. Categorizing. Cataloging. It wasn't even a conscious effort. He registered the whooshing sound of a hornbill's wings as it flapped through the canopy, the distant peeping of the rain frogs, the low grunts of a troop of mona monkeys and the sound they made leaping from limb to limb, like surf crashing against a stony shore.

He saw a giant katydid stride on spindly legs across a leaf, a woodpecker creeping up a massive trunk, a Maxwell's duiker—a small forest antelope—crouching in a muddy depression, hoping he wouldn't spot it.

There was very little Trey missed.

He paused for a moment to squat beside a colony of slave-making ants in the midst of a raid. The attacking horde of big, red ants was routing the nest of smaller black ones. Corpses were strewn across the ground, and the victors were carrying off the eggs and larvae they would hatch out and enslave.

He wondered whether human slaves passing by here— Senegal had been full of them—had ever watched a slave-maker raid and thought: All life on earth is the same.

When Trey stood, the sudden movement brought forth a low, angry snarl from behind a nearby tree. A leopard was watching.

Trey was calm. Aware of his heart beating, the blood moving through his veins, the prickle of moisture against his skin. Aware he was alive.

But not the master here. Not the boss.

He had no primacy in the rain forest. He was just a package of meat and bone, a creature with remarkably few defenses. Soft and fleshy, with no hard shell. No sharp claws or teeth. No ability to run fast or climb effortlessly or leap from branch to branch.

How easy it was to kill a human, if you got one away from the big cities, the stone and steel structures the species built as defenses, as hiding places. As easy as killing a worker termite if you pulled it away from its hardened-mud mound.

The leopard snarled again, from farther off. Today, at least, it would let him live.

Trey smiled. Right then, right at that moment, there was nowhere else on earth he would rather be.

\* \* \*

**WHEN HE WAS** five years old, Trey's family went on a trip out west. They visited four states and a half dozen national parks, but Yellowstone was the place he recalled most clearly, with its bubbling mud pits like something from Mars, its big geysers, its bison and elk and moose. One day there was a storm so violent that a hailstone came down from the sky and cracked the windshield of their car.

It was in Yellowstone that Trey first felt that pull, the desire to just walk away from the car, the road, his mom and dad and brother, to get *out* and just . . . see what was there.

They were picnicking in some rest area, surrounded by tall conical evergreens, a clear brook running down a nearby hill. Christopher, who was eight, was fascinated by the chipmunks that raced around the picnic area, standing up on their hind legs, chattering, begging for food.

But Trey found them boring. Why come all the way out here to look at *chipmunks*? They had chipmunks back home in New York. So these ones were bigger, with different patterns of spots. Chipmunks were chipmunks.

He was far more interested in the big gray-and-white bird that picked apart a pinecone with a thick, sharp beak. The salamander, longer than his foot, he found under a rock by the side of the brook. The grasshoppers that went whirring away from him like tiny toy helicopters.

And the enormous creature that moved cautiously among the trees, keeping out of sight of the picnickers.

Trey, who already had sharper eyes than anyone else he knew, was the only one to see it.

A bear. They'd spotted a few during this visit to Yellowstone, though Dad said that he'd seen many more—forty-eight, in fact—during a trip he'd taken here when *he* was a kid. Black bears, they were called (though one had been brownish red), with cute rounded ears and eyes like black buttons.

"Don't be fooled," Mom had said, as they watched one scratch its back against a tree. "They can be dangerous."

Trey had found that hard to believe.

Sitting as still as possible on the edge of the picnic area, Trey watched the bear move through the woods. He could tell that this one was different from the others they'd seen. Its gray-brown fur, tipped in silver, was thicker, longer. Its eyes, as it focused on Trey, were dark and deep. When it moved, the muscles rippled along its legs and its thick, humped shoulders.

Trey stood to get a better view.

Watching him, the bear made a low grunting noise that he could feel in his chest. He expected someone else to notice, to shout, to come running, but no one did. They were all too busy laughing and tossing peanuts to the begging chipmunks.

The bear backed away deeper into the shadows of the pine trees. Without hesitation, Trey followed.

Missing the caution gene. That was how his mother already described him.

The bear grunted again as Trey came up to it. He could feel the heat radiating from its body, smell its earthy odor when it blew its breath out through strangely delicate lips.

Then it reared up on its hind legs and peered down at him. To Trey, it seemed as tall as the pine trees, as massive as a hillside. It was unbelievably big and powerful, so Trey did what he would have done with anything whose existence he doubted, despite the evidence of his own eyes.

He reached out and touched it.

The bear's fur was coarse, thick, oily but still as scratchy as his dad's cheek when he didn't shave for a few days. It felt hot to his touch, though Trey never knew whether the heat was the bear's or his own.

But mostly what he sensed was the power radiating outward from beneath the fur. The incredibly strong muscles, and beneath them, the engine, the core of the beast beneath his palm. An unharnessed energy that he'd never sensed in his family, in any person, and for the first time he realized that the world was not a pyramid, with humans sitting on top.

The bear flinched and let out a strange, whining cry, but did not move.

Trey closed his eyes. The pure connection between the two of them did not require vision.

But apparently the bear's cry had been loud enough to attract the attention of others. After that, Trey's memories were blurred. He remembered screams, shouts, being knocked down—by human hands—his head banging against the ground. Being carried by someone running, then thrown into the backseat of the car, the feel of vinyl against his cheek.

His mom saying, "Oh, my God, oh, my Christ," over and over.

Both Mom and Dad touching him, lifting his shirt, holding his hand, checking his legs, again and again, as if trying to discover wounds they'd somehow missed the first twenty times they'd inspected him.

Or maybe they were just trying to make sure he was real, just as he'd done with the bear.

The grizzly. That was what Christopher told him it was called. A grizzly.

IT WASN'T UNTIL years later, when he found some newspaper clippings hidden in the bottom of his father's desk drawer, that Trey learned the fate of the giant bear.

Turned out it already had a criminal record, that bear, having previously been convicted of wandering too close to campgrounds and picnic areas. It had never been aggressive, had done nothing more than watch, but you never could tell with grizzlies, so twice it was anesthetized and taken to more remote parts of the park to be released.

Its encounter with Trey was the third strike. The National Park Service brought in a marksman with a high-powered rifle, and the curious bear was shot no more than a mile from the picnic ground.

Reading about the bear's death, alone in his quiet house, Trey felt his eyes prickle. And at that moment, at age eleven, he made himself a promise.

Not to avoid the presence of the wild creatures on earth, but to seek them out.

And to keep them safe by going alone.

TREY WALKED THROUGH the dim forest for nearly two hours. Then, when and where he'd known he would, he saw it:

a brightening in the forest ahead, as subtle as the first wash of light in the eastern sky an hour before dawn.

But nothing as natural as that.

Trey stopped for a moment, looked, listened, and went on.

# FOUR

**HE DREW CLOSE** to the dying forest. The green, stained-glass light that glowed through the unbroken canopy behind him gave way to something brighter, harsher. The wind changed direction for a moment, blowing into his face, and with it came the now-familiar bitter odor.

Only then did Trey realize that the forest around him was silent. Even healthy rain forests can be surprisingly quiet, but this was different. He heard no birdsong, no frogs calling, not the midday shrill of cicadas or whisper of crickets. It wasn't the quiet of a vast natural engine concealing its secrets, but a stillness more like death.

Perhaps a hundred yards ahead he could see a tangle of underbrush. Inside a healthy forest, very few plants grow in the understory; not enough sunlight reaches the ground. Only where a great tree falls, creating a light gap, do vines and thorn bushes and saplings sprout.

Only where a great tree falls, or all the trees are stricken.

What the hell was going on here?

**HE STOOD IN** the angled afternoon sunlight beside peeling trunks, beneath bare, twisted branches. Every step he took, he was forced to kick through piles of leaves, sodden and rotting.

Something was out of whack, and Trey couldn't figure out what. This pissed him off.

He knew that people tended to think of natural landscapes as immutable, never-changing, but of course it wasn't true. Through time—eye blinks, really—glaciers had carved pathways across the world, forests had sprouted and withered, oceans had turned to desert. Nothing stayed the same forever.

And the balance was fragile, especially in the rain forest. Clearing for farmland or industry, the arrival of an invasive pest from elsewhere, humans hunting out keystone species—any one, or a hundred others, could doom an entire ecosystem.

So what was messing with this one?

Only one plant seemed to be thriving in the gap created by the blight: a kind of sprawling, woody vine that Trey had never seen before. Its leaves were a dark glossy green, and here and there he could see its tiny, fleshy fruit, red like a cranberry but smaller and more oval.

The vines spread from tree to tree, sometimes climbing five or ten feet up a trunk before reaching out toward the next. Examining the tree nearest him, Trey saw that the vine didn't appear to be the cause of its blight, at least not in any way he could see.

It gave off a spicy odor that reminded him of ginger.

A hundred feet ahead, directly in his path, lay a thick wall of half-dead brambles, yellow-green leaves and spiky branches interwoven like a cage. Again, this was something Trey had never seen in the healthy forests he'd explored.

Another unfamiliar plant taking advantage of light gaps in this forest. Though, unlike the glossy vine, the brambles didn't seem immune from whatever was killing the trees.

Something jumped near Trey, right at the periphery of his vision. His pulse quickened, but he did not flinch. With careful, slow movements, he turned his head. A pair of bright black eyes regarded him from the depths of a tangle of the vines. A squirrel, it was, a small forest squirrel, its fur mainly dark gray but with a rufous patch on its back.

It stared at him, curious but seemingly unafraid, for a good ten seconds before it turned, revealing a thick, bushy tail, and disappeared into the tangle. Unseen, a second one greeted it with a chuckling call.

Then the forest was silent again. Even the wind had died.

Silent . . . until Trey took two more steps forward. Then he heard it, a sound that made the back of his neck prickle.

Not a rustle like the one the squirrel had made. Not birdsong, or the crash of some large animal navigating the thicket of brambles ahead.

No: a low humming, almost beyond the reach of even

his exceptional hearing. He felt it, a vibration in his bones, in the tips of his fingers and deep in his skull, more than heard it.

Moving silently, he came up to the brambles. The thorny branches wrapped around each other and the trunks of the nearby trees. Though their leaves were yellowish, scraggly, sickly, they were thick enough to block the view.

Ahead, the humming sound rose in pitch and intensity, then quickly died away.

Trey glanced around for some way to climb over the wall of brush, but saw none. The only way through was . . . through.

He began to edge his way into the mass of thorns. One step at a time, clearing the tendrils away, letting them go when they were behind him. Feeling them tugging at him, restraining him, as if in warning.

The smell was much stronger here.

After a half hour, scratched and bleeding, he was almost through. Hidden by the ten-foot-tall stump of a dead tree, he stopped moving and, with great care, pulled away one last half-dead shoot and peered in.

Circled by the wall of thorn bushes was a clearing measuring about twenty-five feet in diameter. The sandy ground within the clearing, as clean and leafless as if someone had just raked it, was molded into strange little hills and hummocks. Atop each mound was a hole, perhaps two inches around.

For ten seconds, fifteen, Trey had no idea what he was looking at. Then something ejected a spurt of sand from the hole nearest to where he stood, followed by a tiny pebble and a piece of twisted root.

And he did know. Partly.

It was the home of a colony of some kind. But of what? The holes were far too big for any ants he knew of, any bees, any wasps. Maybe some minuscule mammal?

Too many questions.

He crouched down beside the stump to wait. Ten minutes later, the answers started coming.

IT BEGAN WITH a rustling on the opposite side of the clearing. At first little more than a slight, dry sound, like fabric rubbed between a thumb and forefinger. Then it grew louder, and a patch of brambles began to shake. Something big was coming through them, something that let loose with a moaning sound as it approached.

For a moment it paused, as if resting. Then, with a last squeal, it burst through the brambles and staggered across the ground into the middle of the clearing.

A monkey. A red colobus, and a big one.

There was something wrong with it. As Trey watched, it stumbled and fell, lying spread-eagled on the ground for a moment. Then it struggled back to its feet, its legs shaking, and turned slowly toward him. When it did, he could see that the skin over its stomach was hugely swollen, as if it were carrying a large tumor beneath its fur.

He drew a little farther behind the tree stump, then held his breath to stay as still as possible. He didn't know what to expect. Would it panic if it knew he was there?

When it turned its face toward him, he saw that its eyes were a silvery white. Was it blind? He couldn't tell.

The monkey took three wavering steps across the clearing before its foot caught on one of the mounds and it fell. This time it just lay there, its patchy fur rising and falling in time to its breath.

Again something moved at the edge of Trey's vision. He shifted his gaze to the nearest mound, the one whose hole he'd seen being cleaned out a few minutes before.

As he watched, a triangular head topped with bulbous, iridescent green eyes emerged. A freakishly thin, black, arched body topped by a pair of crimson wings followed, the wings flickering so quickly they seemed to leave a bloody smear in the air.

It was a wasp. An enormous wasp, maybe three inches long. Trey had never seen one like it before, of any size.

He felt something wriggle in his stomach. There was something about the way it tilted its head to regard the fallen monkey. Something alert, intelligent, calculating.

The wasp perched for a moment atop its mound, unmoving. Then it flew up on humming wings and swooped low over the colobus.

The monkey twitched. Perhaps it could see through its silvery eyes, or perhaps it sensed or heard the vibrations of the wasp's speed-blurred wings. It seemed, in an abject, helpless way, terrified.

The wasp returned to its perch, and only then did Trey notice that it was no longer alone. Others had emerged from their tunnels while he was watching the first. Six more, each seemingly identical, bloodred wings flickering like flags, green eyes turned toward the monkey.

The first one traced a few steps, changed the rhythm of its wing beats, and lifted three inches into the air before settling back onto its mound. When it was still, a second one took flight, streaking upward so quickly that Trey felt his stomach twist.

A moment later the wasp reappeared, plummeting toward the colobus, landing with an impact that came to Trey's ears as a dull, dead thud.

The monkey's eyes opened wide, and its mouth gaped as well. Its arms and legs flailed, as if it were trying to run, or fight back.

Moving on spiderlike legs, the wasp ran back and forth over the monkey's back. Then, without warning, it lifted the skinny black tube of its abdomen. Its stinger slid out, as white and sharp as a needle made of ivory, and plunged deep into the flesh of the colobus's neck.

The monkey cried out. Its eyes wide, its mouth hanging open, it grew still, and Trey wondered if the sting had killed it.

But then it stirred, the wasp still perched on its neck. Stretched its legs, drew in a deep breath, and slowly got back to its feet. It seemed, if anything, less shaky. Stronger than it had been. When it turned, Trey could see that red-tinged drool was dripping from its open mouth.

The wasp rose into the air, flew back to its mound, landed, and took a few seconds to clean its front legs with its mandibles.

Then it turned its head to look at Trey.

At that moment he realized that it had known he was there all along. All the wasps had. They'd just had more important business to conclude before dealing with him.

Trey stood as still as possible, but he knew it was hopeless. Wasps' eyesight was much keener than humans', and, unlike some lizards and other animals, they didn't rely on their prey moving to be able to see it.

The wasp leaped in the air and flew arrow-straight at his face. At the same moment, the colobus snarled and, moving with startling speed, rushed across the clearing toward him.

Even though Trey's brain was telling him he'd get trapped in the brambles if he didn't plan his escape carefully, his body wasn't listening. He recoiled and felt the thorns scratch the skin of his neck and arms and grab hold of his clothes. In an instant, he was trapped.

The wasp came on. Reared up. Hovered three inches from his face. Behind it, the monkey crouched to leap. Then it paused, silvery gaze on him, froth bubbling around its mouth, as if waiting.

Waiting for orders.

The wasp's green eyes stared into Trey's. Its thin abdomen, the sheath for that needlelike stinger, pulsed.

Any second, Trey expected to see the stinger slide out, expected the hovering wasp to swoop forward the last three inches, expected to feel the needle puncture him, expected . . . what?

Agony.

For five seconds at least, however, the wasp made no move toward him. Instead it stayed virtually still, swinging just a little this way and that in the air, its triangular head swiveling so that its multifaceted eyes never left his face.

Almost, Trey thought, as if it were figuring something out.

Making up its mind.

Then it did. Swinging upward, it paused for a moment at its apogee, then swooped down like a dart.

Trey closed his eyes.

And heard a crashing sound in the brush behind him.

He opened his eyes to see the wasp draw back. It

swung away, made a big loop around the clearing, and vanished down its tunnel. The others, too, had disappeared. The colobus was clambering through the tangles at the farside of the clearing.

The crashing got louder. Now Trey could recognize it: the sound of a blade meeting wood. A moment later, he felt the brambles tear away from his hair and clothes.

A hand grabbed his arm and pulled. Half stumbling, he fought his way out through the brush, then stood there, his legs shaking.

A slightly built woman in black pants and a ragged, long-sleeved white shirt stood before him, machete hanging by her side. Its blade was stained with thick sap that pooled and dripped from its sharp edge.

She was looking away, toward the clearing, but when she turned her head Trey knew who it was. Mariama Honso, her eyes wide, her expression filled with alarm mixed with a kind of exultation.

Before he could say anything, she stepped forward and hugged him. Enveloped him in her arms for a moment before letting go.

It wasn't a hug of relief, he knew, or affection, or any emotion he recognized. He didn't have any idea why she'd done it.

He said, "What—"

But Mariama was listening to something else. Trey heard it, too: the humming of wings.

Her gaze found his.

"You fool," she said. *"Flee."*

# FIVE

**THE PLAN HAD** seemed simple when Mariama hatched it. She'd go after Gilliard, that brave, foolhardy, strange American visitor. Arriving in time, she'd prevent him from getting himself killed, then bring him back. On the way, they'd stop someplace quiet, private.

Mariama had thought the Etoile Bar in Ziguinchor would serve. There her father, Seydou, would join them. Together, they would explain to Gilliard what it was he'd seen, and what it meant.

What it meant for the world.

Soon. If not this month, then next, or the one after. They were sure of this, Mariama and Seydou. It had already begun.

And then, once he believed, they would tell him what he needed to do.

And pray that he understood.

\* \* \*

**MARIAMA WAS YOUNG,** but already she knew many ways that a seemingly foolproof plan could go wrong.

This one began to go wrong with the phone call. The call Trey had received after visiting the health clinic and seeing the dead soldier. Mariama and her father, still at work in the clinic, didn't learn of the phone call for more than two hours. By then Trey was gone, heading on his suicidal mission to the forest.

Already almost beyond her reach, and very likely doomed.

Still, she had to try.

Too much depended on his staying alive.

**THEN HER CAR,** her beloved 1983 Peugeot 305, ran over a sharp stone on the Massou-Djibo Road and had a flat tire. Thirty miles from her destination. Listening to the flapping of the slack rubber against the washboard dirt as she guided the car to the edge of the empty road, she almost despaired.

In her mind, she saw Trey moving in his strange, cat-like way through the forest. She'd followed him once, and thought he was quicker and quieter than anyone she'd ever seen, besides herself.

She'd even thought he might have spotted her, and *no one* ever saw Mariama if she didn't want them to.

She imagined him now, following the hints, the clues he'd picked up these past few days. The dying forest. The dead man on the clinic table. The smell.

Using his unusual skills to race to his death.

And she wouldn't reach him in time. It was hopeless. She knew that. She hoped his pain wouldn't be too overwhelming before the end came.

But Mariama Honso had never given up on anything, hopeless or not. She was as hardheaded as a rhino.

All life was hopeless, but you kept living anyway.

She changed the tire, got the car back on the road, and drove.

**SHE FOUND GILLIARD'S** Land Rover where she'd thought she would: where some long-vanished logger had given up his foolish attempt to build a drivable track to the giant, immensely valuable hardwood trees that grew deep in the forest. The end of the road.

Mariama climbed out of her car, bringing only her recently sharpened machete with her. As she went past the Land Rover, she placed her palm against its hood. It was cool to her touch.

More evidence that she was too late.

She went on.

**TREY HAD LEFT** few signs that he'd passed this way, but still Mariama was able to follow. A broken branch, flower petals scattered where he'd brushed against them, half a footprint in a patch of mud. She knew where he was going, into the part of the forest that no outsider should ever enter.

And then, at the very heart of the forbidden place, she saw him. Standing there on the edge of one of the colonies, trapped in the thorns of the volor plant. But alive. Still alive. She was amazed.

As she drew closer, she could read his expression. A mix of fear . . . and fascination.

That was unusual. Most people, facing what he was, showed only pure, unadulterated terror.

She felt like shouting at him, but that was the worst thing she could do. He would jump, struggle, become so enmeshed in the volor that it would take hours to extricate him.

Worse, *they* would be startled by her voice as well. And when they were startled, they attacked. They bit and stung. Paralyzed or killed.

They. The thieves.

So, even as her brain screamed at her to hurry, to run, to yell, she moved slowly, carefully. Coming up behind Gilliard, she cut through the brush with her sharp blade. Clearing a path for him, if he would only take it, if he would only notice.

Beyond him, the thieves retreated. They knew her. They knew Mariama.

But this still might not be enough.

Finally he was free. Waking as if from a dream, he turned to look at her. His eyes were wide. She could see that he understood what had just happened, how close he'd come.

He took a couple of steps away from the colony. Mariama went up on her toes and wrapped her arms around him, just for a moment. He stiffened, pulled away from her, but she held on a little longer before letting go.

He had no idea why. Of course he didn't.

It was one of the things she needed to tell him.

Only not now.

"You fool," she said, to make sure he was listening, but also because it was what she thought of him. *"Flee."*

When he was gone, she turned to face the thieves, hanging in the air, watching her through those green eyes that seemed to understand everything.

But then again, she did, too.

EVEN THEN, EVEN after Mariama had saved him, her luck was bad. She hadn't thought to tell him to wait for her where they'd left the cars—and he hadn't. She shouldn't have been surprised. She'd already seen that this odd American spent as little time with other adult human beings as he possibly could.

Then a storm struck as she was driving back. The Peugeot had to fight through grasping mud, where Gilliard's fancy Land Rover had undoubtedly plowed right through. It took her twice as long to get home as it had taken to reach the forest.

Still, Mariama wasn't worried. There was plenty of time for Trey to hear what she and her father had to tell him.

Only there wasn't. By the time she made it to Mpack, her white car now a spattered reddish brown from the drying mud, he was gone. Gone forever.

The village children were waiting to fill her in. When Gilliard had arrived, he'd been met by a group of soldiers who had flown down from Dakar. Soldiers and a woman, a skinny American woman who'd shown up burning with anger.

Standing where everyone could see them, she'd yelled at Gilliard. Her voice was as high-pitched as a fish eagle's (she also resembled one, the children said), and she talked so fast that even those who understood some English couldn't follow her.

When she'd taken a breath, Trey had turned and walked away from her. He'd gone into his hut. Five minutes later, he'd emerged, carrying his pack and some other things, and climbed into the car with some soldiers and the angry woman.

"Do you think he'll come back?" the children asked. They liked Gilliard. He was strange and generous, two things they appreciated in outsiders.

"No, I'm afraid not," Mariama said. "I think he's gone for good."

As she spoke the words, she felt a black space open in her chest, just around her heart.

"HAVE THEY PUT him in jail?" she asked her father that night. They were in the empty clinic. It was clean, scrubbed down, disinfected. You could only detect the thieves' odor if you sat still and breathed deeply.

Seydou Honso shook his head. There might even have been a glint of amusement in his eyes.

"No," he said. "The government has no interest in keeping him. They just want him out. The soldiers were the lady's idea."

"That was Kendall? The one who was always calling?"

He nodded. "I think she believed the only way to get him to listen was to bring men with guns."

Mariama said, "That was probably true."

They sat in silence for a while. Now there was no expression on Seydou Honso's face except for a kind of grim certainty.

"I fear we have missed our chance," he said.

Mariama had known he would feel this way. She said, "No."

"But who else will listen? Who else will understand what is taking place?"

"There are others," she said. "But Gilliard is the one to tell them."

She thought about his expression when she found him in the forest. Yes, he would understand.

"But how?" Her father turned his palms up. "He's gone, and he won't be welcomed back. Ever."

"I know," Mariama said.

"And calling him on the telephone won't work, no more than it did for that Kendall lady."

"No."

"Then what?"

"I will go see him," she said.

Seydou's eyes widened. "But how? You have no passport."

This was a fact. Mariama's outspokenness had led to her losing her right to travel anywhere outside Senegal. She even required permission to leave the Casamance region.

Legally, that was.

"You know how," she told her father.

He stared at her. Then he said, "You cannot."

"I can. I must." She reached out and put a hand on his strong arm. "Papa, I have no choice."

He argued with her. Finally, almost breathless, he said, "You'll die."

She smiled. "Perhaps I won't," she said. Then, "Or perhaps I will. You know I have never feared death."

Nor had he, not for himself. She knew that. Every day he risked malaria, dengue, river blindness, and a hundred diseases that had no name, in order to treat the clinic's patients.

He had no fear for his own life. For hers, though, yes. Of course.

Mariama said again, "I have no choice."

In the end, he knew it was so. "But not right away," he said. "There are people I can talk to, people who will help you."

She nodded. Though she didn't speak, she knew he understood her gratitude.

"If I'm lucky," she said, "how long will it take to reach him?"

"Weeks." He grimaced. "If you're very lucky."

"Will they get there first?"

He flicked a hand eastward, toward the vast rain forests of Central Africa and the savannas and deserts beyond them. Then west toward the Atlantic Ocean and the New World.

All the places the thieves had already reached, or soon would.

"First, second," he said. "Does it matter?"

Mariama said, "I have to believe it does."

Seydou Honso smiled at his daughter, his expression full of love and grief.

"I know you do," he said.

# SIX

*Ujiji, Tanzania*

**THE FIRST THING** Sheila Connelly's gaze always sought out, every time she rode the Lake Tanganyika ferry from Kalemie, Congo, to Ujiji Port, was the mango avenue beyond the marketplace.

The mango trees had been standing for two centuries or more. By now they were bent and twisted, their branches hung with weaver birds' nests, their trunks riddled with holes where the ravages of time and weather had rotted them out. But still surviving, still flowering each year, their boughs still heavy with fruit in the right season.

Ujiji's mango avenue had long provided shade for the caravans of goods that crossed the lake from the vast, untracked forests of Central Africa and headed east. Sculptures and tapestries and weapons of many kinds, and foodstuffs, and slaves.

Countless thousands of slaves. Men and women captured in the forests of the Congo, carried across the lake in the bilges of ferries like the one Sheila was riding now, then driven on a death march across the plains and deserts of East Africa to their ultimate destination: Arabia.

Sheila wondered if the captives had known, as they stumbled, bound and whipped, past the fruiting trees, that these mangoes would be the last reminders of their tropical home they would ever see. Did any of them ever reach up and pluck a ripe, sun-warmed fruit as they passed, or had they been too terrified that they'd be punished if they did?

The hulking steel ferry, the *Uhuru*, let loose with a blast from its horn and, spewing dirty white water, approached the wharf. Sheila dragged her eyes and thoughts back to the present and scanned the harbor area. There were plenty of people there waiting for the ferry, but her mother didn't appear to be one of them.

This was typical. Undoubtedly Megan Connelly was somewhere in the crowded marketplace, haggling over something she'd decided she had to own, picking up some last-minute supplies for Sheila's visit, or merely shooting the breeze with vendors she'd known for years.

Sheila couldn't blame her. The markets were still the lifeblood of a port city, of a society. Even now, you never knew what you might find: bins full of tiny bananas, totems wrought of rosewood by artists from some barely known rain forest tribe, wooden spears with stone points.

And, instead of slaves, disease. Mystery pathogens. Unnamed viruses and bacteria brought on the ferry from their birthplaces in the heart of Africa.

Sheila knew more about the diseases than anything else at the Ujiji Market. She was a physician, out of her residency just five years, who'd signed on to work in the overflowing refugee camps of the war-torn countries of Central Africa. She'd thought it important to repay some of the debts owed by the world's wealthy societies to those who'd been dealt a worse hand.

But standing by the rail as the ferry docked, Sheila wondered if this part of her life was reaching its end. She was wearing out, losing interest.

She knew the signs of burnout. She'd seen enough of it.

**MEGAN CONNELLY SEEMED** tired, too. Worn.

"What's wrong?" Sheila said as they hugged. "You look awful."

That was Sheila. She always said what was on her mind and had no patience with those who didn't. This had tended to make her life noisy and tumultuous.

Pulling away a little, Megan smiled up at her. "There's this thing that happens, love," she said. "Experts call it 'getting old.'"

She had a point. How old was she now? Sixty-one? -two? Old enough that the years were beginning to take a toll, laying down lines across her forehead and around her mouth, turning her fair skin papery, bringing out spots on her hands. Megan had been too active throughout her life to ever develop severe osteoporosis, but she seemed a little more stooped than she had six months earlier, the last time Sheila had seen her.

Still. There was more. A gray undertone to her skin. Something odd about the whites of her eyes.

"I'll examine you later," Sheila told her.

Megan laughed. "Oh, you flatterer," she said. "You'll have me in my grave before lunch."

Then she returned to her daughter's inspection. "I like your hair," she said. "What there is of it."

Since they'd last seen each other, six months earlier, Sheila had gotten tired of her long coppery ponytail. So she'd cut most of it off, giving herself something approaching a pixie cut.

"How about this?" she asked, half turning to reveal the new tattoo on the back of her left shoulder, peeking out from under her sleeveless white shirt. A regal sunbird with wings spread, all glittering green and yellow and red.

Megan's eyes widened. "How many is that?"

"Just three."

"I remember," her mother said, setting off toward the market, "when Ariel stickers were enough for you."

"Long time ago," Sheila said.

"Seems like yesterday to me."

THEY STOPPED AT the stand run by the same old woman who'd been selling fried corn cakes with cane sugar sprinkled on top for as long as Sheila had been coming to the market. Twenty years it was now, ever since her mom and dad moved here on a three-year mission with the Presbyterian church, fell in love with the place, the people, the African light, and decided to stay.

Twenty years out of Sheila's twenty-nine. She could hardly imagine what it felt like not to live in Africa, which was another reason why, after graduating from medical school, she'd come back.

She'd also wanted to be close to her parents, though not too close. On the same continent, at least.

"A *shilingi* for your thoughts," her mother said.

Sheila smiled.

"I'm still hungry," she said.

The market stalls sold corn cakes, wooden carvings, textiles, weapons . . . and bushmeat.

The bodies of wild animals taken from the vanishing forests to the west and denuded savannas to the east. Hunted with bows and arrows and wire snares and Kalashnikov semiautomatics, then brought back to the towns and cities.

Too many Africans still considered the eating of wild game a birthright, and would do so until all the game was gone.

The crowd around the bushmeat tables was large and boisterous. Sheila, pausing, saw whole baby crocodiles; rain forest rats, piled four to a stick, with their mouths pulled back into rictus grins; civets smelling like swamp water; tiny antelopes with legs as delicate as green sticks; a sliding pile of algae-scummed river turtles, still barely alive.

On the next table over were piles of smoked monkey meat, brown and dry like old leather. The guenons had been transported whole, their heads bent back over their bodies by the smoking process, while the larger mangabeys and colobuses had been hacked into steaks and burned-fur-covered limbs.

Sheila had lost her appetite.

Her mother's hand touched her arm. "Let's go, honey."

Sheila hesitated. Then, just as she made to turn away, the crowd stirred, parting before something new. Three living baby chimps, tied together with ropes, pulled by a slab-faced man in dusty cotton pants, a shirt that had once been white, and a faded old baseball cap with what looked like a bullet hole just above the brim.

Orphans of the bushmeat trade, these babies were. Worth more alive to zoos or medical laboratories than for the meat on their bones. Two of them seemed merely exhausted and terrified, clinging to each other and staring up at the faces in the crowd. They were making little moaning sounds, calls to their family that would never be heard.

The third had had a rougher time. Its eyes were glassy, its arms and legs quivering. Its stomach was swollen, Sheila saw, most likely from malnutrition. It wouldn't last long now.

"Sheila," her mom said, more insistently, "I've seen more of these than I'd like, these past months. Let's go."

The sound of the baby chimps' cries followed them almost to the edge of the busy marketplace.

**"OKAY," SHEILA SAID.**

Dinner over, they were sitting with their coffee on the porch of the compact house Megan and Scott had built here, outside Ujiji. The sun was dipping toward the horizon, and the cool evening breeze was chasing away the afternoon's huddled storm clouds. It would be another gorgeous starlit evening, perfect for the kind of companionable quiet that Sheila craved.

But first there was something they needed to take care of.

It was a ritual. Her parents hadn't believed in visiting doctors except in emergencies. There had been a few of those over the years, a fracture here, a kidney stone there, that had necessitated the hour-long drive to the nearest hospital, in Kigoma. Since Sheila had become an M.D., the Connellys had waited for her occasional visits for more routine checkups.

This system had worked fine until Sheila's father had died of a sudden heart attack two years earlier. Sheila had always wondered if waiting for her visit had cost her father his life.

Megan, face a blur in the encroaching darkness, said, "Can't we do this tomorrow morning?"

Sheila knew that if they waited, some obstacle would come up in the morning, another in the afternoon, and soon enough she'd be back on the ferry and Megan would have escaped her checkup.

"I don't want to know" was Megan's mantra.

"Nope," Sheila said. "Now."

With a sigh, her mother got to her feet.

"You're not going to find anything, you know," she said.

Sheila thought, *I hope not.*

**MEGAN'S BLOOD PRESSURE** was low, as were her pulse and temperature. None of them outside the normal range, but all lower than usual.

Sheila sat back and thought about this. Her mother stayed silent.

They were in the small room, once a study, that Sheila had insisted they turn into an examining room and storage area for medical supplies. Clamps, scalpels, forceps.

Splints and bandages. Antibiotics to ward off infection, epinephrine in case of allergic reactions, rabies vaccine, gamma globulin. Pills for fever, for stomach disorders, for Megan's migraine headaches, for whatever other treatable malady Sheila could think of.

Nothing to treat a sluggish pulse and heart rate, though. Not until she knew what was causing it.

"Diagnosis, doc?" Megan said lightly.

Sheila shook her head. "I'm thinking we'll have to pay a visit to Nyerere."

The hospital in Kigoma.

"No need. I'm fine."

Sheila didn't bother to argue. "Off with your shirt," she said. "I want to listen to your lungs."

With a shrug, Megan unbuttoned her blouse. Slipped it off. Half turned to drape it across the table beside her. Turned back and gave her daughter a bright-eyed look, as if to say, "Can we get this over with?"

But Sheila barely noticed. She was staring at the exposed skin between the bottom of her mother's white bra and the top of her blue cotton pants. And trying to breathe.

Megan's belly was swollen, round, as if someone had surgically implanted an inverted bowl under her skin. Dead center in the swelling was a round black hole, perhaps a third of an inch across.

*Tumbu fly larva,* Sheila thought. *It must be a tumbu fly.*

Anyone who lived in tropical Africa for any length of time had encountered tumbu flies. The adults were innocuous, just one among a billion small winged creatures that infested the tropics. But they had a clever survival trick: They were parasites. And they used large mammals to host their young. Horses, cows, antelopes, and gazelles. Dogs.

And humans.

The eggs, laid on the ground or in wet laundry, would hatch into tiny larvae. As soon as one came into contact with a potential host, it would grab hold and then eat its way through the skin and into the flesh.

It was a perfect home, the mammalian body. Warm, safe from predators, providing abundant food and moisture as the larva matured.

The first sign of tumbu fly infection was usually a myiasis, a tumorlike swelling that indicated where the tunnel lay. A round opening in the skin, which the larva used as an airhole, confirmed the diagnosis.

But tumbu fly myiases were tiny, since the larvae rarely exceeded a few centimeters in length. This swelling was different. Judging by the size of the swelling and the airhole, the larva within would have to be huge, a couple of inches long. The biggest Sheila had ever seen.

As she watched, something wriggled just below the surface of her mother's skin.

"Sheila?"

She raised her eyes. Megan was staring at her curiously.

"Sheila, what's wrong?"

Sheila wet her lips, but still her voice was a croak when she spoke. "Mom," she said, "why didn't you tell me? You should have gone to the doctor days ago!"

Megan blinked. "Tell you what?"

Sheila ground her teeth so hard she could hear them. "This," she said, pointing. "This!"

Her mother's gaze followed the direction of her finger.

For a long moment she stared at her swollen belly, but when she lifted her head her face showed no comprehension.

"I don't know," she said.

Sheila felt a kind of cold fear spread outward from her heart. But she had to set it aside. There would be time for more questions later. She had a job to do.

"Well," she said, "let's get this thing out of you. I'd guess you've got an allergic reaction going on there, too. I'll put you on prophylactic antibiotics and an antihistamine. The swelling should go down fast once it's out."

Talking to herself, that was what she was doing. Her mother was simply staring at her, as if she hadn't understood a word. There was definitely something strange about her eyes.

Sheila stood, stepped over to the supply cabinet, found two ampules of lidocaine hydrochloride. The first she injected near the airhole, to anesthetize the area.

"Don't."

Surprised, Sheila glanced up into her mother's face. Megan had always been a stoic. Once, though gray-faced from the pain of a broken arm, she hadn't protested as Sheila had rigged a field splint, nor during the long, bumpy ride to the hospital.

"Almost done," Sheila said, trying but failing for the same light tone she used with her young patients. "Just sit still."

Megan said, "No. Please. *Sheila*."

Sheila wanted to put her hands over her ears. Without responding, she squirted the second dose of lidocaine through the airhole to calm down the larva. It was a lot easier to pull out a sleeping worm than a wriggling one.

As the anesthetic sluiced into the burrow beneath the skin, she saw a flash of writhing white come to the surface of the airhole, then something black, and then white again.

Her mother spoke no more. Nor did she make a sound when Sheila reached in with her sterilized thumb forceps, got hold of the larva, and slowly pulled it out of the hole.

She could see at once that this grub came from no tumbu fly. Those were oblong, resembling white kidney beans.

This larva, however, was two inches long, with an opalescent white body; big eyes like pearls made of onyx; soft, half-formed legs; and curved black mandibles. Even as she stared, it twisted its body into a U shape and, seemingly unaffected by the lidocaine, bit viciously at the end of the forceps.

Sheila felt her heart thud against her ribs. Over the years, she'd evicted her share of scorpions from various bedrooms, bathrooms, and tents, often using forceps much like this one to transport them safely. She'd always marveled at the tensile strength of the armored creatures, an inherent will to survive that she both admired and feared.

But she'd never felt anything like the strength that seemed to course through this writhing larva. It mashed away at the forceps with its powerful mandibles, creating a vibration that Sheila could feel through her fingers and all the way up into her forearm. Without thinking, she tightened her grip on the handle.

And then, just like that, the larva died. Some grayish goo came out of its jaws, and suddenly it was just a limp wormy thing hanging from the forceps' metal tips. A bitter smell filled the room.

"Christ," Sheila said. "Mom, what the hell *is* this?"

But Megan didn't respond with words, only with a low, guttural groan.

Alarmed, Sheila looked up, but even as she did Megan's eyes rolled up so only the silvery whites were showing. Her mouth stretched wide.

Sheila had barely dropped the forceps and begun to reach out when her mother toppled sideways and fell to the floor.

# SEVEN

*Manhattan*

THERE WAS A big cockroach in Trey's subway car, a water bug like the ones you see scattering from the light in the bathrooms of third-rate hotels all over the world. Not a native New Yorker—an invader of a species from the forests of Asia—but it didn't seem to care. To a roach, one warm, dirty, food-rich environment is as good as another.

Trey watched it scuttle over to investigate some sticky yellowish stuff, maybe spilled soda, on the orange plastic seat across the car from his. Tan in color, flat as something that had been stepped on, it looked alert, energetic, fully alive.

And alien.

Somewhere in our nervous system is an inherent belief that all other creatures are in some way like us, that we can relate to them, understand their thinking, get inside their heads. We make cats, dogs, parrots, even lizards human in our eyes, ascribing our emotions to our pets to justify the food, housing, and love we offer.

But the truth is, if you got inside a cockroach's head, you'd find plenty of nothing. No brain, no control tower for the central nervous system. In fact, if you decapitate a roach, it doesn't die. It doesn't even take a break from running around. True, it can't see, but the only severe damage you've done is to deprive it of the ability to eat. A headless roach will live on until it starves to death.

This is not a creature we can relate to, no matter how hard we try.

The train pulled into the 81st Street station. As it jerked to a halt, the cockroach hustled across the seat and inserted itself into a crack that Trey doubted he could have slid a dime into. He got to his feet and saw, as he stepped out of the car, a young woman sit down right in front of where the roach was hiding.

Most likely the bug was now going to hitch a ride home in the woman's Coach bag or in a pocket of her North Face jacket or snuggled in the fleece lining of her Uggs.

It was perfectly adapted to life in this big city.

Certainly better adapted than *he* was.


"HEY, HAMLET," JACK Parker said. "What are you pondering?"

"Cockroaches," Trey said.

Jack stared at him for a moment. "Well," he said, "you're in the right building, the right floor, but the wrong office. Cockroaches are down the hall."

He laughed. "Cockroaches *and* the men who love them."

Jack was a senior scientific assistant in the Department of Entomology at the American Museum of Natural History. Short, squat, bearded, with a bald head and a barrel chest, he looked like a battering ram and had a personality to match.

The two of them were sitting in Jack's office on the fifth floor, where most of the museum's staff scientists worked. Its anthropologists and paleontologists and ichthyologists and experts in biodiversity and extinction, all laboring away here, mostly hidden from the public.

And entomologists, too. The people who studied insects, bugs, and spiders.

There were more entomologists at the museum than scientists in any other field. This made sense, since at two million species (give or take thirty million), there were more insects, bugs, and spiders than all other creatures in the animal kingdom combined.

"They should make a permanent exhibition about cockroaches," Trey said.

Jack growled. This was a sore subject for him.

No visitor to the museum would realize the abundance—or importance—of entomology at a glance, since there wasn't a single permanent exhibit anywhere in the public areas dedicated to bugs. Dinosaurs, of course. African mammals, sure. Meteors and gems and ancient peoples and even New York trees. But no cockroaches or butterflies or walking sticks or rhinoceros beetles. When it came to arthropods—insects and spiders, basically—no nothing.

Jack had a simple theory about why this was: People were idiots.

"They fear what they don't understand," he said. "And you don't go to museums to see things that terrify you. You make horror movies about them."

Jack would know. He could recite the dialogue from just about every grade-Z movie ever made.

The people who were terrified of bugs would have fled screaming from Jack's office. It had originally been a nondescript room like so many others in the building: four peeling walls, linoleum floor, grime-streaked windows overlooking Central Park West and the park across the way. Just another chamber in the hive, until Jack had decorated it with mementos of his own area of expertise: the order Hymenoptera. Bees, wasps, and ants.

Specifically: wasps.

On his big oak desk were trays of specimens borrowed from the collections room, each containing rows of little yellow-and-black hornets whose black-eyed gazes seemed filled with rage even in death. The bookcases were filled with everything from reference books to penny dreadfuls ("Attack of the Wasp Woman!"), and every other surface was covered with sculptures, postcards, beer cans, and other knickknacks, all variations on the theme.

"What have arthropods ever done to deserve their evil reputation?" Jack asked.

"I'm about to tell you," Trey said.

**THE TWO OF** them had met more than a decade earlier. Trey, emerging from four weeks assessing a vast, empty stretch of foothill thorn scrub in northern Peru, had encountered a multidisciplinary museum expedition that included Jack. No one there ever forgot the contrast between Trey's dirty, ragged, half-starved condition and the opulently equipped expedition.

Unexpectedly, the chance meeting had also marked the beginning of a friendship. Just about the only lasting friendship Trey could claim, and one that most people didn't understand. How could the explosively, unstoppably enthusiastic and talkative Jack have anything in common with Trey, who spent so much time observing and analyzing the world around him that sometimes you forgot he was there?

Trey had wondered about that himself.

Jack's thick arms were crossed over his chest. "What are you talking about?"

Trey didn't answer.

After a moment, Jack said, "People are whispering about you, you know."

"Yeah?"

"Yeah. They're saying you had your butt kicked out of Senegal and got fired by ICT."

Trey was quiet.

"They basically disappeared you, except you ended up here instead of Guantánamo."

This was true enough. A short flight on a military airplane and Trey had been in Dakar, three hours after that he'd left Senghor Airport on a Senegal Airlines 747, and less than seven hours later he'd disembarked at JFK.

Feeling disoriented. More disoriented than he'd ever felt before, and he'd been traveling his whole life.

And also curious. When he'd gotten into trouble before, he'd always known why. But not this time.

He brought himself back and looked at Jack. "ICT can't fire me, since I don't work for them."

"They can stop giving you assignments."

This was true as well.

Jack blinked. "Jesus," he said. "Jesus, Trey, you're, like, famous. You're the guy who always does whatever the hell you want, and always gets away with it."

Trey closed his eyes. He saw the wet gleam of the ivory white stinger. The agonized monkey. The wasp hovering just in front of his face, deciding whether he should live or die.

He opened his eyes again to find Jack staring at him. "Shit, Gilliard," he said, "what the hell happened out there?"

Trey said, "Get your pencils."

**JACK WAS A** brilliant draftsman. Two centuries earlier, he might have been an itinerant artist-scientist, traveling the world with paints and collecting jars. Producing works like those that now hung on the office walls. A John James Audubon of the insect world.

But those times had passed. In the modern era, his artwork was known only to those who read his journal articles. And to his friends, who were often faced with the challenge of finding the perfect place in a small apartment to hang a portrait of, say, a tarantula-hawk wasp attacking its prey.

Over the years, Trey had often seen—but not captured—insects that didn't yet exist in the scientific literature. Jack's crystal-clear reproductions based on his descriptions had existed long before actual specimens were collected, when they were at all.

Knowing the drill, Jack sat down behind his desk,

rummaged, pulled out his case of artists' pencils and a sketch pad. Then looked up and said, "Okay. A bee?"

"Wasp."

A gleam in Jack's eye. He loved wasps. "How big was it?"

Trey held his thumb and forefinger three inches apart.

Jack's mouth turned down at the corners. "Come on, Trey."

Trey's fingers didn't move.

"You sound like a civilian, the kind who mistakes a housecat for a mountain lion."

Trey said, "But I'm not, am I?"

"Not what?"

"A civilian."

Jack stared at him, and now there was a kind of desperation in his expression. "Trey, the largest known wasp on earth, *Scolia procer*, isn't that big!"

He made a gesture over his shoulder at one of the old prints hanging on the wall. It showed a fat black-and-yellow wasp whose wings extended from its back like an airplane's.

"That's not what I saw," Trey said.

"I know! But—"

"The ones I saw were bigger," Trey said. "Can we get started?"

Jack drew in a breath. His face was a little red. After a moment, though, he lifted a hand and held it over the pencils. "Okay," he said. "Color and shape of the body?"

"Black," Trey said. "Skinny like a mud dauber. Arched abdomen."

Sitting in an old armchair across from the desk, he spoke. For twenty minutes, the only sounds other than his voice were the distant hum of traffic down on the street, the scratch of the pencils, and Jack's questions making sure he was getting the details right. The color of the wings. The angle of the head. The size of the mandibles.

When he was done he held up the picture, a nearly perfect representation of the wasps Trey had seen. All that it was lacking was the sense of menace, of calculation, of intelligence that came to Trey whenever he closed his eyes.

The soul.

"You *saw* one of these," Jack said, as if he still couldn't quite believe it.

"I saw a colony of them." Trey sat back a little in the chair. "In a forest that was dying."

Jack stared down at the drawing, and when he raised his head his eyes had a different look. Trey had seen it many times before. It meant his friend's mind was engaged. It meant he was ready for the hunt.

"The whole story, please," Jack said.

**AGAIN TREY TALKED.** It was a requirement of his occupation, talking—if someone was paying you to go look, they expected you to tell them what you'd seen—but one he hated. Usually when he was done being debriefed, done talking to fund-raisers and scientists and whatever press was interested in his explorations, he'd disappear into the wilderness again. Making up for a few days of noise with weeks of silence.

Jack was quiet, looking down at his desk, at the drawing. For someone who loved the sound of his own voice, he knew how to listen, too.

Only when Trey was done did he look up. "That smell," he said. "Was it formic acid?"

The characteristic odor of ant colonies, the acid found in their stings . . . and wasps', too.

Trey frowned. "No. Not quite. It was . . . stronger."

He was much better describing what he'd seen than what he'd smelled.

"And the dead man you saw had the same odor."

"The room did, at least."

"And you think the wasps were going to kill you."

"I think they were considering it."

Jack frowned. Opened his mouth as if there was something he wanted to say, then shook his head as if he'd changed his mind. What he finally said was, "But the sting didn't kill the monkey. You said being stung made it . . . more alert. Aggressive."

Trey said nothing, just turned his palms up.

"Do you think they attacked that woman after she rescued you?"

Trey shook his head. "I tried calling the village to ask about her," he said, "and no one there will speak to me. But—"

"But she didn't seem afraid?" Jack widened his eyes. "Suicidal?"

"No. Determined." He struggled to find the right word. "Powerful."

Jack grimaced. "I hate this shit."

"What?"

"Having a few pieces of the puzzle, but not enough. And not having access to the rest of the pieces."

"I know." Trey felt weary. "But I'm not getting back

into Senegal anytime soon, and I don't know how else to get the other pieces."

Jack stared at him for a few seconds. Then he gave a sudden grin. "You're so clueless, you make me seem like Stephen Hawking. I admire that in you. You really don't know what to do next?"

Trey shook his head.

Jack's eyes flicked over to the laptop computer that sat open on his desk. The screen saver showed not wasps but, unexpectedly, a litter of golden retriever puppies.

"Well, I do," he said.

# EIGHT

*Nouadhibou, Mauritania*

THERE WAS NO space on the dhow for Mariama.

She'd spent days with the Ndoye family, hiding from officials amid the donkey carts surrounding the market-place and among the villagers mending fishing nets down near the beach. Waiting, just waiting, for someone to sell them transport out of the country.

The Ndoye family: an old father and mother, both of them thin, tired, and gray before they'd even left the shore. Their grown children and younger ones, too, along with some cousins, or maybe they were friends, or simply people they'd met along the way as they'd met Mariama. A dozen in their group at least, maybe more, including one girl, perhaps fourteen, who stood out for her quick smile, friendly manner, and unquenchable optimism.

The girl reminding Mariama of children she'd known in Mpack, children she doubted she'd ever see again.

None of them here expected ever to see again the places where they'd been born. All that mattered now was that they'd scraped together the thousands of francs needed to commission an old fishing boat and its captain. A boat like the dhow the Ndoyes got, so rusty in the fittings and wormholed around the hull you marveled that anyone would trust it beyond the ocean's blue edge.

Mariama wanted to warn them, to tell them to wait for a sturdier craft. But it would have been useless. You took what you could get, and if hunger and thirst and storms and those European Union patrols—ships from Portugal and planes from Italy and who knew what else— if they weren't going to stop you from trying, then a leaky old boat wouldn't, either.

If the Ndoyes hadn't taken the dhow, then the next group would have. The next group being Mariama and other men and women she'd met here in Nouadhibou. The next batch of the uncounted refugees who came here every year from Senegal and Morocco and Mauritania itself, all with a single goal in mind.

To reach the Canary Islands.

Islands that for some reason were part of Spain, even though they were located right off the western coast of Africa. Once you made it to the Canary Islands, the refugees had been told, it was easy to reach the real Europe, where there were jobs, food, a new life.

For most of them, this was their first trip from home. Not for Mariama, who had visited Paris, Johannesburg, and New York with her father. A few years earlier, when she still had a passport, she wouldn't have had to travel this way. She would be stepping aboard a comfortable jet at Senghor Airport.

Instead she'd come to this little port town, just another body hoping for passage out. Carrying with her nothing but a few pieces of clothing in a cloth satchel, extra money in a leather belt under her shirt, and just one memento from home: a locket containing a photo of her father, hanging on a tarnished silver chain around her neck.

**MARIAMA ENDED UP** on the *Sophe*, a twenty-foot wooden boat that she thought seemed sturdy and strong enough. There were twenty-two of them on board, packed tightly against the rails and across the slippery wooden deck. Twenty-two plus the captain, who had a sharp face and quick eyes that didn't miss anything.

They departed from an unlighted dock on a pitch-black night speckled with cold rain. Staking a place by the rail near the back, Mariama helped an old man and a mother with a little daughter settle beside her.

Prayers rose and tears fell as they left shore, but Mariama stayed silent and dry-eyed.

**DURING THE FIRST** two days, they saw three EU patrol boats and one spotter plane. None were close, and none noticed their little boat amid the waves.

On the third morning they came upon the old dhow carrying the Ndoye family. It had set off two days before them, but there it was, foundering in a patch of choppy ocean under a slate gray sky. They could hear the engine grinding, but it wasn't making any progress.

"It's taking on water," someone said.

They could all tell that.

"What do we do?" someone else asked.

They were only a few hundred meters away. Some of the dhow's passengers had noticed them as well and had begun waving cloths and shirts to get their attention. Mariama thought she saw the teenage girl she'd met on-shore.

"We must rescue them," said the old man beside Mariama. "Otherwise they will all die."

Their captain shrugged. "That is not our concern." His canny eyes were cold. "Look at us," he said. "Look at our boat. Can we take on more passengers? Even one more? No. We would just sink as well."

Everybody looked. He was right: There was no space.

"We will make room for some," the old man insisted. "We cannot leave them all."

Already they could see that the captain was guiding their boat away from the dhow. "Which ones?" he said. "Which will we choose? No. They will all try to climb aboard, and we will all die."

Behind them they heard a splash, another. Two of the young men had abandoned the dhow and were swimming toward the *Sophe*. But they were too far away, much too far, and how much strength did they have? If they were like Mariama, they had been eating little but rice and plantains for days—weeks—on their journeys.

The captain didn't look back, though Mariama saw his mouth tighten at the sound of the splashing. The old man's gaze caught Mariama's, but he did not speak again, and nor did anyone else.

Behind the swimmers, beyond their pumping arms and kicking legs, Mariama could see the ones that had stayed behind. Some were bailing, throwing water off the dhow's deck with their cupped hands. But others, the old and the children, were still waving, and some were just sitting there, staring at the departing *Sophe*.

It happened quickly. First the two swimmers gave up. One turned back, but the other, perhaps the victim of cramps or dizziness, began to splash around in circles. Soon he was thrashing in one place, and then, as they watched, he slipped below the surface, leaving behind only a tiny crease in the water, and then nothing at all.

The boat itself followed just a few moments later. Echoing over the water came a dull cracking sound, followed by a puff of black smoke that rose a little way into the air before being blown away by the wind. The front of the boat rose from the water, as if it were being pushed upward by a hand. It stood still for a moment, looking like the fin of some sea creature. Then it slid down and back, smoothly as a blade, and was gone.

Mariama had twisted around to see small forms leaping into the water before the dhow disappeared. Now she turned away and looked up at the captain.

But he stood straight, staring at the western horizon.

**AS THE SUN** sank, the swells grew larger, the clouds thicker, the winds sharper. The boat labored forward against the confused currents. Even the ocean itself was fighting to keep them in Africa.

The old man beside Mariama had fallen into a kind of wordless trance after the sinking of the dhow. On her other side, the mother, a tough, wiry woman from Mauritania, tended to her daughter, who looked about six.

The girl seemed unwell. She'd spent most of the journey with her eyes closed, and her dark skin seemed underlain with gray.

"She does not like the motion of the boat," the woman said. "She will be fine when we reach land."

Mariama did not speak. She knew the truth, but there was no point in sharing it.

The woman said she was headed to London, where she had family. She shook her head as she said it: In this small boat, miles and miles from land, it was hard to imagine a place like London even existing.

"And you?" she asked Mariama.

"New York."

"So far away. Why?"

Mariama hesitated for a moment before saying, "There is a man I need to find."

"In that whole big city?" The woman laughed at her. "Good luck!"

It seemed impossible to Mariama as well.

**ON THE AFTERNOON** of the fourth day, as they shared the last of their water, Mariama spotted a brown stripe on the horizon to the north. "Fuerteventura," the captain said.

Their destination.

No. Their way station.

As the sun headed toward the horizon, the stripe grew larger, longer, became the coast of an island, a distant beach. Behind the beach they could see a jumble of houses painted in bright colors and, farther away, the gleaming white and pink towers of tourist hotels.

The captain pulled back on the engine, left it rumbling just strongly enough to keep the boat in place, bumping in the gentle swells flowing out from the island. "We will make land after dark," he said.

So they waited, watching the sun sink and the big jet planes coasting into the airport.

Mariama sat with the mother and daughter. The little girl was worse. Though she seemed to be awake, and would nod or shake her head when asked questions, she rarely opened her eyes.

When the sun dipped below the horizon, the captain aimed the *Sophe* at the beach. The houses and hotels were lit like stars, constellations, and still the jets came in from Portugal and England and Italy. The same countries that supplied boats and planes to keep Africans out of the Canary Islands sent thousands of their own citizens to the same place.

The woman looked down at her daughter, then back up. "Will you help us get to shore?"

Mariama paused and then said, "Yes. Of course."

The woman's smile reflected the light of the hotels, the silvery water. "Then we will finally be safe."

Mariama thought, No.

No, we won't.

WHEN THEY WERE perhaps fifty feet from the beach, the captain brought the boat to a halt. Over the subdued mutter of the idling engine, they could hear music. But the beach itself seemed deserted.

"The tide is low, and the water is shallow," the captain said. "I cannot go in any farther."

One by one, stiff on their feet, the men and women

clambered over the side of the little fishing boat and splashed into the water. Some made little sounds of fear as they went, but none hesitated. They could see their goal just ahead.

No one said good-bye.

Soon just the three of them and the captain remained on board. "Hurry!" he said. "Or I will take you back with me."

Mariama went over first, landing in warm, calm water that reached barely to her waist. The woman, struggling, lifted her daughter over the railing and into her arms. Getting a grip on the limp figure, Mariama felt the girl's rounded, swollen belly bump against her side.

She thought: *If I were truly brave, I would drop you now. I would swim away and let you drown.*

*It would be a blessing.*

Instead she kept the girl's head above the surface as the mother splashed into the water. Then, together, they made their slow way through the placid ocean and up onto the beach.

**TWO HOURS LATER** Mariama had showered and changed into a colorful print skirt and a dark blue blouse and was sitting in the living room of a small house in Fuerteventura. The house's residents—mother, father, and five daughters—perched on chairs and the sofa and stared at her.

They were making sure she was eating well, as they'd promised Mariama's father they would.

Seydou Honso might have been confined to Senegal, but he still had plenty of friends elsewhere, including here.

People who owed him allegiance (or favors) and were willing to hide his refugee daughter from the authorities and make sure she was dressed and fed.

Especially if Seydou paid, which he had. Money needed no passport to travel.

Mariama was grateful, but impatient. She wanted to move on right away. The sick girl on the boat had shown her how much she needed to hurry.

But the family told her that her transport onward wouldn't be departing for three days. There was nothing they could do to speed it up. And anyway, as the mother pointed out, she would do no good if she died from exhaustion or starvation on the way.

So she stayed, and she rested, and she ate well. The fish-and-tomato stew they called tieboudienne, the baobab drink bouyi, and other Senegalese specialties that made her miss Mpack with an ache that filled her chest.

She spent most of her time thinking about the enormity of the task that lay ahead. Every once in a while, when no one was looking, she took the locket from around her neck and popped it open.

Just looking at it gave her strength.

LATE THE THIRD night, she was woken by a knock on the door of her bedroom. She'd been dreaming of the boat, and even when she awoke, disoriented, she felt like her bed was rocking on treacherous swells.

One of the daughters leaned in through the doorway and said in an apologetic tone, "You asked to be called if there were any messages for you."

Mariama said, "Of course. Thank you. I will be right there."

After washing her face, she followed the girl into the kitchen. A computer sat on the table, its screen bright in the dimness. Without a word, the girl turned and left. They were willing to shelter her, these nice people, but they didn't want to know a thing about her plans.

She sat down in front of the computer, marveling. Just days ago, on the boat, she'd been dangling like a puppet over the very edge of the world. How easily she could have fallen off, sharing the fate of the people in the doomed dhow.

And yet here she was, all the miracles of the modern age at her fingertips.

It was absurd.

She bent over the screen. The name of the person who'd sent the message was unfamiliar, but the code she and her father had agreed on was there. The message was from him.

Only there was no message. Just a link. Compressing her lips, Mariama clicked on it.

At first it *still* didn't make any sense. It was just an article about the death of some American expatriate in Tanzania. Only when Mariama read through did she begin to understand what it meant and what its consequences might be.

She felt cold. While she sat here, events were spinning on—and out of control—without her.

She took in a long breath to calm herself. Then leaned forward over the keyboard and began to compose a message of her own.

# NINE

*Manhattan*

**TREY COULD BLAME** his relentless yen to travel on his parents.

His father, Thomas, was a specialist in respiratory diseases, but unlike most doctors he'd never chosen a sedentary life at a hospital, HMO, or university. Instead, as if something were chasing him, he stayed on the move, spending a few months here, a year there.

He'd had a willing conspirator in Trey's mother, Katherine. She was a writer, and her ongoing series of columns for *Adventure Travel* magazine, detailing life on the run with a husband and two young sons, had proven very popular.

By the time he was fifteen, Trey had visited more than thirty countries. If his family never stayed put long enough for him to make friends, to learn what it was like to live in human society instead of just skim over it, he didn't mind. He was sure that the trade-off was worth it.

His brother, Christopher, disagreed. "You just don't know any different," he told Trey when they were teenagers. "You've never learned how satisfying it is to grow roots."

"You haven't, either," Trey pointed out.

"That's true." Christopher thought about it. "But there's a difference. As soon as I can, I'm going to. Deep roots."

And then Christopher went out and did it. Grew roots. When he reached the age of eighteen, he went back to Australia, always his favorite among the places they'd visited, got a job, and settled down in Port Douglas, Queensland. Eventually he fell in love with a woman there and got married.

Just like normal people did.

Christopher and Margie still lived in Port Douglas and had produced two children. Twin girls, whom Trey had seen only a handful of times over the years.

On his most recent visit, three years earlier, he found himself driven to explain himself to his brother. They were sitting on the porch of Christopher's house at dusk, drinking Fourex Gold and watching a steady stream of flying foxes winging past, dark silhouettes against a celadon sky.

In halting words, he tried to describe why he couldn't stay still. How the world seemed like such a fragile place, and that by going where it was most fragile, most endangered, he might be able to make a difference.

Christopher smiled at him over his beer. "Dad used to use exactly the same excuse when he dragged us around."

Trey was struck silent.

"But that's okay." Christopher leaned his head back and looked up at the darkening sky. "He was who he was, and you are what you are." He laughed. "At least you're not inflicting your compulsions on your own kids."

Right then, the twins came home from a play date, and Christopher's face lit up. He looked happy in a way that made Trey feel ashamed of himself.

But not for long. The next morning he was off again, spinning round the world, just as his father had.

**WOULD THOMAS AND** Katherine have been proud of him? He liked to believe so, but he'd never know for sure.

Early in his career, Thomas had seen the field of respiratory medicine morph into something almost unrecognizable. Every year seemed to see the emergence of a new or resurgent respiratory disease. AIDS-associated pneumonias. Legionnaires' disease. SARS. Bird flu. Even tuberculosis, once considered nearly eradicated, came roaring back, more deadly than ever.

Not all the diseases sprouting like vile mushrooms all over the world had names. Some unidentified ones were so ferocious—and so little understood—that the physicians hurrying to study and treat them knew that doing so might be suicidal.

When Trey was in his second year of college, Thomas Gilliard was summoned to Guangdong Province in China to investigate one such newly hatched disease. Katherine went along, as she always did.

Three days after seeing his first patient, Thomas fell ill. His lungs filled with fluid, then with blood, and less than forty-eight hours later he was dead.

Katherine had been warned to stay away from him, but ignored this advice. Even before Thomas died, she'd begun to experience the same symptoms. Her death came three days after his.

And Trey, world traveler, just nineteen, found himself accompanying his parents' bodies back to the United States.

Back home. As if they'd ever truly had a home.

**"YOU LOOK LIKE** a poster for Reading Is Fundamental," Jack said.

Trey looked up. The open books before him bore titles like *A Young Man's Grand Adventures in Afrique Ouest Français* (Colonel Fitzwilliam Wallis, First Bengal Lancers, Ret., 1878) and *Into the Jungles of the Camerouns with Gun and Knitting Needles* (Lady Mary Maurice Smith, Women's Goodwill Society, 1904). Books that were mirrors of a time when the world was an empty map, where grand adventures were still possible.

"Found nothing, huh?" Jack said.

Trey shook his head. No mention of monkey-killing wasps in the rain forests of Senegal or anywhere else the peripatetic Victorian authors had traveled.

He lifted the book by Lady Mary and watched as fragments of the deteriorating, yellow-orange pages drifted down onto his lap. Books like these were another thing in the process of vanishing, unnoticed and unmourned. When they were gone—and libraries were relentlessly clearing shelf space to make room for computer terminals—they'd be gone forever.

If something wasn't at the tip of your keyboarding fingers, it wouldn't exist.

Jack, who considered Trey sentimental about such things, moved easily back and forth between the two worlds. Entirely comfortable in the wilderness, chasing after new species on mountaintops, in swamps and forests, he was equally content traveling across time and space on the Internet.

He saw Trey looking at the paper dandruff on his lap and said, "Get used to it. Scientists can't survive without technology."

"Then I guess it's lucky," Trey said, "that I'm no scientist."

"Lucky for us, at least." Jack's gaze moved to his computer. "Come here."

When Trey stood behind him, he gestured at the screen.

"Here's what I've done," he said. "Should I send it out?"

He'd created a kind of garish advertisement, like something that might have touted an old-time Coney Island sideshow. At its center was Jack's drawing of the wasp. Above the illustration were the words "Have You Seen This Bug?" in big red-and-white letters, and the space below contained a description of the wasp's size and where Trey had seen it, a smaller sketch of one of the colony's mounds with a wasp perched on top of it, contact information, and a warning ("Dangerous! Do not approach.") that Trey was sure would be ignored.

"Who will receive this?" he asked.

"Well." Jack took a second to think about it. "I'll send it to every bug hunter I know, for starters. Every entomology department in every university, of course. Nature-travel and bird-tour companies. I'll also be posting it on my bug blog, Facebook and Twitter of course, my Tumblr and Pinterest—"

He grinned at Trey's expression. "Social-media sites

where not only scientists, but real people, will see it. That's the key, I think. I want someone I'll never meet to tell someone else I'll never meet, 'Hey, doesn't this look like the wasp you stepped on when we were playing tennis at Club Med this spring?'"

Trey was silent.

"Gotta look for help," Jack said. "Way of the world."

After a moment, Trey nodded. You couldn't always do everything yourself. He understood that.

Hated, but understood.

"Send it," he said.

SOON AFTERWARD, HE headed back to his apartment in Brooklyn's upscale Park Slope neighborhood. His parents had bought it once he and Christopher grown, a place on the ground floor of a four-story yellow-brick building just a few blocks from Prospect Park. Worth a fortune these days because of the neighborhood, but it was nothing glamorous: one bedroom, one bath, a foldout couch in the living/dining room, separated by a counter from the tiny kitchen.

More a place for stopping off to do laundry between trips than a real home.

After they'd died, Trey and Christopher had inherited it jointly. Christopher, just twenty-two but already settled in Australia, had wanted nothing to do with it, even refusing Trey's offer to buy out his half.

"You sell it, give me my share," he'd said. "Till then, feel free to live there."

So that was what Trey did, as much as he lived anywhere.

\*   \*   \*

**HE SAT AT** the little table in the dining area and powered up his laptop. Despite Jack's jibes, he knew his way around the Internet.

He had no choice. The ability to use a computer was nearly as essential to his (tenuous) relationship with his employers as his skill at returning from the wilderness with data no one else could obtain.

He got no pleasure from computer literacy. But all Jack's talk about social media had reminded him that days had passed since he'd been online. With a sigh, he logged on.

And then, right away, almost deleted the most important e-mail of his life because it looked like spam.

It had come from a travel company in the Canary Islands. Unsurprisingly, Trey had ended up on countless travel e-mail lists, and at first he assumed this one was just another advertisement.

Except for the subject heading. It didn't advertise cheap vacations in Majorca, time shares on Grand Canary, easy hops to Casablanca.

It just said: "This time . . ."

Trey looked at it and thought, *What does* that *mean?*

So instead of deleting the e-mail unread, he opened it.

It contained three short lines of text. The first said, ". . . you don't have to flee."

The second: "Sheila Connelly."

And the third: "Find her."

Trey sat looking at the screen. Thinking.

Then he reached for his phone and called Jack.

# TEN

DESPITE THE HOUR, Jack was still in his office. No surprise to Trey, who knew that Jack frequently stayed at work long after the museum closed, even through the night.

This had always been true, but even more so since his divorce had eliminated his main reason for setting foot outside.

Not that he was ever alone in the vast building. Jack was far from the only museum scientist at work during the dead of night, when the streets outside were quiet but for an occasional bus or taxi, and even Central Park itself seemed to sleep. You could concentrate better, they believed. Gain perspective that was impossible in the glaring light and endless noise of the city day.

Trey didn't need convincing. It was his favorite time at the museum as well. With only scattered emergency bulbs casting a feeble glow, the tigers and gorillas in their darkened dioramas, the shadowy dinosaur skeletons, the great blue whale dominating its ocean room, all managed to capture some of the magic—some of the awe—of the living creatures they evoked.

Plus, when he visited at night, the place was deserted. That was always a good thing.

**ONLY THE COMPUTER** screen and a bumblebee-shaped child's night-light illuminated the office. Jack had opened a window, and Trey felt the night's cold, damp exhalation as a prickle on his skin. Taking a breath and holding it, he could detect, at the very edge of his hearing, a series of staccato, high-pitched cries: the contact calls of a flock of birds—he heard orioles, tanagers, and grosbeaks—migrating north over the city.

Trey had forwarded the e-mail to Jack. Now they stood looking at it again, though they'd both long since memorized the brief message.

"It's Mariama," Trey said.

Jack frowned. He'd been frowning since Trey arrived. "And you're sure of this how, Sherlock?"

"The word 'flee,'" Trey said.

Jack's frown deepened into a scowl. "But why go through"—he gestured at the screen—"this gobbledygook? Why use someone else's account? Why not just say, 'Hey, Trey. It's Mariama. How ya doin'?"

Trey said, "I don't know. Maybe she's protecting herself . . . or someone else."

"And maybe you're grasping at straws, Scarecrow."

Trey just looked at him, and after a moment Jack sighed. "I argue with you," he said, "because it feels so good when I stop."

Sitting down at his computer with a thud, he muttered,

"Sheila Connelly, huh. There must be a ton of people with that name out there."

He tapped at the keys. "No. I was wrong. Most of them use a second *o* instead of an *e*. At least we're not looking for a single ant in a hill."

A moment later, he said, "This one? Tanzania Sheila? The one whose mother died?"

"I think so."

Jack swung around to look up at him. "You searched this yourself, didn't you? Before you came in?"

Trey nodded.

"And?"

"I didn't find anything that meant a thing to me." Trey hesitated. "I thought you might have better luck."

"Because I live in this century? Or just because I'm awesome?"

Trey didn't bother to say anything. Grinning, Jack went back to the computer. "Still, don't expect too much. I think it's a snipe hunt."

Trey said, "Just look."


MEGAN CONNELLY'S DEATH had received a burst of attention in Tanzania's tabloids, mostly because it involved an American who'd been living in the country for decades. The death of an American anywhere on earth also seemed to warrant a few lines in the wire services, which had meant a bit of international newspaper and cable news website coverage as well.

Long or short, though, the articles all said basically the same thing, and it wasn't enough.

Connelly, who had come to western Tanzania as a

missionary, had—along with two Tanzanians—died in a suspicious fire that consumed her house in Ujiji. Her daughter, Sheila, a physician working for the nongovernmental organization Les Voyageurs, had been hospitalized due to distress. And also (several of the articles hinted) because officials suspected that she might have had something to do with the fire.

"When did this all take place?" Trey asked.

Jack looked. "The fire, five days ago. The most recent article is dated yesterday."

"And Sheila is still hospitalized?"

"As far as we know."

Trey said, "For 'distress.'"

"Yeah. Sounds more like detention than treatment to me." Jack gave a sympathetic grunt. "Though I'd be distressed, too, if my mother had just died and I was being held in a Tanzanian hospital."

He shrugged. "But I still don't see anything here about wasps."

"Keep looking," Trey said.

**NOTHING. JUST THE** same few details regurgitated again and again.

*Damn.* Trey hated when he couldn't find what he was searching for. When he couldn't *see*.

"Told ya," Jack said. "Snipe hunt."

"No." Trey found that his hands were clenched. "We're missing something."

Jack shrugged. "We've read every word of every story."

"Then why did Mariama point me here?"

Jack opened his mouth, then closed it again. *Maybe she didn't*, he'd begun to say. *Maybe it wasn't even her.*

Trey said, "Could there have been a story up when Mariama looked, but that's gone now?"

Jack went still for a second. Then he said, "Sure."

"Can it be retrieved?"

Again a pause. Then, "Maybe."

Jack went to Google, typed, clicked. A page of results unfurled. The first four led back to articles they'd already read, but the fifth took them to a page that, under the heading of a newspaper called the *Kigoma Dart*, said, "Error 404: The article you are looking for no longer exists."

"Huh," Jack said.

"We need more than a dead link," Trey said.

"Yeah, I know. Let me see if this article's been cached." A few more clicks. "Damn. No."

He sat back in his chair and pulled at his beard. Then he leaned forward again. "Let's try the Wayback Machine."

The name awoke vague memories of cartoons Trey's father had shown him on DVD when he was young. A dog and a boy who traveled back in time to famous historical events.

"The what?" he said.

"The Wayback Machine." Jack was tapping at the keyboard as he spoke. "This site that stores deleted Web pages." He laughed. "Everything on the Internet lives forever, if you know where to look. Just ask any politician."

Ten seconds later he said, "Bingo." And there the article was, as if it had never been taken down, under the title "New Details in Tragic Ujiji House Fire."

Trey scanned it, finding nothing unexpected until the next-to-last paragraph. There, directly beneath the sub-head "Daughter Speaks" were the only words from Sheila Connelly he'd seen in any of the articles he'd read.

Even these were not direct quotes, just a paragraph written as if the reporter had actually talked to Sheila. "Miss Connelly claims to have no knowledge of the fire," the passage said. "She claims that her mother was ill from a tumbu fly larva, which she extracted. During the minor operation, her mother died, she believes of an allergic reaction. The body of Mrs. Connelly was too badly burned to confirm her daughter's statements. Police hope to question Miss Connelly further as she recovers."

"Claims this," Jack said. "Claims that. They've as good as convicted her of arson and murder."

Trey said, "Sure. But that's not what's important."

"Yeah." Jack pulled at his beard, which by this time of the night stuck out in wiry tufts. "But her story doesn't add up, either. No one's ever died of an anaphylactic reaction to a tumbu larva."

Trey was quiet. It was late, and Jack's mind wasn't working as quickly as it usually did.

He'd get there eventually, though.

Trey watched it happen. First, Jack closed his eyes. Then he said, "Wait a second. Wait."

Then his whole body grew still. His intense concentration made him resemble a statue, a monument. A figure from Easter Island, flesh captured in stone, but not flesh itself. He didn't seem to be breathing.

As commanded, Trey waited. In the silence, he heard a car honk down on the street. He glanced over at the bee clock hanging on the wall. Four thirty. Already traf-

fic was beginning to build toward rush hour. The freedom, the wildness, of the New York City night was
retreating. Soon the city would be filled with human
voices once again, sounds as meaningless to Trey as the
gabble of flamingos.

Jack opened his eyes. They were dark with comprehension. "That colobus monkey you saw," he said. "You don't
think it got stung because it was threatening the colony.
You don't think it was there by chance. You think it
was . . . a host."

"I saw the swelling, but thought it was a tumor."

"And that man in the clinic, the one who was shot in
the stomach. You think he was, too. A host."

"Yes."

"And Sheila's mother as well."

Trey let him work it out.

"You're saying that your wasps are parasitic. That they
use primate hosts to hatch their young." Only Jack's
mouth moved. The rest still seemed rooted to his chair,
to the earth.

"And not just lower primates," he said. "*Homo sapiens*
as well."

"We need to know what Sheila Connelly saw," Trey
said. "We need to know what that larva looked like."

Jack stared at him, unblinking. Then, drawing in a
huge breath, he shook his shoulders like a bear or a dog.
In that moment, he was flesh again.

He turned back to his computer. Within a few seconds
he'd called up a website for booking airline reservations.

"Today or tomorrow?" he asked.

Trey stood, stretched, walked over to the window. The
predawn light made the leaves on the trees across the way

look like fog, like smoke. It reminded him of mountain forests he'd visited, the clouds wafting through, the deepest of mysteries made briefly tangible.

A familiar feeling pierced him, stabbing like a blade. The thrill of the hunt.

*You are what you are,* his brother had said to him. Meaning: *You'll never change.*

Trey might never know whether it was a curse or a blessing, or both.

"Today," he told Jack. "Now."

# ELEVEN

*Kigoma, Tanzania*

**TREY HAD NEVER** worked in Tanzania. The reason: The country was too well trodden. With the exception of a vanishing patch of forest here, a remote mountain range there, all the wild areas had been extensively studied by scientists before he was even born.

For Trey, that was a deal breaker. Nothing was more boring than walking in somebody else's footsteps.

He'd visited, though. Just once, with his parents and Christopher when he was fourteen. In and around the tuberculosis conference Thomas and Katherine were attending, the four of them had followed vast herds of wildebeests in the Serengeti, witnessed lions bringing down a zebra in Ngorongoro Crater, and climbed Mt. Kilimanjaro.

It was this last that Trey remembered most vividly. Even now, he could bring back the breathless thrill of standing amid ice fields at nineteen thousand feet on the summit at dawn, all of Africa at his feet, the fading stars above close enough to touch, brilliant meteors tracing across the purple sky.

He remembered his parents flanking him, his mother's arm around his waist, his father's draped across his shoulders.

**TREY WALKED DOWN** the stairs and onto the tarmac at Kigoma Airport a little after noon two days after his departure from New York. The atmosphere was noticeably wetter, more tropical, than in the savannas to the east. Clouds piled up on the horizon, replete with moisture picked up over the Congo rain forests to the west.

To the first European explorers, Africa had been an unimaginably vast continent. More than a single place, it was a thousand that didn't even overlap or intersect. Trackless swamps, endless forests, sourceless rivers. Going in, you knew you were going to get lost.

You could disappear for years, or forever. As David Livingstone did before being found by Henry Morton Stanley in Ujiji, only a few miles from where Trey was standing right now.

But that was then. Nothing was far enough apart anymore. You could move from desert to forest, from mountain to savanna, in just a few hours. The mystery was all but gone, the teeming plains little more than gigantic zoos filled with semidomesticated animals, idling minibuses, and clicking tourist cameras.

The taxi stand outside the terminal building was starved for business. Trey chose a canny-eyed young man from among the dozen importuning drivers and climbed into the backseat of his 1970s-era Peugeot. It had once been red, most likely, but the sun and rain had turned it a grayish brown.

The driver glanced at Trey in the mirror. "Yes?"

"Nyerere Hospital."

Without a blink, the driver pulled away from the curb. If he had some idea why Trey was here—and Trey thought he did—he didn't show it.

The hospital was located on the outskirts of town. It was a relatively new building, rectangular, made of whitish stone and steel. The polished sandstone floor of the lobby had ammonite fossils in it.

As he walked in, Trey saw a squarish young white man in a gray suit, blue tie, and sunglasses sitting in the waiting area. Instead of going to the reception desk, he walked over to the man, who looked up at him (or at least in his general direction) without taking the sunglasses off.

Trey had seen a thousand just like him in a hundred countries. It didn't matter to them if they were walking clichés: Embassy men, CIA officials, and (increasingly) private contractors almost always dressed like this.

Trey read this one as embassy.

"You're making sure that Sheila Connelly gets out of here with no fuss," Trey said to him, not phrasing it as a question.

Embassy was a little softer than Trey had expected, with a round face behind the dark glasses. His sandy hair was thinning on top, even though his smooth cheeks marked him as no more than thirty.

Trey guessed he was unhappy to have been posted here, and Trey couldn't blame him. Since the end of the cold war, East Africa's global importance had dwindled. Tanzania was far from being prime territory.

Finally Embassy shifted in his seat. "You a friend of

hers?" His voice, too, was unexpectedly soft, the accent showing South Carolina origins.

Trey said, "Hope to be."

He introduced himself, then sat down opposite and said, "Didn't think she'd need protecting by you guys."

Embassy's sunglasses were trained on him. Trey waited, giving the man the chance to decide how much he was willing to say.

CIA agents were never worth talking to. They were always looking to dump you in some secret prison and forget about you. Nor did embassy men open up when their mission was dangerous or high profile.

But this kind of mind-numbing assignment? Babysitting a hospital waiting room? There was a chance.

Eventually Embassy shifted a little in his seat and said, "Well. There's been some rumblings from the families of the other people who died." He paused. "We're just making sure she gets on her way safely."

He licked his dry lips. His forehead gleamed with sweat. The lobby wasn't air-conditioned, and it must have been hot inside that suit.

Trey got to his feet. "I'm getting myself something to eat and drink," he said. "Want anything?"

"Not allowed to eat while I'm on duty," Embassy said darkly.

Trey waited.

"Cafeteria here is under renovation."

Trey smiled. "I'll figure something out."

**FIFTEEN MINUTES LATER,** he was back from a market down the street, carrying Cokes, coffee, sandwiches, and a paper bag full of passion fruit. Keeping a chicken sandwich, coffee, and the passion fruit for himself, he handed the rest of it over.

Embassy dug into a sandwich, then said through a mouthful, "Nice try. But I still can't tell you anything."

Trey said, "'Course not."

The man took another bite, followed by a gulp of soda. His sunglasses were a little fogged up. "Real good," he said.

Trey said, "No one really believes that Sheila burned down her mother's place, do they?"

Embassy lowered his sandwich and looked across at Trey. "People who set fires go to jail," he said.

"And?"

"We're putting your friend on an airplane today and waving 'bye. Then everyone's happy and I can go back to my place in Dar."

Trey said, "What killed Sheila's mother?"

It was worth a shot. But the sunglasses were as blank as blacked-out windows. Trey knew he wasn't going to get any more.

He stood. Embassy looked up at him and said, "She gets no visitors. Sandwiches won't get you through the door."

"I know." Trey hesitated. "She goes home today, you said."

Embassy nodded.

"Can you tell me about what time?"

Trey watched him think about it before saying, "The last flight back to Dar."

Trey said, "Thank you."

Looking down again at the remains of the food Trey had brought, Embassy added, "And the first flight tomorrow to Rome, and then New York."

At the door Trey turned and said, "You going to be here when I get back?"

Embassy sighed. "Yeah."

"Okay."

"But they won't let you talk to her then, either."

**TREY CLIMBED INTO** the taxi and handed over a passion fruit, which the driver accepted without comment. Getting a knife out of the glove compartment, he sliced off one end of the purple fruit's tough skin. Then he handed the knife to Trey, who did the same with one of his own.

The driver slurped up some of the seeds and pulpy fruit, then said, "Yes?"

Trey said, "Ujiji. The house that burned."

The man shook his head. "Nothing left there."

Trey took a moment to eat some of his passion fruit, sour enough to make his eyes half close.

"The house," he said. "Please."

The driver seemed to be considering whether to say no. But it was a quiet day, Trey had hired him for hours—and was paying well—so eventually he sighed, finished sucking out the innards of his fruit, engaged the gears, and pulled away from the curb.

**THE FIRE HAD** done a thorough job. Where the house had stood, all that remained was sodden rubble. Even the nearby trees had been scorched.

But it didn't really matter. Trey knew what had happened here, or at least most of it.

He stood in the midst of the rubble and breathed in

deeply through his nose. Nothing but the odor of smoke and wet wood.

He turned and walked past the scorched trees to the edge of the clearing. Breathed in again, but smelled only the forest itself.

Somewhere in the distance, a trumpeter hornbill let loose with its raucous call.

He went back to the waiting taxi. Climbed inside, slamming the door behind him. Before he was even settled in his seat, the car had pulled out and was leaving the ruin behind.

"Ujiji Market," Trey said.

The driver grunted.

**THEY PASSED BENEATH** an avenue of mango trees lining the road. People were clustered in the shade, eating lunch or sleeping or just sitting in twos or threes, talking. Some of them looked up at the passing taxi, but without much interest.

"It's not a market day," the driver said. "No ferries today."

Trey didn't reply. In silence they headed past the mango trees and toward the market, the docks, and the shore of Lake Tanganyika, its surface ridged with whitecaps under a looming sky.

**AS THE DRIVER** had said, the market was quiet. But not deserted. Many of the stalls and tables were open, selling piles of bananas, stacks of brightly colored textiles, or wooden sculptures of elephants and giraffes.

Trey bought a little carved warthog made out of

rosewood, then walked over to a woman selling *kanga*s, traditional garments made from cotton. She was wrapped in one herself, blue with a pattern of big gold leaves on it.

Trey knew that *kanga*s always came with a *jina*, a kind of motto or aphorism, stitched into the fabric. From a distance, he couldn't make out what hers said.

She was an old woman, somewhere between seventy and eighty, with a wrinkled-nut face and white hair cropped close to her scalp. Her eyes were sharp, though, watching Trey approach. Sharp and suspicious.

He was used to that.

"*Habari,* Mama," he said.

She inclined her head. *"Mzuri."*

Now he could read her *kanga*'s *jina*. It said, *Majivuno hayafai*: "Greed is never good."

He smiled, and again when she bargained fiercely with him over a red-and-blue *kanga* patterned with fanciful birds and a motto that read, "Humanness is better than material things."

Finally he handed over twenty thousand *shilingi*— about ten dollars, more than the woman had asked—and made a "keep it" gesture when she looked at him with raised eyebrows.

The money disappeared into her *kanga*, and she handed over his purchase. Then, with a sigh, she lit a cigarette and said, "Yes."

Yes. Ask your questions.

Trey said, "Mama, what killed the missionary lady and those other people?"

"Fire," she said at once.

When he didn't reply, argue, push, she watched him.

"Have there been other such fires," he said after a while, "in Ujiji and Kigoma?"

After a pause, she nodded.

"Many?"

She shrugged and made a back-and-forth motion with her hands. "Some here. Some there. Not so many."

She looked up to the sky, where only a pair of vultures circled.

"Not yet," she said.

Trey leaned against her table, looking out at the quiet marketplace before turning back to her. "Have you seen them?" he asked. "The wasps?"

She nodded.

"I have as well."

Her eyes were very dark. "I was . . . afraid."

"Yes. Me, too."

"Yet we both still live," she said.

He looked back at her. "Mama, why burn the house? Why blame the daughter?"

For a long time, many seconds, she didn't answer. Then she said, "They do not want anyone to know what happened."

"They?"

"If people learn about this, who will be blamed?" she said. "We will. Tanzania. Aid will stop. Tourists will no longer come here."

"And everything depends on tourists."

"Yes." She looked down at her pile of *kangas*. "We will go hungry."

Again they were silent for a while. Then Trey said, "The wasps. Have they always been here?"

"The *majizi*? No. Of course not. Four months. Five, maybe." She gestured at the oily lake beyond. "They came across. With the bushmeat and the live animals. The monkeys. And the hunters, too."

Trey took a breath. "What did you call them?"

"*Majizi.*"

*Thieves.*

Trey said, "What is it they steal?"

But the old woman only shrugged.

Then, as she looked over his shoulder, he saw her face set. "Enough questions," she said. "Go now."

A young man in a military uniform was standing at the other end of the uncrowded market. He was chatting with one of the vendors, laughing.

"Just tell me," Trey said. "The thieves, are they still here?"

"Yes, of course," she said. "They will never leave. But not only here."

"Where else?" Trey asked, although he knew the answer.

She opened her arms wide.

Out there.

In the world.

**AS HE'D SAID,** Embassy was still at the hospital. He looked around hopefully to see if Trey had brought more food, then shrugged in a resigned way.

"You almost didn't make it in time," he said. "They'll be down in a minute or two."

"Sheila and who else?"

"My boss and this lady from the NGO."

"Les Voyageurs?"

He nodded. Then, for the first time, he reached up and took off his sunglasses. His eyes were very pale blue underneath sparse lashes.

"I told you," he said. "You're not allowed to talk to her."

Trey was quiet.

"Yeah. You can follow her like a lost puppy from here to Dar to Rome, but you can't interact with her till you're at JFK. Ignore that and you'll be grabbed."

Trey didn't even bother to ask on what grounds. When did that ever matter?

Across the lobby, the elevator door opened and four people came out: two more embassy men (one of whose gray hair and more expensive suit indicated his seniority) and a fiftyish woman in an expensive suit. And Sheila Connelly.

Tall, skinny, her skin pale, her short copper-red hair ragged. Dark hollows under her eyes. She was wearing black pants over hiking boots and a cheerful flowered blouse that she'd buttoned wrong.

The woman from Les Voyageurs was holding on to Sheila's arm, guiding her. Both embassy men had seen Trey immediately and were looking at him hard as they shepherded the two women toward the front door.

Trey got to his feet and walked toward the group. Behind him, he heard Embassy sigh and rise as well.

Sheila's gaze shifted his way, but she showed no interest. Her eyes, which were large and an unusual dark blue-green, had a blankness that might have been drug induced or might not.

Trey reached a decision. *Hell*. He hated being forbidden to do something.

"Sheila," he said.

Her gaze sharpened a little as she looked at him.

"I know that larva wasn't from a tumbu fly," he said.

Already the two younger embassy men had him by the arms. But Sheila said, "Wait!" And her voice had so much authority that everyone stopped still.

She took a step closer and stared into his face. Her eyes, irises so dark as to be almost black, seemed enormous in her gaunt face.

"Do you know what it was?" she asked. Her voice was deep, hoarse.

"I think so."

Red spots rose to her ashen cheeks. "Why did my mother die?"

"I don't know yet," Trey said. "But I'll find out."

"Okay," the senior embassy man said. "That's enough."

The two others spun him around. Trey twisted in their grasp. "Wait for me at JFK," he called out as they yanked him toward the door. "Don't leave there without me."

"I won't," she said.

Her voice was little more than a breath, but he heard it.

# TWELVE

**DURING HIS CAREER,** Trey had stalked rare birds, elusive frogs, poisonous snakes, a scorpion nearly the size of a lobster, even a shadowy, half-glimpsed pack of bush dogs in Suriname that he eventually realized was also stalking *him*.

Never a human, though.

Not until now.

**HE SAT ON** a blue plastic seat amid hordes of tourists in the spacious waiting area of Nyerere Airport in Dar es Salaam. Every once in a while, he'd raise his eyes from the battered paperback he was reading—a novel by Lee Child—and look across at Sheila Connelly.

She was sitting beside the gate for the overnight Emirates Air flight they'd both be taking to Rome. From what Trey could see, she was dressed in the same clothes she'd been wearing earlier in the day.

Beside her was the elegant woman from Les Voyageurs. Her outfit had probably cost more than a typical Tanzanian earned in a year.

On Sheila's other side was another embassy man, one Trey hadn't seen before. He wore a gray suit and a white shirt and a red tie and sunglasses.

Sheila and the Les Voyageurs lady seemed oblivious of Trey's gaze, but not the embassy man. Every time Trey looked in his direction, he turned his head and gazed back, the lenses of his glasses like two distant blacked-out windows.

Trey felt a lot like a stalker.

He didn't like it.

HE KILLED THE time by watching the tourists. Tanzania's lifeblood. The only thing preventing the Serengeti, the Selous, the Ngorongoro, and the other fabled wilderness areas from being plowed under and converted to cattle pasture. The last thing keeping its famous herds of wild game alive.

The tourists on their way into the country wore freshly bought khakis and were excited, anticipatory. The tourists on their way out looked exhausted, bug bitten, and deeply satisfied. They'd seen giraffes and wildebeests and lions and, if they were lucky, leopards and rhinos. Now they could head home, their adventures over, and get back to whatever they did with their lives.

Trey felt a sense of dislocation a lot like sorrow. For a moment he envied those who could look upon the wilderness—or what was left of it—as a temporary break from real life, not life itself. For all the joy he got from hopscotching around the globe, from taking his life in his hands while sitting beside Malcolm in rattletrap prop planes, from trekking through disease-ridden and rebel-haunted forests, sometimes he wished that he could unlearn what he knew.

That he, too, could dress up in adventurer's clothes and choose to be blind.

**THE HOURS PASSED.** Trey read his book. Lee Child's protagonist, Jack Reacher, was enormous: six-and-a-half feet tall and 250 pounds of pure muscle. He was smart and clever and relentless, but in the end he tended to solve problems with his fists. No one had fists like Reacher's.

Trey thought of his parents. His father had been tall and slender, nonviolent, gentle to the core. His mother, short and compact, had possessed a strength and volatility that made those around her instantly treat her with respect. Trey had never seen her lose her temper, not fully, but he always knew she would be a force to be reckoned with, to be feared, if she did.

Still, neither she nor his father could have survived a single blow administered by any of the villains Jack Reacher shrugged off in a typical day's work, much less by Reacher himself. There was something comforting in that superman's strength, a sense that the world could be measured, controlled. That all it took was smarts and brawn to make things right.

On the other hand, all of Reacher's power would do him no good at all if he happened to run into the kinds of enemies Thomas and Katherine Gilliard had faced in *their* typical day. Their enemies, the villains in their stories, didn't aim at you with a gun or stand toe-to-toe with hands clenched into fists.

They attacked you as you sat eating dinner, as you drove to work, as you talked to a friend, as you made love, as you slept. They bit you or stung you—you might not even notice—or they simply entered your body in a mouthful of food or a breath of air. Then they got into your bloodstream and killed you before you even knew you'd been attacked.

Jack Reacher could make the world right because all of his enemies were human.

And humans were easy.

**SHEILA AND HER** chaperone were among the first to board. The embassy man watched them as they went through the gate and down the walkway. Then he spun on his heel and came over to Trey. His mouth was a line as he looked down through his sunglasses.

"Not a word to her until you get to JFK," he said.

Trey smiled. "Yeah, I've been told."

"There'll be an air marshal on board. You won't know who he is, but he'll be keeping an eye on you the whole flight."

Trey didn't say anything.

"He's got orders to restrain you if you so much as approach Sheila Connelly. You'll be detained in Rome, and you'll never see her again."

That sounded like a threat, but not necessarily aimed at him. Trey said, "Why do you have your pants in such a bunch over this?"

Of course the embassy man, scowling at the question,

didn't explain. But Trey knew anyway. It was obvious. They—the Tanzanian government, the U.S. Embassy, and Les Voyageurs—wanted her out of the country. They wanted Trey out of the country. And they wanted no complications in the meantime.

He thought about the old woman in the marketplace, her gesture when she'd indicated where the thieves had gone. *Out there. Into the world.*

All the cover-your-ass on earth wouldn't be enough if she was right.

"Don't worry," Trey said to the embassy man. "I'll stay away from her."

The truth this time.

He could wait a few more hours.

**TREY WAS ONE** of the last to board the 777. Already some of the tired tourists were asleep under mounds of blankets, while others were frowning at their iPads or getting ready to watch movies on their seatback screens. The atmosphere had a festive feel, as was typical of the onset of these long flights. A "we're all in this together" vibe that would last for a while, until everyone started getting bored and cranky.

Trey's seat was on the aisle about halfway down the plane. He looked back and saw Sheila leaning against a window near the back, her pale face peaceful in sleep. Her chaperone, sitting next to her on the aisle, watched Trey, an unreadable expression on her face. He raised his hands in a placatory gesture, and after a moment she nodded.

Trey took another quick look around.

It took him about fifteen seconds to identify two plainclothes air marshals, one male, one female. The way they peeked at him reminded him of meerkats popping up from their burrows.

He made sure not to let the marshals know they'd been spotted. He didn't want them to feel bad.

**TREY HATED SLEEP.** Hated how much time it sucked up that could be better spent doing more productive things. Hated how it eventually won every battle, no matter how strong you were, no matter how hard you fought it.

He hated being . . . *away*.

But there was one thing he'd learned after hundreds of flights: If you didn't sleep on airplanes, you were an idiot. Whatever else you could do on a plane, you could do better almost anywhere else. Sleep was the most productive thing you could get out of the way while strapped to a seat.

So on both flights, all the way till the announcement came of their final approach to JFK, Trey read his book and ate airplane food, but mostly he slept. Knowing that when they arrived, and the important work began, he'd be ready.

**HE GOT OFF** the airplane in New York before Sheila and her chaperone. Waited by the gate as the hordes made their way past, faces bleached gray by the barren lights of the terminal. It was only eleven at night here, but most of these travelers' bodies were stuck in the timeless limbo of jet lag.

The two women finally came through the door. Sheila's face was slack, but her eyes were alert. Beside her, despite her expensive clothes, the older woman just looked worn out.

They came up to Trey. He said to Sheila, "I almost thought they'd spirit you away. Make you disappear."

The chaperone straightened and stared at him. "Are you nuts?" she said, her incredulity sounding funny expressed in such a crisp, cultured tone. "I'm handing her over to you, and now I'm *done*."

She brushed her hands together, the age-old gesture of dismissal. "One night in the airport hotel for me, and back home tomorrow."

Then, unexpectedly, she switched her gaze to Sheila, and her expression softened. "Are you sure of your decision, dear?" She looked back at Trey. "We were supposed to be met by someone from the New York office, but she didn't want to."

"I'm sure," Sheila said. "You can go."

The woman looked at Trey. Her expression said, *Are you sure?*

No, Trey wasn't. But he knew he had no choice. He nodded.

"Thank you," she said.

Which really meant, *Better you than me, pal.*


**THE EX-CHAPERONE WAS** barely out of earshot, her heels clicking away down the quiet terminal, when Sheila said to Trey, "Tell me what it was."

He reached into his pocket and pulled out a copy of Jack's drawing.

Sheila stared down at it. "You've seen these?"

Trey nodded.

"Where?"

"In southern Senegal."

He watched her take in the new information. It seemed she hadn't been completely undone by her days of confinement, by exhaustion and grief. He shouldn't have been surprised: You had to be strong to work with ill and dying refugees.

"That's where they're native?" she asked.

"We think so."

She blinked. "Who is 'we'?"

Trey looked around, saw a café still open at the far end of the terminal. He pointed to it and said, "Let's sit, and I'll tell you what I know."

First at the café and then, when it closed, on adjacent seats at a deserted gate, they talked. By the time they were done, it made no sense to try to find her a hotel room.

"People coming through the city stay in my place all the time," he said.

Her gaze was unblinking. "'People'?"

"Folks I've met along the way. Scientists. Field researchers. Aid workers. People like you who have business here but can't afford the rates."

"People like me," she said.

Trey waited.

"Okay." She paused. "Thank you."

Her acquiescence came a little quicker than he'd expected. He wondered whether it was because she already trusted him or whether she didn't much care whether he was a friend or a psychopath.

He thought she hadn't quite decided, not yet, whether she had anything left to lose.

# THIRTEEN

*Aboard the MV* Atlas

**HIS NAME WAS** Arjen. He was tall, at least a foot taller than Mariama, and as skinny as a fig sapling, with big knotty hands and a prominent Adam's apple that moved up and down when he laughed. Which he did often.

And a thin, bony Scandinavian face that lit up whenever he saw her. Green-blue eyes that glinted with amusement as he told tall tales of his years aboard freighters like the *Atlas.* Stories of sea monsters, ancient as dinosaurs, rising from the calm surface of the horse latitudes at dawn. Of a wooden house floating a hundred miles from the mouth of the Amazon River, a family of monkeys clinging to its roof. Of a flying saucer hovering over Hong Kong harbor, illuminating thousands of upturned faces on the boats below before ascending and disappearing at unimaginable speed.

Laughing when Mariama mocked him. Saying, in his thick and joyful accent, "Yes, you doubt me. But can you *prove* I am lying?"

Arjen, the *Atlas*'s first officer, knocking on Mariama's

cabin door when his shift was over. Sometimes this was at 4:00 A.M., but Mariama was always waiting for him.

Sweet Arjen. Doomed, she thought, like all those others who spent their lives on ships like the *Atlas*.

The coal mine's canaries.

**WHEN HER HOSTS** in Fuerteventura told her about the next stage of her journey, Mariama sighed and shrugged.

"The slow boat," she said.

But she wasn't surprised. With no passport, she could not fly. When you couldn't fly, and governments knew who you were, the world became a huge place once again. A huge place where you had to move slowly, quietly, to avoid notice.

For enough money, though, you could always find a freighter that would take you aboard. No passport necessary, and entry to any of a hundred port cities. It was hardly even a risk. No one would be paying attention.

Mariama's hosts chose the MV *Atlas*. They knew the captain, knew that he and the crew would look the other way. They'd done it many times before.

But it could just as easily have been another ship. The port of Las Palmas, where Mariama embarked, was overrun with freighters. At least half would cross the Panama Canal, the next step on Mariama's slow journey.

And then? As the ship made its transit across the Atlantic, and she laughed with Arjen, and shared her bed with him, and talked with the other passengers aboard the *Atlas*, Mariama allowed herself to dream.

To dream of cold, and the safety cold could bring.

\* \* \*

**"VALPARAISO," ARJEN SAID** to her one night, close to dawn. He stretched in her little bed, years of experience somehow allowing him to lie comfortably without crowding her. Too much.

She wasn't sure she'd heard of it.

"In Chile. A beautiful city on the Pacific Ocean. All hills. Staircases and outdoor elevators and these little trains that take you up and down."

He grinned in the dim light that came through the porthole of her cabin. "And the *curanto*! The best seafood stew you will ever eat."

"Where is it?" she asked.

"I told you. In Chile."

"No. I mean the latitude."

He turned his head to look at her across the pillow. "Thirty-three degrees south, more or less."

"Not far enough."

Not cold enough.

Arjen stayed silent for a few moments. Mariama was still, feeling the motion of the boat across the Atlantic's long swells as a pull on her bones. The first night or two, the unceasing movement had bothered her, but now she only noticed it in quiet moments like this.

Then he propped himself up on his elbow. "Every day," he said, "you walk the decks, even going places you should not. Some of the crew believe you are a terrorist, but I don't think so."

"Thank you," Mariama said.

"Me, I just think you are strange."

She smiled. "Thank you very much."

But now his expression was serious. "When you walk, Mariama," he said, "what are you afraid of?"

She felt her chin lift. "I am afraid of nothing."

He didn't smile. "All right. Then what are you searching for?"

For a long time she just looked into his eyes. Then, deciding, she reached out and took his rough, callused hand in both of hers.

"Listen to me," she said.

**WHEN SHE WAS** done, he was silent for a long time. Then he said, "I have seen birds, rats, spiders, snakes on board. But never one of these—"

"We call them thieves."

"No. Nor smelled them."

Mariama sighed. "Not yet."

"But I will?"

"I don't know," she said. "Maybe not on this ship, but others, certainly. Airplanes, cars. Any place they can hide."

"This is happening already?" he asked. "Now?"

She said, "Oh, yes." Then paused. "I am standing still, and they are not."

"But you know of a way to stop them?"

She was silent.

He thought for a while. Finally he said, "Valparaiso. I know why you asked where it is."

She waited.

"You wondered if you would be safe there, because it is cold. Those . . . thieves could not live there."

Mariama shook her head. "No. Not there. It would need to be farther south."

"Magallanes?" he said. "Tierra del Fuego?"

She did not reply.

Again he thought. Then he said, "Would you do this? Know what you know, and run away?"

Again Mariama was silent.

*Gatun Locks, Panama*

**SHE SMELLED IT** soon after she stepped off the ship. Drew in a single breath and felt her heart flip inside her chest.

Arjen was there, walking her past the Customs officials who met every ship, but who also looked the other way if provided with the proper inducement. The *Atlas* was in dock for two days, maybe three, and his plan was to enjoy all the delights Panama City offered for every minute he was free, starting immediately. He'd asked Mariama to come along, but hadn't seemed either surprised or disappointed when she'd smiled and shaken her head.

Now he was looking at the expression on her face. "What?"

She breathed in again, then said, "Come with me."

They walked past the visitors' center, the big concrete-and-glass building that overlooked the locks, the carts and trucks selling candy and Coca-Cola and batteries for your camera. Beyond lay a row of ramshackle stone and wood buildings that, like thousands of others throughout the Canal Zone, had belonged to the Americans before they handed over control of the canal to the Panamanians in 1999.

Mariama told Arjen to stay where he was, then walked up to one building, another, a third. She rattled doorknobs, looked inside when the doors were unlocked, stood still and breathed in.

At the sixth building she tried, a one-story stone structure little larger than a shed, she saw what she knew she'd find. Closing the door again, she gestured for Arjen to join her.

"Stay beside me," she said as he came up.

She swung the door open. Inside were jugs of cleaning fluid, bottles of bleach, mops, brooms. The bitter odor she'd detected was stronger, making Arjen wrinkle his nose.

"There," she said.

The thief moved forward, out of the shadow and into the rectangle of sunlight that splashed through the open door. Seeing it, Arjen cursed.

Mariama saw at once that there was something wrong with it. With its wings, which twitched and whirred but did not lift it off the concrete floor.

The injured thief crawled toward them. Mariama knew it could have been close to death, missing half of its body, and it still would never think to hide. Thieves attacked.

Its head was tilted, and its shining green eyes were focused on Arjen. She sensed his anxiety, his desire to run, and did not blame him for it. There was something about the intensity of a thief's gaze that terrified even the bravest men.

But Arjen stood his ground.

When it was about two feet away from him, it reared up on its long legs like a demonic spider. Arjen gave a sudden gasp, as if awakening from a daze. He took one quick step forward, shifted his weight onto his left leg, and lifted his right boot into the air.

The wasp's eyes were like multifaceted mirrors, but somehow they still conveyed . . . fearlessness. Rage.

Arjen brought his boot down.

In the last instant, he altered his aim. The wasp's long body was the obvious target, but all its venomous intelligence seemed to radiate from the creature's head. So it was the head he crushed with his heel.

His foot hit the stone floor with a crack. Instantly the bitter odor intensified a thousandfold. Mariama heard Arjen gag, but again he held his ground. When he lifted his foot, they looked down at the black-and-green pulp smeared across the floor.

Beside the remains of the wasp's head, the nearly intact body writhed, first on its belly, then its back. The long black legs stretched and twitched, grasping at air. The abdomen pulsed, and as they watched, the needlelike white stinger emerged from its tip, then withdrew, leaving a drop of black liquid gleaming like an evil jewel on the floor.

"Let's go," Mariama said.

Arjen didn't move. She had to say it again, and then put a hand on his arm, before he allowed himself to be led away.

OUTSIDE HE SPENT more time than he needed scraping the bottom of his shoe in the dirt. "The smell is all over me," he said.

"It just seems that way," she told him. "It will fade, I promise."

Eventually he straightened and looked at her. His face was pale. "You were not afraid," he said.

Mariama didn't reply.

"You said you did not fear anything, and you were telling the truth."

She made a gesture of frustration with her hands. "I am standing still," she said. "And soon they will be everywhere."

Arjen didn't seem to absorb what she was saying. Again he stared at the shed's closed door. "That thing," he said, "it wanted to kill me."

Mariama laughed. He gave her a surprised, nearly offended look.

"Yes," she said. "Of course it wanted to kill you. I told you. That's what the thieves do."

Then her amusement ebbed.

"One of the things they do," she said.

**AS THEY PARTED**, he asked, "You need a place to stay?"

She nodded.

"For how long?"

A shrug. "A few days."

Every stop just another way station.

His eyes had cleared, though his gaze was still troubled. "And when you move on, will you be heading south like you said? To Magallanes? Tierra del Fuego?"

She shook her head. "No. That was just a dream. I have a job I must do."

"You alone?"

Mariama closed her eyes for a moment.

"I hope not," she said.

# FOURTEEN

**FIVE MINUTES AFTER** they pulled away from the airport, Sheila fell asleep in the taxi. Trey had to shake her awake when they reached his apartment, and though her eyes were open he had to keep his hand on her arm to make sure she didn't crash into any walls.

Most visitors who stayed at Trey's place used the sofa, but he let her take his bed. He knew at least some of what she was going through. Knew that it was more than jet lag. What she was seeking, embracing, wasn't sleep, but freedom from consciousness, and the comforts of a bed might help, at least a little.

He remembered his own experiences too clearly. It had felt like he'd slept for days after his parents died. But he always woke up, which was a blessing and a curse.

The blessing was that for an instant or—if you were very lucky—a few, you did not know who you were or what had happened to you. The curse, of course, was that you remembered, and then had hours to wait until you could sleep and forget again.

There were other alternatives, of course. Trey had never been tempted to go to sleep after making sure he wouldn't awaken, but he could understand why others were. He'd known a few over the years, people who craved the kind of timeless freedom the waking life could never provide.

He could understand it, but not sympathize with it, not much. Humans were the only species with the inclination to commit suicide, and he thought it was a strange evolutionary quirk. A herd that culled itself.

Sitting at his table, wide awake, Trey wondered what kind of person Sheila was.

**HE SHOWERED, PUT** on clean clothes, stayed up the rest of the night. He'd had enough sleep on the airplanes.

Every once in a while he stood to stretch and to check on Sheila. Though she never seemed to change position, he could see the lightweight sheet that covered her rising and falling.

It was strange, having her in his apartment. Strange having anyone there. Most visitors used it when he was on the road. It was little more than a hotel to them, and to him, too.

**HE WOKE HER** at eight. But instead of retreating beneath the covers, trying to hold on to oblivion, as he'd expected, she merely opened her eyes and looked at him. Her eyes, that strange blue-green, were at once clear, alert, though her face was so gaunt that the tendons along her jaw stood out. The hollows under her eyes were bruises.

She sat up. "We'll go see your friend at the museum." Then, looking down at the dirty, rumpled clothes she'd slept in: "Soon as I have a shower."

Trey nodded. "Okay." Then, "There's coffee."

He hesitated. What else? He had little experience as a caretaker, and no particular desire to learn how.

"We'll stop for something to eat on the way," he said finally.

Sheila's mouth compressed. "I'm not hungry."

He suppressed an unexpected flash of anger, though from her expression it must have shown on his face. "What's the first rule for you guys, the aid workers in the refugee camps?" he asked.

She stared at him but didn't answer.

"Stay healthy, right? Something like that? Stay hydrated and well nourished." He stood and walked to the bedroom door, then turned back to her. "Otherwise you'll just get sick, too. Die. Be of no use to anyone, only make more work for the others. Right?"

Sheila's eyes were still on his. Her face was stone. Trey thought he might not be grading out to an A in this caregiving thing, but he didn't much care.

"We have a lot of work ahead," he said. "Jack and me. With you, if you want, or without. But the one thing you're not going to do is slow us down. You want to walk away, do as you please. Prove a point. Starve yourself. You want to help, then we'll stop to eat on the way."

Before she could say anything, he pointed. "The shower's that way," he said and went back to the living room.

* * *

SHE EMERGED FIFTEEN minutes later, scrubbed, her hair in place, the application of soap and shampoo only making her look more fragile and unhealthy. Trey felt a moment's regret for his sharp words, but only a moment.

"Coffee's over there," he said.

She nodded, went to the coffeemaker, and poured herself a mug.

"Cream?" he said. "Sugar?"

"This is fine."

Taking a sip, she looked around the apartment. "None of this looks familiar. Guess I didn't notice much on my way in last night."

"Yeah. Hard to see much with your eyes closed."

She glanced into his face, away. Her expression softened, and suddenly she seemed almost embarrassed.

"Well," she said, "you know . . . all this? Thanks."

Trey said, "You're welcome."

After a moment, she walked over to the bookshelves that lined the interior walls. The mystery stories that his father had read almost exclusively (the last chapter invariably first, because he didn't like surprises). The complete collections of Dickens and Twain that his mother had inherited from her mother. And Trey's own contribution: row upon row of nature books, travel books, field guides, and explorers' and scientists' memoirs.

Sheila picked up an Inuit sculpture of a grizzly bear carved from green serpentine, looked at it, put it down. "Your place," she said. "It's nice."

Something in her tone caused Trey to say, almost without realizing, "It belonged to my parents."

"Yeah?" She looked over at him. "Where do they live now?"

It was a casual question, but he couldn't mask his reaction, the tightening of the skin across his cheekbones. And she noticed.

"They died," he said.

Her hand went to her mouth. "Oh! I'm sorry."

"It was a long time ago."

She nodded. Then he saw something in her face change. "Wait," she said.

Trey sighed. He hated when this happened.

"You're *that* Trey Gilliard."

"Never met another one," he said, as he had before.

"The doctor's son."

"Yes."

She looked at him. He held her gaze, waiting. Knowing what she'd say.

The repertoire was limited. People always said one meaningless—or even cruel—thing or another. Some said, *Your father was a real hero.* Others, *What was your mother thinking? I'd never take risks like that if I had kids.*

Trey had a gracious, meaningless response to each. He never rose to the bait.

But Sheila said, "Do you ever get over feeling like an orphan?"

After a long pause, he shook his head.

**JACK WAS WAITING** impatiently when they walked into his office. Jaw set, beard bristling, he was standing behind his desk, and Trey could see that he already had his pencils and sketch pad ready.

He'd probably been standing like that, waiting in that exact position to make sure they saw and felt guilty, for an hour.

"You ready?" he said. "Or maybe you want to go to a movie first."

Sheila didn't seem to be listening. She was looking around the office, taking in the ramshackle furniture, piles of old books, and Jack's collection of wasp-themed junk.

"Cool," she said. Then, "I got stung sixteen times before I was twelve years old."

Jack blinked, then looked at her with something approaching respect. "Thirty-seven times by the age of ten," he said. "But thirteen of them came at one time."

Sheila walked to the streaked windows and looked out at the park. "I used to love this museum," she said, as quietly as if she were speaking to herself. "Especially the Hall of African Mammals."

"You from New York?" Jack asked.

When he met someone new, Jack usually had one polite question in him before he got impatient. Trey thought this was probably it.

Still looking out the window, Sheila shook her head. "When I was little, we lived in Boston. After that, Tanzania."

She paused. "Shit," she said. "Where do I live now?"

"I heard Trey's place." Jack's eyes gleamed. "Knowing him like I do, I'm sure he'll welcome you there for as long as you need. Stay a year!"

Both Trey and Sheila looked at him, and he laughed. "Now that we've settled *that*," he went on, "can we get to work?" He looked down at his pad and pencils. "I fucking hate a blank piece of paper."

As Sheila sat down across the desk from him, he looked at her out of the corner of his eye. "Heard about your mom," he said. "Sorry."

Sheila said, "Thank you, Jack."

**SHE DESCRIBED THE** larva she'd extracted and Jack scratched away with his pencils and erased and asked questions. Trey did not look. He wanted to see it fresh, complete, not as a work in progress.

While they worked, he sat in an armchair across the room. Taking an old book from the pile he'd gathered, he paged through another tale of adventure, discovery, and high tea among the itinerant aristocracy of nineteenth-century Europe.

He found descriptions of everything from white ants to elephants, but nothing that even resembled the wasps he'd seen.

As he put the book down, a thought struck him immobile for a moment. Something he'd forgotten to mention to either of them.

"A woman I talked to called the wasps *majizi*," he said. "Thieves."

"What woman?" Jack asked.

"A vendor at Ujiji Market."

"And she sounded like she knew what she was talking about?"

Trey nodded. "Yeah. She'd seen them."

"Huh." Jack pulled at his beard. "Thieves. Interesting. So what do they steal?"

The question Trey had asked the old woman, who hadn't answered.

"Maybe . . ." Sheila sounded unsure. "I think maybe . . . your awareness."

They looked at her. Color rose to her pale cheeks, but she didn't waver. "My mother couldn't recognize that she'd been"—a breath—"parasitized. Even when she was looking right at the spot where the larva was, she didn't seem to see it."

There was silence as they all thought this through. Then Jack gave a shake of his head as strong as a wet dog's. "Wait. You're saying that these wasp larvae can . . . *disguise* themselves? Cloud men's minds?"

Sheila didn't answer.

"Like *stealth babies*?"

Sheila's expression hardened. "I'm just telling you what I saw."

"Could it be," Trey said, speaking carefully, "that you're putting two different things together? Maybe your mother had something else, a second condition, that prevented her from seeing clearly."

"You mean like a stroke?" Sheila was shaking her head. "I wondered about that, but I'd seen no other signs. We were together for hours. No symptoms of stroke. Just . . ." Her certainty seemed to vanish. "Just that she didn't seem to understand she'd been infected."

Even Jack looked uncomfortable with the direction the conversation was taking. "A stroke might also help explain why she—passed away so suddenly."

Again Sheila shook her head. A muscle in her jaw jumped.

"All we know for sure," Trey said, "is that we don't know enough."

"You're right, Yoda." Jack picked up the half-finished drawing and shook it. "So let's get this done with."

*  *  *

**FIFTEEN MINUTES LATER** Trey heard Sheila say, "Yeah. That's it."

He looked up just as Jack lifted the drawing so he could see it.

Trey looked at the elongated white body, eyes like pearls, black mandibles. "There's no reason to believe that's *not* the larva of what I saw," he said.

"Yeah." Jack scowled. "You know what fucking sucks? I'm the only one sitting here who actually gives a damn about wasps. And I'm also the only one who's never seen one of these guys in the flesh—larva *or* adult."

Sheila sighed.

"I wish it had been you," she said, "instead of me."


**THEY SHOWED SHEILA** the poster Jack had e-mailed around the world. "Any response yet?" Trey asked.

Jack said, "No. Just mostly people asking if I missed April Fool's Day."

For a moment he looked disconsolate, but then his face brightened. "But it's early yet. Most of the people likely to see these beasts aren't spending all their time on the Internet. They'll get to it."

He walked over to a cluttered table in the corner of the room beside the windows. "Meanwhile: Look!"

They looked. He was holding a multicolored map of the world mounted on corkboard. Poster sized, at least three feet by two. Big enough to illustrate all the world's countries and plenty of cities and geographic land-marks.

He pointed at a red pushpin stuck into the Casamance area of Senegal. As they watched, he moved a poster of the movie *The Wasp Woman* off the wall and hung the map there instead. Then he stuck a second red pin into western Tanzania, right at the edge of Lake Tanganyika.

"The story thus far," he said.

Sheila said, "Two pins."

Trey thought again about the old woman, the gesture she'd made that had encompassed the whole world.

"Just wait," he said.

# FIFTEEN

*Canal Zone, Panama*

**IT WAS A** dance.

That was what Mariama decided. A long, involved dance, with everyone following the steps that had been assigned to them. Even Mariama herself.

Maybe Mariama especially. She was learning that you could be aware of the dance and still be trapped by your role in it.

By now, every stage of her journey here, from the surreal trip on the fishing boat all the way through her nights with Arjen aboard the freighter, seemed as if it had been preordained. Choreographed. All her forward movement, all her plans, all her cleverness and good fortune, seeming to exist at the whim of some master puppeteer she could not even visualize, much less see.

Standing in the fat man's office, Mariama wondered: Is this how the dreaming ones feel?

She didn't know. No one had figured out how to ask them.

\* \* \*

**THE FAT MAN'S** name was Bannerjee. He looked at her across the desk and said, "And why should I help you?"

Mariama suppressed a sigh. Arjen had sent her here, telling her that this Bannerjee was the best in the Canal Zone if you needed a passport. He'd also told her to watch out for him, this man. She hadn't needed to be warned.

"Because I can pay," she said.

He appeared to think about it. Yet she knew that Arjen had gotten word to him as well. He had been expecting her.

He would do what she wanted, when they'd completed their portion of the dance.

"Your friend," he said now, "he has told you that I am the best."

"How much?" She kept her eyes on his. "For the best?"

"Two thousand."

"And I will get . . . ?"

"A Panamanian passport and a valid visa to the United States. They will get you into New York. After that—" He shrugged and pooched out his lips, as if to say, *You will no longer be my problem.*

"Fifteen hundred," Mariama said.

They settled on seventeen, five hundred now and the rest when she got the passport. She retrieved the cash from her money belt, counted it out, and handed it across the desk. Bannerjee counted it for himself, then bent over and put it in a safe or lockbox somewhere near his feet.

In a back room furnished only with a wooden chair and a big camera, he posed her against a white wall and took her picture. "Don't smile," he said before pressing the button. "Since September eleventh, it makes them suspicious when they see people smiling in their passport pictures."

Mariama wondered if this was so, and why, but didn't question it. She didn't feel like smiling anyway.

"When do I come back?" she asked.

"You don't," he said at once.

"Then where?"

"I will send someone to deliver it in three days. Just tell me where you are staying."

She told him.

He blinked but didn't comment, saying only, "Have the rest of the money ready."

She was staying in a place Arjen had told her about, a stone building that had once been a one-room school-house built and used by the Americans. It was part of a subdivision of structures that had boasted houses, shops, and restaurants, but now contained only ruins.

Although it was only about fifteen miles from down-town, when you were there you felt a thousand miles from anywhere. The hum of distant traffic was often obscured by the calls of crickets or the wind rattling through the empty buildings.

In the schoolhouse itself, there were still blackboards and the smells of chalk dust and the sweat of children. Spiders in the corners and mice squeaking at night. But a cot, too, and a functioning well outside, not far from the door.

More than Mariama had expected.

Best of all, the windows had long since been bricked up. The only way in and out was through a reinforced steel door. The outside walls were crumbling, leaving chunks of stone scattered across the ground. But the long, slow ruin still had a ways to go: The interior walls still stood. There was no way in through the cracks, not even for something small and clever and determined.

With care, she could be safe there.

Safe as you could be anywhere. Each night, she checked every inch of her windowless chamber, her schoolhouse tomb. And then lay sleepless for hours on the sagging cot. Thinking. Planning.

When she was outside, she watched the skies. But saw, heard, smelled no sign of them at all.

She knew this meant nothing. Less than nothing. But she did it anyway.

TREY GILLIARD WAS so near. It was infuriating. She could almost reach up from the Canal Zone and touch him in New York City. Almost shout loud enough for him to hear her.

But not close enough. And she couldn't risk contacting him from here.

No one knew she was in Panama, she was almost sure of it. It was possible that the government of Senegal did not even know that she'd left the country.

But they hadn't forgotten who she was and what she knew. And since they'd expelled Trey, too, they must be aware of what he knew as well.

Someone would be watching him, she was certain of that. Listening in on his calls, reading his e-mails. It was legal for the government to do that in the United States these days, or so she'd heard.

No, it wasn't worth the risk. The message she'd sent him from the Canary Islands had been her one shot.

Had he understood?

Phone calls, e-mails, they were close to useless now anyway. She needed to see him. Needed to be in the same room with him, telling him what he didn't know. Showing him. In person.

The three days she had to wait for her passport felt like years.

**ON THE SECOND** day, she had a revelation. She couldn't risk calling Trey, but she could learn more about him.

She went into town, bought an international phone card, and paid for private access to a phone in a downtown real-estate office whose owner was on vacation. Alberto Castro would never know she'd been there, and no one else would think to be listening in on Castro's line.

She sat at his big steel desk. Alongside piles of paper sat a photograph of a cheerful-looking young man with a serious-faced wife and two smiling children, a girl of about ten and a boy of perhaps seven.

Mariama felt an unexpected jolt of something like sorrow. She wasn't sure what caused it. Maybe it was the fact that she would never have a life like the Castros'.

Or maybe it was that the Castros' dream of a life would too soon come to an end.

Swiveling around in her chair, Mariama picked up the phone and dialed the international operator. When someone picked up, she said, "Rockefeller University in New York City, please."

Mariama had never visited Rockefeller University or even seen a picture of it. She imagined a gigantic apartment building filled with geniuses and their technology.

Winners of the Nobel Prize. Inventors of new machines to replace failing organs, of new medicines, of new ways of looking at the world.

The sort of people who would laugh at the health clinic Mariama's father ran in the Casamance.

To the receptionist she said, "Elena Stavros's office, please."

Elena Stavros, the one person in the building full of geniuses Mariama knew wouldn't scoff at her.

**MARIAMA AND ELENA** had met just once, two years earlier, at a conference in Cape Town, South Africa. Mariama had attended with her father, back when they were allowed to travel.

Mariama remembered Elena Stavros vividly. How could she not? Elena, a microbiologist, was small, like Mariama, and just a few years older, but in all other ways so different that people had laughed when they saw the two together.

Mariama was self-contained and slow to smile, with a quiet voice and a face whose expressions were hard to read. Elena, on the other hand, flaunted a great mass of black hair, expressive eyes, and a face that always seemed to be gripped by one rampant emotion or another.

She was also loud. In fact, she was so loud that three times during symposia and panel discussions she'd been warned to keep her voice down.

Somehow the two of them had decided they liked each other. They'd spent hours one night sharing experiences and memories, and among the topics of conversation they'd touched upon was Trey Gilliard.

Mariama had mentioned that the International Conservation Trust was planning a months-long mission in the Casamance rain forest. Elena had blinked and said, "Hah! That means you'll meet Trey. Lucky you!" She'd paused. "Unless they've gotten sick of him by now and fired his ass."

Elena's face had reddened as she spoke, something Mariama had pretended not to notice. She'd just said, "How do you know him?"

"Oh, our paths have crossed." Then, as if acknowledging her discomposure: "He's absolutely brilliant about nature. With people? Not so much."

Later, as the future's path became inexorably clear, Mariama had thought of those words often. Brilliant with nature, that was important. She didn't care how he was with people.

"When you see him, tell him I said hi." Then Elena's gaze had sharpened. "And also tell him that the door to room 33 is shut."

Mariama had promised. But by the time Trey had finally shown up in Senegal, ICT's mission delayed again and again, Mariama had become persona non grata, warned to stay far away from all visitors.

The times she'd managed to get close to Trey, they hadn't had the chance to exchange pleasantries, jokes, or cryptic references to the past.

Or anything important, either.

"STAVROS," THE VOICE on the other end of the line said. "Who is this?"

Her voice instantly familiar. Mariama found herself

smiling. "My name is Mariama Honso," she said. "From Senegal. We met in Cape Town. Do you remember me?"

There was a brief pause. Then the voice came again, louder. "Mariama! For God's sake. Of course I do! The lion kill!"

Mariama remembered the lion kill. It had been on a field trip to Kruger National Park and the victim had been a zebra.

"Where are you?" Elena went on. "Here? In the city? Let's get dinner. There's this great Ethiopian place—wait, do you like African food?"

Mariama laughed. It was amazing she could still laugh.

"I'm not in the city," she said. "Not yet. Soon, though, and then—dinner."

"But I'm hungry for injera bread *now*." Elena's sigh came down the line. "Okay. Deal. Why are you calling?"

"I have a question."

"Shoot."

"Are you still in touch with Trey Gilliard?"

Elena was silent for a few moments. Then she said, "No. Not recently." She made a sound that might have been a laugh. "People don't stay in Trey's life for very long, you know. But I do keep an eye on him from afar."

"You do?"

"When I can. God knows why."

Mariama took a breath. "Do you know if he's there? In New York?"

"To the best of my knowledge." A pause. "I heard he was in Tanzania recently, but I think he's around again. Him and some woman he met there."

Mariama felt something loosen inside her chest. This was good. This was better than she could have prayed for.

Elena was saying, "That's not typical of Trey. He doesn't often bring anyone home."

When Mariama didn't speak, Elena laughed. "Sweetie, why do you want him?"

Mariama said, "I'll tell you when I see you."

"You want me to give him a call, tell him you're coming to town?"

Mariama kept her voice calm. "No, thank you. I'll get in touch with him myself."

When it's time.

Once she hung up, Mariama sat for a while in the unfamiliar office, beside the photograph of a family she would never meet.

She'd taken a risk, but it had been worth it.

Maybe, just maybe, there was still a chance.

# SIXTEEN

**ONE MAN CAME** through the door. She had expected two at least.

They'd underestimated her, as people always did. Thought she was merely a girl, and therefore easily handled.

And thank the gods they had, because one man was almost more than enough. She'd been so consumed with her plans that she'd lost some of her instincts, some of her alertness.

The knock on the schoolhouse door came when she expected it. But as soon as she unlocked the door, it swung open so violently that she didn't get out of the way in time. Next thing she knew, she was on her knees on the floor, dazed, looking up at the man who came striding in.

He was a brute, a huge white man with a scowling face and thick legs and bare arms like slabs. Quick on his feet, though, grabbing the front of her blouse and yanking her up, his left hand already under the shirt and against her bare skin.

When she tried to knee him in the groin, he turned his hips just far enough to take the blow on his thigh. If it hurt him, he showed no sign.

He wasn't reaching for her body. She heard the latch of her money belt click. A moment later, he'd tossed her across the room as effortlessly as she might have tossed a cushion.

Waking up finally, she protected her head when she crashed onto the stone floor near the cot. Still, she lay there, breathless, for long seconds while he inspected what was inside the belt's zippered compartment.

When she struggled to her feet, he pointed at her, a casual warning to stay still. He didn't seem to be paying much attention to her, but she knew how quickly he would respond if she went for him.

Not that it mattered. She barely was able to get enough air into her lungs to say, "My passport—"

"Shut up," he said.

He was holding a big wad of bills in one thick hand. Almost all her money.

"Here's what happens," he went on. His accent was American. Not all of them had gone home.

"I'll take this," he said. "You want the passport, you find another thousand. Give it to my boss, and you can have your passport."

"But how—"

He shrugged. His face rearranged itself into something that appeared to be a grin. "Who cares? Fuck for it, kill for it, whatever you need to do. But the price is another thousand. You don't have a choice."

Eyes still on her face, he jammed the bills into his pocket, tossed the belt onto the floor. Then his gaze dropped a little and he focused on something.

"That, too," he said.

For an instant Mariama thought again that he meant her body. Then she realized it was her silver necklace, her locket, that had captured his attention.

"Give," he said, holding out a beefy palm.

Mariama shook her head.

He wasn't much for explaining himself or asking twice. She was learning that. He came across the room at her, again much faster than she'd anticipated, his hand grabbing for the chain, clearly not caring if he yanked her head off with it.

He was fast, but this time she was faster. His hand had not yet reached her neck when she brought up a chunk of rock that had come from the crumbling wall outside. One of several she'd brought in and hidden.

She swung her arm in a short arc and banged the stone against his temple. That stopped him in his tracks, but he didn't go down. Instead, his face took on a thoughtful expression, his eyes suddenly vague. She could feel the tips of the fingers on his outstretched right hand brushing her neck and the links of the silver chain.

She hit him again, harder, and this time he did fall. Onto his knees, at first, and then all the way, toppling onto his side. His eyes closed.

She studied him for a few moments, waiting to see if he would awake and leap at her, whether he might be pretending. But he didn't seem like the kind to engage in subterfuge. He was unconscious.

There was already a huge purple bruise on his swollen

forehead, and some blood seeped out of the abrasions where the rough stone had broken the skin. Nothing gushing, though. Good.

Kneeling over him, she searched his pockets. She took back the money he'd stolen from her, but found nothing else. No wallet, no identification, no money of his own.

There was one thing: a knife with a spring-driven folding blade. Mariama tested it a couple of times, pushing the button that released the blade and folding it back in again. Then she slipped it into her pocket.

When she was done, she walked over to the door, which was still open, and looked out. Heard no one. Light pollution from Panama City brightened the western sky, and a half-moon and smeary stars cast some light on the falling-down buildings and patchy brush of the old sub-division. Somewhere out in the darkness, a dog or coyote yapped.

His car was parked out front. She knew the keys must be in it. And why not? He'd assumed that he would be the only one going in, the only one coming out.

Returning to the fallen man, she took both his wrists in her hands, pulled his arms over his head, and dragged him to the door. He snorted and once his right foot kicked, setting her heart racing, but he didn't awake.

It was hard work. She was dripping with sweat well before they reached the spot she'd chosen. Behind a pile of rubble a hundred feet from the school, a spot that no one would likely ever visit, but for the dogs and carrion birds and insects.

When she had him lying there, illuminated only by the moonlight, she paused to catch her breath. Then she squatted beside him and reached out with both hands.

One pinched his nose shut while the other covered his mouth.

He fought back. Or, rather, his body did, flailing its arms and kicking its legs. But the organizing principle, the conscious mind that would have resisted her in some specific way, that would have gone for her eyes or her throat in return . . . that was missing.

All that was left was the organism's inherent desire to live. And that wasn't enough.

Soon his movements grew weaker, more sporadic. Then they ceased entirely. When she was sure, she stood one last time, stretched her weary arms, turned away, and walked over to his car.

In the past, she might have spared his life. Tied him up and later, when she was safe, told someone where he was.

But they were living in a new world, one that permitted no unnecessary risks.

SHE HELD THE edge of the blade against Mr. Bannerjee's neck. His mouth opened and some saliva dropped out of it and onto his desk.

She knew she must have looked like a creature from a nightmare to him: sweaty, disheveled, bloodthirsty, fierce. He must have guessed what had happened to the man he'd sent for her.

"Where is it?" she asked him.

A few minutes later, she was holding a green Panamanian passport issued to Maimouna Wade, complete with her photo and a U.S. tourist visa. After looking it over, she put it in her belt and squatted beside Mr. Bannerjee, who was again sitting slumped behind his desk.

"You're very lucky," she told him. "I'm letting you live. But if you tell a single person about any of this, I *will* send someone to correct that error."

He looked at her but said nothing.

"Do you understand?" she said.

He nodded. His mouth and chin were quivering.

She wasn't satisfied, but it was as much as she could expect. She couldn't afford to leave this man's body behind where it might be found.

Some chances you had to take.

**THE FLIGHT TO** New York City was uneventful. Not crowded, so Mariama had a two-seat row to herself. She'd brought a book to read, just like the other tourists (though most of them spent their time staring at their laptop computers), but she looked out the window for much of the flight, her mind far away.

She still had so much planning to do.

The plane landed on time. The passengers disembarked and headed to Immigration. In her modest skirt and flowered cotton blouse, Mariama looked like any other West African woman coming to the world's melting pot city.

She waited on the line, and soon enough it was her turn. Somewhere deep inside she could feel a flutter of nerves, but on the surface she appeared completely calm. Compared to everything she'd been through, this was easy.

The young man in the Immigration booth looked tired. He glanced at Mariama's face, then at the passport. Typed something into his computer. While he was waiting, he asked her if she was there on business or pleasure.

"I'm visiting my family," she said.

"So some of both, eh?" he said.

Mariama smiled. She wondered how often he made that joke.

He stamped her passport and handed it back to her. "Enjoy your visit."

"Thank you," she said.

Done. All she had was a carry-on bag, so she wouldn't even have to wait for a suitcase to come trundling out on the baggage loop. Nothing left to do but to disappear into New York City, get in touch with the people whose apartment she was going to share, and—at last—go see Trey Gilliard.

**SHE WAS STILL** a few feet from the door labeled *Ground Transportation* when she felt the tap on her shoulder. "Excuse me, ma'am."

Her first instinct was to run, but she knew that would be disastrous.

Instead she turned to see two men in uniforms with black pants and bright blue shirts. They were big, strong, polite. In the way of security officials everywhere, they stood a little too close to her.

On their blue shoulders were labels saying *TSA*. Mariama knew what that stood for: Transportation Security Administration.

"Yes?" she said.

"Come with us, ma'am, please," said the one who had spoken first.

And the other said, "We have a few questions to ask you."

Mariama went with them. What choice did she have?

**ALL THIS TIME**, with all the dangers she'd faced, she had never truly believed that her part in the dance would end so soon.

# SEVENTEEN

" 'NATIVE SUPERSTITIONS RUN wild in this fever-ridden black heart of the Dark Continent, where God has never smiled and people worship the spirits of the teeming forest whose grasping tendrils they never escape.' "

"Is that purple prose getting all over your fingers?" Jack asked.

Sheila said, "Go on."

By now, Trey had become sure he'd never find what he was looking for in the old travel memoirs. So sure that when he did find it, in a book called *Beasts, Bugs, and Bedouins: A Journey through the Slavelands*, he turned the page before what he'd read filtered through to his conscious mind.

Then it got his full attention.

" 'The native witch doctors tell tales of pythons large enough to eat a young hippopotamus—or a large man— whole, then retiring to digest their meal for two full years before stalking a new victim,' " he read out loud. " 'Of strange doglike creatures, seen only in the shadows, that howl outside a village the night before the wretched victim of a mystical curse perishes. And of a winged demon that, in the guise of a wasp, preys on monkeys, and even on the most unfortunate of men.' "

"Hey," Jack said.

Sheila was standing very still and straight in her spot by the window. "Keep reading," she said.

" 'Once they find you,' " Trey went on, " 'your life is forfeit. There is no surcease, no restitution, no cure. Neither escape: These demons act in unearthly concert, as with a single intent. There is only the summoning, the long dreaming days, the last terrifying madness, confronted only at your own mortal peril, and then the inevitability of death.' "

He stopped reading. Very quietly, almost under her breath, Sheila said, "Long dreaming days."

"The last terrifying madness." Jack grunted. "Anything else?"

Trey shook his head. "No, that's it."

"I guess it would've been too much to expect an illustration." Jack turned his palms up. "I don't know. It all sounds like a Victorian flight of fancy." He grimaced. "I mean, in the same passage we have hippo-eating snakes and mystical doglike creatures that foretell your death with a woof."

No one spoke for a while. Then Trey stirred. "No," he said. "I don't think so. If I hadn't seen the thieves myself, I'd agree it was myth, legend. But the thieves do exist, so we can't assume there's no truth at the heart of this description."

Jack was still frowning. "Then tell me: What are 'dreaming days'?"

"Something we haven't seen yet."

"That's helpful." Jack leaned back in his chair and stared at the ceiling. "Okay, let's go through this methodically. The madness is last—"

"The inevitability of death is last," Sheila said.

"Well, besides that. But 'summoning' comes before. What's that?"

Trey said, "I wonder . . ."

"Silent wondering not allowed," Jack said. "Spill."

Trey was remembering. The colony. The thief hovering in front of his face, deciding.

Even here, even after all this time, the memory made his skin feel cold.

"At the colony," he said. "That monkey I saw."

Seeing again the colobus's terror, its white-rimmed eyes and desperate cries as it staggered into the clearing.

"You think it was going . . . against its will," Sheila said. "Not that it was just disoriented?"

Trey said, "Yes."

"But how? Who was summoning it, and how?"

Jack brought his feet back down to the floor. "Well, I could come up with a theory about *that*." He seemed suddenly more cheerful. "Fungus," he said.

Sheila said, "What?"

"Fungus," Jack said again. "Specifically, *Ophiocordyceps*."

Trey was nodding. "Yes, that could be it."

Sheila looked at the two of them and frowned. "Please tell me what you're agreeing about."

"Various species of *Ophiocordyceps* fungi are found in tropical forests all around the world," Jack said. "They have a diabolical way of dispersing themselves, colonizing new territories."

He was enjoying himself. "It all starts when an ant, a grasshopper, or another bug breathes in some of the fungus's spores. The spores lodge in the bug's lungs and the fungus starts to grow, to spread through the body. At the same time, it releases chemicals that affect the insect's brain. Basically, it turns its victim into a zombie."

Sheila said, "You're making this up."

Jack grinned. "Nope. The bug's behavior suddenly changes. It finds a bush and climbs to the top, a place it would never normally go. An ant that has never left the ground, for example, might climb six or eight feet up. Then, with its last strength, it grabs hold of a branch with its strong mandibles. And dies."

Sheila was staring at him. "Why on earth does it do that?"

"So when the fungus sprouts through the dead ant's eyes, mouth, and other openings, it can release its spores out into the breeze, to drift down and be breathed in by another ant, or a hundred, or a whole colony."

They waited while she absorbed this. Then Trey said, "In some forests, you can find them pretty easily. The remains, I mean. These white fungus stalks and sprouts catch your eye—they gleam among the green leaves—and there, clinging to the bush, is something that was once an insect."

"Oh, did I mention?" Jack was grinning at Sheila's expression. "The fungus liquefies the host's innards and converts them to sugars. Food!"

Again they waited. After a while Sheila said, "Okay. I have a few questions."

Her voice crisp, like she was taking a patient's history.

"Are mammals ever infected by these fungus spores?" she asked.

Jack looked a little less happy and said, "Not that anyone's found yet, no."

She nodded. "What you described to me is a pretty straightforward parasite-host relationship. But do these fungi ever work with other species to their mutual benefit? Are the relationships ever symbiotic?"

Jack scowled.

"And if the thief-fungus relationship is symbiotic, the fungus has to get something out of the deal. Unless the infected monkey climbs to a treetop before it dies." She looked at Trey. "Does that seem likely to you?"

Silence. Then Jack, looking a little disconsolate, shook his shoulders. "Okay," he said. "As a theory, it needs work."

"We don't have enough of the pieces yet." Sheila paused, the corners of her mouth turning down. "And if something *was* 'summoning' the monkey Trey saw, yours is a much better theory than I could have come up with."

For a moment her eyes went out of focus. She pointed at the old book Trey was still holding. "If she'd lived, would my mother have been summoned as well?"

Neither Trey nor Jack spoke. It didn't matter. Sheila went on without waiting for an answer.

"And was Mom going to experience the dreaming days?" she said. "The madness? Was her death inevitable?"

Her voice shook a little on the last sentence. Then it firmed.

"I *hate* not having the answers," she said.


THE PHONE RANG about an hour later, a loud, clattery sound in the silence. Jack answered on the third ring and said, "Yeah?"

And then, "Yeah."

And then, straightening, his face lighting up, "Yeah?"

He listened for another second, then said, "Hang on. Let me put you on speaker. There are people here who'll want to hear this."

He pushed a button. The speakerphone kicked in just in time for Trey to hear a voice say, "—Gilliard there?"

"Yes, I'm here," Trey said.

"Gilliard! Hey. Remember me?"

A familiar British accent, nasal voice. Trey could see the storklike frame, the long, indolent face, the blue eyes like chips of glass.

"Sure," he said. "How you doing, Ranny?"

Randolph Whitson, one of the countless field biologists whose paths had crossed Trey's over the years.

"You still at La Tamandua?" Trey asked.

"Always. That's why I'm calling."

La Tamandua Tropical Research Station, set amid the cloud forests below the peak of Monte Blanco in Costa Rica. Trey remembered it well from his single visit a decade earlier. The dense, wet forest had been filled with jewel-like poison dart frogs, iridescent birds, and foliage of more shades of green than even Trey had ever seen before.

Ranny, a mammalogist associated with the University of London, had built the research station, beam by hardwood beam, and since then he'd rarely left. His specialty was bats, but by now he knew everything that lived in those forests.

"Finally got a phone in there?" Trey asked.

The crowing laugh came down the line. At the beginning, Ranny hadn't allowed a radio or satellite phone to be installed on La Tamandua's premises. Word was he'd chosen the station's site, in a little valley, because cell-phone service didn't penetrate there.

"No effing way," Ranny said. "I'm calling from Rio Viejo."

The small town an hour's drive from the station.

"And you drove all that way just to chat?" Jack asked. It was time to get to the point.

"You kidding? We were running low on beer, and any-way it's Graciela's time of the month, so she needed some shit."

Over by the window, Sheila gave a quick blink and an unmistakable roll of the eyes.

Trey didn't bother to ask who Graciela was. With Ranny, there was always a girl. Always a different girl.

"But I figured, long as I'm here, why not call? 'Cause I think I caught one of those buggers you've been look-ing for."

Jack rose onto his toes. "You just told me you'd *seen* one!"

The laugh. "Saw it and caught it. Hang on."

Garbled noises over the line before Ranny returned. "Last time I was in here, somebody showed me that Wanted poster you sent around on the computer. Ugly bugger. Give me a bat any old day.

"But then damned if I didn't find your beast chewing through one of my mist nets maybe three mornings later." A pause. "Most bats give up once they're tangled in the net, but not this guy. He had determination, that one."

"And you collected it?" Jack looked like he couldn't believe what he was hearing.

"Yeah." Ranny seemed to hesitate, and when he spoke

again his voice had a different tone. "Yeah. Tell you the truth, I didn't want to go near it. Wanted to leave it alone, let it get away and go back to wherever it came from. But I knew you were on a kick for these guys, so I maneuvered around and squeezed it till it gave up and died."

A sound, maybe a cough, came down the line. "You didn't mention the smell in your ad, I notice. That thing effing stinks. It's bothering Graciela. So when are you going to come pick it up?"

Jack said, "What? Send it to us."

"Yeah?" Ranny was laughing. "Sure. No prob. I'll just stick it in a box and courier it up your way."

Jack growled at his tone.

"Sorry, pal," Ranny went on. "Maybe that's how it works at your museum, but not here. Here we carry out our specimens. I'm not leaving for six more weeks, and there's nobody else around."

When no one spoke, he said, "The way this thing smells, if you don't come for it in the next two days, I'm putting it outside. And you know how long it'll last in the wet here."

Trey was remembering how he'd felt the first time he'd encountered the thieves. He said, more quietly than he'd intended, "I'll go."

Then, louder, "Ranny, I'll be there by tomorrow night."

Sheila said, "Trey, no."

At the same time, Ranny was saying, "Great. If I remember right, there's a direct flight to San José from Kennedy at around six in the morning. Drive fast, and you'll be here before nightfall."

"I'll drive fast," Trey said.

Ranny laughed. "My man. Bring more beer."

He disconnected. Jack was already sitting behind his computer, clicking the mouse. After a few moments, he looked up. "Six twenty-five on LACSA. From Kennedy, like he said."

Trey nodded, but he was looking at Sheila. "What's the problem?"

"Those things," she said.

Jack raised his eyes from the screen. "Only one of them, and it's dead."

"Come on, Jack," she said, her voice suddenly harsh. "Give someone else credit for a little intelligence. We all know that where there's one, there'll be more."

Jack stared at her. His mouth moved, and Trey was sure—certain—that he was about to say something like, *I guess it's your time of the month, too, huh, Sheila?*

Trey didn't let that happen. "Both of you," he said, "pipe down."

Their eyes went to him. Neither of them looked happy to be interrupted, but it was Sheila who spoke. "Trey, you'll be walking into too many unknowns. I don't think it's worth the risk."

Jack said, "As opposed to his usual M.O.? We need that specimen."

Trey saw the wasp hovering just before his face, the others staring at him from the mouths of their burrows.

"I'll be back as soon as I can," he said.

# EIGHTEEN

*Costa Rica*

## TREY DROVE FAST.

He'd gotten an old black Jeep Cherokee at the airport rental counter in San José, dented and dinged and with chipped paint and a touch of rust. The agent had been apologetic. It was all they could find for him on such short notice, in a country filled with tourists seeking shiny SUVs equipped with air-conditioning and powerful sound systems to keep the smells and sounds of the tropics out.

But it was just what Trey wanted, with plenty of power and four-wheel drive. These were the only requirements for a region whose roads were composed of mud, rutted dirt, turtle-backed all-weather gravel, and—worst of all—pothole-ridden asphalt that hadn't been resurfaced in twenty years.

Under dripping skies, he left San José behind and, weaving in and out of traffic, made his impatient way through the capital's suburbs and onto the Pan-American

Highway. Driving north past steaming volcanoes and lowering clouds punctuated by flocks of circling vultures.

Trey had once planned to drive the entire extent of the Pan-American Highway. He'd begin up in Prudhoe Bay, above the Arctic Circle, and not end till he reached Ushuaia, Argentina, just north of Tierra del Fuego. Along the way, wherever he found something interesting, he'd stop. For a day or a year, he didn't know, but always knowing he'd eventually get back on the road.

At the Darién Gap in Panama, where for fifty miles the highway didn't exist, he'd abandon his car and hike through the jungle to Colombia. There he'd buy a new junker, get back on the road, and keep going.

That was the plan, but even as he made it, he knew it was impossible. What about the rest of the world? The Americas weren't enough. He couldn't drive everywhere he wanted to go. He'd miss too much.

The whole way to La Tamandua, Trey drove faster than anyone should. The cautious tourists goggled at him and swerved out of his way. Locals, keeping up on the rutted highway for a while in their old pickup trucks, laughed and honked their horns as they fell back. For twenty or thirty miles, a pair of men on Harley-Davidsons accompanied him, effortlessly keeping pace, a convoy, a motorcade, before peeling off.

Why so fast? He wondered about this later. Because Ranny had told him to, threatening to destroy the specimen if he didn't arrive by nightfall? Or because after days of sitting still in New York, he gloried in the chance to *move*?

Yes. Those were both true. But not the whole truth.

The other part: He was afraid.

And when something frightened you, your only option was to confront it. To race toward it, not to hide.

He sped past farms and villages and factories, leaving the highway and ascending on ever-smaller and rougher roads into the Tilarán Mountains. The Jeep bucking and plowing, sending up sprays of mud but staying on the road.

Two thousand feet. Four. The old Jeep's engine beginning to protest from lack of air. The clouds descending, billows of gray mist blown by a cold, fitful breeze.

He drove through the town of Rio Viejo, where Ranny made his phone calls. Then turned onto the all-weather road that ended at the lip of the forested valley where the field station was located.

The ten-hour drive had taken him barely seven. It was time for him to confront his fears.

**THE CLOUD FOREST** as dusk neared. Low, gnarled trees whose branches hung heavy with mosses, and air plants. Philodendrons and vines climbing up moisture-slick trunks. Clouds sweeping through, coating every surface with droplets that caught the light and gleamed like gems.

A forest out of Middle-earth.

Trey parked the Jeep beside a battered Nissan—Ranny's, he assumed—in the little dirt lot carved out of the brush beside the road. If you wanted to visit the station, you left your car here and hiked down a wet, muddy trail for two miles. If this felt like too much, you were welcome to turn around and go home.

Ranny didn't want it any other way. His goal, he said, was to keep the riffraff out.

Trey climbed out of his car, then reached back in for

his daypack. Before he'd taken ten steps, his skin, hair, and clothes were slick with moisture. As he walked, sure-footed as always on even the wettest, steepest trails, he heard a distant bellbird give its ringing "tonk" call from a treetop and a troop of black howler monkeys welcoming nightfall with their roars.

Eventually he spotted a brighter patch ahead: the clearing where La Tamandua stood. As he approached, he realized that the station was silent, its generator off. No music, no voices. Through a mist-streaked window, he could see a lamp burning inside, but no sign of movement.

Shifting his flashlight to his left hand, he walked forward and pulled the door open.

A puff of warmer air wafted out. Trey breathed it in. It was stale, carrying the odors of overripe fruit, cigarette smoke, and bug repellent.

And the bitter smell of the thieves.

Trey would always know, would always hate, that smell.

**THE THREE ROOMS**—a dormitory-style bedroom, a den/office/living room, and a laboratory—were empty, of humans and anything else living. But they hadn't been empty for long. No more than six or eight hours.

The light Trey had seen from outside came from a goosenecked lamp that craned over Ranny's desk. Even as Trey looked at it, it flickered, reaching the end of its battery backup. He turned it off.

The dirty plates in the sink had once held rice and beans. What was left was congealed, but not yet petrified. Yesterday's dinner or today's breakfast.

There were two plates. One had held more food, eaten more messily, the second a smaller, neater portion.

In the station's dorm room, containing a half dozen cots, two had been pushed together. The room smelled of perfume and sweat and sex.

Ranny's clothes were piled haphazardly on shelves and slung over a rack in the corner of the room. A woman's clothes—Graciela's clothes—were more carefully folded or hung neatly on the rack. She'd brought a large variety of short skirts and colorful slacks, halter tops and sleeveless blouses.

Trey left the laboratory itself till last. It was modest, one of the smallest Trey had seen, but that made sense. All Ranny needed here was a ready supply of collecting equipment and the materials to preserve the specimens. More in-depth study could wait for his occasional trips back to better-equipped laboratories in England.

A half dozen bats in various stages of preservation sat on a work table. Amid specimens of insectivorous leaf-nosed and foxlike fruit-eating bats, Trey recognized a vampire bat, its size, oily fur, and squinting grin distinctive even in death.

None of the bats occupied pride of place on the table, though, the spot right in front of the chair. A small wooden box, perhaps a foot long by six inches wide and the same again deep, sat there. It was open. Its top, waiting to be nailed on, lay beside it.

But there was nothing inside, amid the white-foam packing material that would protect the specimen in transit. Just a depression in the foam, about three inches long. Skinny. Insect shaped.

What had happened to the specimen?

Trey took some air into his lungs. Somewhere outside in the forest, a large branch cracked and fell to earth. It made a sound like a gunshot or the breaking of a mast just before the ship goes down.

Looked at one way, all he'd learned from his search was that the two of them were out. It was nearing dusk, the time that Ranny would have been stringing his mist nets between the trees of his study area. Setting his traps for the bats he hunted and studied. Graciela could well have accompanied him.

Trey could just wait here, and in an hour or so they'd return.

That was the fantasy. But Trey knew better. He knew the reality was different.

He was going to have to go look for them.

He found the station's first-aid kit and put it into his daypack. Near the front door was a row of pegs, three of them holding hard hats with attached headlamps. He took one and put it on.

Last, he went looking for the weapon he knew would be there. It was standing in the shadows by the laboratory door: a shotgun, unloaded, cleaned, oiled, not recently used. The ammunition—a box of #9 birdshot shells—was in a supply closet in the corner of the room.

Trey took the gun and a handful of shells with him and walked out into the cold, dripping forest.

# NINETEEN

**THE ABRUPT TROPICAL** dusk had fallen while Trey was inside. Rain pattered on the leaves above his head, and every once in a while a bigger drop struck his hard hat with a thump.

The bellbird had fallen silent, but in the wet darkness crickets and glass frogs had started calling. A gigantic beetle, nearly as big as Trey's hand, buzzed slowly past. It had two bright green lights shining like headlights from the front of its thorax.

The air was growing even colder. Trey knew that temperatures here could dip into the forties at night, a far cry from the sticky heat of the lowland rain forest.

Trey remembered the trails from his previous visit—he never forgot a trail he'd hiked—but, radiating out like spokes from the field station, they would have been easy enough to follow anyway. The shotgun under his arm, he searched one trail, then retraced his steps and headed down the next.

When full darkness fell, he had no choice but to turn

on his headlamp. He hated using lights. They were like neon signs: For everything you spotted, a hundred things spotted you.

The beam turned green leaves gray. Shadows moved at the corners of the light, and small, unseen creatures rustled through the wet foliage at his feet. The howler monkeys roared again.

Staying patient, he moved slowly along each trail, looking for evidence that anyone had been there. Recently crushed leaves or bent stems, kicked-up leaf litter. And on the fifth trail, as he stepped into a small clearing caused by a tree fall, he caught just a whiff of the thieves' odor. That was all, and then it was gone, chased by the breeze.

He turned the lamp's beam this way and that, but could see nothing in the harsh light. Lifting his gaze, he saw that the mist had risen and a half-moon had emerged from hurrying clouds. That was enough. He reached up and turned off the lamp.

At first the darkness seemed absolute. He was blind.

Amid the forest's rustles and calls, he waited as his eyes gradually adjusted to the diffuse light of the moon and stars. When he could see the movement of a small gray salamander across the trail ten feet away, he knew he was ready.

He turned slowly in a circle in the middle of the clearing, searching for anything unusual, anything out of the ordinary. At the same time, he listened beyond the sound of the night insects and the whisper of the breeze through wet leaves.

Three times he turned before he saw it: the tiniest glimmer, detectable only through the corners of his eyes.

Not the light cast by the stars or moon or the cold luminescence of a colony of forest mites. A gleam from the ground at the far end of the clearing.

And movement, too. A brief, flickering shadow obscuring the light.

Trey walked toward it.

The glow grew brighter as he approached, but only slightly. The feeble illumination it cast revealed drooping leaves, a gray-brown tree trunk, a vine twisted around the trunk like a snake. And a large, slumped form he couldn't make out yet.

He knew what it was, though.

The light he'd glimpsed was a flashlight's beam. Like the lamp in the field station, it must have been burning for hours, because by now it was so weak that he could see the coil itself flickering inside the bulb.

Ranny was lying on the ground, the flashlight attached to his belt.

Trey reached up and turned on his headlamp. The scene before him sprang into full relief, black shadows erupting. A great curassow, unseen in the foliage above, gave a harsh croak and lifted off from its roost, heavy wings making a rushing sound like the wind. The diamond-bright pinprick eyes of dozens of spiders gleamed from nearby trunks.

Ranny lay on his back beside a small tree, his collecting gear—rolled-up mist nets, cloth bags, the harness he used to climb—scattered around him. His eyes were closed, his face gray.

Trey squatted beside him, felt for a pulse. Found it after a moment, just a slight, delicate throbbing in the throat. Ranny's skin was warm, but it had a strange, waxy consistency to it, as if in some strange way it had been molten and was now firming again.

Trey called out his name, shook his shoulder, but Ranny didn't stir.

The long dreaming days.

Trey aimed his beam and saw what he'd expected to: the telltale swelling on Ranny's stomach, pressing against the inside of his shirt. Unblinking, Trey watched it. Half a minute, a minute. Nothing. Nothing.

Then . . . something moving beneath the cloth. A sinuous flutter, quickly gone.

Something coming to the surface of the skin for a gulp of air, then twisting and diving deeper once again.

Trey stood. He let the beam describe a wider arc. Knowing what he was looking for and soon finding it.

The girl lay perhaps eight feet away, on her side, back to him. Under the clear plastic rain poncho, her tight blouse, white with a pattern of flowers stitched in it, was untucked from the waistband of her short ruby red skirt. Her long brown legs were bare and slick with mist. So was her left foot, though she wore a white sneaker on her right one.

Graciela.

Looking at that one bare foot, Trey felt his fear dissipate. It was replaced by a kind of burning determination, the ice-cold certainty that always took the place of anger deep in his core.

He knew that, whatever happened, he would never be afraid of the thieves again.

As he took his first step forward, the shadows shifted. A thief moved, spiderlike, into view on Graciela's hip, then stood there, staring at him. Slender black body shining with dew, wings flickering.

"There you are," Trey said.

The thief tilted its head at the sound of his voice, but did not otherwise react. It was waiting, Trey thought. Waiting to see what his next action would be.

He wondered if it knew what a gun was. Whether it understood what the birdshot could do to it.

Trey tilted his head so that the beam shone directly into the thief's eyes. It merely turned away from the light, watching him instead from the corners of its eyes.

For a minute, maybe more, the standoff continued. Just as Trey knew—knew!—that it was dying to come for him, he wanted nothing more than to pull the trigger and blast its body into rubble and ichor.

He lowered the beam a little. The wasp turned back to stare at him. What was going on in its insect brain? Conscious thought or only the primitive neuronal firings of a simpler species?

There was one way to find out.

He swung the shotgun down and poked the barrel into Ranny's stomach. One twitch of his finger and the larva beneath the skin would die.

Did the thief understand what he was threatening to do?

The wasp sprang a foot into the air. Before Trey could shift his aim, it landed on Graciela's bare leg, closer, facing him head-on. Its mandibles twitched and its wings made a strange chittering sound on its back.

Trey had long since learned not to ascribe human emotions to other mammal species, much less insects. Still, he couldn't help it. In this thief, he saw rage and something more: anxiety, even horror. Yes, it understood.

Trey poked the barrel of the rifle deeper into Ranny's stomach. Up the barrel and into his hand came a quivering motion from within the flesh.

The thief came for him. As he'd known it would.

Even so, even though he'd expected it, the attack was so fast, so unerring, that the wasp almost reached him. He barely managed to raise the shotgun, and if it had contained a single bullet instead of a birdshot-filled cartridge, he would have been dead.

In the headlamp's beam, he caught a glimpse, a snapshot, of the creature. Its reaching legs, green eyeshine, white stinger.

Then he pulled the trigger. The gun kicked against his shoulder. The sound of the shot echoed through the forest. The familiar odor hit his nostrils before mixing with the smell of smoke. And the thief disintegrated before him.

Trey stood still. Even over the thudding in his ears, he could hear the grunting roars of the howler monkeys his shot had startled.

Jacking another shell into the chamber, Trey put his back against a tree and waited. Ten minutes, fifteen, as his hearing returned, the howler monkeys quieted, and the dead wasp's smell hung in the air.

Nothing. Maybe the two thieves—the one Ranny had caught and the one Trey had just killed—were the only ones here. The pioneers. The colonists.

It was time to go. There was nothing he could do for Ranny and Graciela.

Go.

Only . . . he couldn't.


**ABOUT A MILE** back to the research station. Another two up to the Jeep. All along treacherous, muddy trails, illuminated only by his headlamp.

Trey was strong, but strong enough to drag or carry Ranny—who looked to weigh about 180 pounds—all the way, and then return for Graciela? He didn't think so.

Still, he had to try.

Propping the shotgun against a tree, he bent over, got his hands under Ranny's arms, and lifted. His plan was to use some version of the fireman's carry, but he never got a chance.

As he lifted, Ranny let out a cry, a sound of intense pain. Then he said, "No!"

Trey, shocked, almost let him fall, but managed to return him gently to the ground. Only then did he see that Ranny's eyes were open.

Sightless eyes, slicked with an odd silvery sheen. They reflected the headlamp's beam, gleaming like mercury as they shifted this way and that. Random motions, as if Ranny were looking at something no one else could see.

As if he were dreaming.

"Ranny," Trey said, his voice a hoarse whisper.

Ranny's mouth moved. The sheen over his eyes faded a little. "Trey?" he said.

"Yes. I'm here."

Ranny was looking at him. "Trey," he said again.

Trey said, "Yes?"

"*Kill me.*"

**TREY COULDN'T SPEAK** for a moment. Then he said, "I'll get you to a doctor. I promise. He'll help. I'll—"

"*No.*" Only Ranny's mouth moved. "You can't. It hurts. . . ."

"Then I'll bring someone back here—"

"No." Ranny blinked, and when his eyes opened again the silvery shine was stronger. "They're . . . here. In here. Forever."

He drew in a breath. "Trey," he said. "*Please.* Kill me." Another breath. "And . . . her."

His eyes gleamed, and he was gone again. Back inside his dreams.

Trey sat there.

*Kill me.*

He couldn't do it.

**COULDN'T PULL THE** trigger, at least. Was what he did instead any different? Any better? He never knew.

But what other choice did he have? He was out of options.

Unzipping his daypack, he pulled out the first-aid kit he'd taken from the station. Snapped it open and saw, amid the usual gauze pads and antibiotic creams and antihistamines, the scalpel he'd expected to find.

These kits always included a knife or scalpel, a holdover from the days when people believed the first, best response to snakebite was to cut open the spot and suck out the poison-laced blood. Now, even though that theory was long out of fashion, habits hadn't changed.

Trey searched through the kit until he found a pair of forceps. Then, squatting over Ranny's still form, he shoved the man's heavy, wet shirt halfway up his chest. A couple of moves of the knife, one quick snatch with the forceps, and he was holding the larva up to the light.

It was as Sheila had described: long, white, tensile, with black mandibles and large eyes and an almost unbelievable strength for something its size.

Beneath him, Ranny stirred, drew in a ragged, gasping breath, and died.

**TREY KNEW THAT** he should keep the larva. Kill it and preserve it and bring it home.

It was important. It might tell them things they had to know.

But . . . no chance. With a movement that was like a spasm, he threw it to the ground. It writhed and twisted and bit at the earth until he ground it to pulp with the stock of his gun.

For long minutes he stood there, not moving, hearing nothing but the roaring in his ears. Then, carrying the scalpel and forceps, he walked over to where the girl lay. Graciela, with her brown legs and bare foot, her face turned away as if she'd chosen to avert her gaze from what lay ahead.

Trey rolled her onto her back, then pushed her shirt up, exposing her swollen belly.

Under her skin, something moved.

\* \* \*

**"NO SPECIMEN?" JACK** said.

Trey was calling from the airport in San José. He was still covered in mud and sweat, and smelled of rotting vegetation and a bitter stink he thought would never leave him.

He knew he looked like a madman. Felt like one, too.

"No," he said. "It was gone."

"And Ranny and the girl?" Sheila said. He hadn't known that he was on speakerphone, that she was listening.

"Gone."

Nothing but the crackling line. Then Sheila's voice, closer. "Trey," she said, "did you see them?"

He didn't answer.

*"Shit,"* she said.

Still he didn't speak.

"There was nothing you could do." Her voice was strong. "Remember that. Remember what you told me. Whatever happened, whatever you had to do, you had no choice."

He was silent.

"Trey," she said. "Come home."

# TWENTY

*Marco Island, Florida*

**KAIT HAD BEEN** watching for days.

As soon as school ended each afternoon, she'd leave Mrs. Warren's fourth-grade class at Tommie Barfield Elementary and hurry home. Once there, she'd barely pause for a snack before heading out the kitchen door and down to the boat slip.

"You give it a name yet?" Ma had asked one time, when she had Kait's attention for more than thirty seconds.

Kait had just shaken her head. Inside, though, she'd thought: That was stupid. You didn't name wild creatures.

They had their own names, she was sure of it, names they used for each other. Names you'd never know. You could decide to give them any name you wanted, but it wouldn't mean anything.

Now that she thought of it, maybe that was true for your pets, too. Their two dogs, for instance. Their setter, Fire (named by Da because in some lights his coat looked almost like flames), and their mutt, Chester (Ma had named him because she said he looked like a Chester). Maybe they called each other something completely different and wondered why people used such strange sounds to call them.

Anyway, when Kait went down to their boat slip and looked at the dolphin, she decided not to give it a name. It was just the dolphin. Her dolphin.

If it felt like telling her its true name, it would.

It had first come to the slip two years before, when Kait was eight. Almost every day, the dolphin had been there, lazing in the warm water near Da's boat. Sometimes it would dive for something to eat, but mostly it would just lie on the surface, its breath coming through the hole in its head like little explosions, surprising Kait every time.

She would sit there for hours after school, watching the dolphin until dinnertime. Watching and drawing. That was what Kait did best, draw. She didn't like to talk that much, but she loved to draw what she saw.

Often the dolphin would look at her with its bright eye. She wondered what it thought when it saw her.

"Is it sick?" she'd asked Ma and Da.

They'd smiled at each other, who knew why, and Da had said, "No, it's not sick."

"Then why is it always there?"

Ma had given her a hug. "Keep watching, sweetie, and you'll see."

And just a few days later, she *had* seen. She walked down to the slip early one Sunday morning and saw that now there were two dolphins, hers and a tiny little one, no bigger than some of her stuffed animals, lying in the water beside it.

* * *

**NOW, ALMOST EXACTLY** two years later, it was back. The mama dolphin. Alone again, but looking just the same and acting just as she had the first time. Lolling around in the calm blue-green water between their boat slip and the one next to it. Looking as happy as any creature on God's green earth. (As Grandma Mary put it.)

"Is she going to have another baby?" Kait had grown a lot in the past two years, and had a better idea what kinds of questions to ask. Actually, it was hard to believe how little she'd known, back when she was eight.

"Sure looks that way to me," Da said.

So Kait spent every moment she could down there, by the slip, hoping to see the birth. Over the years she'd witnessed her share of rabbits and hamsters being born, chicks hatching from eggs, and even, once, a garter snake delivering itself of a mass of squirmy black-and-yellow babies that formed themselves into a knot before heading their separate ways.

But never a dolphin. Kait wondered how many people in the whole world had seen a baby dolphin being born. Especially in the wild. Ones in aquariums or SeaWorld didn't count. She didn't think you should ever keep dolphins in a big tank of water, or orcas, either.

But a wild one? Maybe she'd be the first ever.

So, sitting on the edge of the dock, her legs dangling over the water, she watched and watched. And drew, of course. She might have changed a lot in two years, but she hadn't lost her love of drawing.

Sometimes other kids would come and stay for a little

while, but Kait didn't have that many friends and didn't care when Amanda or Isabelle would drift away to do something they thought was more fun. Watching a lazy dolphin wasn't their idea of how to spend a warm spring Saturday, and that was fine with her.

She kept it company after dinner every night till dark, when Ma called her for bedtime. Then she'd pretend not to hear until Da came down, hoisted her up—laughing and complaining at the same time—and carried her back to the house. (She was ten now, and much too big to be carried. That was her opinion, at least, but Da didn't share it.)

She'd always known that she wouldn't be able to watch every minute—even if her parents had let her camp out on the dock, she would've had to sleep sometimes. So she wasn't especially surprised when she ran down to the water one morning before school and saw, floating at the mama dolphin's side, a new baby, even smaller and more perfect than the one from two years earlier.

With a rush of emotion that squeezed her heart, Kait instantly fell in love with the rubbery, gray creature, with its tiny beak and bright eyes. If she'd spent a lot of time at the slip before it was born, now she was there every single possible minute.

Watching and drawing.

**FOR THE FIRST** week, the baby grew in leaps and bounds. Every day it seemed stronger, more active, following its mother farther from the shore and dock, diving a little deeper. Still it stayed mostly at the surface, happy, comfortable, the water rolling off its shiny skin.

Then, one morning, something was different.

No one else noticed, not the neighbors who stopped by to take a look every day, not the sea kayakers who put slip 173 on their regular route, not even Ma and Da.

Only Kait saw. The baby dolphin stopped growing. It spent more time sleeping. Its dives were less deep, and it no longer ventured as far as it had just a few days earlier.

The mama dolphin pushed it with her nose, urging it away from the dock. She looked around for the baby as she dived, rocketing to the surface out in the channel as if trying to capture its attention.

But the baby just drifted.

"Is it sick?" Kait asked Da as they sat side by side on the edge of the dock late one afternoon.

"I'm sure it's not," he told her, though the look on his face said something else.

**THE NEXT DAY** Kait noticed the swelling. A bump on the baby dolphin's back, a few inches from its blowhole. There was a round black mark in the middle of the bump, like a second, tiny blowhole.

"Huh," Da said when she called him to see. "Maybe it's got an infection."

"Call the doctor." Kait hated how her voice almost squeaked over the words. If ever she had wanted to be bigger, stronger, it was now. So Da would listen to her.

"Please," she said.

Da listened. He called. But it didn't make a difference.

"Bunny," he said, "they won't come. If it was abandoned, maybe, but not if the mother is still with it."

"But it's sick."

Da looked unhappy. "They say dolphins aren't endangered. They say it's just the cycle of life."

Kait heard: the circle of life. She'd seen that movie, *The Lion King*, on the Disney Channel. She understood what it meant. Despite what the movie said, it didn't seem very noble to her.

"So he'll die," she said. "Fish will eat him."

"Maybe you should stop watching," Da said.

Kait felt her chin lift. She crossed her arms over her chest and stared into her father's eyes.

He knew that expression of hers and didn't argue.

**THE SWELLING GOT** bigger. The baby dolphin grew weaker. It was spending all its time on the surface now. It didn't nurse as often, or for as long.

Its mother stopped trying so hard to teach it. Kait thought she was giving up.

Nobody else came to watch now. The neighbors were busy, and the kayakers paddled right on past.

Kait didn't sleep well at night. She picked at her food at breakfast and dinner and gave away most of her sack lunch at school. Her parents looked at her, and frowned at each other, and suggested movies, dinner out, a trip across the state to see Harry Potter at Universal Studios.

But they didn't push. They knew Kait had to see this through.

**EARLY ONE MORNING** the baby dolphin wasn't floating anymore. It was half pulled up on the flat wooden platform that bobbed off the end of the dock. Da had built this platform when Kait was littler so she could step from it straight into their canoe to go paddling with him.

The baby looked as if it had been on the platform for hours. Its skin was all dry except for its tail, which hung unmoving in the water. The one eye she could see was a strange silver-white color.

At first Kait thought it was already dead. Then it gave a long, slow breath through its blowhole.

Kait looked down at the swelling on its back and saw movement beneath the baby dolphin's skin.

She ran to get Da.

**SOMETHING WAS COMING** out of the black hole in the swelling.

Da said, "What the hell?"

He scrambled down the wooden steps to the floating platform. Kait followed.

The baby dolphin flinched a little at their footsteps, but made no effort to push off, swim away. Right then, Kait realized that its mother was gone. She'd abandoned her baby.

The thing was about halfway out of the hole now. Kait saw red wings, a head that looked to be too big for the black, wormlike body. Everything about it was droopy, wet. Drops of some liquid ran off it and speckled the baby dolphin's back.

Kait's hands covered her eyes, but then she spread her fingers. She had to look.

"What is it?" she asked.

"The damnedest thing." Da squatted down. "Some kind of bee? No, a wasp. One heck of a big wasp."

Kait had watched plenty of yellow jackets and cicada

killers, even caught some in her butterfly net. She knew what a wasp looked like. This wasn't a wasp. Or . . . it wasn't *only* a wasp. It was also something else, some other kind of thing.

She could see its mouth parts moving. A whitish drop formed; with a twitch of its big head, it flung the drop away.

"Shit," Da said, forgetting that Kait was there, speaking to the wasp-thing instead. "Where the hell did *you* come from?"

The baby dolphin breathed. The wasp-thing dragged itself farther out of the hole. With one last pull, it was free.

The baby dolphin's body quivered, all the way up and down. Its blowhole gaped open, and its sad little droopy beak twitched. Then it was still, and Kait knew it was dead.

The wasp-thing raised its heavy body high on its skinny black legs. It stood still for a moment, and then a stream of the whitish liquid began to pump out of its rear end. It turned its big triangle head and looked at them, at Kait and Da.

It's deciding what it wants to do to us, Kait thought.

Da made a funny gulping sound. His hand whipped out, faster than Kait could follow, and the next thing she knew the wasp-thing was flying through the air. It landed on its back in the water beside the dock.

Kait watched it struggle, its legs waving around, its wet wings twitching. A mackerel came to look at it, but swam away again.

Just a few seconds later it was dead, bumping against the pilings alongside some seaweed and a bit of newspaper.

Kait looked back at the baby dolphin. Already its eyes were glazed over, like the dead fish you saw at the market.

Everything was dead.

Da put his hand on top of Kait's head for a second, just like he'd done when she was little. "I'm sorry, Bunny," he said. "I wish we hadn't seen that."

Kait didn't say anything.


**GRANDMA MARY WAS** at the house. Ma must have called her while Da and Kait were down at the slip.

Da went upstairs to take a shower.

"You and me, we're going out for breakfast," Grandma told Kait.

"I have school," Kait pointed out. The first words she'd spoken in a while.

"Hang school!" Grandma talked like that. She wasn't that much bigger than Kait, but she could be a lot louder.

Ma said, "I already called to tell them you'd be late."

"I'm not hungry," Kait said.

Grandma gave a big shrug. "Okay, fine, you can watch me eat, and after that we can do a little shopping."

Grandma Mary loved shopping.

"Go," Ma said.

So Kait went. They ate at Breakfast Plus (Kait ended up getting French toast, and even eating some of it), then went off to Marco Walk, where they visited every store. At Richard's Reef, Grandma insisted she buy some earrings. Kait was quiet, but Grandma didn't make her talk.

By the time they got back home, it was almost noon. "We'll make sandwiches," Grandma said. "And then, if you feel up to it, I'll take you to school."

Kait didn't say anything, but she thought she might be able to manage school.

While Grandma went in the front door, Kait squatted down beside the front step to watch a small lizard that was sunning itself. An anole. When it saw her looking, it puffed out a pretty red pouch under its throat.

"You don't scare me," Kait said.

That was when she heard it. At first she thought it was the sound of a bird, a gull or maybe even an eagle. But then she realized it was coming from inside the house, a high sound unlike any she'd heard before.

And then she figured out what it was: someone screaming. A kind of scream she'd never heard before.

Grandma Mary.

**MEN. DOZENS OF** men. Maybe hundreds. A couple of women, too, big women with fake smiles, at least one of them sitting with her at all times.

Grandma Mary was in the hospital, they told her. But she would be fine. Fine.

They promised.

It took them a long time to say anything about Ma and Da. But Kait knew. She'd known from the moment she'd heard Grandma start to scream. That sound she'd never heard before, but which still echoed in her ears.

The men asked her a thousand questions, or maybe it was the same question in different words a thousand times. Kait didn't say anything. She didn't feel like talking.

But she *knew*.

# TWENTY-ONE

**IN THE TWO** days Trey was gone, some kind of floodgate seemed to have opened. Or perhaps there was an algorithm for how long it took people to notice Jack's alert on the Internet, go out looking for thieves, and report back on what they'd seen.

Or maybe, Trey thought, the algorithm was a darker one. Maybe the first people to go out looking for thieves didn't make it back to their computers. Maybe there was some magic number of searchers that overwhelmed the wasps' ability to stay hidden or to kill, and what the three of them were seeing was the overflow.

Whatever the equation, he returned to Jack's office to find pins sprouting from the map on the wall. Each pin marked a spot where a sighting had been reported, and the pins steadily clustered more thickly and spread more widely.

Some of the reports were sketchy, others likely hoaxes. But enough were certain—a scrap of video taken from

Ivory Coast, a photo from Thailand, a detailed description from an entomologist in southern Italy, a series of images from somewhere in South America, showing a thief standing astride what looked like the still form of a capybara—to make the overall picture clear. To make the conclusion inescapable.

The thieves had spread across the world. More than that: Their spread was explosive. They were moving like the Spanish influenza had in 1918, like malaria-carrying mosquitoes before that, like countless other pests and epidemic diseases throughout human history.

But even more easily than those of the past. "They're fucking turbocharged," Jack said. "There's, what, tens of thousands of airplane flights taking off and landing every day? How many have these beasts on board, hitching a ride?"

Trey stayed silent. Sheila, sitting at Jack's computer, didn't appear to be listening.

"And not just planes," Jack went on. "Planes, trains, and automobiles. All we're missing is Steve Martin and John Candy."

"No reports from the United States yet?" Trey asked. "That's strange."

"Must be that border wall they've been building in Texas." Jack rolled his eyes. "The president should give a speech touting its success. It might help him win reelection."

He gave a dismissive shake of the head. "Nah. It's just a blip. Nobody's reported it to us yet, but they will. Soon."

He looked at the map, at the scattering of pins in South

and Central America. "Put it in the books. The thieves are already here."

Sheila merely raised her gaze from the computer screen.

"You're right," she said. "Look at this."

**SHE HAD A** series of windows open on the screen. Most showed variations on the same headline: "Bee Attack Leaves Florida Couple Dead."

"Already saw that," Jack said. "'Africanized Honeybees Claim Another Victim.' 'Killer Bees on the Prowl.' 'Young Couple Stung to Death.' 'Family Dogs Victims, Too.'"

He scowled, as if not proud of his tone, then shrugged. "Killer bees have been spreading throughout Florida and Texas for decades. These aren't the first deaths."

Trey was reading the first paragraphs of the different stories. "They all say the same thing."

"Not this one," Sheila said.

She clicked the mouse and brought a new page to the front.

The *Marco Island Sunrise*, a local online newspaper filled with stories about shopping deals and fishing charters and a new real-estate development. And the deaths of two island residents.

Trey read the sad details. The attack on the parents. The daughter surviving due to being out shopping with her grandmother. The grandmother being kept overnight in the hospital after discovering the bodies of her son and daughter-in-law.

"Look here," Sheila said.

It was a link to a video, a black rectangle in the middle of the page. The heading was, "Orphaned Daughter Speaks."

"Yuck," Jack said.

Sheila clicked on it, and after a few moments the video began. It showed a reporter, a slim young woman, standing in front of a Florida scene: white houses with red roofs, palm trees, blue water shimmering in the distance. She was holding a black microphone.

"In a *Sunrise* exclusive, we were able to talk with Kaitlin Finneran, daughter of the couple whose tragic death is the talk of Marco Island," the reporter was saying. Under her suitably solemn expression, she looked thrilled. "Kaitlin's story will shock you."

"Double fucking yuck," Jack said.

The camera focused on two figures sitting on a bench: an exhausted-looking seventyish woman with white hair and a ten-year-old girl with fair skin dusted with freckles, black hair pulled back into a long ponytail, and big dark eyes. She had a hollow, thousand-yard expression in her eyes that Trey had seen too often before.

And too recently. He glanced at Sheila, who was leaning forward as if she wanted to climb through the screen.

"It's too soon," she said. "The grandmother should never have allowed this."

"She's in shock herself," Trey said. "I doubt she knows what's right."

Sheila grunted.

"So, Kait," the reporter was saying, "you've said that you don't believe killer bees killed your parents."

Kait shook her head.

"Then what did?"

Kait stared into the camera. As Trey watched, some banked flame lit behind her eyes, and suddenly she seemed completely focused and aware.

"The wasp-thing," she said.

The reporter said, "The what?"

Kait didn't blink. "I watched it hatch out of the baby dolphin," she said. "Da killed it." She bit her lip, and when she spoke again, her voice was choked. "That's why they killed him and Ma."

"So you're saying—"

But Kait's grandmother had had enough. She stirred and put her hand on the girl's arm. "We're tired," she said. "Do you think you can leave us alone now?"

The scene went back to the reporter in front of the island scenery. "We talked to Derek Franks of the Collier County Sheriff's Office about Kait's extraordinary claims. Should the residents of Marco Island be afraid of wasps, as well as killer bees? His response: 'Residents should not be afraid of either.'"

Sheila clicked the mouse, freezing the reporter with her mouth open. They were silent for a few moments, and then Jack said, "The little girl must not have understood what she was seeing."

Trey said, "Why?"

"Because wasps don't parasitize dolphins."

Neither Sheila nor Trey spoke. Jack's face turned red. "Okay," he said. "Fucking sue me for being scientific, okay? Wasps are *not* such generalists."

"They are in their diet, aren't they?" Sheila said. "I mean, some are."

"But not in their breeding methods."

Sheila shrugged. "Yeah, and viral diseases couldn't

jump from species to species. It was a natural law . . . until this one virus took the leap from African chimpanzees to humans a few decades back. You know, the one transmitted during sex. That rule breaker has managed to spread pretty well through the population. What was it called again?"

Jack's beard bristled. "I love it when you condescend to me," he said. "Makes me feel all tingly inside. Still . . . a *dolphin*?"

"It's not impossible," Trey said. "A newborn dolphin stays at the surface. It's not strong enough to dive yet. A larva needing only an occasional breath of air could grow inside one, hatching out before it would be in danger of drowning."

"So these things can parasitize any mammal," Jack said.

Neither Trey nor Sheila answered.

Jack was looking at the map. "We're going to need more pins."

**"ONE THING I** don't understand," Trey said a while later.

Jack said, "Only one?"

"Kaitlin says her father killed a thief. If there had been any others around, wouldn't they have attacked right away? Why wait?"

Jack turned his palms up. But Sheila said, "No. You're looking at this the wrong way."

They waited for her to explain.

"If there'd been any other thieves in the area when Kaitlin's father killed the hatchling, he and Kaitlin would have been dead at once," she went on. "The ones that attacked—they came later."

"Later?" Jack asked. "Like, for tea?"

"Jack—"

"No, tell me. Why?"

"That's obvious," Sheila said. "For retribution."

*"Retribution?"*

"Revenge," Sheila said.

**TREY TOOK A** breath and watched Jack carefully. He knew what was going to come next.

Jack's eyes narrowed and red spots rose to his cheeks. He raised both hands and rubbed his face. The air whistled through his nose as he gave an explosive breath out, like a whale clearing its lungs through its blowhole.

All as expected.

Less expected was the wiry, snarling tone in his voice as he said, "Sheila, shut the hell up."

Sheila blinked. "What?"

Jack's face was dark. "Listen to you. 'Revenge.' Don't be an idiot."

She stared at him.

"You know where revenge comes from?" he went on. "Conscious thought. Calculation. *Human* attributes."

"Okay," Sheila said, her voice flat. "I misspoke."

"No," Jack said. "You didn't misspeak. You're ignorant. And you still don't understand."

Trey said, "Jack, you've made your point—"

"No," Jack said again. "Both of you. *Listen.* It's simple. Wasps, like all insects and most living things, are motivated by two things: the instinct to survive and the need to procreate. *That's all*. Nothing else."

"I know that," Sheila said.

"No, you don't." Jack's voice was quiet now, but no less fierce. "No . . . you . . . don't. You're watching me freak out, and you want me to stop, but inside you haven't learned a thing."

He ran his hands again over his face. "You know what intelligence is? Let me tell you: It's the ability to ponder, to think things through, to see both sides of an issue. To change one's mind."

He paused for a moment, but when Trey began to speak he raised a hand in warning. "Shut up, Trey," he said. "I'm not done. You still don't get it. Neither of you. 'Intelligence' is the greatest weakness afflicting the human species. We insult the thieves when we attribute it to them."

He took a breath, and when he went on, his voice was calmer. "Worse than that, we underestimate them. Because lacking intelligence sets them free. They don't ponder, equivocate, mull things over. They act. They survive. They procreate. That's all. But it's enough."

He looked back and forth from Sheila to Trey. Neither spoke.

"Wasps evolved more than a hundred million years ago, and they're still going strong. They haven't much missed being 'intelligent,' have they?"

TREY THOUGHT THAT would be the end of the discussion, but apparently Sheila didn't. She crossed her arms over her chest and said, "So tell me: How did they do it?"

Jack blinked. "How did who do what?"

Sheila didn't answer his question directly. Instead, she stood very still, and when she spoke again there was a wondering tone in her voice. "And I'll bet it was the same thing at my parents' place, too."

Her gaze sought Trey's. "Listen. I killed the larva. My mom died. I was taken to the hospital. I've been trying to figure out: Why did the house burn down, and who were the other people who died there? No one would ever tell me."

Trey said, "Well, we know that the local governments in Kigoma and Ujiji have been aware of the thieves for a while. Weeks or months."

"Yes." She paused. "Here's what I think happened: Someone was in my house when the thieves came back. Maybe some policemen investigating the scene. Maybe looters or squatters who knew I was gone. Whoever it was, the thieves killed them."

"And you're still alive because you weren't there," Trey said.

She nodded. "Like Kaitlin Finneran."

"Then who burned down the house?" Jack asked.

"The authorities, I'd guess."

Trey thought of the old woman in the market. "Killer wasps being bad for tourism and foreign aid."

Sheila nodded, frowning. "But the question still is: How did the thieves know to come back to the house? How did they *know* I'd killed one of their young?"

"Oh, that's easy," Jack said, his good mood restored.

Sheila looked at him.

"The hive mind."

* * *

**SHEILA KEPT LOOKING** at him, adding a minuscule shake of her head.

"Come on, you must have heard of it," he said. "Consciousness shared instantly within a population of a social species."

"Well," Sheila said slowly, "yes, I'm familiar with the term, but I always thought it was kind of science fiction. You know, pod people? *Invasion of the Body Snatchers?*"

Jack smiled, pleased with the reference. Then he shook his head. "Haven't you ever seen those nature documentaries, *Planet Earth* or something, that show a flock of sparrows or school of anchovies when a predator comes along?"

"Of course," she said.

"Well, watch them again. They're brilliant. And listen to what David Attenborough says in the narration. When the flock or school tries to escape, what happens? They all make the same decision at precisely the same instant."

After a pause, Sheila said, "But that's because they all read the situation the same way. They all receive and process the same information, and react identically. That doesn't seem very 'hive-mindish' to me."

"That's because it isn't." Jack smiled at her. "It's also not what's going on here. You're doing it again, you know, forcing your feeble human theories on something far more beautiful and profound."

Sheila compressed her lips but didn't say anything.

"Listen. The fish in a school don't all react the same way to the same information . . . because they're not all *receiving* the same information. Think about it. Not every member of the school is under the same threat. If they were each reacting to what they were seeing, the ones on the edges of the school would flee in opposite directions, while the ones closest to the predator would plunge or head for the surface. No coordination. Every fish for itself."

Sheila nodded, beginning to understand. "But that's not what happens."

"No, it's not. The movement of the school is exquisitely—and instantaneously—coordinated. And the goal is for the most members of the flock or school to survive, not any one individual. In fact, you could argue that some individuals sacrifice themselves for the greater good."

Sheila was quiet.

"*Invasion of the Body Snatchers* wasn't the half of it," Jack said. "*That's* the beauty of the real hive mind at work."

There was a long silence. Then Sheila looked at Trey. "You know about this?"

Trey nodded. "You spend as much time out in the woods as I do, you see it in action."

"Okay. I buy it." She paused. "But that leads to the obvious question."

The corners of Jack's mouth turned down. "I know," he said. " 'How does it work?' "

"Yes, that's the one."

Now Jack was scowling. "I fucking hate obvious questions."

"Why?"

"Because the answer to this one is: We have no idea."

\* \* \*

**"GEORGE SUMMERS IN** Ag," Jack decided.

They'd been figuring out what their next step should be. No one wanted to sit around, sticking pins in the map.

"Ugh," Trey said. "The government?"

"I know. But Agriculture is in charge of keeping track of invasive species."

Sheila didn't look impressed. "Things like wood-boring beetles and aphids."

"George is kind of an asshole, but he's not stupid. He might listen." Jack looked Sheila up and down. "Especially if it's you doing the talking. He likes a bit of skirt."

"'A bit of skirt,'" Sheila said.

Jack grinned.

"Anyway, forget it," Sheila went on. "Despite such inducements, I'm not going."

Jack looked surprised, but Trey had seen this coming. "You're planning to go see Kaitlin," he said.

Sheila nodded.

Jack thought about it. "Makes sense," he said. "We might learn something."

She frowned. "I'm not going to learn, but to teach."

Jack said, "What?"

Sheila was looking at Trey. "You came halfway across the world," she said to him, "to tell me that I wasn't crazy. That I hadn't killed my mother." She paused. "You saved my life."

Trey could think of nothing to say in return. But Sheila wasn't looking at him anymore. She was facing the computer screen.

"This poor little girl," she said. "Kaitlin. She deserves someone to do the same for her, doesn't she?"

# TWENTY-TWO

*Washington, D.C.*

**"LET ME GET** this straight," George Summers said. "You rode the Acela all the way down here to tell me about a bug."

He was sitting behind his desk on the fifth floor of the Department of Agriculture building. A disgruntled-looking man in his late forties, with a face like a hatchet, narrowed eyes, a permanent five-o'clock shadow, and a mouth with a lifetime's experience in turning down at the corners, as it was doing now.

Jack was looking back at him. It wasn't a friendly look. "The Metroliner," he said. "On our own dime. You're forgetting that not everybody's lucky enough to have the American taxpayer springing for his travel."

Trey stayed quiet. As far as he was concerned, the best thing you could do when dealing with government officials was keep your mouth shut.

Especially when you were skew data like Trey. Someone who went off the grid, traveled for a living, got in trouble.

Governments hate skew data.

"I don't know," George Summers was saying to Jack. "The American Museum still pays you, don't they? Seems to me they use plenty of taxpayer money, too."

Jack's mouth was a grim line behind his beard. "I took a vacation day."

"Well, then, I'm afraid you wasted one. We should have just wrapped this up on the phone." Summers pointed to a stack of thick files on his metal-topped desk. "And then I could have added your report to the pile without wasting time with this lunatic social call."

After a moment Jack sighed and said, "George, if you'll just listen—"

But Summers didn't seem to be in the mood for listening. It got in the way of his talking.

"Tell me something," he said, his eyes on Trey. "How many foreign insects and plants do you think make it into the U.S. each year? Let's just say each year since 2001. A rough guess will be fine."

Trey just shook his head. But Jack shifted in his seat and said in a whiny approximation of a child's voice, "Papa, tell us about the effects of September eleventh again!"

Summers's mouth turned down, but the jibe didn't stop him. "One of the first things the new Department of Homeland Security did after 9/11," he said, "was re-assign hundreds of Ag scientists who'd been focused on stopping the spread of invasive insect and plant species. Overnight, presto, they became members of Customs and Border Protection."

"He always forgets," Jack said, "that I was there."

Summers stared at him. "Were you? Funny, I don't recall that. I don't recall seeing your face back then, when people who'd spent their whole lives fighting troublesome bugs suddenly found themselves being told to learn the twelve signs of a suicide bomber." His face darkened. "Know what? Surprise! Most of our people didn't want to become cops. You should have seen them heading for the doors. Homeland Security didn't get its new border protectors, and we didn't keep our inspectors."

Summers took a deep breath, and when he went on his voice was calmer. "After that, the pests went wild. Our borders were closed to anyone with swarthy skin, but they were wide open to *them*. Chilli thrips. Emerald ash borers. A thousand others. *They* didn't need passports—"

"Oh, for God's sake," Jack said, "shut up."

Summers stared at him.

"If you don't stop living in the fucking past and start paying attention," Jack went on, "you're going to be dreaming of the days when chilli thrips were your biggest problem."

This was the part of the conversation where, in other countries Trey had visited, he and Jack would have been spun around and frog-marched to the nearest windowless room with bars on the door.

Here though, George Summers merely sat back and gave them a grim-eyed look.

"Why should I listen?" he said. "I already know what you're creaming your jeans to tell me about."

Jack blinked. "Yeah?"

"Yeah. A wasp. A big black wasp."

"YOU THINK I didn't hear?" Summers said. "With all the noise you've been making? You're as bad as cicadas in August, you two."

Jack looked disgusted. "Then why are you jerking us around?"

Summers's dark gaze was unyielding. "Because I don't buy it. I think you're lumping a few truths together with a bunch of guesses and suppositions and wild surmise. With the result that, like all paranoiacs, you're seeing bogeymen everywhere."

Jack said, "We think—"

"I know what you think. And I know how it went." He pointed at Trey. "*You* encountered a new species of wasp in Senegal, along with a lot of mumbo jumbo." Now at Jack. "When Gilliard came back to New York, having screwed his reputation even more than before, *you* took his slender thread of evidence—though that's an insult to slender threads—and ran with it."

He sat back. "And then the two of you hijacked that poor young lady doctor whose mother had been killed. Encouraged her delusions. She's the alcoholic and you're the 'friends' who keep refilling her glass. You two should be ashamed of yourselves."

His expression was bleak. "And where is she now, your damaged friend? Heading to Florida, so she can spread your delusions to another vulnerable victim. Disgraceful."

He stopped, and for a few moments the room was silent. Then Jack reached down for his laptop. "Watch the videos—"

"I've seen them. I watched them all after you called. You think I don't do my homework? Yes, there's a wasp. Hooray."

"And—" Jack said.

Summers ran over him. "And the population is spreading. Surprise! Welcome to the world. Species move around, especially these days, or hadn't you noticed?" He gestured again at the pile of folders on his desk. "What do you think I work on every single frackin' day?"

"They've made it here to the U.S.," Jack said.

Summers's face tightened for a moment. "First of all," he said, and now his voice was quiet, icy. "First of all, I don't believe you. You're doing it again, taking every tragedy you can find and claiming it for your wasp. Leave that poor little girl in Florida alone."

He fixed his gaze on Trey, who stayed silent.

"What killed those people on Marco Island was Africanized bees, one of the pests that fell through the cracks after 9/11," Summers said. "They're not part of your story. But say you're right about the rest. Your wasp's here. The point is: *So what?*"

He looked again at his stack of files. "That just makes it like thousands of other invasive species. Those killer bees we've been talking about. Anacondas. The giant African land snail. You want more? I could go on all day."

His eyes went back to Trey's face. "You want reassurance, Gilliard? Here it is: We'll get to your wasp, I promise, just as soon as we've dealt with all those others."

Trey said, "Wasn't my idea to come here. Fact, I bet Jack ten dollars you'd be completely useless."

Now Summers was quiet. Trey held out a hand, and after a moment Jack, scowling, got out his wallet, extracted a bill, and handed it over.

"Easiest money I've made in months," Trey said.

Summers stood. "Okay, you two clowns. We're done here. I have actual work to do. You know, important work in the *real* world." He pointed. "Close the door on your way out."

Trey stayed where he was. "Three days ago, in Costa Rica, I saw 'my wasp' in action," he said. "I saw it kill two people."

Something flickered in Summers's gaze. "Explain."

Trey explained. When he was halfway through, Summers sat down again.

He didn't speak until Trey was done. Then, his voice hoarse around the edges, he spoke four words.

"I don't believe you."

And five more.

"Get out of my office."


**JACK AND TREY** left the enormous Agriculture building, wended their way through the concrete barriers strewn along the sidewalk to prevent a car bombing, and crossed Independence Avenue to the Mall. The day had grown hot, the afternoon sun hanging heavy in a smeared sky.

They had time to kill before catching their train home. At a food truck that was still selling lunch, each bought a falafel and a can of soda wrapped in a wet napkin. Then they sat on a bench amid purposeful men and women in business suits, meandering tourists in shorts and T-shirts, and runners whose neon shoes shone like beacons as they went past.

Jack took a bite of his sandwich, then wiped a hand across his mouth and said, "Think they've made it here yet?"

Trey shrugged. "Maybe. Only a matter of time."

"They'll love it." Jack watched the oblivious crowd. "Perfect weather and so many hosts to choose from."

They ate in silence for a while. Then Jack said, "What's your take on our friend George?"

Trey finished his sandwich before answering. Then he said, "He was trying too hard."

"You think?"

"Yeah. You could hear it in his voice."

Jack nodded. "Agree. Overrehearsed, right? And all those pat phrases: 'Disgraceful.' 'You should be ashamed.' Yadda."

"He didn't expect to hear about my face-to-face at La Tamandua, though."

"Yeah. That shook him."

A busload of Chinese tourists passed, heading toward the Capitol Building. Eyes on them, Jack said, "Question is, why try to throw us off?"

"That one's easy," Trey said.

He was thinking about his taxi driver in Kigoma, who'd been reluctant to take him to see the Connellys' torched house. The old woman in the marketplace, wary about talking to him, always watching to see who might be listening. And Sheila's guards at the hospital, making sure no one talked to her.

He thought about governments and what they would do to protect their investments. The money they made from tourism, foreign trade, imports-exports, and other markets that would crash if word of the thieves got out.

He thought about the way governments made the same mistakes over and over again. It was what they did best.

"They're going to try to keep the lid on," he said.

Jack's mouth tightened, making his beard bristle. "For how long?"

Trey shrugged. "Forever?"

"Least till Election Day."

The two of them looked out at the passing crowd. All the government workers chatting as they walked by. All those moving mouths. Over on Constitution Avenue, a TV news truck was setting up a remote shoot. Another news camera was set up in front of the Reflecting Pool, the Capitol Building in the background.

"Election Day or forever," Jack said, "I don't think it's gonna work."

# TWENTY-THREE

*Marco Island*

**ON A TRIP** to the United States when Sheila was a child, her parents had brought her to Florida. She had only the vaguest recollection of Disney World and the various restaurants and beaches they'd visited. Only one memory remained vivid two decades later.

They'd taken a walk at dusk from their hotel in one of the cities on the North Coast. Daytona, maybe, or Jacksonville. Their path had taken them down street after street filled with small, newly constructed wood-frame houses built on plots of what until recently had been wetland. Every single square foot of the natural world had been filled, leveled, cleared, and "reclaimed" for humans to develop.

*Reclaimed*. Killed, was how Sheila had thought of it. People had killed Florida.

But then they'd come to a single undeveloped plot, one that still contained trees and brambly bushes and muddy water. There was a big white sign saying *Land: For*

*Sale*, and Sheila guessed that within a year there would be a house there, just like the ones that stood on either side.

For the moment, though, a remarkable abundance of wildlife was using this tiny stretch of unspoiled land as a refuge. A dozen white egrets perched in the branches, their nighttime roost. Turtles were stacked on a log, catching the last warmth of the day, and butterflies and dragonflies flitted here and there.

The For Sale sign was streaked with bird shit.

That was when Sheila had the thought she still remembered two decades later. People could—and would—do everything they could to kill Florida, to kill the world, but that it was ridiculous, hubristic, to think they'd succeed. Nature would find a way to survive.

These birds, turtles, butterflies would have to move when this land, too, was cleared, but they'd find someplace to go. Some would probably die, but not all.

The rest might even return to the plots where the first houses had been carved out of the swamp. Sheila had noticed that some of the buildings were already overgrown, sagging, their wood rotting in the relentless humidity and heat.

**THE FINNERAN FUNERAL** was at a Catholic church that looked like it had been built the week before. Hot white light poured through the clear windows up near the top, cooler blue and green through the stained glass lower down.

Sheila saw that the beams running across the ceiling showed signs of termite damage.

The sad, shocked crowd had too many young parents

in it, and far too many children. Girls, mostly, dressed in whatever dark clothes they owned, their faces sallow under permanent Florida tans. Short skirts were in style here, rows of bare legs swinging in the pews.

A young priest spoke of seasons, of forgiveness, of love. Sheila didn't bother to follow what he was saying. She was looking at the two simple wood coffins that sat before the priest and thinking about her own parents.

Then her gaze sought out the gray-haired woman in the front pew and the girl in black beside her. Mary Finneran and her granddaughter, the child of the deceased. Kaitlin.

Kaitlin was bent over, focused on something in her lap, her right hand moving. Writing? No. Sheila thought she was drawing.

**AFTERWARD, SHEILA WENT** to the end of the line to pay respect to the mourners. At the head, Mary Finneran was pale, red eyed, but she seemed calm and composed. Strong. Beside her, Kaitlin looked thinner than she had in the video, with her grandmother's sharp chin and a watchful gaze.

Hanging from her right hand was a piece of white paper with a drawing on it. In her left was a ziplock bag containing a few colored pencils.

Sheila couldn't make out what the drawing showed, just its range of colors. It seemed that the girl had mostly used silver or gray, with a little blue as well.

The line moved slowly forward. Nobody was speaking until they reached the Finnerans, not even the children shuffling along. It was quiet. Silent as a church.

Eventually Sheila's turn came. Mary Finneran locked eyes with her. "Dr. Connelly?"

Sheila nodded. "I'm so sorry," she said.

"Thank you." The older woman looked Sheila up and down, as if deciding whether to trust her. Kaitlin's quick glance held the same cautious judgment.

Mary looked over to where the hearse, the limousine, and the diminished crowd of family and friends waited for the trip to the cemetery. The priest and a man in a dark suit stood nearby, exuding mournful impatience.

"We have to go," she said, still indecisive. Then, sighing, she reached into her black handbag and withdrew a square slip of paper. "Come to this address at five o'clock," she said. "Can you find it?"

Sheila said yes.

Without another word, Mary Finneran put her hand on Kaitlin's shoulder. Together they walked out the door and into the light.

As the girl turned, Sheila caught a glimpse of what she'd been drawing during the service. It was a dolphin. No, two: an adult and a baby, pearly blue-gray and alive in the gleaming silver water.

SHEILA HAD CALLED the day before. Without giving any details, she'd told Mary Finneran that she thought the official story of the Finnerans' death was wrong.

"Why should I believe you?" Mary Finneran had said. "Why do I need you in my hair? You can't imagine the number of calls I've gotten, and plenty of them have been from cranks. Why should I trust you're any different?"

Sheila had thought it over before saying, "You were

the first"—struggling with the words—"on the scene, right?"

"Yes."

"Did you see any dead bees?"

"*What?*"

Sheila, certain that the grief-stricken older woman was about to hang up on her, had hurried on. "Listen," she'd said. "Africanized bees are deadly, but they're still honeybees. When they sting a person, they leave their stinger behind. Then they die almost immediately. Someone who's been attacked will be surrounded by dead bees."

There'd been a long silence over the line. Then Mary Finneran had said, "You're telling me Kait was right."

Before Sheila could answer, she'd gone on. "No! No, I need to hear it face-to-face. Can you come here?"

And Sheila had said, Yes. Yes, of course.

FIVE O'CLOCK. THEY were sitting on Mary's back porch, the hot day edging into a cooler evening.

Mary went to get something to drink. Sheila leaned back in her chair and watched first a white egret and then a small flock of ibises flap past.

Unkillable Florida.

When Mary returned, she was carrying a tall glass filled with ice cubes and a light brown liquid. "Iced tea," she said, "with a kick."

"Thank you." Sheila took the glass, cool and sweaty in her hand. She sipped it. There was gin in it.

"Where's Kaitlin?" she asked.

Mary sat across a glass-topped table from Sheila, sipped her own drink, and said, "She goes by Kait. She's inside drawing something, I imagine, but I'm sure she'll be out soon."

Then her mouth firmed. "Which makes it a good time now to spit out what you came down to tell me."

Sheila nodded. Before she could speak, though, the door slid open. Kait stood there, wearing yellow shorts and a red T-shirt with some restaurant's name on it, her face without expression. All coltish arms and legs, unruly mop of hair, and dark eyes staring into Sheila's own from across the deck.

She was holding something in her hand: a sheet of paper.

Mary said, "Kait, what have you been drawing?"

Still the girl hung back. As Sheila watched, she saw her body gradually grow rigid. When she finally moved, it was on stiff legs. An angry stride. She slapped the drawing facedown on the table in front of Sheila.

"They won't believe me," she said, almost spitting out the words. "They say I'm making it up."

Sheila turned the drawing over. It was what she expected it to be, but even so the sight made her heart pound.

A portrait, almost scientifically accurate, of a thief. The head, the bloodred wings, the aggressive posture, triangular head tilted, the way it stood high on its legs—all were unmistakable.

Only its abdomen was too thick, but the whitish liquid Kait had drawn dribbling from the end explained that, too. This was a newborn thief, still attaining its final adult shape.

"Well?" Kait was staring at Sheila. "Do *you* believe me?"

Instead of replying, Sheila bent over, reached into the shoulder bag at her feet, and withdrew a copy of Jack's drawing.

She placed it on the table beside the other. The two thieves stared up at them.

"My God," Mary said. Her hand was over her mouth.

"Yes," Sheila said to Kait, "I believe you."

Kait stared down at the drawings. "The wasp-thing," she said.

**THEY TOLD THEIR** stories. Only once, as Kait described watching the life and death of the baby dolphin, did she grow teary. The rest of the time, she spoke in a sober voice that betrayed, Sheila thought, too little emotion. As if the girl had already spent too much time thinking about what she'd seen. Or had already dissociated herself from it.

The same way Sheila sounded as she described what had happened to her mother.

Mary mostly listened. By the time the two of them were done, she looked older than when they'd begun.

"You say these creatures started in Africa," she said.

Sheila nodded. "As far as we know, yes. West Africa."

"But now they're here."

"Yes."

"Why?"

Sheila gave a shrug. "You must know how easy it is for invasive species to spread in this day and age." She paused. "They used to have to hitch rides on the wind or on islands of floating vegetation. These days it's effortless."

Mary was frowning. "That's not what I meant." She gestured at the drawings. "These creatures were happy to live—and stay—in their forests for, what, thousands of years. Millions. Why are they spreading *now*?"

"We don't know yet," Sheila said. "Declines in population of food and host species in their home range? A change in their biology, some evolutionary leap that's led to increased aggressiveness? Pure chance? Any answer is just a guess."

"It doesn't matter why," Kait said.

Sheila said, "You're right."

"It just matters that they're here." Kait looked up at her. "They're in Africa. They're here. Are they everywhere else, too?"

Without thinking, Sheila put a hand out and brushed a lock of hair out of Kait's eyes. The girl flinched a little, but didn't pull away.

"I'm afraid so, honey," she said.

**WHEN KAIT WENT** inside to get ready for bed, Mary said, "Why were they attacked? I mean, my son and his wife. Was it just a coincidence?"

Sheila looked at her, trying to decide how much speculation to share. Finally she said, "That's possible, but I think it might have been something else."

"What?"

"Retribution."

Mary stared at her. "You mean, like payback? They come back and punish you?"

"Yes."

"Sounds like a crackpot theory to me."

Sheila thought of Jack's similar—though less temperate—response and didn't say anything.

"But how would the other ones know?" Mary's gaze shifted toward the sky, where a big heron was winging in front of darkening clouds. "Are they always watching?"

Sheila opened her mouth to say something like, *We have no idea*, when she heard Mary say, "Oh, God."

Sheila lowered her gaze.

The older woman's face was contorted. "Kait was there," she said. "When Tim killed that one. *She was there*."

Sheila understood. Somehow the idea hadn't occurred to her. The idea that Kait might still be in danger.

"I think," she said and hesitated. "I think that, if it was going to happen . . . it would have already."

"But you don't know, do you?" Mary was on her feet. "You're just guessing."

She stopped beside the door. "I have a friend with a place in Charleston," she said, half to herself. "I'll call her from the road."

Then she paused, her eyes widening. "But will that be enough? These creatures. You said they're everywhere." She seemed almost to be begging. "Sheila—tell me where to go that will be safe."

But Sheila had no answer.

Fifteen minutes later Kait was sitting in Mary's car. "Grandma," she was saying, "we'll be fine."

Mary, ignoring her, made sure Kait's seat belt was securely fastened.

When Sheila had loaded two suitcases into the trunk, Mary handed her another square piece of notepaper. There was a phone number written on it in green ink.

"Call me when you know it's safe," Mary said. "When you're sure."

Sheila just looked at her, and after a moment Mary, amazingly, laughed. It was a bitter, self-mocking sound, but still, it was a laugh.

"All right," she said. "Don't wait *that* long."

# TWENTY-FOUR

*Manhattan*

BURUNDI. MADAGASCAR. FIJI. Ecuador. Mexico.

Trey stuck the last of the morning's pins in the map, then stood back to look at the ever-thickening and growing clusters.

"Useless," he said under his breath. Then, more loudly, "I'm useless."

Jack looked up from his desk. After their encounter with George Summers at Ag, he'd admitted that he had to get back to work. To his real work, the kind the museum paid him for. He was still gathering data on the thieves, but an increasing amount of his attention was focused elsewhere.

In front of him lay a tray from Entomology's collections room. Rows of black-and-yellow wasps stuck on pins, a yellowing card scrawled with ornate fountain-pen handwriting identifying genus and species beneath each one. *Philanthidae*, the drawer was labeled. And the English, too: *Beewolves*.

Beewolves, wasps that preyed on bees, were Jack's specialty.

"What did you say?" he asked.

"I said that I'm useless here." Trey wriggled his shoulders. "Looking at YouTube videos, reading blogs, checking out the latest picture pinned on—"

"Pinterest," Jack said.

"Whatever. A million people could do all that better than I can."

"Look on the bright side," Jack said. "Your girlfriend will be back soon. She can take over the job of sticking pins in the wall, and you can go back to staring out the window. You're a ninja master at that."

His eyes widened a little at Trey's expression. "Okay, don't bite me. Ix-nay on the ins-pay. What are you going to do instead?"

Trey was silent for a few moments, but he'd already thought it through. He'd known for days where his path was leading.

"I have to find out what the thieves are doing," he said, "and I can't do that here. Not via computer. Not with—" He held his hands out. "Not with *pins*, real or virtual."

Jack gave a half grin. " 'Obsessive Traveler Flies the Coop,' " he said. "I read it in the paper, just below 'Dog Bites Man!' "

His expression grew more serious. "How, though?" he asked. "How do you know where to go?"

Trey had been figuring that out, too. He looked at the telephone, a technology even he was comfortable with, though he hated it, too.

"I know where to start," he said.

*Kinyare, Uganda*

**"EIGHT WEEKS," THOMAS** Nyramba said.

Fortyish, thickly built, with a shaven head shaped like a bullet, he was sitting behind the desk of his wood-paneled office in the Kinyare police station. Trey occupied a wooden chair opposite him.

The sunlight coming in through the windows was tinted green by the surrounding forest. Over the rattling of the ceiling fan, Trey heard the nearby shrill of crickets and, farther off, the loud calls of a great blue turaco, a dinosaur-like bird that lived only in these African rain forests.

"Eight weeks, or a little more." Nyramba shrugged. "That was when we first saw them. How long were they here before that?" Another shrug. "Who knows?"

Trey nodded. Yes: Who knew? He'd spent four months in this region some years back, surveying the area for ICT, and he knew that the dense, wet forests guarded their secrets closely. The people of Kinyare might have detected the thieves just two months earlier, but that didn't mean the wasps had just arrived. They could have been hiding out for years, picking off a colobus here, a golden monkey there. A chimpanzee. A human.

"But it does not matter," Nyramba said. "They are here now, and they will stay."

Another cry echoed through the room. Not the call of a turaco this time, or any other bird. A man's shout.

Thomas Nyramba tilted his head. "John Ndele," he said. "Do you remember him?"

Trey did. A loud drunk, with small, yellow-shot eyes and a propensity for using his fists. You couldn't have spent much time in Kinyare without knowing John Ndele.

"He finally killed his wife," Nyramba said. "So now he is down the hall."

In a cell, that meant. In many villages, in many countries, killing your wife was not much of a crime. But in Kinyare, Thomas Nyramba's rules applied. You broke them at your peril.

Ndele shouted again.

"That would wear on my nerves after a while," Trey said.

"Yes. It does." Nyramba's sudden, wolfish grin showed white teeth against dark skin. "But not for much longer."

**JOHN NDELE LOOKED** up from his cot when the cell door swung open. His expression said, *About time!*

But then, as he pushed himself into a sitting position, he saw who had come for him. His squinty eyes widened, and his face paled.

Along with Trey, Thomas Nyramba had brought his two deputies, beefy young men in khaki shirts and sunglasses. "You thought we would let you walk free?" Nyramba said. Then, "Stand up."

His voice prickled the hair on the back of Trey's neck.

Ndele didn't move. The deputies looked at Nyramba, saw him nod, stepped into the cell, and hauled the prisoner to his feet.

For a moment Trey thought Ndele would faint. He slumped in the deputies' grasp, and his eyes rolled, showing the yellowish whites.

Nyramba took a step forward and slapped his face. That woke Ndele up. He began to weep.

Trey stood still and did not speak.

\*    \*    \*

**"HOW MANY IN** your village have died?" Trey asked.

They were heading down the Nkuru Trail, which led south away from town and into an undisturbed stretch of forest. The deputies went first, pushing Ndele, his hands cuffed, before them. Trey and Nyramba followed, far enough behind that they could talk.

"Too many, before we learned." The police chief sighed. "Our doctor. A nurse. Others. Five of our hunters never returned from the forest."

Trey grimaced. "I think hunters are always among the first," he said. "They're alone. Unprotected."

Nyramba walked a ways without answering. Then he gave Trey a sidelong glance. "That is not the only reason."

Trey waited.

"The *majizi* and the hunters, they want the same things. Bushmeat. Monkey meat."

Still Trey was silent.

"They will not accept anyone else in their territory," Nyramba said. "Unless—"

"Unless what?" Trey said.

Nyramba gave him an amused glance. "You know the answer," he said. "You've figured it out."

He was right.


**THEY WALKED. THE** forest grew darker. The trail was a muddy, winding stripe alongside a lowland stream strung with waxy white flowers and mushrooms that smelled like rotting meat, like death. Ndele, stumbling, struck dumb by his fate, needed more encouragement from the deputies, so progress was slow.

"Not so much farther," Nyramba said. "Twenty minutes, perhaps."

"How many have you brought here?" Trey asked.

"Fourteen. So far."

Trey kept his face a blank, but Nyramba smiled anyway.

"That many," Trey said finally, "from Kinyare alone?"

The police chief laughed. "No, only one from the village before this. Mattias, who assaulted women, and would not stop."

Trey said, "From where, then? I don't understand."

"Why must all bad men come from our village?" Nyramba was still smiling. "The world is full of those who deserve to be condemned."

When Trey was silent, he went on. "The first four came from the Lord's Resistance Army. Together, they had probably killed a thousand people here in Uganda and in Sudan. Another was a member of Al Qaeda, plotting against our president. Fool! Another, from the town of Inomo, has not been able to stay away from young boys. Children, I mean."

He stopped and faced Trey. "Tell me," he said. "What else should I have done? They had to die. Should I have let them die without purpose? Without use?"

Trey didn't answer.

"And, at the same time, let the innocent get taken by the *majizi*?"

THE END OF their trail was a small clearing not far from the stream. Ndele was only half conscious by now.

There was the stump of a fallen kapok tree beside the trail. Someone had plunged a large spike deep into the stump and attached a chain to the spike. The deputies attached the end of the chain to Ndele's manacles, shook them so the chain clanked, then stepped back. The prisoner didn't even test the strength of his bonds, merely lay back with his eyes closed.

Their job done, the deputies went past Trey and Nyramba and back down the trail. Their faces were expressionless, and they were walking fast. They didn't look back.

Trey watched until they were out of sight, then said, "How did you choose this place?"

"It is where I first saw the *majizi*." Nyramba sighed. "Emmanuel, a bushmeat hunter, he was here."

Trey drew in a breath through his nose. He thought he might have caught the slightest whiff of the familiar scent.

"Are they here now?" he asked.

"Yes." Nyramba looked around. "Somewhere. They always stay downwind. And you only see them when they want you to."

Then he stiffened. "There."

Trey followed his gaze. Saw one thief, two . . . four of them. Two moved to hover over the trail, right at eye level, perhaps fifteen feet away. Two others flanked them, one on a small bush to the right, the other half hidden in the foliage on the left.

*Standing guard*. That was what those two were doing. Cleverly, too, using a formation that didn't allow you to keep your eyes on all of them at once. You couldn't kill them all with one shot—not even with #9 birdshot—or strike them down with a single blow.

If you killed one, or even two, the others would reach you before you had time to adjust or protect yourself.

Trey stood still. The two that were hovering seemed to be looking straight into his eyes.

"You interest them," Nyramba said. There was an edge to his voice that might have been alarm. "We must go."

Trey didn't want to take his eyes off the wasps. Most of all, he wanted to see what would happen next to the prisoner, cowering beside the stump.

"Now," Nyramba said.

Still Trey was reluctant to leave. The same reluctance that had pulled at him when he stood beside the thief colony in the Casamance. Looking over his shoulder as he walked, he watched as the thieves swooped toward Ndele. One landed on the prisoner's shoulder and skittered around behind his neck, while the second perched on his ragged white shirt just above his belly.

The trail curved and Ndele was out of sight. Still Trey hesitated, wanting to go back, to see it through till the end.

He felt a hand on his arm. "No," Nyramba said. "They do not like to be watched."

Trey turned away, listening as intently as he could for any sign from the hidden scene behind them.

But he heard no sound at all.


"NOW I WILL show you something else," Nyramba said. "If you think you are strong enough to see it."

Trey didn't reply, just followed as the older man led the way back up the trail. This time, though, they turned onto a smaller path that headed west through wet, silent forest.

Less than a quarter of a mile down the path, Trey heard the clanking of chains ahead and some deeper, grittier noises he couldn't identify. Sounds that grew louder as the two of them approached a bend in the trail.

"Slow," Nyramba said, his voice and expression both grave. "Take care."

Trey nodded and stepped around the bend. Then he stopped where he was, his heart giving a convulsive leap in his chest.

Ahead stood another stump, another spike, another chain. Another prisoner. Two adult thieves guarded it from low-hanging branches, alert but not alarmed by Trey and Nyramba's appearance.

But the similarities to the last scene ended there. This prisoner was a naked man, his body filthy, his skin covered with oozing cuts and scrapes, his stomach grotesquely swollen. He was standing in the middle of the path and staring directly at Trey with a silvery gaze. His chin was slicked with blood—maybe his own—and his breathing came in tortured grunts.

*The last terrifying madness,* the old book had said. *Confronted only at your own mortal peril.*

Trey thought about the colobus monkey at the thief colony in the Casamance. The way it had gotten to its feet after being stung. Its bared teeth as it had come across the clearing at him.

"What is in the venom," he said, "that causes this?"

"You have seen it before?" Nyramba asked, stopping a stride behind him.

Trey didn't reply. Calculating the length of the chain, he stepped forward to get a closer look.

"Any farther," Nyramba said, "and I will be returning to Kinyare alone."

Trey said, "How near is he to the end?"

Before Nyramba could answer, the prisoner straightened and, without any warning, leaped forward to the limits of the chain. Gasping and growling, more blood spilling from around bared and broken teeth, he reached for Trey's throat with his right hand.

Trey, holding his ground, saw that the prisoner's left arm, the one attached by the chain to the stump, was dislocated at both the elbow and shoulder, turned nearly inside out. But the man—the host—seemed to feel no pain.

"At this time," Nyramba said, "they will kill you if you try to harm the young. And sometimes even if you do not."

As if called, the wormlike creature nesting inside the snarling man came to the surface. Trey saw a flash of white in the black circle of the airhole before it retreated deeper into the tunnel of flesh.

The host ground his teeth, yanking at the chain, grasping with clawlike fingers. Pink froth dripped to the ground.

Trey turned away. Nyramba was watching him closely, something in his expression that might have been amusement.

"You asked a question," the police chief said. "After the final sting, the convicted grow worse and worse, but they only become like this at the very end. This man's punishment will likely end tonight, and then he will have peace."

Trey didn't speak, just walked past him and back along the trail. Behind them, the prisoner howled at the sky.

## "SO . . . FOURTEEN."

Thomas Nyramba smiled. "Fifteen now."

They were back in his office, drinking Nile Specials.

"And the thieves, they stay away from the people of the village?" Trey said.

A nod. "We have made a treaty, and both of us respect it."

Trey listened to the language, the choice of words, and thought of what Jack's response would have been. It was all about survival and procreation.

He said, "But what happens when you run out of . . . offerings?"

Nyramba laughed. "What? Run out? People are bringing us"—he paused, searching for the word—"*troublemakers* from every town that the thieves have left alone so far. Four more will come tomorrow from Fort Portal."

He sat back in his chair, still smiling. "We will never run out."

"Is the same thing being done in other towns?"

"Of course. Where it is needed." He gave a shrug. "But none of us will ever lack for people who, like Ndele, deserve what they get."

Trey was silent.

"And you in the United States?" Nyramba said. "In New York? What is your response?"

Trey shook his head. "There've been very few reports so far anywhere yet, and none in New York."

"There will be."

"I know."

"And when there are, when the *majizi* come," Nyramba said, "you Americans will do the same things."

Trey was silent.

*Or worse*, he thought.

"Or worse," Nyramba said.

# TWENTY-FIVE

*Jabiru Wetland Preserve, Queensland, Australia*

**"YOU LOOK OLDER,"** Christopher Gilliard said.

Trey looked at him. He'd been thinking the same thing: Some last spark of youth in his brother had been extinguished since they'd last seen each other. He'd always been more solid, more settled, than Trey, but now time had thinned his sun-bleached hair, broadened his paunch, and lent his face the solidity of encroaching middle age.

He was thirty-nine. Trey was thirty-six. Neither of them were kids anymore.

Only one of them had chosen a life that allowed him to pretend he was.

Christopher said, "When were you last here?"

Trey thought back. With all the traveling he'd done, all the countries he'd visited, he'd made it to this corner of northern Australia just a handful of times, most recently three years ago. Actually, closer to four.

"Too long," he said.

"And it took all this to bring you back here."

"Yeah."

Christopher turned his head to look over the wetlands he'd been hired to preserve, to protect. He breathed in through his nose, and though there was no smell other than that of damp earth and waterweed and, from farther away, dust carried by the wind from the Outback, Trey guessed what odor his brother was searching for. He'd been searching for it himself.

"You can't stay here," he said. "You and Margie and the girls."

Christopher didn't reply at once. Trey saw the corner of his mouth twitch upward and caught a glimpse of the boy he'd adventured with in a dozen different countries while their parents were otherwise occupied.

Still without looking at Trey, he said, "Yeah? How about you? You don't stay anywhere. You spend your whole life running. Do *you* feel safe?"

Trey was silent. After a few moments, Christopher did turn his head. There was affection in his expression, and amusement, too. Even after all this time, he was still the big brother, Trey the child. And they both knew it.

"The world's too small," Trey said at last.

"For you. For most of us, it's just right." Christopher smiled. "And anyway, I think you're missing something: I'm safer from those bugs than you are, no matter how far or fast you run."

Trey blinked. "You are? Why?"

"Because they need me."

**THEY WERE STANDING** on a grassy bank, the freshwater marsh at their feet stretching toward a row of forested hills in the distance. The calm surface was green with algae, silvery where the sun caught it. Black swans and Australian teal and magpie geese paddled across the water and dabbled in the weeds, while lily-trotters ventured across giant lily pads on long-toed feet.

Not just swans and geese relied on the marsh for water and food. Driving in, Trey and Christopher had passed a big gang of gray kangaroos near the preserve entrance. Honeyeaters and other small birds flitted in the underbrush, and a flock of cockatoos clad in graveyard black circled overhead, letting loose with mournful honking cries.

The wetlands were a human creation, kind of. They had been here for thousands of years until the Europeans colonized the area during the nineteenth century. In an eyeblink, the flow of water was diverted, put to other uses, and the wildlife died out or went elsewhere.

On Trey's last visit, Christopher had explained the system of damming and water diversion that had restored the original marshes. Now he said, "These days, we need to keep pumping or the wetlands will dry out again." He snapped his fingers. "Like that."

He gestured again, this time taking in not only the green hills that bordered the marsh, but what Trey knew lay beyond. The vast Outback, hundreds of thousands of square miles of searing heat and spiny grassland and red-rock desert, where wildlife was scarce and water almost nonexistent.

"These bugs of yours, they value the wetlands," he said. "Like every living thing, they need water. Also food and hosts for their young, both of which congregate here. This is an oasis for them, too."

Trey saw where he was going.

"If it weren't for me and my team," Christopher said, "the oasis would vanish. The bugs don't want that."

Trey thought about Thomas Nyramba, so certain that he and the *majizi* understood each other. That, like two warring societies, they'd reached a deal.

Trey had seen nothing to prove Nyramba wrong, or Christopher, either. Not exactly. What neither of them seemed to understand, though, was that the deal wasn't between two equal partners. It wasn't a treaty, signed and witnessed and understood, that happened to exist between two different species.

No. It was the same deal as the one enslaved ants made with their captors: We'll do what you command. In return, you'll let us live.

For now.

"How do you know this?" he said to Christopher. "How can you be sure?"

For a long time his brother didn't answer. He stood without moving, and when he finally spoke his eyes stayed fixed on the glimmering surface of the marsh.

"Brian Pearce," he said. "He managed the preserve along with me. They killed him—or, I guess you'd say, used him. When he died, I sent the rest of the staff home and shut this place. Two days later, the pumps broke down."

He watched a heron stalk along the shallows, hunting for fish. "I couldn't stand it, to let it all go to hell. So I came back, just me, and fixed what was broken."

His expression bleak, he waited long enough that Trey said, "And?"

"And they watched me, the whole time I was here

working. Six of them, maybe, or eight, when I was outside, at least two whenever I went in."

Trey made a sound in his throat.

"Yeah." Christopher managed a grin. "I'd prefer not
to live through another day like that one, ta very much."

He shook his arms and shoulders. "Anyway, they figured out what I was doing, or at least that I was necessary
to this place, and since then they've left us alone. All of
us. I can tell they've taken a few of the kangaroos, and
who knows how many smaller mammals, but they're
hands-off the humans for now."

He tilted his head and laughed. "I guess I owe my life
to these waters, just as much as the lily-trotters, ducks,
and herons do."

Then he turned his back on the wetland. "Let's go,"
he said. "There's something I want to show you at home."

Trey said, "Okay."

Christopher paused and added, "And also, Margie and
the girls would love to see you."

Trey smiled and nodded, but Christopher looked a
little embarrassed.

He was embroidering the truth, and they both knew it.

MARGIE GILLIARD WAS tall and willowy and blond, with a firm
jaw, blue eyes, and a no-nonsense manner. She greeted
Trey with wariness, her behavior reminding him why:
She'd always worried that whatever wanderlust infected
him would spread to his brother. But she seemed pleased
enough to bring him a beer and insist that he stay for
dinner and the night.

He accepted the offers. "Thank you."

Her eyes betrayed a glimmer of amusement. "Well, we could hardly make you stay in a hotel, could we? You're Kit's brother."

"I hear unspoken words," Trey said, smiling. " 'Even if not much of one.' "

She laughed. "You'll do," she said, "until someone better comes along."

In the living room the seven-year-old twins, Jaida and Nicole, long limbed and tan in shorts and T-shirts, stopped playing a video game to look him over. They claimed to remember him and proved it by recalling the time he'd dropped a pitcher of water that had shattered all over the deck outside.

Despite the years, they seemed comfortable with him in about thirty seconds. Trey found himself remembering—with the same surprise he always felt—that he enjoyed being around children. He often found it easier to talk to them than to adults.

Regardless of anything else, the fact that he lived in New York City part-time made him golden to the two girls. They asked him endless questions about shopping on Fifth Avenue, celebrity sightings, and other subjects he knew nothing about, and thankfully forgave him his cluelessness.

When they'd relinquished him, Christopher jerked his head toward a door off the living room. Trey followed, and they entered a small, dim study containing a desk, a bookshelf, and a computer.

" 'Kit'?" Trey said.

Christopher smiled. "Got a problem with that, Thomas the Third?"

Then his expression darkened. "You need to see this,"

he said, sitting down at his computer. "An old friend of mine in the Southern Highlands sent it to me."

The Southern Highlands were on New Guinea, the enormous island that lay just a short flight north of Port Douglas. Before settling in Australia, Christopher had worked on water projects in that area.

Trey had visited him there only once. He retained vivid memories of the Huli Wigmen, with their painted faces and elaborate wigs of human hair twined with flowers and the feathers of birds of paradise. A proud, warlike people, they'd been more than willing to show off their ceremonial dress to outsiders, but had kept their age-old ceremonies a secret.

"The video was raw when I got it," Christopher was saying. "I've done a little editing, but it's still pretty rough."

It began with a close-up on a man's face. An old man with dark skin and fierce eyes, staring straight into the camera. "I am Isaac Agiru," he said. "Listen to what I am about to tell you."

"Agiru. I've known him for years." Christopher gave a snort of amusement. "He was a rebel until the government changed. Now he's a member of the National Parliament. Tough old bugger."

"He's speaking English," Trey asked. "Not New Guinea Pidgin."

"Agiru wants this to be seen and understood."

"Two months ago," the old man went on, "the *stilmen* came to the highlands."

"*Stilmen* is the Pidgin word for thieves," Christopher said.

Trey knew.

"We did not understand how to fight them, and at first many died throughout the district." Agiru's expression turned fierce. "But soon we learned."

"Look at him!" Christopher's voice was admiring. "Don't cross the Huli. Don't even steal a pig from them."

"Today we will go to war," Agiru said.

For a moment the screen went black. "How does he know?" Trey asked.

"Watch."

The screen lit. It showed two men lying on their backs on a grass mat on the floor of a hut. When the camera came in close, Trey could see that their eyes were half open. Light from offscreen caught a silvery sheen.

He took a breath. Beside him, Christopher said, "Seen this before, too, have you?"

Trey nodded. "Too often."

"Today we will take out the worms that live inside these men," Isaac Agiru was saying, though the camera remained focused on the dreaming men. "Later, the *stilmen* will come. They will want revenge, as they always do, but we will defeat them."

Trey thought about Sheila, about the little girl Kait and her parents, and about revenge.

The video's view shifted to a dusty village square ringed by wooden huts and an elaborately ornamented longhouse, the building where all the important—and secret—Huli rituals took place. A steady stream of men was emerging from the front door. Sixty, or perhaps even more.

They were dressed for battle, with painted faces beneath their large, triangular wigs. They looked powerful, unafraid.

Trey could see a pile of wooden and metal objects in the corner of the screen. He leaned in closer to inspect the image.

"I've studied that," Christopher said. "They had guns, clubs, nets, and canisters and sprayers of what I imagine is DDT."

DDT, the pesticide banned for forty years in the United States but still available in other countries.

"You can't see when the battle starts, but I think they rigged mist nets to arrows, and shot them over the first wave of *stilmen*."

Trey nodded. It was a clever strategy. Still . . . "How many attack?" he asked.

Christopher shrugged. "A lot."

The screen showed the closed door of the hut where the two infected men lay. After a moment, the door opened, and a young man came out. He walked up to the camera and showed what he held in his hands: the limp white bodies of two thief larvae.

Agiru's voice. "And Jonathan and Tiken?"

The young man shook his head. His face was grim. "It has been too long," he said.

The camera returned to the old man's face. "Now we will wait," he said. "They will come."

"How do the thieves know?" Christopher asked. "I'm guessing they have a sentry that goes and warns the colony. Something like the ones who were watching me."

Trey said, "Maybe."

There was a jump in the video. When it focused again, Trey could see that hours had passed. Dusk was approaching. The longhouse cast black shadows across the ground.

Whoever was carrying the camera put it down on a

wall or other structure, aimed at the plaza and the waiting men.

Most of the warriors had been sprawled on the ground, but now they got to their feet and went to the pile of weapons. A moment later they had moved out of sight of the lens, some heading to the front of the plaza, some to the sides.

"They come," Isaac Agiru's voice said.

Trey leaned forward, his ears straining to hear the hum of wings, his nose prickling as if somehow he could smell the thieves' odor.

A moment later, someone screamed, a sound of agony. There was a flurry of movement on the right side of the screen—a man staggering, his hands clutching at his face as he fell to the ground. This was followed by disordered shouts, the twang of unseen bows, the sound of gunfire, the sharp crack made by birdshot shells.

And then someone knocked into the camera. The view jolted and spun, coming to rest aimed upward at a patch of treetops.

Trey said, "Don't tell me—"

Christopher sighed. "Sorry, yes."

More shots, more cries, another scream. The hum of wings close to the camera's microphone. A glimpse of a thin black body. Nothing else. No one reset the camera's aim.

All Trey could make out were the trees against a darkening sky. He wanted to climb inside the screen. He needed to *see*.

The scene leaped forward again. Hours had clearly passed, and now it was nighttime. It seemed the battle was over.

"That's it?" Trey said.

Christopher nodded.

The camera was again focused on Agiru's face, just as it had been at the beginning. Illuminated by the harsh light of an offscreen lantern, the old man was still wearing his full Huli regalia. His face was painted yellow, with red slashes under each eye and beneath his mouth; a white line ran down his forehead and nose. His beard was blue, his wig ornamented with brilliant red-and-yellow bird-of-paradise feathers.

"It is done," he said. *"Mipela I paitin ol stilmen na killim olgeta."*

We fought the thieves and killed them.

His eyes glinted. "Seventeen of our warriors are dead. But the *stilmen* will not return."

"How can he say that?" Trey said.

"Listen."

"We are not the first to fight them. The first to defeat them. The *stilmen* attacked the people of the lowlands and islands, Kambaramba and Karkar and Imbonggu and Margarima, first. The warriors of those places fought back. They drove the attackers away, although many men died.

"The lowland peoples warned us, the men of the Southern Highlands, the Huli and the Duna. They told us to watch the forest, to watch the skies. And we did. So when the *stilmen* came here, we were ready. We knew what we must do.

"And, like them, we are victorious. The *stilmen* will be gone from here. This was the last big battle, and we defeated them.

"Together, the people of Papua New Guinea have discovered: The *stilmen*, they like to kill, but they do not like to die."

He leaned toward the camera, his face a totem of strength and certainty. "If you are watching this," he said, "this is what we have taught you."

He sat back and made a dismissive gesture, a flick of one hand.

"Remember," he said, "they are still just *binatang*."

Bugs.

"And they do not like to die."

**THE VIDEO CAME** to an end. Christopher stood, stepped away from the computer. "Plenty to ponder in that," he said.

Trey said, "Yeah."

"Mostly, it makes me think that in New Guinea, on the islands and in the mountain valleys, victory is possible," he said. "But here in Oz, we don't have a chance."

Trey looked at him.

"Think about it. We're a huge, empty country. Not very many people, most of us clustered in a few areas, and hundreds of millions of rabbits and other potential hosts. We couldn't be more outnumbered."

He shook his arms and shoulders, the same gesture he'd made when overlooking the wetlands. Trey recognized it as a sign of acceptance.

"No, this war is over," Christopher said again, "and we've already lost."

"Then leave," Trey said, the words emerging almost before he'd thought them. "Take your family and go to the Southern Highlands."

Christopher smiled. "I've been in touch with Agiru. He said they will welcome us when the time comes."

He looked into Trey's face. "Come with us."

Trey was quiet.

Christopher took a breath to calm himself, a familiar habit Trey had forgotten. When he spoke again, his tone was lighter.

"I know. What was I thinking? You'll race around, trying to save the world, until the last possible minute. Beyond."

His gaze burned into Trey's. "But then what?"

Trey was silent.

"We'll be safe in New Guinea. Where will you go?"

# TWENTY-SIX

*Dry Tortugas, United States*

**WHEN THE MEN** from the U.S. Department of Homeland Security met her at Kennedy Airport, Mariama assumed her counterfeit passport had tripped her up. Perhaps the fat man back in Panama City had alerted the authorities. Maybe this was his revenge.

Or maybe her number had just come up. She *had*, in fact, entered the United States illegally. No matter how porous the borders were, sometimes you just got caught.

As she sat across the table from the three men who would question her, her mind was racing. She had to be able to keep going. They had to allow her to go on. What could she say that would make them unlock the door and set her free?

But then it turned out not to matter. As soon as the questioning began, she realized she had it all wrong. They didn't give a damn about her passport.

The leader, a man with a strong jaw and unblinking

gray eyes, said, "You are from Mpack, in the Casamance region of Senegal."

Not a question.

Mariama recalculated. "I am."

He reached into a briefcase and pulled out a single sheet of paper. Laid it down on the table between them. "And you are familiar with these."

She looked down at the paper and saw a drawing of a thief.

Mariama laughed. All three men, their careers built on unflappability, showed their surprise in subtle ways: a blink, a slight clenching of the jaw, the fingers of a hand flexing for an instant.

"Yes," Mariama said. "Quite familiar."

"Do you know how to stop them?"

Getting to the point more quickly than she expected. *They must be very afraid,* she thought.

Yet she was unsure how to respond.

She could say yes, she knew. But what would happen then? She'd get absorbed. Become merely a cog.

Disappear into the machine.

Or she could say no and . . . perhaps complete the task she'd traveled across the world to accomplish.

The three men's eyes were fixed on her. Even with the lag she demanded due to a (feigned) difficulty with English, she had barely a second left before her hesitation became obvious, before their suspicions were raised. And once that happened, there would be no turning back. They'd break her to find out what she knew.

*Decide.*

"Of course not," she said. "I came here to escape them."

She saw the disappointment on their faces. And, for a moment, she almost weakened, told the truth.

But she'd never been much for playing on a team. Her philosophy: A team was only as strong as its weakest player. And in Mariama's opinion, almost every player was weaker than she was.

**IT WAS THE** wrong decision. Catastrophically wrong.

She'd thought at worst they'd send her home. Then she could start trying again.

But they didn't. After two days in New York they flew her here, to this rock in what had to be the Caribbean Sea, with its old fort and manicured lawns and boatloads of tourists coming to see the ruins and watch the seabirds circling above, white against the blue sky.

None of them knowing there was a small prison on the island, too, a featureless building a stone's throw from where the crowds wandered, and a world away.

For the first few days, Mariama expected to be interrogated. To be tortured. Why else would they bring her to a prison off the mainland?

But as the days passed, Mariama realized that she was here just so they didn't have to worry about her. But why? She was no threat, was she? Why had they neither sent her home nor questioned her further?

She was treated well enough. A cell to herself, with a cot, a small table, and a barred window overlooking a patch of scrubby salt grass, a stretch of sky, a single palm tree, and one end of the small paved runway used by the airplane that had brought her here. The window admitted, along with sunlight in the late afternoon, the sounds of the wind and birds calling, and even sometimes the crash of waves.

Between the window and the overhead electric bulb, the light in her cell was always strong enough to read by. That was most important of all. As Mariama had long known, the greatest punishment a jailer could inflict was to take words away from her.

They wouldn't let her read newspapers or magazines, or listen to the radio or watch television. Instead, they brought her books. Novels, books about ancient history, mystery stories.

But nothing that would give her a clue about what was going on in the real world.

She asked. Of course she did. She asked the people who brought her meals. She asked those who accompanied her during her two hours outside every day, the walks she took within the courtyard, under the brilliant blue sky and circling white birds. She asked the guards who stood outside her cell day and night.

No one would tell her a thing, so eventually she stopped asking them. And there was no one else to ask. If she wasn't alone in this jail, they kept her separate from any of the other prisoners.

Whenever she was outside, the trade winds would be blowing. Every day, she'd take in a deep breath, searching for the familiar smell but detecting nothing.

Not yet.

SHE STOPPED ASKING, but not wondering.

Why am I here?

It wasn't the foundation for a philosophical disquisition. She wasn't questioning her place in the universe. No. It was:

Why am *I* here?

Why am I *here*?

That led to another question: Who had condemned her? In the darkness of her solitude, Mariama even allowed herself to believe it might be the thieves themselves. That somehow they'd infiltrated the highest reaches of the United States government and commanded that Mariama Honso must be neutralized.

Even in the darkest moments, her essential sanity made Mariama laugh. Even at her maddest, she would never believe herself to exist at the center of the world.

No, not the thieves.

Who, then?

There was only one answer that made sense.

**THE WEEKS PASSED.** She told the guards she'd changed her mind, that she wanted to talk, that she had important things to reveal. But it didn't help. No one ever responded.

The guards, young men and women in uniforms she didn't recognize, brought her food. Maids cleaned her cell while she was outside.

Summer turned to fall. Even here, the air had a chill to it in the late afternoon.

One day she had a revelation: She'd been forgotten. She'd slipped into the system, but now no one remembered she was here, why she'd been sent, why requisition slips were still being signed and manpower still being allocated to guard her and keep her alive.

Late at night, sleepless, she thought: I will know when

the world comes to an end. On one sunny day the tourists will stop coming to visit the fort. Then the guards and those who keep me fed will disappear.

And then it will be only me, me alone, the last person left on earth.

The last untainted human. Until the thieves find me, too, as they someday will, and pollute me, and finish the job they've already begun.

**THAT WAS THE** worst day.

The beginning of the worst days.

# TWENTY-SEVEN

*Washington, D.C.*

"THIS CAN'T GET out," the chief of staff said. "Not a whisper, not a breath."

Harry Solomon didn't bother to stifle his laugh. How often had the old guy called with something desperate that needed fixing? How many assignments had he prefaced with this same tired demand?

It was dumb on so many levels. If Harry or his people had ever let a story leak, even a whisper, even a breath, then the COS wouldn't ever have called again.

So why did he always say it? Harry thought he knew. The point was to make the old guy feel better about himself, to help him justify going ahead and telling Harry what he needed done.

What the Big Man needed done.

Okay. Thought about that way, it made some sense. "'Course," Harry said. That wasn't enough, so he added, "You know me and my guys. We don't talk."

Harry knew he'd still have to wait while the COS wrestled with his fears and needs. Usually after about fifteen seconds, the latest tale of woe would come pouring out.

This time, though, the hesitation lasted longer. Much longer. Long enough that Harry actually found himself saying, "Hey, you still there?" over the secure line.

"Yeah." The old guy's voice sounded different, like he was having second thoughts.

"Then talk." Now Harry's curiosity was piqued. Usually the call involved some brushfire that needed extinguishing before it could bring the Big Man down. Harry would listen and roll his eyes. Only in public life, and only in this country, would the sort of thing he was asked to clean up require much more than a laugh or a shrug.

Squashing some figure out of the past with a new claim of presidential drug use. (Regardless that the Big Man had been open about his "youthful indiscretions.") Stoppering up some new embarrassment perpetrated by the First Lady's alcoholic brother. Infiltrating and sterilizing some group of fringe nuts killing time by developing theories that the Big Man was a Manchurian Candidate.

Easy stuff.

"Call me back when you got the cotton wool out of your brain," Harry said and made to disconnect.

"Wait—"

Harry waited. He'd always intended to wait. He was interested.

Then, as the chief of staff finally began to explain, more than interested. As the stream of words, delivered in a rush, went on, Harry felt sweat prickle on his neck. A muscle jumped in his jaw.

When the COS took a breath, Harry said, "Where, again?"

"Fort Collins."

"At the DVBID?"

The Centers for Disease Control's Division of Vector-Borne Infectious Diseases.

"CDC was involved, yes. Under the auspices of the MRIID."

The United States Army Medical Research Institute of Infectious Diseases, that was. Did someone actually get paid to come up with these names?

"But not at Fort Detrick?" Harry said.

The main offices and labs of MRIID were housed in Fort Detrick, Maryland, a lot closer to Harry than Fort Collins, Colorado.

"No."

"Why not?"

"There were reasons."

Meaning, *You don't need to know the reasons.*

Harry could feel his blood pulsing in his throat. This was no DUI to be kept out of the newspapers.

"How many are there?" he asked.

A pause. Then, "Six."

*Shit*, Harry thought. "What happened?"

Silence.

"Listen," Harry said. "I'm not going into something fucked up by the MRIID without knowing what I'm stepping into. I read *The Hot Zone*, yeah, and saw *28 Days Later*. You want to expose a crew to Ebola or the rage virus, find somebody else."

Even then, a couple of extra seconds of silence over the line. Then the COS said, "No virus. No pathogens. These men were . . . stung."

Harry couldn't believe it. *"Stung?"* he said. *"Bit?* You

mean, like bees? I think I saw a movie once about that, too."

The old guy wasn't laughing. When Harry was finished, he just said, "Yes. Stung. And you're going to clean it up. Tonight."

Then he explained how.

As he did, Harry felt his unease return. Whatever it was, it sounded like an emergency. An F5. A 9.1.

Harry didn't ask why. Didn't ask what it was about. Those weren't the kinds of questions he could ask, especially not in an election year.

They weren't even the kinds of questions he was supposed to wonder about. But by the end of the conversation—the COS's monologue, really—he felt, for the first time in a long while, a little shaken. He'd never show it, of course, but there you were.

He had only one question left. Only one he could ask.

"Whatever stung those six men," he said, "is it still there?"

"Of course not."

Meaning: *We hope not.*

Okay, one more question. "You killed it?"

Silence.

Meaning: *No.*

*Fort Collins, Colorado*

**IT WAS THE** damnedest government laboratory Harry had ever seen.

He'd been in others, and they were all basically the same. Squat buildings on university campuses or in office parks. Concrete or brick on the outside. On the inside, linoleum, fluorescent and halogen lights, glass and steel. Disposal boxes for sharps and other hazardous materials in every room. Plenty of bottles of Purell.

People in white coats and eyeglasses hurrying around clutching pads and clipboards and cell phones and little handheld computers.

But the building where Harry and his team were sent late that night was none of these things. It was a two-story shingled house way out toward Horsetooth Mountain, in the shadow of Roosevelt National Forest. On the outside, just a house, out of sight of any neighbors, hidden away in the forest. The kind of thing a family might use for ski weekends in another season.

The nodding leaves of the aspens caught the panel truck's headlights when they pulled to a stop at the end of the long dirt driveway. Beyond the dark house, the surface of a stream glinted silver, reflecting a high, cold three-quarter moon.

Harry felt uneasy out here. He wasn't used to being spooked. It pissed him off.

The man in the seat beside him, Trent, craned around. "Too bad I forgot my fly rod," he said.

Harry didn't bother to reply. He swung the door open and climbed down. The breeze was cool—it felt like fall here already—and he could hear the stream trickling over pebbles and, farther off, an owl hooting.

No people talking, no cars, no dogs barking. The officials who'd chosen this location had wanted solitude, isolation, and they'd gotten it. Harry didn't like how dark it was.

*Why at night?* he'd asked.

There were advantages to working at night, he knew. Fewer eyes watching, for one. But also disadvantages: If some eyes happened to be open, they'd be more likely to notice you, to notice the truck labeled *Central Moving & Storage* rumbling past.

And also, when you got to the site, no matter how isolated it was, at night you had to bring lights. Lights where people didn't expect to see them often meant local police where you didn't want to see *them*.

*Why at night?*

Getting back the usual bullshit.

*Why else?*

A last long pause, and then the chief of staff had spoken. One more sentence.

*We think they mostly come out during the day,* he'd said.

That hadn't made Harry feel any better.


**THE FIRST TWO** were lying in the front hallway.

"Holy fuck," Trent said.

The dead men were wearing the same white lab coats government scientists always wore. But their lab coats were no longer white. They were red. Red shading to black in the beams of the men's flashlights.

Their coats and the floor around them, too. The smell of blood was very strong, and so was another, less familiar odor.

"What the fuck *is* this?" Trent said.

Harry hadn't told them, any of them, what they were going to see here. That was how it worked: No one knew any more than they had to.

Not that knowing in advance made the sight much

easier to take. Harry had heard *stung* and had looked up the after-effects of bee stings on the computer. People who died of shock, who gasped and clutched their throats, who died, eyes popped out, when they swelled up and choked to death.

That would have been bad enough, but this was worse. Much worse. These men's eyes weren't still, protruding, staring, as Harry had expected. They were gone. Torn out of the sockets. Nothing left but white flecks and globules across their cheeks.

The other four, scattered across the floor of the lab itself, were the same. Eyeless, with every exposed portion of skin—faces, necks, hands, shins above their socks— covered in red, swollen speckles and slashes. And some deeper gouges where, Harry thought, something had fed.

The crew's flashlight beams kept returning to the eyes. "What the hell did this?" someone asked.

"Some kind of bee," Harry said.

Knowing he shouldn't have said anything, but feeling shook up. His tongue a whole lot looser than it should have been.

"A *bee*?"

"A shitload of them, I guess."

The beams went this way and that, crisscrossing, inter-secting, as everyone looked in every corner of the room. Harry saw that, regardless of the building's modest, decep-tive exterior, the laboratory was well equipped with scan-ners, scopes, centrifuges, who knew what else. Important research had been going on here, until the bees came.

"Get to work," Harry said, "and let's get the hell out of here."

He didn't have to say it twice.

\*   \*   \*

**HE AND TRENT** put the dead men into body bags, carried them out to the truck, hoisted them into the coffin-shaped coolers that ran half the length of the truck. When they were done, they'd drive to the rendezvous point halfway to Denver. There they'd find a car waiting for them, and the truck and its contents would no longer be their responsibility.

While he and Trent lugged the bodies, the other two were focusing on their area of expertise. This involved a lot of careful carrying of liquids, some precise wiring, and plenty of quiet cursing.

Harry often dismissed what they did as no harder than splashing lighter fluid on charcoal, but he knew the two men earned their pay. A few hours from now, when they were all safely far away, this isolated little house would erupt. By the time it was done burning, there would be nothing identifiable left.

Nothing to make the story blow up, costing Harry his job.

Or worse than just his job. He was under no illusions.

Not in an election year.


**IT WAS TIME** to clear out.

First, though, and as he always did, he took one last walk through the premises. One time there'd been a body in a closet that he hadn't found till that last moment. He would've had a lot of bad days if he hadn't thought to open that closet door.

But he also had another goal for walking through the

scene one last time, alone. He was always on the lookout for something, anything, that he might find useful later.

Did anything here qualify? He wasn't sure. But he did find something: an index card, on the floor near where one of the workers had fallen.

Harry picked it up. There was blood on it, but it was still readable. Four short lines, half typed, half handwritten in black ink.

Beside the typed word *Family*, a handwritten *Philanthidae?*

Beside the word *Genus*: *Philanthus???*

Beside *Species*: ????

And beside *Type Specimen*: *Patagonia, AZ*.

Harry said, "Huh," tucked the card into his pants pocket, and went out to join the rest of his crew.

# TWENTY-EIGHT

*Manhattan*

**"WE'VE LOOKED AT** this video, like, twenty-seven times since your brother sent it," Jack said. Slumped in the chair at his desk, he was scowling. "And it pisses me off just as much this time as the first."

He wasn't happy that the camera had mostly been aimed at the sky.

"The people who shot it had other things on their minds," Sheila said.

"Yeah? Well, next time, hire a cinematographer. I heard there's quite a crowd of them in PNG."

Sheila looked at him. "You of all people should know that we make do with what we've got."

"Yeah." He glowered. "Doesn't mean I can't piss and moan about it."

Sheila had returned from Florida the day before. Trey had come straight from the airport to the office after his flight back from Australia, not even stopping at home to drop off his bag and change clothes. Now here they were, the three of them: Jack at his computer, Trey in a chair beside him, Sheila looking over their shoulders at the screen.

Together again, as if that made a difference.

Trey thought about his visit with his brother. At the airport in Cairns, Christopher had smiled and said, "Things go the way I think they will, you won't be able to spin around the globe so easily anymore."

Trey had shrugged off the words, but now he was seeing the truth in them and wondering how he'd react. How would he handle waking up every day in the same place?

Sheila was looking at him. "You okay?"

He nodded. "Sure. Why?"

"You seem tired."

Jack laughed. "The mighty Trey Gilliard with jet lag? After just eighty hours on airplanes over five days? You must be getting old."

He looked up at the clusters of pins on the map. "I'm getting pisssed off. Those things are everywhere, and we still know damn-all about them."

He grasped the arms of his chair. "We fucking need to get some fucking specimens of this fucking species, and fucking soon."

"Yeah," Sheila said. "But until then, what have we learned?"

Trey, who had been slumped in his seat, straightened. "Agiru says that the people of the Southern Highlands weren't the first in PNG to fight off the *stilmen*."

"Makes sense," Jack said. "Look at the map. The first arrivals to PNG most likely came by boat to the islands and ports, or via airplane to Port Moresby, which is also on the coast." He shrugged. "Those are the places the thieves would colonize first, before moving up into the mountain valleys."

"Plus the lowlands are hot and humid, friendlier turf for them," Sheila said. "It must get cold in the highlands."

"Though they seem able to withstand the cold pretty damn well." Jack waved a hand. "Look at the fucking map. They can survive almost everywhere."

Trey had only been half listening. Now he said, "My point is, how could those islands and villages have been battling the thieves, and no one has noticed?"

Jack went still for a second. Then he was bending over his keyboard. A moment later he said, "Here's how."

It was a little article on CNN.com dated about a month earlier. Just two paragraphs under the headline, "Papua New Guinea Violence Flares Anew."

Trey bent closer to look at the tiny type. The story was datelined Kambaramba, East Sepik Province. "'This long-restive region was riven again by battles among different factions of the Kambot people,'" he read out loud. "'Twenty-two were reported dead, local authorities said. The outbreak of violence follows others in Madang, Karkar Island, and elsewhere. Authorities blame the violence on heightened tensions following disputed parliamentary elections.'"

Jack looked impressed. "That's actually kinda brilliant," he said. "If PNG is famous for anything, it's for tribal violence. Nobody would think twice about a report like this, and nobody would double-check."

Sheila was nodding. "Another government wanting to hush up bad news."

"Until the chief sent around this half-assed video and spilled the beans."

"If it wasn't him, it would've been someone else." She

shrugged. "Governments always think they can hide things, and they're always wrong."

"I have an idea," Jack said. "They could pull their heads out of their asses and fight back, like the villages did."

"Not all people are as fearless as the Huli, and governments are cowardly by nature. Most would prefer to ignore a problem and hope it becomes someone else's."

Trey took a deep breath and said, "My brother believes that, in Australia at least, humans have already lost that war."

Or at least he *thought* he said this. He saw both Jack and Sheila staring at him, and then Sheila was taking his arm and pulling him to his feet.

"I'm bringing you home," she said.

He tried to shake her off. "I'm fine."

"Sure you are." Jack was standing there, too. "You look like one of the zombies from *Night of the Living Dead*, and not one of the handsome, debonair ones, either. And that last thing you said? It made zombie sense."

He looked at Sheila. "Malaria?"

She shook her head. "He's cold, not feverish."

"Home or hospital?"

She hesitated, then said, "Home first. Then we'll see."

"Go."

They went.

By taxi, or at least that was what Sheila told him later. But Trey couldn't have said one way or another, since as far as he could tell, he wasn't there.

**HE ROUSED A** little when they went through the front door of his apartment. He was aware, at least. Aware of lying down, really more like falling. Of someone—Sheila—taking off his shoes and pulling a sheet up over him as he shivered and shook.

Then he lost some more time, with no idea whether it was minutes or hours. When he awoke, he was a little more alert and realized where he was. His bed.

But not his. It was Sheila's bed now. Its contours didn't match his body's anymore.

He was supposed to sleep on the sofa.

He saw that she was sitting on a chair beside the bed. He caught the expression on her face. Concern. Worry, rearranging itself into a smile when she saw he was awake.

"Hey," he said.

She seemed to understand that. "Hey."

He saw her stretch, as if her muscles were stiff and cramped. "I'm going to get myself a cup of tea. I'll get you one, too. You'll be okay for a minute without me?"

He nodded, watched her leave the room.

His room. Hers.

Why was he in here?

He'd ask when she came back.

BUT BY THE time she did reenter the room a few minutes later, carrying two mugs and a steaming teapot on a tray, he'd forgotten what he'd been thinking about.

Her eyes were on him as she came through the door. He saw her stop so suddenly that the mugs clattered against each other, nearly toppling.

"What are you doing?" she said, in a tone of voice he hadn't heard before, hoarse, twisting upward in pitch at the end.

"Doing?" he said. His mouth felt fuzzy, his words indistinct in his ears. "I'm not doing anything."

She put the tray down on the floor—another clatter—and was sitting on the bed beside him before he could move. He felt her grab his right hand, and only then did he realize that he'd been scratching his stomach under his shirt.

Sheila's face was a mask of horrified realization as she pushed the shirt up. He lifted his head off the pillow and looked down at his body.

They both saw it. The small swelling. The tiny black airhole.

Something moving beneath his skin.

"Oh, God," Sheila said, her voice a gasp. "Oh, no. *Trey.*"

# TWENTY-NINE

*Albuquerque, New Mexico*

## JEREMY AXELSON SIGHED.

Here they were again. How many nights had been spent this way since the campaign started? A thousand? Ten thousand?

It felt like a million.

Axelson could probably have figured it, the real number, or close, if he'd wanted to. But why bother? It would just depress him, and right now his brain was fried extra crispy anyway. The last thing it needed was a math problem to solve.

A million nights. A million hotels. Not that it made a difference. Wherever they stayed, it always felt like the same room. You could only tell where you were by the subjects of the paintings hanging on the walls.

In Iowa the paintings showed towheaded kids among ripening fields of corn. Vineyards or the Golden Gate Bridge in northern California. Leaping dolphins in Miami. Here in Albuquerque? Mountains and canyons.

Of course, you didn't ever get the chance to see the actual scenery. Just the paintings.

The three of them were watching four televisions. Or not watching. The speech was over, and now it was time for the political consultants to offer their opinions, the spinners to spin, and the panelists in the studios to sit in middle-aged rows and pontificate.

The TVs were muted. Not that it mattered: Each of them, two men who'd pushed past fifty and a woman a decade younger, could have recited the words being spoken on-screen. No need to hear them.

"Guy puts me to sleep," the rumpled, bearlike man sitting across from Axelson complained.

He wasn't talking about the anchors, the consultants, the spinners, or the panelists.

He was talking about the man who'd just given the speech. Sam Chapman.

The president of the United States.

"You say that every time," Axelson pointed out.

"He does it every time."

The woman—tiny, sharp-eyed—stirred in her chair. "If he does it another ninety times between now and November," she said, "he's going to win."

The three of them stared at the silent screens, and for a while nobody said anything.

Ron Stanhouse, the campaign manager. Chief pollster Melanie Hoff. And Axelson himself, tall, angular, with a narrow face and a beaklike nose and a general air of geniality belied by the glitter of intelligence and calculation in his eyes.

Axelson was the communications director. Which meant it was his job to make the world think that the smell arising from their campaign was imminent victory, not flop sweat.

Not their campaign. Tony's.

Senator Anthony Harrison, the man who, in two weeks, would be nominated to run for president against Sam Chapman.

And who, eight weeks later, was going to lose.

"Give me today's numbers," Stanhouse said.

Hoff sighed. "Nationwide, likely voters, we're behind 49–43–8. Make them choose, it's 53–47. Likeliest screen, a little closer: maybe 52.2 to 47.8. Not good enough." She grimaced. "You know all this. The numbers haven't budged in weeks."

"Think they'll budge a little after tonight," Axelson said.

Tonight the president had delivered what amounted to an out-of-season State of the Union speech from his desk in the White House. The supposed excuse was to reassure America over instability in the Mideast. The truth was that Sam Chapman knew that whenever he demonstrated the trappings of the presidency, his numbers went up.

The results of the first instant poll appeared on one of the screens.

More likely to vote for: 31%.
Less likely: 13%.
No difference or no opinion: 56%.

"Tomorrow's numbers will be worse," Hoff said.

At the beginning of the cycle, Chapman had seemed vulnerable. The unemployment rate had risen in his first year and had stayed stubbornly high, gas prices had been spiking, the housing market continued in its endless stay in the doldrums.

And though he was still seen as likable—it was one of the things that had gotten him elected in the first place—nobody had ever claimed that the earth shook when he spoke. Support for him had been broad, but only an inch deep.

Almost by definition, Chapman was the kind of incumbent who might fall to a strong challenge. And among the usual gaggle of senators, ex-governors, and hopeless gadflies, Anthony Harrison, former governor of Colorado, had an excellent shot at the nomination.

That was why Stanhouse, Hoff, and Axelson had signed on with him.

Almost immediately, though, the breaks had started going the incumbent's way. None of the potential challengers, including Harrison, had emerged unscathed from a long, tedious, and expensive primary season. The recent laws allowing for nearly unlimited anonymous corporate donations had given even the fringiest wannabes life and staying power.

Another ex-governor had, as was her wont, gobbled up far more than her share of media oxygen before declining to run.

Now, at the end of the circus, as Harrison was finally emerging with the nomination, a skeleton or two had been unearthed from his closet. Nothing the campaign hadn't known about, and nothing they couldn't deal with, but still, the news had occupied too many cycles.

The point was: To defeat a sitting president, you had to get all the breaks. Or just one, if it was big enough.

But neither was happening for Harrison. For them.

"Swing states?" Stanhouse said.

Hoff shrugged. "Today we'd win Florida, Georgia, North Carolina. Colorado, of course. But we'd lose most of the others: Pennsylvania, Virginia, the industrial Midwest—maybe even Missouri."

She switched her gaze to Axelson. "Your guys better write him one hell of a convention speech."

When he didn't reply, she drained her drink, mostly just ice and water now, and got to her feet. Stretched, yawned, and walked to the door.

"Figure out a way to change the game," she said, "and I'll give you better news."

**A KNOCK ON** the door.

Axelson didn't move. It was late, dark-night-of-the-soul late, but he was still up. He hadn't moved since Hoff and Stanhouse left, except once to freshen his drink and turn off three of the TVs. The television that was still on, tuned to TCM, was showing an old Bob Hope–Bing Crosby movie, the one where they went to the North Pole.

*The Road to Utopia.* Axelson laughed and drank. Could he go along? Utopia was sounding pretty good right about now.

The knock came again. For a moment Axelson considered ignoring it. But he knew he wouldn't be able to hide from whatever news lay on the other side of the door. Not forever.

With a groan, he got to his feet, walked over, and swung the door open.

A young man stood in the hall. He was wearing a

pinstriped gray suit, a crisply pressed sky blue poplin shirt, and a patriotic red tie. With his fair skin, open expression, and studious black-framed eyeglasses, he lacked only an American flag pin to be ready to appear on camera.

No, wait. He *was* wearing a flag pin, on the lapel of his suit jacket.

Perfect.

"Do you sleep in that getup?" Axelson asked him.

The young man smiled. "Gary Kuster, sir," he said. "Can I talk to you?"

Axelson knew who he was. A member of the field staff, an advance man whose job it was to lay the groundwork for campaign appearances.

He was good at it, too. A rising star, keen minded, and not nearly as guileless as his fair-haired-boy looks would have you believe.

Axelson didn't move. "What about?"

He was tired. He didn't want to hear any more complaints. Nothing that this irritatingly bright-eyed boy had to say could possibly be of any interest, not tonight.

"Sir," Kuster said, "I need to show you something." He looked Axelson straight in the eyes. "Something that will win us the election."

Axelson sighed. He'd outgrown dramatic pronouncements from underlings twenty-five years ago. They always thought they'd found the faux pas that would sink the opposition, the angle that no one else had seen. And they were always wrong.

He swirled the Scotch in his glass. It needed more ice. "Do I have to go somewhere to see this 'something'?"

Kuster lifted his left hand. He was carrying an iPad. "No. Here's fine."

Finally Axelson moved out of the doorway. As he fished the last shards of ice from the bucket, he watched Kuster push a button. The iPad lit up, revealing a YouTube page.

"What are you going to do," Axelson asked, "show me rock videos?"

## HE COULDN'T BELIEVE it.

The guy *was* showing him videos. And not stuff of any interest, either. Not even old Allman Brothers performances, Bugs Bunny cartoons, or trailers for the movies that Axelson would miss this fall, when every minute would be spent staving off electoral humiliation.

Not even the cute amateur shit that he'd watched during the endless down hours every campaign had to endure. Cats running on treadmills, monkeys pulling dogs' tails, the guy who traveled all around the world dancing. (Axelson would have traded jobs with *that* guy in a heartbeat.) That old one, with the little kid biting the finger of the other little kid.

No. None of that. Videos of wasps.

Big wasps. Axelson had grown up in Texas, not that far from the Rio Grande, and the wasps down there, the cicada killers, they could be huge. But these ones looked different, skinny and black, with legs that made them look like they were half spider. These ones were spooky.

One of them crawled over a branch and stared at the camera. Axelson felt like it was looking right into him.

Damn spooky.

"What's the point?" he said.

Kuster didn't reply. The camera zoomed in so that the wasp's face filled the screen. Watching, Axelson could have sworn that he could see intelligence in its gaze. The way its mouth moved, it looked like it was licking its chops.

When the video ended, he said, "Okay, you've put me off my feed. Now tell me why the hell I should be interested."

Kuster smiled at him. "I told you. These bugs are going to win us the election."

Then he began to explain. His voice staying calm, but with an edge of excitement, of triumph, behind it. Euphoria.

Sometimes he paused to show Axelson evidence. Proof. Another video, a newspaper article, notes he'd made on a legal pad.

At first Axelson remained skeptical, out of sorts. Then his attention sharpened. He found himself leaning over Kuster's shoulder, peering in at the screen or down at the neat handwriting on the pad. His heart thumped, and again.

And then, finally understanding, seeing exactly where this was going, Axelson felt his legs get weak. He sat down, his drink forgotten. But he still didn't say anything. He just listened. Listened for more than an hour, until Kuster was finally done.

At last the young man said, "That's it. What do you think?"

Axelson cleared his throat. He wondered what his face looked like.

"Who else knows?" he asked. His voice was scratchy. "Who else knows the whole story?"

"No one," Kuster said. "No one else has put it together yet, much less figured out the White House's role. Just you and me."

Axelson was already reaching for his phone. "Let's fix that," he said.

He knew what he'd just heard. He understood what it meant.

He punched a button and said, "Ron? Wake up and get back in here. Melanie, too. Everybody. The whole senior staff. Roust 'em."

Normally Stanhouse would have bitched about it. It was late, it'd been a bad day, and why the hell was it his job to track everyone down? But he merely said, "Okay," and disconnected.

He recognized that tone in Axelson's voice.

Soon enough, no more than fifteen minutes later, everyone was there. In rumpled clothes, some of them still rubbing their eyes, but ready. Eager. It was amazing how fast a staff's morale could turn around, if they sniffed a change in the wind.

Axelson surveyed the room. A dozen faces. His team.

Then he looked back at Kuster, who was still sitting in the same chair, and said, "Go over it again."

Kuster smiled and began.

# THIRTY

**"TAKE IT OUT,"** Trey said.

His heart was hammering, as if he'd just climbed a mountain and was standing at twenty-seven thousand feet. But he hadn't moved. Couldn't move.

Understanding at last what had happened to him. His mind clearing for an instant, just an instant, then clouding over again. Like a tide sweeping in, obliterating everything in its path, before being sucked back out, leaving only ruins behind.

A battle. A war.

His heart was his enemy. With every beat, every liquid leap inside his chest, every surge of blood in his veins, his consciousness dwindled.

Sheila stood beside the bed. Frozen. Stunned. He could see that. As if through a smeared window, he could see the anguish on her face.

His heart thudded. He was disappearing inside his poisoned blood.

"Take it out," he said, or thought he said. *"Now."*

Only knowing he'd actually said the words, and not just dreamed them, when Sheila, her bloodless face half obscured by the hand over her mouth, shook her head. Hard. In terror.

"I can't," she said.

Trey reached out and grabbed her arm. He could still feel it. It was cold.

"Sheila," he said, "there's no time. It's . . . taking me."

His blood rushed. Something was chewing at the edges of his consciousness, dropping crimson veils over his vision. Winning the battle. Winning the war.

"Trey." She was sitting on the edge of the bed, holding his hand in both of hers. "You'll die."

Her voice tiny through the roaring in his head, the rattling of his heart.

"No." His tongue felt swollen in his mouth.

In some remote, untouched corner, he thought, *It's trying to stop me. It knows that if we wait just a little longer we'll be too late.*

*It.*

With an effort almost beyond his imagining, he wrenched his shattered thoughts back into an approximation of something whole. His vision cleared. A little.

"Sheila, no," he said. His voice wasn't his own.

"You don't die," he said. "Not—yet."

He squeezed her hand. *Listen to me.*

*Save me.*

Her face was a mask of grief and indecision. Tears streaked her cheeks and dripped from her chin. "My mom—"

"Sheila," he said, "I don't know—when this happened. *I don't remember.* But not long. Look—"

He couldn't breathe. His lungs were filling.

"Look." He was speaking underwater. "It's so small."

Still she did not move.

"Agiru—" he said. His words tumbling out in gasps. "The old man. He said they weren't in time—"

Was she listening? Would she *understand*?

"Do you see—" Despairing. "That's why you don't remember you were infected. Not at first. Because you won't die . . ."

It was hopeless. She would not go. She would not try.

It was already too late.

He felt something flutter inside him. A tiny wriggle within his flesh.

For one last instant, everything was silent, calm. He sat in the eye. The center of the vortex.

He could see. He could hear.

He could breathe. He inhaled and said, his own voice, his own words, "Sheila. *Kill it.*"

The creature wriggled again, more strongly. Diving deeper. Releasing its poison.

Saving itself.

Sacrificing him.

Trey's mind burst apart. His mouth moved, he could feel it moving, but the roaring of his heart kept him from knowing if he spoke words or if the words made any sense.

With his bloodred gaze, he saw Sheila put her hands over her face. Then she took them away, and, when she did, her expression had changed.

She got up from the bed. He saw her, could still see her, as she ran for the bedroom door and out of view.

The creature dug.

The veil fell, and he was blind. No: blind on the outside. Inside, he could still see.

Seeing, he glimpsed . . . something.

Huge. Monstrous. Shapeless.

At that last instant, Trey knew what it was.

And what it wanted.

**FAR IN THE** distance, he felt . . . something new.

Pain.

A dart of pain as clear as crystal.

Light danced before his eyes. The aurora borealis. The height of a migraine's aura. Twisting, whirling fragments of light, but through them he could again glimpse the real world. The world outside, the one that the monster deep in his brain could not yet control.

The tide pulling back.

He looked down at his body. It lay on the bed. Still. Waxen. Someone else's body.

Sheila sat on a chair, leaning over it. Leaning over the body. She was wearing latex gloves from the first-aid kit he kept in his bathroom.

Trey could see the side of her face, see that she was calm now. A doctor. Doing what she had to do.

She held a small knife in her right hand. A paring knife from the kitchen. In her left hand, rubbing alcohol in a brown bottle.

The bottle spilled. The liquid was cold on the body's pierced skin.

Somewhere in the center of his brain, Trey felt something new rise. Something jagged.

Fear. Rage.

Not his own.

Trey watched as Sheila swabbed first the knife blade with the alcohol, then the body's bare belly. Her face intent, she bent over him. The blade caught the light as it sank into his swollen flesh.

In the moment before the two warring worlds inside his brain collided, merged, burst apart again, Trey saw the larva wriggle in the parted lips of the cut. He glimpsed its black head, saw its mandibles reaching in vain for something to attack.

Sheila lifted it from the body. It twisted on the points of a gleaming pair of forceps.

Trey felt terror erupt inside him. Something shrieked inside his head.

Who was it?

What was he?

The world inside flew. Shattered.

He was gone.

# THIRTY-ONE

**ONE MOMENT WAS** a dreamless blank, and the next Trey was lying in his bed, aware of the sheets against the bare skin of his back and arms, the pillow against his head. The body he'd been watching from a distance was once again his own.

He lay there, unmoving. His eyes were closed, but the shadows projected on them came from the yellowish light illuminating the bedroom.

He could feel himself breathing, his lungs pushing the bellows of his chest up and out, down and in. He could feel his heart beating, but more gently now, set free from its adrenaline frenzy.

He could feel the pain in his stomach. In the skin of his stomach.

Still he didn't move. These sensations were all reassuring. He was alive. He'd been right. Sheila had gotten the larva out in time. Whatever poison it had released to stop his heart, it had not yet possessed in sufficient quantities to succeed.

It had tried. It had done its best, and he still lived.

But . . .

Somewhere deep inside his brain, something had changed.

Something was different.

He explored, like you search for a missing tooth with your tongue. He probed, and found . . .

Something gone?

Something new?

He didn't know.

Maybe both.


TIME PASSED. THEN he awoke again and, this time, opened his eyes.

Sheila was sitting in a chair beside the bed, elbows on knees, head propped on her hands. The latex gloves were gone, her hands scrubbed clean. But she'd neglected to wash her face. Tearstains had left tiny streaks on her cheeks, like the paths the first raindrops leave down a dusty windshield.

No tears now, though. Just an echo of terror in her eyes. Trey could see it. It was still there. He wondered if it would ever leave.

Her gaze found his face. "There you are," she said, and it sounded casual until her breath caught on the last word.

She reached out and took his hand. Just as she had done before, when he was falling. Before she pulled him back.

Her hand still felt cold in his, and she didn't want to

meet his eyes. He could only imagine the horror she must have gone through as she made that first incision, as she removed the writhing larva from his flesh. She must have been sure, certain, that he would die.

That she would kill him, as she believed she'd killed her mother.

But she'd gone ahead anyway. She'd done what he'd asked, what he'd pleaded for.

Trey moved his mouth. Making words seemed strange, as if he didn't quite know the language anymore.

"Thank you," he said.

Now she was looking directly at him. "If you ever make me do that again," she said, "*I'll* die."

He shifted his gaze to the window and saw that night had fallen. The light he'd seen through his closed eyelids had come from the bedside lamp, not the sun.

He realized he didn't even know when—or how— they'd come back to the apartment. The entire day seemed obscured, covered in fog.

Was that what every victim felt? Every host? Was that the preamble to the dreaming days, and death?

"I was asleep," he asked, "for how long?"

Sheila looked at her watch. "About four hours."

"God," he said, remembering his dreams. No. They hadn't been dreams.

He'd have to tell them about what he'd seen, what he'd felt. Sheila and Jack. Even though he didn't want to. Even though something inside him, inside the part of him that had changed, fought against the telling.

Sheila raised her eyes to his. "Once you'd survived the initial procedure," she said, only the slightest quaver in her voice betraying her resolve, "I wondered if you'd live, but never awake." Her mouth turned down at the corners. "Whether all I'd done was turn your dreaming days into dreaming years."

She rolled her shoulders, winced. "I thought about calling an ambulance, taking you to the hospital." Both her voice and gaze sharpened. "But Jack's right. We don't understand *anything* about this. Maybe moving you would have killed you. I didn't know."

Her mouth twisted, a grimace, not a smile. "So I kept you here and stayed beside you." A pause. "And . . . *prayed*."

Trey drew in a breath, remembering the maelstrom inside his head. His fear. All the pain. Dimming now in the memory, becoming surreal, as pain always did.

"I'm . . . glad you stayed with me," he said.

Her hand tightened in his. "After about two hours, you began to give the signs of someone emerging from deep sedation. That's when I thought you might be all right. But still . . . it took so long."

Trey tried to push himself up into a sitting position. He couldn't stop himself from making a sound in his throat.

Sheila frowned. "Stay where you are. I rigged up a butterfly bandage for the incision, but you really need a couple of stitches."

He shook his head and kept trying. Finally, with her help, he propped himself against the headboard. He was sweating, light-headed.

Sheila said, "Oh, so you're *that* kind of patient."

He reached for the water bottle that stood on the bedside table and took a drink.

His belly hurt. He looked down and saw a large white

sterile pad—a little stained with yellowish red—covering where the swelling had been and, underneath it, the edges of the butterfly bandage.

Seeing it made the bile rise in his throat. That was where it had been. The invader. The parasite.

Sheila said, "I'm sorry if it's a mess." For a moment her gaze turned inward again. "You're not exactly equipped for surgery here."

Trey nodded. He felt cold.

"But if we keep it clean, I don't think there'll be much risk of infection. Since the larva was"—she struggled for the word—"comparatively undeveloped, it hadn't gotten in very deep."

Deep enough. Trey could remember the sensation as it dove beneath the surface. It had felt like it was digging into his center, his core.

He made to swing his legs over the edge of the bed, to get to his feet. Sheila put a hand on his shoulder and, without effort, kept him where he was.

"Overruled," she said. Then, more gently, "Give your-self a little time. You're still clearing all that junk out of your system."

She frowned. "I wish I had some way of measuring your kidney function. Don't be surprised if your pee comes out some strange colors the next few days. Your blood is likely full of debris."

"I'm fine," Trey said.

She kept her hand on his shoulder. "Then why are you shivering?"

After a moment, he lay back down.

"Better," she said.

For a moment he thought he might drift off again.

Then, almost before it became a conscious thought, the question was out of his mouth. "Where's the larva?"

Sheila's mouth turned downward. "In a jar, in the bathroom." She gave a little grin. "I didn't want to be in the same room with it."

"Is it—"

She nodded. "As a doornail, about thirty seconds after I pulled it out. And I didn't squeeze it." She widened her eyes. "I don't think those things can live long away from their hosts. Not until they're ready to hatch."

She got to her feet and walked out of the room. Trey watched her go, that strong stride on long, slender legs causing her knee-length skirt to swish back and forth as she moved.

Her skirt. Had she been wearing a skirt earlier? Trey didn't think so, though his dreaming hours made him unsure of what he knew and what he didn't.

She came back in carrying a little jam jar. Trey noticed that she was wearing a white sleeveless blouse with a network of small flowers around the neck and down the sides. She'd washed the tearstains off her face.

"You look beautiful," he said, surprising them both.

Sheila's face colored. Then she gave him an askance look. "Calm down, cowboy. I'm still telling you to stay in bed till tomorrow."

She sat down in the chair and showed him the jar. At its bottom lay the dead larva, a limp white tube with oversized head, staring black eyes, and those familiar, vicious mandibles.

Trey had seen two of them before, alive and then dead, in the cloud forests of Costa Rica. Bigger, those had been, and more deadly. But seeing this one made his heart pound again, as if it were still inside him, still spreading its poison.

The top of the jar was screwed on tight. Sheila saw him looking. "Can't hurt to be sure." She gave a little laugh, shaky around the edges. "I would have glued it shut if I'd found where you keep the glue."

"Jack will be happy," he said.

She frowned. "I've been trying him, but for once he's not at the office, and his cell phone's off."

Trey leaned closer, but the larva had nothing else to tell him.

Or maybe it did. Finally his head was clear enough for something else to occur to him. Something he should have thought of as soon as he awoke.

His gaze shifted to the window, which was closed, the shades drawn. To the door of the room, closed as well. To the shadows cast across the ceiling by the lamp at his bedside. To the dark closet and shelves in the corner.

Sheila, watching him, nodded. "I wondered when you'd think of that."

"But—"

"Nothing." There was something blurred in her expression. "Let me tell you, Trey, I wanted to lock myself in the bathroom, the minute I was done." She closed her eyes for a moment, then turned her gaze on him once again. "But I couldn't. Not with you here."

Trey didn't say anything. "Thank you" was not enough for everything he owed her.

She leaned over, reaching down out of his line of vision. When she straightened, she was holding a kitchen knife, a claw hammer, and a big hardcover book.

"The place needs more weapons," she said. "And better ones."

Trey looked at her armaments and said, "Yeah. Pretty pathetic."

Sheila's gaze shifted to the door. "Still," she said, "sometimes they don't come for hours for . . . revenge."

Trey nodded but didn't speak.

"It could still happen at any moment," she said. "Couldn't it?"

Trey raised his eyes to look at her. "Yes. It could. But I don't think it will."

"Why not?"

"Because it's a lot easier for a thief to plant a larva in me than to hitch a ride here."

"I don't know," Sheila said. "They seem like pretty caring parents to me."

Trey shook his head. He was missing something, some revelation that lay just beyond his conscious mind.

Something he'd learned from the creature, the *presence*, inside him.

He was reaching for this knowledge when he heard Sheila gasp. He focused on her and saw that her face was bloodless.

"What?" he said, alarmed. "What's wrong?"

"Trey," she said, "where's your suitcase?"

He looked around, as if he expected to see it on the floor. Even as he did, though, he felt a tide of horror rise inside him.

"I went straight to the museum," he said, his voice a whisper. "It's still there."

But Sheila was already standing, half turned toward

the door. Reaching into her bag, pulling out her cell phone, dialing.

Saying, even before Jack's phone began to ring, "Answer me this time, you idiot. *Answer.*"

# THIRTY-TWO

**ONE RING OVER** the speaker. Two. Three.

Trey remembered reading that the first few rings you hear when making a call on a cell phone are phony. They're generated by your phone to keep you occupied while the signal is bouncing off various satellites and cell towers. The person you're calling doesn't hear them.

Five rings. Seven. By now Jack's cell phone would be ringing.

Trey could see that Sheila's eyes were growing frantic and knew his own expression must be a mirror of hers.

The squawk of Jack's voice. "Yeah?"

"Where the hell have you been?" Sheila's voice was breathless. "I've been trying to reach you all afternoon."

"At the movies."

Sheila rolled her eyes. "Where are you now?"

"Walking down Eighty-first Street. Heading back to the office."

"Turn around."

"Say again?"

"Just listen to me." Sheila took in a breath. "Trey was infected. I removed the larva—"

"Holy shit—"

"Jack, he's okay."

She held up the phone. Trey called out, "I'm fine. Now shut up and listen to her."

"So the old man was right," Jack said. "If you remove the larva early enough, it can't set off a sufficient immunocascade—"

"Yes," Sheila said. "We'll tell you everything when we see you. Now—"

"Trey, what did you see while you were dreaming?"

"Jack—"

"'Cause I have some theories about that, too."

Sheila was holding the phone tightly. "Wait—are you still walking?"

"Sure. Told you: I'm heading to the office."

Sheila squeezed her eyes shut for a moment. Then she opened them and said, spacing the words out as if she were speaking to a child, "Jack, listen. Trey left his bag, the one he took to Australia, there. In your office."

That shut him up for a moment. Then he said, "Ah."

"Yes," Sheila said. "Ah."

After a pause he said, "Trey, do you have any memory of seeing the adult? In your rental car in Port Douglas, maybe?"

Trey worked through his dim memories of the past few days. Or were they visions? Created by the presence he could still feel shifting at the edges of his consciousness?

Finally he said, "I don't know."

"Doesn't matter." Even over the phone, Jack's excitement was evident. "This is so fucking cool. Come right in so we can talk."

"Jack, that's not—"

They heard his muffled voice speaking to someone else.

"Jack!" Sheila's voice was like a whip crack. "Where are you?"

No answer for ten seconds. Then Jack's voice: "Inside. Now I'm waiting for the elevator to the fifth floor."

"Are you listening to me?" Sheila said.

"What? Oh, hang on, I'm getting on the elevator. Cell service sucks in here."

"What are you doing? Stop!" Red spots had risen to Sheila's cheeks, and her left hand had, unbidden, risen to pull at her hair.

In other circumstances, Trey might even have found it funny: Sheila's powerful force meeting the immovable object that was Jack Parker.

But not here, not now.

Jack's voice came over the line, clearer.

"On five. What were you saying?"

Sheila's voice was despairing. "We're saying there might be an adult thief in your office."

They heard him laugh. "Yeah, I got that part."

"So don't go in."

"Don't go in my office?" He sounded disgusted. "The hell I won't."

Trey said, "I've seen those bugs, Jack. They're fast, and they know what they want. If one's in there, even if you think you're ready, it could still get the jump on you."

"Blah," Jack said, "blah blah. Trey, could you keep it down? I'm listening at the door here."

Trey stopped talking.

Jack said, "I don't hear any angry buzzing coming from inside."

"They're pretty close to silent, Jack," Trey said.

"It was a joke."

Trey said, "Ha."

"There you go." Static on the line. Then, "I'm going to put the phone down and go in."

Sheila closed her eyes. "Oh, Jack."

"I know. You don't know what you miss till it's gone."

A clunk as the phone was placed on the floor. The creak of a door swinging open. Footsteps.

Sheila said, *"Shit."*

They could hear Jack's voice in the distance: "That smell—"

Sheila's eyes opened wide. Trey was sweating.

Jack said in a singsong tone, "Oh, *ladrón*, where are you?"

Then, in a different tone: "Hey!"

A crash. Another.

"Hulk, smash!"

A hissing sound.

Silence.

Thirty seconds of silence that felt like forever to Trey. What was he doing here in bed? He should have been there with Jack.

He was supposed to be on the front lines. He was *always* supposed to be on the front lines.

A rustling sound over the phone, and then Jack's voice, much closer. They could hear his breath. He was panting.

"Got her," he said, "before she got me. She's dead."

Unmistakable triumph in his tone.

"You're okay?" Sheila asked. Her voice was strained.

"Told you, I'm fine." A laugh. "More than fine. I'm great."

"Hulk smashed it?" Trey said.

"No. That was a joke. We need it undamaged."

"You sure it's dead?"

"Oh, I'm sure. It's dead. It is no more. It has ceased to be. It is an ex-thief."

"How did you do it?"

"Come in and I'll show you."

Sheila said, "Trey can't travel yet."

But Trey was already swinging his legs over the side of the bed. He still felt shaky, but far stronger than he had when he'd first awoken. "I'm fine," he said, getting to his feet. "Just give me a minute and we'll go."

"Good," Jack said. "Get a move on."


"TAKE OFF YOUR shirt," Sheila said the moment they walked into the office.

Jack looked at her. Opened his mouth to make a joke, then quailed a little at her expression. "I told you, I'm fine. She didn't get near me."

Sheila crossed her arms. Jack's beard bristled. Then he caught a look at Trey, all sallow skin and shaky legs, and his expression turned thoughtful.

"Okay," he said.

It was hard to see the skin of Jack's round belly underneath its generous covering of black hair. After a close inspection, though, Sheila pronounced him unmarked.

"For now," she said.

"Told you," Jack said.

"Yeah, well, that doesn't mean we can be sure. We'll check again every few hours."

"Can't get enough of me, huh?"

He walked up to Trey and gave him a once-over. For a moment his expression turned serious.

"I feel better than I look," Trey said. "A little. I'll feel even better when my pee isn't dark brown, though."

"I want every detail." Jack paused. "Well, except the pee part."

Trey nodded.

"But first—look."

It was Trey's bag, where he'd left it on the floor near the windows. There was a ragged hole just beside the zipper, where the thief had chewed its way out.

Trey drew in a deep breath. How many hundreds, thousands, of other thieves had already traveled the same way?

"Here she is," Jack said.

The dead adult lay on her back on Jack's desk, her bloodred wings folded, black legs crossed in death like any insect's. Her body seemed undamaged.

"How did you kill her?" Sheila asked.

"Take a breath and guess."

Trey breathed in deeply. Under the harsh smell of the thief, he could detect another odor. After a moment, he figured out what it was.

"Pyrethrum," he said. Then, to Sheila, "What they use to fog trees and plants when they're collecting bugs. Deadly, but only to its targets. Plus it breaks down fast and doesn't harm the specimens."

"Kills them without harming them, a neat trick." Jack

nodded toward a half-full plastic plant sprayer sitting on the corner of his desk. "Mixed up a little of my own solution before walking in here, and knocked her out of the air when she came for me."

He frowned. "She was damn strong, I'll give her that. It took a couple of shots."

"Still, they can be killed," Sheila said.

Trey said, "They're just *binatang*."

"It's easy to forget," Jack said, "but it's true. Individually, they're easy enough to defeat."

"Individually," Sheila said.

Trey's hand crept up to his shirt. He touched the sterile pad on his belly and felt something stir deep inside his brain.

Sheila reached into her shoulder bag and took out the jar containing the dead larva. Opening the jar, she tipped it out onto the desk beside its parent.

In silence, they all looked at the two still forms.

"That's all they are," Sheila said in a wondering tone.

"Smaller creatures than these have brought civilizations crashing down," Trey said.

Jack shrugged. This sort of conversation didn't interest him.

He brought his face close to the two thieves, larva and adult. "Okay," he said to them, "tell us everything you know."

*That* was what interested him.

# THIRTY-THREE

*Charleston, South Carolina*

**MARY FINNERAN SAT** in the shade under the live-oak trees in White Point Garden and looked out at Fort Sumter. The hazy summer sun, high in the sky at midday, had turned the harbor shimmering silver. The ferryboats and yachts left meteor trails across the choppy water, and farther out a cruise ship heading for land caught the sunlight and flashed white like a semaphore flag.

The skies were nearly as crowded. Wide-bodies brought tourists from all over the world, corporate jets carried executives for a round of golf or festivities at a plantation, and fighter jets and huge, creeping C3 cargo planes, which seemed as unlikely to achieve flight as snails, shuttled back and forth between nearby military bases.

Whenever Mary looked at these airplanes, *any* of them, she wondered whether they were carrying stowaways. What was aboard that no one knew about.

She let her gaze fall, come to rest on her hands. They looked like claws to her. She knew she'd lost weight since they'd come here, which was ironic in a town where you couldn't walk twenty feet without tripping over a place that served shrimp and grits, mac and cheese, barbecue, and gallons and gallons of sweet tea.

She felt her lips compress. She knew exactly what happened to you when you were old and lost too much weight. You got shaky. Your mind started to wander. You fell, breaking wrists as fragile as dry sticks and hips as sharp as bone knives. You lay in bed for weeks, as one system after another—heart, kidneys, brain—gave out, shut down.

You died.

If you wanted to live, if you wanted to be there to protect your granddaughter, who had nothing and no one without you, you kept eating. You kept the weight on. You made sure that you didn't waste away.

Maybe later they'd stop by Jestine's for fried okra and fried chicken. Hush puppies and Co'Cola cake. You couldn't waste away at Jestine's.

In the meantime, Mary rummaged for the plastic bag of pretzels she carried around. At the same time, her eyes sought out Kait, who was sitting perched on one of the shiny black cannons that aimed so bravely out toward the water.

Mary rarely took her eyes off her granddaughter, even though she knew full well that watching never saved anyone. It was magical thinking, but still you fell for it. A kind of deal with God: If I never look away, she will never come to harm.

And if the worst happened anyway, Mary was going to be there, right beside her. The last thing Kait was going to see was the face of someone who loved her more than life itself.

Kait put her cheek against the rough, freshly painted metal of the cannon's barrel. There was something about powerful weapons that drew kids, even girls. Even Kait, who usually just wanted to stay home reading or drawing pictures.

Pictures that she kept in a folder that resided deep in the back of a dresser drawer.

Mary ate a pretzel, then sighed and sat back against the bench, sweating in the shade. It was a hot day. They were almost all hot days in Charleston in the summer, hotter even than down on Marco Island. The kind of wet, unmoving heat only gulls and pelicans could love.

She wasn't complaining. It was nice here. The people were friendly enough. Mary's standards were based on how they treated Kait, and most of them—guessing that there was some tragedy in the story somewhere, but far too polite to ask about it—were unfailingly kind to the near-silent ten-year-old.

There had been more open arms than Mary could count, more attempts to bring Kait together with other children her age. Failed attempts so far. Kait preferred her own company. She always had.

"Grandma! Look!"

Mary's old heart pounded. She'd allowed her attention to wander.

But Kait's voice held no fear. She was standing balanced halfway down the barrel of the cannon. A tightrope walker, a high-wire artist, arms out, face split by the wide grin that used to come so often, and now so rarely.

The slippery barrel. Even as Mary swore she wouldn't, she found herself calling out, "Be careful, Bunny."

*Damn.* Let the girl have some fun.

Kait frowned. "I will." Then she took another step, wobbling a little before setting herself again. The grin returned, unbidden, as she concentrated and reached out for her next toehold.

A movement at the edge of Mary's vision. Her alarms went off. Again. Adrenaline flooded her poor worn-out system. Again.

As Kait reached the end of the barrel and jumped back down to the ground, Mary forced herself to turn her head. A man was coming in their direction, moving with purpose through the sunstruck tourists and moseying dog-walkers.

A tall, shambly sort of man wearing an expensive gray suit and carrying a leather briefcase. Perhaps fifty, the length of his legs and the way he held his head reminding Mary of an egret. On the street behind him, at the curb outside the building where Mary and Kait had rented a one-bedroom apartment, a black limousine idled.

Somehow she knew immediately that he was coming to see her. She looked back and saw that Kait was standing still, her face a blank but her hand up near her mouth. Her position and expression of stress, worry, not so different from when she was little and sucked her thumb.

The man stopped, far enough away not to be seen as a threat. Mary had the sense that he'd chosen the distance carefully.

"Mrs. Finneran?" he said. It was a question, barely. He knew who she was.

There was something familiar in his stance, in his face, as well. "I am," she said.

Kait hopped down and came trailing up to them. Using that hesitant way of moving she'd developed, every stride containing an escape clause.

"My name is Jeremy Axelson," the man said.

A familiar name, too, but she couldn't remember where. "Can I help you?"

He said, "Perhaps I could sit and explain?"

Again, not really a question. Mary frowned. "If I said no, would you sit anyway?"

He smiled at her. There was kindness in the smile. Or maybe he was just wooing her.

"Most likely," he said.

"Then go ahead and sit."

He folded his skinny frame onto the bench. Close enough that their talk would be intimate, private, far enough away that she didn't feel crowded.

The man was good at what he did, Mary realized. Whatever that was.

Kait dipped past them, picking up her Totoro backpack and taking it to a bench across the path. In Mary's sight lines, but far enough away to be separate. A moment later, she had her sketch pad and colored pencils out and was bent over, drawing.

Mary hoped she wasn't drawing another picture of those creatures. She'd sneaked a look at Kait's hidden trove. Almost all of them were of the wasp-things.

The man was sitting there, patient. Mary had the unsettling feeling that he'd been able to read her thoughts while her attention was elsewhere.

She looked into his calm face. "I do know you," she said. "From somewhere."

"Television, perhaps. I show up on the news shows a lot, since I work for Anthony Harrison." He paused. "The presidential candidate."

"I know who Anthony Harrison is," she said with asperity. "And now I know who you are. You're his . . . mouthpiece."

He seemed unoffended. Rummaged in his pocket and pulled out a photo ID.

"Communications director," he said. "So, yes: mouth-piece."

"You," she said, taking a moment before finding the word, "spin."

He smiled. "I prefer to put it another way: It's my job to make sure my candidate's thoughts and views are presented properly to the press and understood fully by the public."

She tilted her head. "Q.E.D."

He laughed.

"You're convincing on TV," she said, "but I don't envy you trying to spin your man's chances."

Axelson looked into her eyes. There was something in his expression beyond the calm intelligence he projected. Something eager, electric.

"Oh," he said, "there's plenty of time for things to change before Election Day."

It was in his tone, too. Mary felt a spiderlike sensation creeping across her stomach. Dread.

She said, "Speak your piece, Mr. Axelson."

"I will. But first let me show you something." Yet even as he reached into his briefcase and pulled out a small sheaf of papers clipped together, she knew. Maybe she'd known from the first moment she'd laid eyes on him.

The first page showed a photo. A lousy one, most likely captured from a computer screen. Lousy but recognizable.

Mary didn't even have to look at the rest, but she did, paging quickly through them. The last was a drawing, stiff and far from lifelike. A drawing done by a bureaucrat, not an artist.

"You want a halfway-decent picture of one of these creatures," she said, "get my granddaughter to do it."

Axelson nodded, but didn't directly respond. "You know what really killed your son and daughter-in-law, don't you?"

Yet again a statement couched as a question. Spoken in a quiet voice, but Mary knew that Kait had heard. People always underestimated how well she listened.

"You know what's going on," Axelson said.

Mary said, "Why are you here?"

Again instead of replying, Axelson reached into his case and withdrew another pile of papers, a thinner stack. Not a hodgepodge of photocopied photos and drawings this time. A memo. A briefing.

He handed it to her. Across the way, Kait put her art materials into her backpack, stood, and came over to stand beside Mary. One hand rested lightly on her grandmother's back, as much physical contact as she granted these days. Mary moved the papers on her lap so she could read them, too.

Axelson shifted a little in his seat, but didn't intervene.

The title of the briefing was "Spiderweb." Below this heading was a series of bulleted paragraphs, each beginning with a location and date in boldface. Patagonia,

Arizona, in May. Anza-Borrego Desert State Park in California, and Galveston, Texas, early in June. Later the same month, Biloxi, Mississippi.

This data was followed by a few words of description. "Two seen by birders at Falcon Dam." "Found dead inside town hall." "Host: Rhesus monkey." "Possible human involvement."

*Possible human involvement.* Mary raised her eyes.

Axelson gave a tiny nod.

"Look," Kait said. "There's us."

Marco Island, Florida. "Host: Bottlenose dolphin. Emergence? Yes."

On the next line: "Probable human involvement."

Mary felt sick to her stomach. She said to Axelson, "These witnesses, survivors—are you visiting all of them?"

"Someone on my staff is, yes. I wanted to see you two myself."

He pointed at the papers. "Keep reading."

The locations on the first two pages were almost all from the southern tier of states. Nothing north of Georgia or Oklahoma or New Mexico.

"Any in South Carolina?" Kait asked. Her face was a shade paler than usual, but mostly she looked merely interested. Unlike Mary, she'd always liked lists.

"Nothing that's risen to a level of certainty," Axelson said.

She looked at him as she worked out what his words meant. "You're saying," she said at last, "that you've heard they're here, but you don't know if the stories are true."

His look was thoughtful. "Yes, that's exactly what I'm saying."

"But they are," Kait said. "If they're in all those other places"—she pointed one slim forefinger—"they're here, too."

Axelson said, "Read a little further."

Mary turned a page. More reports. More sightings. More "human involvement."

In northern California. Baltimore. Portland, Oregon, and Portland, Maine.

Outside Chicago.

In Davenport, Iowa, and Sioux Falls, South Dakota.

More than two dozen reports from nearly as many states. Southern, northern, coastal, and landlocked.

A C3 rattled the ground as it cruised overhead. Mary raised her gaze to watch it, then met Axelson's eyes.

Kait got it, too. "They're everywhere," she said.

Axelson nodded. "Two dozen reports might not seem like that many," he said, "but those are only the ones we know about, only the ones we've confirmed. How many others have gone unreported? And how many more will we hear about today? Tomorrow?"

Mary and Kait were silent.

"It's an invasion," he said. "Our country's being invaded, right here, right under our eyes, and nobody's doing a thing about it."

Mary gestured at the papers. "So many reports—why aren't the newspapers and TV all over this?"

"Two dozen reports over many weeks in a country as big as ours—well, that's not quite an avalanche," Axelson said. "Especially not when the deaths are reported to be from 'natural causes,' allergic shock, or killer bee attacks."

Now there was an edge of anger in his voice. "But the government should know what's going on. The question we need to ask is, Are they asleep at the switch? Or is it something else?"

Mary said, "What do you want from us?"

He gazed at her. Calculated sincerity and hope and compassion mixed in his expression, and beneath them, excitement. Avidity.

It was the look of a spinner who's seen the opportunity of a lifetime.

"Come with me," he said. "Come meet Governor Harrison, and he'll tell you."

# THIRTY-FOUR

CLARE SHAPIRO WAS a biochemist and a lab rat, which wasn't hard to guess when you met her. She was tall and thin, with knotty hair pulled back in an unfashionable "I don't give a shit" ponytail and unsettling, pale-gray eyes that looked at you as if you were wasting her time before you ever uttered a word.

Maybe because you were.

Trey and Jack hadn't come to Rock U to analyze the limitations of Clare Shapiro's charm. They were there because she was better than anybody else on earth at one thing: analyzing the chemicals in wasp venom.

Trey knew that scientists around the world were working to develop new antivenins, new drugs, even potential weapons, from wasp venom. But before they could get to work, they had to understand what they were working with. For that, they went to Shapiro and her team.

Trey and Jack had done the same a week before, when they'd sent the two thief specimens to her.

After getting a call that she was ready to talk, they'd come to her dingy little office on Rock U's fourth floor. It had a view of an airshaft and pigeons promenading around on the windowsill. Trey doubted that Clare cared. She probably never even looked out.

As they entered, she said, "Parker."

"Hello," Jack said. Trey could have sworn he looked a little shy.

Her gaze shifted. "And you're Gilliard? The one who served as a host to a larval wasp?"

"Yes, that one," Trey said.

She regarded him with interest. "Mind if I get a blood sample from you?"

"Sure." He began to roll up his sleeve.

She gave a hint of a smile. "When you leave will be fine. I'll tell you where to go."

Trey wondered if a blood sample would reveal the changes in him. The presence, the other, that he was beginning to think would be with him forever.

He was most aware of it when he awoke in the dead of night, when there were no distractions. At those times it felt most like a being, a *consciousness*. Half formed, incomplete, but there, living inside him.

Trey had gone through every detail of his experience with Jack and Sheila, except this one. He wasn't sure why he was keeping it a secret.

Maybe it was telling him to stay quiet.

Shapiro's cold gaze held him. "Gilliard, how much do you understand about the chemistry of wasp venom?"

"Let's assume I understand nothing," he said.

Her expression tightened, and he thought she was biting back some choice words. Instead, she said, "You know we have the tools to decode genomes across the animal kingdom, right?"

He nodded. Beside him, Jack said, "I'm still getting asked if there's any dinosaur blood in our amber-trapped mosquitoes, so we can unravel the dino DNA and clone new ones."

Shapiro ignored this. "A few years ago, we successfully decoded the genome of *Nasonia vitripennis*—that's a parasitic wasp, though not closely related to yours," she said. "We were able to map out the constituents of its venom and compare it to the venom of other wasps."

Her expression had lightened a little. This was no surprise. Trey knew that even the most contrary people liked to talk, as long as you stuck to what interested them.

"So we used a two-dimensional liquid chromatography electrospray ionization Fourier transform ion cyclotron resonance mass spectrometer—"

"Assume I understand nothing," Trey said again.

She looked at him, sighed, put her hands flat on the desk. "It's a device for analyzing the chemical constituents of substances like wasp venom. Will that do?"

"Yes."

"Good. What its analysis showed us was that *N. vitripennis*'s venom contains at least seventy-nine different proteins—half of which were never previously associated with insect venoms, and nearly two dozen of which weren't similar to *any* other proteins we'd ever seen. They were complete mysteries to us."

She stared at him with her unearthly gray eyes, making sure he understood. "These proteins are as alien," she said, "as ones we might find in insects discovered on Mars."

Silence spread in the room. Then Trey sighed. "You're warning me that seven days hasn't been long enough for you to solve all the mysteries of thief venom."

"No," she said. "Not quite enough."

Her eyes brightened. "But I wouldn't have called if we'd found out nothing about your beast." She blinked like a cat. "Logically, first we used a bioinformatic approach, employing amino acid sequences of known venom proteins to search for transcripts—identifiable patterns—of proteins in your wasp's venom."

"Let me guess: The problem with that approach," Trey said, "is that it only recognizes previously known proteins, not any 'Martian' ones."

"Yes." Shapiro gave a quick nod. "But it's a useful first step."

"And the next one?"

"A combination of two techniques: The ion cyclotron resonance mass spectrometer I mentioned and—" A glint of amusement in her eyes. "And an off-line two-dimensional liquid chromatography matrix-assisted laser desorption and ionization time-of-flight mass spectrometer as well."

Trey said, "You had enough venom for all these analyses?"

"Just. We're lucky that your beasts have exceptionally roomy venom sacs and that this adult specimen hadn't stung anyone recently."

"I'm the luckiest!" Jack said brightly.

Trey and Shapiro both ignored him. "What did you find?" Trey asked.

"Mass spectrometry showed the presence of more than one hundred proteins—significantly more than we uncovered in *N. vitripennis*. Again, about a third were unrecognizable—we don't yet know *what* they do. We'll keep working on those."

"And the rest?"

"Some, like an allergen 5 protein, are quite familiar. They represent well-known venom constituents that appear in many different wasp species."

She gave her quick smile. "Which tends to indicate that your wasps did not, in fact, originate on Mars. They evolved here."

Another blink. "Of the rest, some are merely translational or transcriptional." She noticed his expression and said, "Proteins that help the venom gland function. They're the grease in the machinery."

Trey was beginning to learn what Shapiro's expressions meant. He could see that even as she spoke, her mind was on to the next thing. The next six things. She was like a chess player who can see the forced checkmate fifteen moves ahead.

And now Trey could tell that she had something else to tell them, something more important. "But that's not all, is it?" he said.

"No." Suddenly her face was alight. "In our tests, we kept finding the same protein, again and again. In some ways it resembled ones we've seen in other parasitic wasps, but with significant differences as well."

Her eyes widened a little. "It is highly unusual to see any protein appear so often."

"What does it mean?" Trey asked.

"It means it's important. Crucial. It means that the beast has put the most energy, the most evolutionary effort, you might say, into producing this constituent."

Trey thought that over. "And which known proteins does it resemble?"

She tilted her head and looked at him, then at Jack. "Most closely: phospholipase A1."

Jack sat up straighter in his chair. *"Shit,"* he said.

Trey waited.

"That's a major venom allergen in the genus *Polistes* and others," Jack told him. "When people die of anaphylactic shock from wasp stings, phospholipase A1 is often the culprit."

Trey looked at Shapiro. He had one more question to ask, the most important one. "That same protein," he said. "Did it also turn up in the larva?"

"Yes," she said. "Repeatedly." Again the widening of the eyes. "It's unprecedented to find the same venom in an adult wasp and its larva, but that's what we discovered."

Trey thought about the poison he'd felt pumping through his bloodstream. "Disturb the larva, and it releases the venom."

Shapiro nodded. "Yes."

"Any chance of an antivenin?"

She grimaced. "That's a long way off."

But her gaze was still bright as she looked at him. She had something else to tell him, but was waiting for him to figure it out first.

"You also found," he said slowly, "an explanation of why I didn't realize I'd been . . . infected." He looked over at Jack. "Or Sheila's mother, either."

Jack's eyes were still on Shapiro. "The chemical that clouds men's minds?"

She nodded. "Yes. In a gland in both adult and larva that, as far as we know, is also unique among wasps."

"What does the gland contain?"

"A benzodiazepine."

Jack said, "Jesus."

At last something that was familiar to Trey, too. He knew that benzodiazepines were a class of drugs used as muscle relaxants, to control seizures, as sedatives, to battle anxiety.

And to make patients forget what they'd just gone through. To create amnesia.

"Every symptom of early infestation you've described—the lethargy, the dreaminess, and the inability to remember being implanted—can be caused by benzodiazepines," Shapiro said.

Jack was frowning. "Okay. Phospholipase. Benzodiazepine. You're drugged to the gills. Why?"

"I think I know," Trey said.

They both looked at him.

"Let's tie this together." He paused, marshaling his thoughts. "The fact that I'm sitting here shows that removal of the larva isn't necessarily fatal to the host."

Jack said, "Not when the larva is small."

"A mammal that's been infected," Trey went on. "Especially a primate—and we know that primates are the preferred hosts—when it notices the swelling. Sees the airhole, figures out there is a larva underneath. How does it respond?"

Jack answered. "It worries at the wound. Even non-primates will try to get the larva out. A dog will scratch, a cat will chew, and a monkey will have a friend or family member pick it off."

"Yes. But only if it's aware that it's been infected. Only if it *notices*."

"Which the amnesic properties of the benzodiazepine prevent," Shapiro said.

"That's how it worked on me," Trey said.

"Until Sheila noticed, and even then it was almost too fucking late." Jack sat up in his chair. "You're right. That's it. That's the point. When the larva is implanted, your mind is fogged so you don't mess with it. Then, by the time it's big enough that someone notices it and tries to get it out—well, by then it's almost certain to kill you."

Trey nodded. "Could another sting, late in the process, influence the host's brain to bring on the protective rage response I've seen?" He paused. "Is that even plausible?"

Shapiro gave a shrug. "I don't see why not. The human brain is easily influenced, and there are many known compounds that antagonize the ionotropic glutamate receptors, which mediate rage. Phencyclidine is just one well-known example, but it's far from the only one."

"Phencyclidine?" Trey said. "PCP?"

She nodded. "Angel dust. No, phencyclidine didn't show up in our assays, but there's something there. Now I just have to find it."

This seemed like a cue. Trey and Jack stood. "You've done amazing things," Trey said, holding out his hand. "Thank you."

An eyeblink of a smile, and then she stood and shook his hand. Hers felt like it was made entirely of tendons.

"My team is very skilled," she said.

Then she frowned. "Want more? Want that antivenin? Get us a supply of new specimens. There's only so much we can get out of a single venom sac."

Jack made a sound through his nose. A laugh.

"Soon enough," he said, "that shouldn't be a problem."

* * *

**THEY HEADED TO** the fifth floor, where Trey would leave a blood sample. At the elevator he said, "Hold on. I forgot to ask her something."

When Jack made a move to go with him, Trey shook his head. "Wait here."

As Jack's curious gaze followed him, he went back to Clare Shapiro's office. She was still standing where they'd left her, peering down at some papers on her desk.

She raised her eyes as he entered the room. "Yes?"

"Are there any substances in wasp venom," he said, "that can permanently change the chemistry of the human brain?"

She tilted her head, thinking, then said, "None that I'm aware of. Theoretically, of course, it's quite possible. Why do you ask?"

Trey shook his head and answered her question with another of his own.

"Clare," he said, "what do you know about the hive mind?"

# THIRTY-FIVE

"I GOT A voice mail from Mary Finneran," Sheila said as they walked in the door.

Something in her tone made Trey stop and look at her. Jack, oblivious, sat down at his computer and said, "Who's Mary Finneran?"

Before she could answer, Trey said to Sheila, "The woman you visited in Florida. The one whose son—daughter?—was killed."

"Son and daughter-in-law." Sheila frowned. "She and Kait are living in Charleston now."

"I remember. What did she say?"

Sheila crossed her arms, hugging herself as if she were cold. "She said to make sure we watch Anthony Harrison's acceptance speech tonight."

Jack looked up from his screen and said, "The hell does *that* mean?"

Trey stood still, his mind working. Then he figured it out and felt a hole open somewhere deep inside him.

"It means the deluge," he said.

\*   \*   \*

**THE PRESIDENTIAL CONVENTION** hall looked like any other. Strung with bunting and red-white-and-blue banners, it was brightly lit but carefully calibrated not to make the audience look corpselike. The seats were filled with banner-waving delegates, politicians, reporters, and perhaps even some regular people.

Jack, Sheila, and Trey had met in Trey's apartment because Jack's apartment was always a disaster area, and Trey wanted to watch on a full-size screen, not a computer monitor at the office. He didn't watch much television, but when he did, he needed to *see*, to be able to understand and interpret what he was seeing.

"Can they get to the point?" Jack said after two hours. "Or should I just shoot myself now?"

But still the speeches went on and on, all lauding Anthony Harrison's merits for the presidency. The audience rose to its feet for repeated scripted ovations. Delegates pledged their support to the candidate and showed off their crazy hats and buttons and waved their banners.

Trey barely listened. He was watching the faces and seeing, under the cheers, the laughter, the shouts and ovations, something different: worry.

They were worried because none of them—not delegates, reporters, pundits, viewers—knew what was coming when Anthony Harrison took the stage. Unlike every nominee for decades, he'd declined to release a transcript of his speech ahead of time, or to give even the slightest hint what it would contain.

"This is the most important night of Harrison's

political career," said an offended talking head on MS-NBC, "and we have no idea what he's about to say."

"Well," replied a pundit, "he may be on his way to a crushing defeat, but he certainly has kept our attention tonight."

Jack pointed at the screen.

"Here he comes," he said.

**ANTHONY HARRISON LOOKED** like a politician. He was tall, broad shouldered, and wore his pinstriped steel-gray suit and red tie comfortably but not ostentatiously. His hair was thick and touched with gray at the temples.

As he acknowledged the ovation from the crowd, smiling and waving at this ally and that supporter, Trey watched his face. Harrison didn't have the shifty, angry look of so many career politicians. Nor was he a handsome blank. There seemed to be some intelligence in his gaze, some awareness of the absurdity of the theater he was engaged in.

"This guy was a governor, right?" Trey asked.

Both Jack and Sheila turned their heads to look at him. "Uh, yeah," Jack said. "Of Colorado? For eight years?"

Trey said, "Was he good?"

Jack snorted, but Sheila said, "I think he was okay. Honest enough. Not the brightest or dimmest star."

"How do you know this?" Jack asked. "Didn't you live in the Congo or something?"

She shrugged. "Sure, but I'm still American. This is still my country."

Trey thought about it. Was it still his country? Sometimes he didn't feel like he even belonged to the same species as the people cheering and waving banners on-screen.

**FINALLY THE CROWD** restrained itself and sat down, and Anthony Harrison began to speak. His voice was deep, relaxed, confident. Trey could see how he'd come so far.

The nominee's expression was serious, even grave. "As I'm sure most of you have heard," he began, "I recently discarded the speech I'd planned to deliver tonight. In it, I talked about many of the challenges facing our nation, and why I am the man to confront them."

He looked around the hall. "All of it is still true. But just in the past few days, I've learned about a situation—a crisis of monumental proportions—that demands my immediate attention, and yours. A crisis that my opponent has known about far longer than I have, but has chosen to ignore. *That* is what I must talk about tonight."

The camera panned the confused, apprehensive crowd before returning to Harrison. "My fellow Americans," he said, "I am with you tonight to tell you that our great nation is under attack."

A frightened murmur from the crowd.

"More than an attack," Harrison said. "An act of terrorism."

*So that's his angle,* Trey thought.

"Give me a goddamn fucking break," Jack said.

"We are a strong nation," Harrison went on. "We've faced terrorism on our shores before, and we've overcome it. We've triumphed because we've stood together, proud, strong, united. That's who we are as a people. Nothing can bring us to our knees."

He gazed into the camera. Now he looked angry. Righteously angry.

"Nothing can bring us to our knees," he said again, "except an administration that hides a grave threat to our lives, our freedom, merely so it can win an election."

Though the cameras stayed on Harrison's stern face, Trey could hear sounds of dismay from the audience.

"The lives of your neighbors, your coworkers, your parents, your *children*, are in peril. Too many have died already—and how many more will die before Election Day?"

"Careful, asshole," Jack murmured, "or you'll have them fleeing the hall."

"How many thousands will die?" Harrison said, his expression now one of controlled rage. "Ask the president. Ask the president—and then ask why he is covering up this crisis, this invasion, this terrorist act."

Harrison's voice rose. "Or don't. Don't ask. All you'll hear is what I heard when I contacted him, offering to do everything I could to help confront this new enemy. All you'll hear are lies and obfuscations and denials. Because he doesn't know what to do. He doesn't have any idea."

An accusatory finger. "Instead, our president is trading the lives of American people for votes." His eyes looked into the camera, into the eyes of the American people. "Hoping to keep the news of this invasion out of the newspapers until after he has been reelected."

Harrison's face was red. "I'm sure my opponent and his staff are scrambling for a response as I speak. Well, let me tell you what they're going to say. They'll tell you I've gone off the deep end. They'll say I'm desperate, making it all up, lying. They'll tell you not to believe a word I say."

He took a breath. "And, you know, I can understand that. Why should you believe me? I am, after all, a politician, and though I've been an honest one throughout my career, I certainly wouldn't blame you for being skeptical. We folks don't exactly have the most sterling reputation, and a lot of that reputation is deserved."

A slight ripple of uneasy laughter from the unseen audience.

"But if you won't believe me," Harrison said, "will you believe Enrique Montero?"

The cameras focused on a young man in the front row of the balcony. He had an oval face, dark eyes with circles under them, and straight black hair. He looked very nervous, glancing back and forth at the older woman and man who flanked him—his parents, Trey assumed.

"In many ways, until recently Enrique lived the American dream. The son of legal immigrants who, through determination and hard work, were able to open their own grocery store in Chico, California. While his older brother, Gonzalo, worked at the store, Enrique attended college . . . until two months ago."

The camera came back to Harrison's face. "Two months ago, Gonzalo was killed. And you know who was arrested for murder? Who spent weeks in jail before being released? Yes, Enrique. Yet he was innocent—he *is* innocent. The real culprit? The invader, the terrorist. The threat the president doesn't believe we deserve to know about. But we do. Enrique and his parents do."

The camera went back to the family's faces. They were crying.

"Jesus Christ," Jack said. "Why don't you pick their bones while you're at it?"

Now the camera focused on a pretty young woman with sandy blond hair. She looked angry.

"This is Elizabeth Keaton," Harrison said. "Six weeks ago, she was a newlywed, married just eight months to her high school sweetheart, James. They'd just bought their first house together, in Davenport, Iowa. They were planning on having four children—four, at least."

On camera, Elizabeth Keaton glanced at someone to her left and nodded. Then she faced forward again, and now her eyes were red.

"Then James disappeared. You know what the authorities told Elizabeth? That he'd probably run away with another woman!"

Harrison's face filled the screen. "I am not blaming the Davenport police. They are good at what they do, and we should all be proud of them and grateful for their service. It's not their fault that they weren't given the information they needed—information that might have saved James's life, or at the very least brought an end to Elizabeth's uncertainty. For, yes, James, too, was a victim of these terrorists. Tragically, his life, too, came to an end—and with it, Elizabeth's dreams."

Harrison lifted a hand. "I'll give you just one last example, although I could share a dozen more if I wanted to. No, just one more, to show you how this is a tragedy, a threat, that spans generations."

Sheila made a sound in her throat.

And there were Kait and Mary on-screen. Kait, her thick black hair held back by a headband, wore a blue dress with a big belt around the waist. Her dark eyes stared out from a face that was ghostly pale under the freckles.

In her own simple red dress, Mary, her white hair standing out in the crowd, looked just as resolute. Together, grandmother and granddaughter cast an indelible image, as they'd been intended to.

To Mary's left sat a long-jawed, blue-eyed, blond-haired woman of about forty-five. Her face was perfectly made up, her hair was piled up on top of her head, and her diamond earrings and necklace sent little gleaming stars across the screen.

"Harrison's wife," Jack said. "Samantha."

Two children, a boy and a girl, sat to Kait's right. The boy was perhaps twelve and had the candidate's olive complexion. The girl, maybe eight, was a small, blond replica of Samantha. As the camera focused on them, the girl took Kait's hand in her own and squeezed it.

"On July twenty-third, Kait spent the morning with her father—and Mary's son—Tim, on the dock behind their home on Marco Island, just as she'd done countless times before," Anthony Harrison said. "Together they were watching a baby dolphin who had been born in their boat slip just a few days before—a sick little dolphin Kait hoped to save.

"But the dolphin died. It was killed." Now Harrison's voice rose and became accusatory once more. "A sad story, but not one I would be talking about right now . . . if the same killers hadn't then visited Tim and Joanna Finneran's house and murdered them as well."

Cries from the crowd.

"Yes," Harrison said. "These innocent young parents died without knowing the dangers they were facing. Why didn't they know? Because our government, our president, didn't tell them."

His expression was ferocious. "Tim and Joanna Finneran, James Keaton, Gonzalo Montero—*none* of them had to die. But they did. Now the American people—the voters—*you and I*—need to know why."

He rocked back a little behind the lectern. "You've been very patient," he said. "I know you've long been wondering what I'm talking about. Invaders, I say. Attackers. I can imagine you're all thinking of soldiers in uniforms, of rebels, of people with bombs strapped to their bodies.

"But no. That's not it. What's been attacking us, killing Americans, leaving people like Enrique and Elizabeth and Kait alone in the world is . . . this."

Trey was never sure whether people in the convention center saw the image on a theater screen or television monitors or somehow projected in 3-D into thin air, but what viewers at home saw was the face of a thief projected so suddenly and so large that even Trey jumped. Whatever the audience saw must have been just as dramatic, because loud gasps were mixed with shouts and muffled screams.

The camera focused on the crowd. Some were staring upward, some were averting their eyes, and many were crying.

On-screen, Harrison raised both hands in a quelling gesture. "Ladies and gentlemen," he said, "hear me out. This is not a monster I'm describing, not some ancient beast out of Jurassic Park." He held his right thumb and forefinger apart. "They are wasps, the biggest on earth, but still just this big. That's big enough. Big enough to kill with a single sting."

The screen showed the vicious-looking thief again, then went back to Harrison. "This wasp, this creature," he said, "is hunting us. It wants to kill us. It will not be stopped by locked doors and shut windows. And if you kill one—well, more will come, and more, and more."

He paused for a beat, then said, "And I haven't even told you the worst part of this story."

Jack groaned.

"The worst part—the part that we will never forgive the president for hiding from us—is that these creatures' larvae, their young, are parasitic. They must grow inside mammal hosts to survive. Mammals . . . including humans."

His voice rang out. "One grew inside the baby dolphin that poor Kait tried to save," he said. "One grew inside Gonzalo, Enrique Montero's brother. And one grew inside James, Elizabeth Keaton's husband. Grew inside them, and killed them."

The camera went back to the crowd, which looked shell-shocked.

"Yes," Harrison said. "I am sorry, so sorry, to be the one giving you this news. It should have been the president. This is the president's job, but he won't do it. He's too busy running for reelection."

A breath before he delivered the next blow. "And if, tomorrow, one of these creatures begins to grow inside *you*, you know what he'll do? He'll hide, just as he always does."

His fist struck the lectern. "But *I* won't hide. As soon as I am finished here, my staff—including a team of brilliant scientists and doctors—will be providing detailed instructions on how best to stay safe in these dangerous times. Check our website for fact sheets, videos, and links to important information and advice. Keep watching the station you're tuned to—after my speech, we'll have experts on every network.

"Now and in the coming days, my staff and I will do everything we can to prepare you to face what scientists are calling the most serious crisis of our lifetimes. Perhaps the current administration does not think you are worth it, but I do."

Again his voice grew quieter. "At the beginning of this speech, I spoke of terrorism. I spoke of invasion. Some of you may be thinking, 'All right—he's scared us. But this doesn't sound like terrorism to me. It sounds more like an epidemic. Frightening, yes, but just bad luck. Nobody's fault.'

"Yes, that's how it sounds . . . but it's not how it is. Until recently, no one had ever heard of these creatures—not even the nation's leading scientists. But now the wasps are here. Here, in America, killing our citizens. Where did they come from? How did they get here?"

He leaned forward. "I believe they were sent by our enemies. By those who envy our freedoms, who hate us for our democracy. I believe—I *know*—these creatures were created and hatched in a laboratory and sent here, just as surely as anthrax spores, a dirty bomb, or any other bioweapon would be. And with the same goal: To terrify us. To destroy us."

"Brilliant," Sheila said.

Her eyes were wide.

"This *is* terrorism," Harrison said. "Pure and simple. Who is behind it? We don't know yet. But we will find out." His eyes were fierce. "Elect me, and I guarantee *I* will find out. Find out who has targeted us, and if we have to scour the earth we will make sure they *pay*. Just as we will make sure that every last one of these creatures has been driven from every corner of our great country."

Trey felt something stir deep inside him. An awakening.

"When Election Day comes, and you're deciding how to cast your vote, remember that you face a stark choice," Harrison said. "My opponent, the man who is willingly putting your lives at risk, or me: the one who promises— who *swears*—to clean up the mess President Chapman has left behind and restore our great nation to the strength and honor it has always proudly held.

"Thank you. And may God bless America and protect us in the trials to come."

# THIRTY-SIX

## THE DELUGE.

They kept the television on for most of the night. Jack sat on the sofa and wielded the remote, flicking back and forth among the networks and cable news stations. Sheila had taken over the apartment's one comfortable chair, while Trey, unable to stay still, sat at the kitchen table or on the edge of the sofa, but spent most of his time leaning against various walls.

They watched pundits and commentators and party members spin the political implications of Harrison's speech, as if this were the story of the night, not the threat itself, not the deaths. Scientists—whoever the shows had found willing to pontificate in the middle of the night—offered their learned opinions. Bloggers who had posted videos of the thieves blinked in the harsh light of the movie cameras. Conspiracy theorists weighed in. Instant polls measured the consequences.

And driving it all was the Harrison campaign's carefully

planned publicity blitz. Compelling, sober, terrifying spokespeople were everywhere, on every channel, all reinforcing the same message: This is serious. This is scary. The president has dropped the ball. Trust Anthony Harrison.

Having watched this routine a dozen times, Jack started to growl. "Next they're gonna start sending people door to door," he said, "and I'm gonna slug the first one who rings the bell."

Hospitals and police stations reported being flooded with calls and visits. Hordes of people thinking they'd been stung. Further hordes fearing they were now hosting larvae. False alarm after false alarm.

"Therapists all over the world are thanking Harrison and making down payments on their dream homes," Jack said.

"Hush." Sheila ran her hand through her hair, which had grown out from its pixie cut. "You know what's interesting," she went on. "They all keep going over the same list of attacks, but nobody's managed to come up with any fresh footage of the thieves, or even of someone who's been infected."

"Huh," Jack said. "Well, it hasn't been very long. We'll start hearing shit soon enough."

"I don't think so."

It had been a long time since Trey had spoken. Jack and Sheila both turned to stare at him, as surprised as if a chair had decided to join the conversation.

"Don't think so?" Jack asked. "Don't think so what?"

"I don't think we'll be hearing of many attacks," Trey said. "Not now."

Sheila was watching him closely. "Why not, Trey? You think they're hiding?"

Trey thought about it, then shook his head.

"Then what?"

"Waiting," he said.

**AT SOME POINT** in the evening the president sent his press secretary, a rumpled-looking man who looked like he hadn't slept in a week, out to meet a crowd of reporters. He stood before a microphone in front of a cluster of cameras and tried to convey outrage.

"He looks terrified," Sheila commented. "I think the first he heard of this was tonight."

"No," Trey said. "He's terrified because he *did* know— they all did. But they weren't prepared for the secret to leak."

Sheila's eyes were on him. "How do you see that?"

Trey shrugged. How did he understand anything he saw? Tone of voice, posture, stresses, intonations, expressions in the eyes.

He just did.

"With his reckless, irresponsible speech, Governor Harrison has proven himself unfit for public office," the press secretary declaimed. "He is using family tragedies for personal benefit, something President Chapman—or any person with an ounce of morality—would never do."

Reporters shouted questions. The press secretary said, "Our hearts go out to those who have lost family members and friends, just as we express sorrow over those who die too soon from so many other maladies. We take this new threat very seriously and are utilizing all resources at our disposal, including the Centers for Disease Control and, if necessary, the military, to repel it."

Then, to a cacophony of shouts, he turned and walked away.

"Not enough," Sheila said.

Jack shook his head. "Not close."

Trey felt something move inside him, somewhere near his core.

And stayed quiet.


**TWO IN THE** morning. "It's weird," Jack said.

"What is?" Sheila asked.

"I feel ripped off." He gave a little smile. "I mean, for a while there, this was all . . . ours. We were, like, the only ones who knew. And now, just like that, we're not."

Sheila looked at him. "I wish it had never been mine."

His mouth twisted. "Yeah. And I'm sorry. But you know what I mean." He opened his arms. "As long as it was just us, there was a chance it wouldn't all blow up and go to shit. Now—no."

"I don't think there was ever a chance." Sheila sighed. "People were going to find out, and things were going to start spiraling anyway."

"I guess so."

"It's what people do," Sheila said. "They ruin everything."

"'People ruin everything.'" Jack's voice was approving. "I think I'll make a T-shirt with that."

"Tell me something," she said to him. "*Could* someone weaponize wasp venom?"

"I told you," Jack said. "No. It's bullshit."

He took a gulp of coffee. "Listen," he went on. "Sure, you could make the venom more potent, more deadly—at least, someone like Clare Shapiro could. I'm sure those busy bees at the Defense Department are 'efforting' that as we speak."

He turned his palms up. "But when it's still inside the wasp? Creating a new breed of superwasps? Come on. Crapola."

"But thief venom is so powerful," Sheila insisted. "Powerful enough to kill a human—and much more than would be needed for smaller hosts. Why would it evolve that way?"

Jack grinned at her. "Black widow spiders," he said.

"What?"

"Sheila," he said, "what do black widow spiders eat?"

She shrugged. "I don't know. Crickets? Beetles?"

"Yeah. Stuff like that. Yet their venom can kill a human. Hell, it can kill a horse or a cow. Why?"

Sheila opened her mouth to answer, then closed it again.

Jack was enjoying himself. "The widow's venom is thousands of times more powerful than it 'needs' to be. In fact, if anything, its potency is an evolutionary *disadvantage*."

Sheila thought this over, then nodded. "Because people who see a black widow are likely to kill her, where they might ignore a less venomous spider."

"Exactly. And not only people—other animals will go out of their way to kill widows as well." He crossed his arms over his chest. "We all fall into the trap of seeing nature as infallible, of seeing every evolutionary step as an improvement, an aid to species survival."

"But it's not true?" Sheila said.

Jack shook his head. "Of course not. Evolution isn't a

straight path. It's filled with dead ends, wrong turns, mistakes."

His shrug was eloquent. "Sometimes Mother Nature just deals a wild card."

"And the rest of us pay the price," Sheila said.

**SOON AFTER, JACK** started yawning so widely that they could see where his wisdom teeth had been yanked fifteen years earlier. Eventually he started eyeing Trey's sofa. "At night, I think better prone," he said.

"I certainly hope so," Sheila said.

Groaning a little, he lay back on the sofa. Three minutes later his eyes were closed and his mouth was open, though he wasn't quite snoring.

"Down for the count," Trey said.

Sheila, who'd come over to sit opposite Trey at the table, regarded Jack's sleeping form with something like affection. "How come I feel like we've acquired a teenage son?" she asked.

Trey said, "He'll still be a teenager when he's sixty."

"That's true for most of you research types, isn't it?" Her voice was light. "Heading off into the field, leaving your lives behind, staying forever young?"

"Right now," Trey said before he could stop himself, "'forever young' is about a million miles from how I feel."

Sheila looked at him. There was something new in her expression.

"Talk to me," she said. "Tell me what's happened to you."

Meaning: *Since you were infected. Since I cut that thing out of you.*

Trey took a deep breath. He'd been waiting for her to ask. He'd known she suspected something.

What he hadn't figured out was how he was going to answer. Whether he was going to lie to her—say, "I'm fine," and change the subject—or trust her to understand. Open himself up.

Looking at her pale, beautiful face, the intensity and intelligence of her gaze, he knew he couldn't lie. Subterfuge wasn't in her makeup, and tonight he couldn't summon it, either.

"When you took out the larva," he said, "something got left behind."

Her gaze strayed to where she'd performed the surgery, then back up to his face. "The site was clean," she said.

He smiled. "Yes, you did a beautiful job for someone who expected her patient to die. It's almost healed already—but I didn't mean there."

"Then where?"

Slowly Trey reached up and pointed to his head. "Here," he said.

Then he hesitated and spread his hands over his chest for a moment. "Or here." He shook his head. "I don't know exactly. Just somewhere *inside*."

Sheila's eyes were narrowed. "Left . . . what?" she asked.

"The hive mind," he said.

She kept her eyes on his, steady, unblinking. But the faintest flush rose to her cheeks.

"I asked Clare Shapiro at Rockefeller about it," he went on. "She agrees with Jack that such a thing exists—that the minds of bees and wasps stay connected somehow.

That they can communicate over great distances in ways we don't understand."

Trey paused, remembering Shapiro's unrestrained impatience at having to explain something so simple to a neophyte. "Listen," she'd said. "*Of course* apocritids are capable of communication between members of the colony—that's because each bee or wasp isn't really an individual. Each is a separate part of one superorganism that incorporates data from thousands—or millions—of different viewpoints and makes a decision based on that data.

"A million units," she'd said, "but one controlling mind."

Now Sheila said, "Tell me."

He struggled to answer, as he'd known he would. "I feel like it's watching me, and also looking out through my eyes," he said finally. "Though not always. Not every minute. Sometimes it's quiet." He paused. "Like now."

"It's looking elsewhere?"

He shrugged. "Maybe that's it. But even then, I can sense it. A heaviness. An *awareness*." He raised his hands from the table in frustration. "It kind of . . . moves inside me."

She was silent.

"And when it's fully present," he said, staring down at his coffee mug, "it does more than watch. I feel like it's *taking*."

"Oh, Trey," she said. He looked up to see that her expression was full of sorrow. She reached across the table and took his sweaty hands in her cool ones. Over on the sofa, Jack stirred but didn't awaken. Somewhere in the distance, a car downshifted, its engine roaring, falling silent, then roaring again, much farther off.

Still holding his hands, Sheila broke the silence with a single word. *"Taking,"* she said, her gaze sharpening. The scientist reasserting herself. "That makes me wonder."

"Yes. Me, too."

"We got the larva out early."

He nodded.

"So what does the hive mind take from the rest of its victims?" she asked. "The ones where it stays until the end?"

Trey stayed silent.

"What is it learning about us?" she said.

Still he didn't speak.

"And what will it do with what it learns?"


**AT AROUND FOUR** Sheila started rubbing her eyes, a childlike gesture. "I can stay up with you," she said.

Trey smiled and shook his head. "No. You'll be of more use to all of us if you get a little rest."

She stood, then leaned across the table and kissed him. Just a quick kiss, her lips warm on his, before she pulled away.

Something in her expression made him say, "What?"

"I kiss . . . multitudes," she said and headed off to bed.


**TREY WAS DEEP** in his own thoughts when the phone jangled. It was just past six. After two rings he got to his feet and walked over to the kitchen counter. Jack hadn't moved on the sofa, but his eyes were open.

The call was coming from a blocked number. With a sigh, Trey picked up the receiver and said, "Yeah?"

"Gilliard?" said the voice on the other end. "George Summers." Then, after a brief pause, "Department of Agriculture."

Trey said, "Yeah. I remember you."

"Is Parker there?" Summers's voice sounded stretched, tense, and Trey wondered if he, too, had spent a sleepless night.

"Guy should check his cell phone every once in a while," Summers added.

Trey said, "Yes, he's here." He glanced at Jack, who was sitting up, alert now. A movement at the periphery of Trey's vision showed that Sheila had come to the bedroom doorway and was listening as well.

Trey held the phone out to Jack. "It's Summers."

Jack took it, then pointed and mouthed, "Speaker."

Once Trey had pushed the button, Jack leaned back on the sofa and said, "You knew. All that time bullshitting us in your office, and you knew."

"Jack, I don't have time for this," Summers said.

But Jack did. "And know what else? Trey and me, we saw it right away. But you had to pretend that we were idiot conspiracy theorists, but now that your boss is being hit with a pile of—"

"Fuck you, Parker." Summers's tone was venomous. "First of all, he's not my boss—I'm career here, you know that. Second, fuck you anyway."

Jack was grinning. "Very nice. I'll do anything you ask now."

"We need you to come in. Right away."

"Oh, now you want me? Well, fuck you, too."

"Could you put a lid on it for, like, two seconds, and just listen?"

Jack grinned, but kept quiet. When Summers spoke again, his tone had changed. "You know this is a shit-storm," he said, "and we need your help."

Some of the pleasure drained from Jack's expression. "I don't know, George. I saw the *Bourne* movies. 'Coming in' isn't always such a hot idea."

"We need to know what you know. You're doing nobody any good sitting in your little office in that big stone building filled with rocks and old bones."

Again, a pause and a change in tone. "I mean it. We want to hear what you have to tell us."

Jack moved his mouth around, as if testing arguments, but in the end he just sighed. "Okay," he said. "Say I say yes, what do I do?"

"How fast can you get out to LaGuardia? We have a plane waiting for you."

"Wow." Jack's eyes widened. "You sure know how to woo a boy. Let me just go back to my place for my clothes—"

"We'll buy you some when you get here."

"And I have to tell the museum."

"We already did that."

Jack scowled. "Let me just check with—"

"No," Summers said.

"What?"

"Not your friends. Just you. You're the expert."

Jack said, "You're wrong about that. They know things I—"

"Just you," Summers said again. "Those are my orders, and that's the way it has to be."

Jack looked at Trey. Now he just looked weary.

"You know that part of the movie where someone says, 'You're making a big mistake'?" he said. "Well, we've reached that point. You're making a big mistake."

They heard Summers make a sound. It was probably a laugh.

"I wouldn't bet against it," he said.

**FRESHLY SHOWERED BUT** his hair still a mess, Jack watched the TV as he got dressed.

"Call when you can," Trey told him.

"Sure, if they don't bump me off as soon as they pump me for everything I know."

It came out sounding like a joke, but Trey didn't think he was kidding. Those *Bourne* movies must have made a strong impression.

Jack ran his hands through his hair, then said, "Look, it's that guy again."

"That guy" being Anthony Harrison's communications director, Jeremy Axelson, whom they'd seen on every network the night before. Somehow he still looked awake, alert, ready to face the new day.

As they watched, he looked straight into the camera and pointed. Jack got the remote and raised the sound.

"One piece of advice for the president and his staff," Axelson was saying. "You're in deep already. Don't dig yourself any deeper. Don't obfuscate, don't hide, don't destroy. It's not the crime—or not only the crime—it's the cover-up. Whatever you try, it won't work. We'll find out. It's a guarantee. *We'll find out.*"

The doorbell rang. "Your taxi's here," Trey said.

Jack was still staring at the TV. Then he turned his head and gave them a wide-eyed look.

"Summers is an asshole," he said, "but he's right about one thing."

"There's a storm coming," Sheila said.

For once Jack looked completely serious.

"I don't believe," he said, "that *any* of them—on either side—has the slightest clue how bad this is going to be."

# THIRTY-SEVEN

*Springfield, Vermont*

**IT WAS THE** same crew as the other time, Harry Solomon realized. Fort Collins. Trent and the two young guys, the ones who knew how to make things burn.

Harry wondered what here in Vermont needed burning.

He wasn't sure he'd gotten over Fort Collins yet. It had left a bad taste in his mouth, and in his brain, too.

At least this time they weren't going to have to carry away any corpses. The chief of staff had assured him of this. Harry doubted the COS's word, but the car left for them in this gravel parking lot beside a long-closed factory was a late-model Subaru Forester. Not big enough for the four of them and a stiff, much less multiple stiffs.

Harry didn't know exactly what their job would be. That was new. Ever since Anthony Harrison had made his first speech about those bugs, the COS—the whole White House—had been in full-on panic mode. Harry, and who knew how many others, had been working double-time, calling in favors—and offering money or threats when favors didn't work—from newspaper reporters, police departments, and the general public, all to keep the story from boiling over.

The panic had led to increased security, which meant Harry now got his orders in stages. Today, for instance, he and the rest of the crew had been told to meet here in Springfield, and then drive the Forester to some house a couple of towns away. There they would learn their ultimate destination and what they were expected to do.

It was a pain in the ass, not knowing in advance, but Harry could see why the COS was crapping bricks. Just a few weeks left till Election Day, and their guy's best chance was to convince the voters that the story was being overhyped by the Harrison campaign.

Harry wasn't so sure he believed it. That the story *was* being overhyped. He'd seen the dead guys in that house, and now he knew what had killed them. A few more attacks, someone filming the wasps chewing the eyeballs out of somebody, and all the bribes and threats in the world weren't going to win Sam Chapman the election.

Harry's phone buzzed. He peered down at the screen: the coordinates of their first stop. Pain in the ass.

He looked back up at his waiting crew. "Let's go."


**HARRY DROVE. THE** GPS guided them west on a small highway, northwest on a smaller one, and then onto a dirt road heading due north. They passed dairy farms with black-and-white cows. A pond with people rowing on it. Cabins set back from the road, surrounded by maples and oaks that were already losing their leaves, and some pines and firs, too.

Then three more turns—east, north, east—and onto a small dirt road marked with No Thru Traffic signs. At the end of this road, in a small clearing at the end of a winding driveway, lay their initial destination.

It was a wooden cabin, hand-built a half century or more ago, now weathered to gray. Harry stopped the car and they got out. Other than the pinging of the cooling engine and the whisper of a breeze through the trees, there was no sound. No human voices, no birdcalls, not even the chirp of crickets.

Later, Harry knew he should have understood what this silence meant, but he didn't. He wasn't paying the right kind of attention.

Instead, he was looking around. He guessed this was someone's hunting or fishing cabin. Not a telephone pole or power line in sight. The kind of place you'd come to *because* there was no phone service.

"I could like it here," he said.

Beside him, Trent opened his mouth to say something. Whatever it was, it went forever unspoken, because instead of talking he went flying backward. Flung through the air like some huge hand had flicked him away.

His arms spread out as he flew. He had a surprised expression on his face.

As Harry threw himself to the ground, he heard the muffled snap of a silenced .457, sound traveling more slowly than death, as always. Rolling, twisting, getting back to his feet, he hurled himself toward the edge of the clearing, as far as he could from where the bullet had come from.

Knowing exactly what was happening.

More muffled shots. The other two men dead in five seconds: a cutoff cry and the thump of a body hitting the ground, followed by one last crack of a gunshot, another thump. A wet, hopeless moaning.

Just as Harry made it to the edge of the clearing and dove into the brambles that surrounded it, he felt something riffle through his hair. A moment later, he heard the shot that had barely missed him.

He scrambled forward, feeling the thorns scratch his face and pull at his clothes. It was more like swimming than running. With every passing second—and there were too many of them, far too many—he imagined the gunmen approaching to finish their task. He knew, *knew*, they were drawing near, standing there, aiming.

But somehow he made it through the brambles into more open forest. His skin shrinking away from the expected impact of the bullet, he got to his feet. Stumbling, tripping, falling, pulling himself upright, stumbling forward again. So slow. Someone in a wheelchair could catch him. How could he outrun a bullet?

Fighting for breath, half blind, he didn't see the stone wall snaking through the forest until he nearly fell over it. Stopped in his tracks, he raised his head and saw, perched atop the wall a few feet away, a little girl.

No more than six, she was dressed in blue denim overalls and a pink-and-white-checked shirt. A beam of sun made it down through the canopy and glinted off her blond hair.

"Run!" Harry yelled. Or rather, gasped. Thinking only of what a .457 round would do to her.

She stared at him, mouth open, not moving. Almost immediately, she was joined by three other people: a boy of about nine and an adult man and woman, all standing on the other side of the wall. They were wearing denim and flannel and carrying colorful daypacks. The man held a walking stick.

A young family hiking through the Vermont woods, coming upon this wild-eyed old guy with torn clothes and scratched-up face.

But they didn't run away, as Harry had thought they would. They didn't leave him alone again in the woods. Instead, as he came up to the wall and half climbed, half fell over it, they clustered around him, helping him to his feet, brushing him off, their voices sounding like birdcalls in his ears.

The people pursuing him were still there. He knew it. Right now they had their weapons trained on him, on all of them, as they decided what to do next. Harry's only chance was that they hadn't been cleared to take out any other targets or to kill in front of witnesses.

Maybe, at this moment, the chief of staff was deciding whether Harry—and this innocent family—would live or die.

Maybe it was the president himself making the decision.

The family was staring at him, all four of them. He knew he had to answer their questions, had to say something. But what? What? He'd never been in this position before. He'd never been the prey.

Finally he came out with, "Someone in the woods. A hunter. Took a shot at me. More than one shot."

The boy and little girl seemed to think this was pretty exciting news, worth investigating further. But the mom gasped and put her hand to her mouth, and the man dropped his walking stick and swept his daughter off the stone wall and into his arms.

"Come on," he said to his reluctant son. "Let's go. Now!"

After taking a few steps, the woman looked over her shoulder. "Come with us," she said.

A nice lady. She had no idea that if Harry went with them, the threat of death came, too.

**THEY MOVED THROUGH** the woods for fifteen minutes. The father tried and failed repeatedly to get cell-phone service. Harry found himself noticing the golden and orange leaves spinning to the ground in gusts of wind, the sun gleaming on dew-soaked spiderwebs, a white-tailed deer stopping to stare at them before trotting away, its tail lifted in warning.

He began to understand that the gunmen weren't going to kill him. Not here, not now.

The forest thinned. They climbed over another stone wall and reached a road, a different one than Harry and his doomed crew had arrived on. Dirt, but graded and graveled, with SUVs and a scattering of cars parked along the edges. On the other side of the road a small lake glinted in the sun. A Volvo with a pair of kayaks on its roof came down the road, slowed, and turned onto a muddy track that led down to the lakeshore.

The father was on his phone, presumably with the police, reporting the presence of a dangerous hunter in the woods. When he finished the call, he turned his eyes

on Harry. The man wanted to be rid of him, it was obvious, but he only said, "Did you park along here?"

Harry shook his head. "No—my car's back in there,
near where you found me." He widened his eyes. "I'm
not going back for it, not yet, no way."

The father frowned, but couldn't argue with this. "You
have someone you can call? Who can rescue you?"

*Rescue you.* Harry almost laughed. "Sure."

Then he patted at his pockets. "Oh, hell," he said. "My
phone's back with my stuff."

Gone, along with everything else his team had brought.
His team itself. Their bodies long gone by now. By the
time the police arrived, there would be no sign he and
his men had ever been there.

No, that wasn't true. An expert forensic team would
surely be able to find evidence that people had been shot
there, but who was going to call out a forensic team after
a report of some hunter mistaking a hiker for a deer? The
cleanup would be good enough to fool the forest ranger
or low-level badge the state of Vermont would send to
check out the scene.

"Listen," Harry said, "is there any chance you could
give me a ride to someplace with a phone?"

Thinking, *Someplace with lots of other people around*.

The man frowned again and exchanged glances with
his wife.

"Don't worry about it," Harry said, starting to turn
away. "I can walk or hitchhike."

But the wife was shaking her head. "Of course we'll
take you," she said, smiling. "We can't abandon you here
after you almost got shot. We're going to Ludlow. Is that
okay?"

"That's just fine," Harry said.

He had no idea where Ludlow was, but it didn't matter. Anyplace was better than here.

**LUDLOW WAS CARS**, cafés, art galleries, a ski mountain gearing up for the season, and hordes and hordes of leaf-peepers wandering around.

Perfect.

Thank God for Vermont, Harry thought. All these tourists, and still old-fashioned enough to have a line of pay phones outside a supermarket. Someone had even scratched *Worship God* on the silver coin boxes, just like they used to do in New York City back when there were pay phones everywhere.

Harry had memorized the number he was about to call. He'd been thinking about using it for days, ever since Anthony Harrison had given that speech. Telling Axelson about the stiffs, about the secret lab that had been operating all those weeks ago. Showing him the card he'd had found, the one that said, *Philanthus*???

Proving that Anthony Harrison was right: The president's men had known about the bugs for weeks or months and hadn't told anybody.

Of course, back then Harry had been interested in the financial side of things. He'd thought his information would be worth a fortune.

Now it was all about survival.

He dialed the number. It went to voice mail, a calm voice saying merely, "Axelson."

When the beep came, Harry said, "My name is Harry

Solomon. You know who I am. I got something to tell you you'll want to hear. Call me within ten."

He read out the number, then hung up and stood there. Years ago, you had to guard your pay phone from all the other people who needed to use it, but no longer. Now half the crowd milling past were stuck to their cell phones, the rest patting their pockets to make sure theirs were still there.

He didn't think the COS's men would kill him in public, not now. But he knew they'd have no qualms about muscling him into a car, driving him away, and making sure no one ever saw him again.

It was just a matter of time.

*Call me back, you bastard,* he thought.

The phone rang.

# THIRTY-EIGHT

THE FOUR OF them sat in a corner booth in a chocolate restaurant down below Union Square. Until Mary Finneran had said that Kait wanted to eat at one, Trey hadn't even known that such a thing existed.

To him, a restaurant that came equipped with bubbling vats of chocolate near the entrance, napkins made to look like milk, dark, and white chocolate, and a menu offering little but chocolate foods seemed like a sign of a civilization about to crumble. Then again, a lot of things did.

The four of them: him, Sheila, Mary, and Kait. Uncharacteristically, it was Sheila who was doing most of the talking. Sheila and Mary. Trey guessed that Mary did her part to keep any conversation going, but it was strange to see Sheila so relaxed and animated.

Or maybe "relaxed" was the wrong term. "Comfortable" would be more accurate. In between sips from a nonalcoholic chocolate martini, she was describing everything she and Trey had been doing these past days. Every once in a while she'd ask Trey for a detail, or for backup on some assertion she was making, but mostly he was extraneous to the conversation.

This was fine with him. He was all talked out. If he never had to utter a word again, it would still be too soon.

For two weeks, he and Sheila had done what they could to bring reality—or at least a touch of it—to the media coverage of Anthony Harrison's blockbuster speech. They'd called the networks, CNN, MSNBC, public radio, positioning themselves as experts, offering to describe the process, the risks, the way those risks could be minimized.

When you could safely remove an implanted larva, and when you couldn't.

At first they'd been a hot item, in demand, but soon attention had begun to drain away. Trey wasn't surprised. Absent some new infusion of energy, some new headline, no story captured the public's attention for long. Not an epidemic, a tsunami, a terrorist attack. Nothing. Not these days.

When reports of new attacks fell off, then stopped almost entirely, he had known their time was up.

They were sitting in the chocolate restaurant waiting for a science reporter from the *New York Times*. Trey hadn't put it into words, but he had the sense that this interview would be the last big one, a postmortem for all of their efforts.

He missed Jack. But Jack was gone, in some secret research lab in Florida. Since the government had spirited him away, they'd heard from him just once, a voice-mail message saying he was fine and working hard.

"Not that it's gonna make the slightest bit of difference," he'd added.

* * *

**WAITING, TREY DRANK** his coffee—at his insistence chocolate-free—and watched Kait, who was sitting opposite him by the window, taking sips from a cup of hot chocolate filled with melting marshmallows (and served in a marshmallow-shaped white mug) and working on a chocolate pizza. She was a neat eater, cutting the gooey brown crust into bite-size chunks before transporting them, one by one, via fork to her mouth.

"When I was your age," Trey said, "I would have been wearing that thing by now."

Kait's eyes flickered to his face for an instant. "Grandma told me to keep it off my blouse," she said. Her quiet voice matched her solemn, oval face, dark eyes, and fair skin. Her blouse was white and dotted with little yellow, blue, and red flowers.

Mary, in the midst of her own conversation, heard and said, "You're darn tootin' I did. That shirt is new, and I'm not made of money."

She turned back to Sheila. Trey and Kait looked at each other, and Trey said, "Grandmas are always listening, aren't they?"

"They sure are," Kait said.

Her gaze strayed over his shoulder. He turned to look and saw that there was a TV perched above the restaurant's counter. It was tuned to ESPN, which was showing highlights from a soccer game. A player in a white uniform scored a goal with his head.

"I play soccer on my school team," Kait said. "My new school. In Charleston."

Trey nodded. "What position?"

"Striker," she said. Then, hesitating, she added, "I score a lot of goals."

"That was my position, too," Trey told her.

Kait's brow knit. "Really? But—" She closed her mouth again.

Trey thought he knew what she'd been about to say. "You're surprised that I played soccer, because most people my age didn't."

Kait nodded. "That's what my da told me."

"Your da was right. Most kids in the United States didn't. Not back then. But I didn't spend all my time in the U.S. when I was a kid."

She thought about that. "Where, then?"

"Brazil," Trey said. "Kenya. England. Other places, too. My dad was a doctor, and we traveled a lot. But the places all had one thing in common."

"Football."

Trey smiled. "Yes, their football. Soccer. I knew when I was, like, six, that if I was going to fit in, I had to play."

"Me, too," Kait said. "Now."

Her eyes growing distant.

"Is it helping?" he asked. "Soccer?"

She hesitated, then said, "Yes. I think so. But—"

Again the words cut off. Trey said, "But what?"

She compressed her lips, her gaze reaching his eyes, then quickly away. "It's just," she said, "you know? The other girls? They're like, you know, all really . . . blond."

Trey smiled. "Well, you can't blame them for *that*. Some people are just unlucky."

She stared at him for a moment, then actually laughed. Beside her, Mary looked startled.

"Being different is only a problem," Trey said to Kait, "if you *want* to be just like everyone else. And who wants that?"

He saw her working it through. After a while she gave a considered nod. "I never did . . . before," she said.

"Then why start now?" He pointed at himself. "Look at me—I'm doing fine, and I'm not like *anybody* else."

"You can say that again," said Sheila, who'd apparently also been listening.

**THE *TIMES* REPORTER** was named Becca Shaw.

Seeing her curly blond hair, Trey glanced at Kait. She gave him a wide-eyed look, and when he raised a finger to his lips, she let loose with a small, stifled giggle.

Becca Shaw was smart, serious, interested. Pulling a chair up to the head of their booth, she withdrew a tiny digital recorder and a well-used notebook from her black shoulder bag and began to ask pointed, relevant questions. She worked through the history of Trey's discovery, touched on Sheila's tragedy without crossing any lines, made sure she got every detail right about the thieves' life cycle.

She also took advantage of the Finnerans' presence to ask about their own encounter with the wasps. Answering, both Mary and Kait were clear-eyed and coherent. Trey wondered if he'd have been capable of as much, if he'd been in their shoes.

"I just wish I hadn't agreed to sit there on TV during Harrison's speech," Mary said, repeating something she'd said to Sheila. "This isn't about politics. It's a health issue."

Becca Shaw opened her mouth to say something, then closed it and, frowning, shook her head.

*It's both,* Trey knew she'd almost said.

*It's always both.*

**"LOOK," KAIT SAID.** "On the TV. It's Mr. Axelson."

"Oh, joy," Mary said.

Trey and Sheila turned to look at the television above the counter. Someone had switched from ESPN to CNN, and on the screen the familiar figure stood in some scrubby field behind a cluster of microphones and a scroll that read, "Breaking News: Statement from the Harrison Campaign."

Becca Shaw was already standing beside the counter, asking a waiter to turn the sound up. He was working the remote as the rest of them joined her.

It was a press conference, and Axelson was listening to a question when the sound came up.

"Look at his face," Mary said.

Kait tilted her head. "He's . . . happy."

It was true. At first glance, Axelson's expression seemed to convey nothing more than his usual interest and intelligence as he listened. But if you looked beneath, you could see more. If you knew what to look for—his posture, something gleaming in his eyes, the way his hands grasped the edge of his lectern—you saw a kind of fierce joy.

"He looks like he's afraid he'll fly right up in the air if he lets go," Mary said.

"Shhh." Becca Shaw was leaning forward, as still as a dog pointing toward the hunter's prey.

On the screen, Axelson nodded. "Yes, that's exactly what I'm saying. President Chapman and his administration have known for weeks—months, maybe—that these creatures pose a deadly threat, but have gone to great lengths, *criminal* lengths, to hide their knowledge."

"Do you have proof?" someone called out.

"Yes, we have proof," Axelson said, pausing between each word and enunciating very precisely. "Incontrovertible proof of a cover-up."

Even through the screen, it was impossible to miss the excitement that rippled through the crowd of reporters at the press conference. Voices shouted out. Axelson let them go on for a few seconds before raising his hands.

"Sorry," he said. "I can't explain yet."

Beside Trey, Becca Shaw was holding her breath.

More shouting voices, angrier now. The communications director was unfazed. "In the Harrison campaign, we believe in doing what's right for America, not just what's right for us," he said. "Or the press."

"As opposed to the Chapman campaign," Mary said in a low voice.

"At this moment," Axelson continued, "our campaign manager, Ron Stanhouse, and other members of our team are meeting with their opposite numbers at the White House. Until we learn the results of this meeting, we consider it unwise—unpatriotic, even—to detail what we've learned in the past days."

He leaned forward, the camera coming in close to his face. "But let this be understood," he said. "I am here today to tell you that the president's reckless actions have led to American deaths. Instead of protecting us—his sworn duty—he has put us, as a nation and a people, in harm's way."

Axelson stared into the camera. "Let it be understood, President Chapman," he said. "Anthony Harrison will keep America safe. And you will be held accountable."

With that, he turned and walked steadily away from the microphones.

When the scene returned to the studio, one of the anchors said, "The White House has just released a statement." She gave the camera a strange look, a kind of half smile. "The statement says, in full, 'The White House will have no statement at this time.'"

"Uh-oh," Becca Shaw said, her voice little louder than a breath. Reaching into her bag, she pulled out her smartphone and glanced at the screen. By the time she lifted her gaze, she was already far away.

"Thanks for all your help," she said. "You'll hear from us with any follow-ups, and we'll let you know when the story will run." Her eyes flicked up to the screen. "I'm guessing sooner rather than later."

Then she was gone, out the door, moving fast.

Mary and Kait headed back to their booth. Sheila, though, was still looking up at the television. The guy behind the counter had switched back to ESPN. A golf ball, shining white against deep green grass, rolled toward a hole. It teetered and then fell in. A golfer pointed his club at the sky.

"'The president's reckless actions have led to American deaths,'" Sheila said, then turned her eyes toward Trey. "What on earth do they know now," she said, "that they didn't before?"

Trey didn't answer. Somewhere deep in his brain, in his gut, in the tips of his nerve endings, something was shifting. Rousing. Coming closer to consciousness than it ever had before.

Flooding him with . . . anger? Fear?

No.

Anticipation.

# THIRTY-NINE

**"I'M SORRY," SAID** the gatekeeper at Rockefeller University's security desk, "but Dr. Shapiro is on leave."

The man didn't *sound* sorry. Trey was silent for a moment. Then he said, "When is she expected back?"

A trace of impatience in the return look. "Dr. Shapiro's leave is indefinite."

"Do you know where she's gone?"

The gatekeeper's mouth tightened. His body language caught the attention of a guard standing near the front door, who fixed his gaze on Trey.

"Never mind," Trey said. He began to turn away, then stopped. "How about Elena Stavros? Is she gone, too?"

"Do you have an appointment?"

Trey shook his head. "Just tell her Trey Gilliard is here to see her."

With a frown, the gatekeeper punched a few numbers into the phone. After a moment, a squawk came across the line.

"Security," he said in a precise tone. "There's a man named Trey Gilliard here to see you, but he's not in the system."

The squawk got louder, so that Trey could make out the words. "Gilliard? Arrest him at once!"

The gatekeeper said, "What?"

"No, no. Send him up."

A loud crunching sound as the phone clattered into its cradle.

The gatekeeper looked at Trey, then bent to print out his security pass. He muttered something with his head down.

Trey thought it was "I hate this goddamn job."

**TREY AND ELENA** Stavros had first met on the Rio Roosevelt, the River of Doubt, in Brazil nearly ten years earlier. He'd been doing his usual thing: walking into the wilderness, then emerging weeks later twenty pounds lighter, engraved with dirt, festooned with bug bites, and brimming with an encyclopedic knowledge of the area's fauna.

Meanwhile, she'd been heading downriver, the microbiologist on an interdisciplinary team studying a new form of leishmaniasis. They'd met, taken measure of each other, and grabbed the chance to share a tent for the nights before their paths diverged.

You took your opportunities where you found them, and you didn't waste time with preliminaries.

In the year that followed, they'd spent two weekends together—one in Bangkok, one in Rio. Both had been memorable, filled with laughter and cigarette smoke (hers) and various other kinds of pleasure and release. Neither Trey nor Elena had asked for or expected anything more.

And then, one day, Stavros had stepped off the carousel. The grapevine said that she'd gotten married. True or not, Trey hadn't seen her again, though he'd heard she'd taken what was basically a desk job here at Rock U. The wheel had spun them to different places.

This, too, was how it worked, most of the time.

**WHEN HE WALKED** into her office, she was standing behind her desk. She looked him over, the same frank assessment she'd given him a decade earlier.

He did likewise. She was almost as he remembered: short, a little stocky, with olive skin and dark eyebrows and all that irrepressible black hair. And eyes that had the amazing ability to actually sparkle. She was the only person Trey had ever met whose eyes did that, and they were doing it now.

It was she who broke the silence, as usual. "Bastard," she said. "You've stayed thin while I've gotten fat."

Her voice exactly the same: deep, a little scratchy from years of cigarettes and retsina. And talk.

Before he could reply, she came around the desk and across the room and hugged him. That was familiar, too, her soft, compact body belying her arms' stranglehold.

Then she pulled away from him and looked up into his face. Up close, he could see that the years had added some lines around her mouth and across her forehead. The hair might now be getting some help staying black. On the other hand, she didn't smell like cigarette smoke anymore.

"You look great to me," Trey said, and he wasn't lying.

"For an old married lady," he added.

He'd noticed the photo on her desk, an eight-by-ten showing Elena with a tall, dark-haired man and two young girls.

"Can you imagine?" she said. "Boring old homebody me, making cheese sandwiches for school lunch every morning."

Trey smiled. He'd seen this so often. The population of itinerant scientists, doctors, and field researchers was always being thinned by those who tired of the constant motion, who sought a more settled life.

Or who thought they did. Plenty then discovered that they couldn't tolerate the lack of stimulation, new sounds and smells, changing colors of light. Who missed the geography of unfamiliar bodies, another kind of terra incognita, as well.

Trey wondered whether Elena ever yearned for her old life.

She went back to her desk and sat down. "You came to see Clare," she said. "To talk about all this foolishness."

Trey sat down in a chair opposite her. "Foolishness?"

"This . . . hoopla." She glanced down at her desk, and Trey knew that she was searching for a cigarette. With a grimace, she raised her eyes to his. "Making it into a political football. Making it about who wins an election."

Trey said, "Because the thing itself, the thieves, that's not foolishness. Regardless of the hoopla, it's real."

She stared at him. He recognized the expression. It meant: Do you remember who you're talking to here?

"Real?" she said. "Christ, Trey, it's more than real. It's the end of everything."

## TREY SAID, "WELL . . ."

Elena sat up straight in her chair. "Oh, come on. You know more about these beasts than anyone. Don't you see it?"

She ticked the evidence off on her fingers. "A new threat we don't understand. A clever, resourceful enemy. An attack we have no comprehensive defense against—and no time to develop one."

She shook her head. "That empty suit Harrison is right. It's an invasion, a war. What he doesn't understand is that we've already lost."

The same words Trey's brother had used.

"Come on," Elena said. "I've seen you on TV. You've been out front on this. You've seen what those creatures are capable of. You know I'm right."

It was true, he thought. He had known, almost from the start, but hadn't allowed himself to face it. Too busy taking one step at a time, just as he'd always done, and not looking at the whole picture.

"Look," Elena went on, impatient as always with a slow pupil. "Let me give you a hypothetical."

Her words awakening a powerful memory in him. Elena had always said, "Let me give you a hypothetical."

Sometimes her hypotheticals were devastatingly true. Other times they were ridiculous. But they always got her point across.

"Listen," she was saying now. "Hurricane Sandy."

Trey said, "What about it? I wasn't here."

"But you remember what it did."

Trey said, "Sure. It knocked out power to millions of people, overloaded satellite circuits, flooded the subways, destroyed entire towns. Hundreds of people died."

Elena nodded.

"That's not quite the end of the world."

She drew in a breath through her nose. "Trey," she said. "All that destruction was caused by a single Category Two hurricane. Now tell me—"

The hypothetical.

"Tell me what would happen to the region if there'd been another hurricane a week later, only this one a Category Five, and another one the next week, and one the week after that? And what if, at the same time, a storm of the same size hit Florida and one hit California, followed by another, and another. And not just in the United States . . . Europe. Japan. China. *Everywhere*, one blow after another, for weeks. What would happen?"

Trey said, "That couldn't—"

"*Imagine*," Elena said.

Trey took a long time before answering. In the silence, he heard—felt, really—an electric hum, a vibration through his bones. It was Rockefeller University's power supply, the whale song of hundreds of powerful computers and the rest of the hungry machinery the university's brilliant scientists needed to do their work.

Trey wondered if the university had generators to provide emergency power in case of a blackout. Most likely. But how long would the fuel for these emergency generators last?

And how brilliant would Rock U's scientists be without their machines?

"It would take months—years—to get back to where we'd been," he said.

She made a dismissive gesture with her hands. "And if those months, years, were characterized by repeated hurricanes, earthquakes, tsunamis? Destroying crops, making huge areas uninhabitable, tearing apart our power grid?"

Trey was quiet.

"The five-hundred-year drought," she said.

This was also Elena. Announce what she was talking about, and leave it to you to catch up.

"I have a friend who's a paleobotanist," she said. "He was studying ancient pollens in Nevada—remnants found along old trade routes—and he uncovered evidence of a drought that lasted half a millennium."

"Droughts don't last that long," Trey said.

"That's what I told him, and he said, 'Why not?'" Elena widened her eyes. "He said just because we haven't seen one during the pitifully short time we've been recording history doesn't mean it's not possible."

Trey was quiet.

"That drought did some serious damage, as you might imagine. Entire civilizations disappeared into the dust. So tell me: In a world that now holds seven billion people, what havoc would a five-hundred-year-long drought wreak?"

Now there was no sparkle in her eyes. "And weather? Drought? They're just blunt instruments. Bad luck helped along by climate change. The threat posed by these thieves of yours is a whole lot more . . ." She searched for the words. "Direct. Clever. *Real.*"

Still Trey didn't speak.

"Think about it," she said. "What happens when there's no one willing—or left—to oversee our communications satellites? Man our hydropower plants? Open the locks in the Panama Canal? What happens when there are no firefighters willing to quell a fire before it goes out of control, or ambulances and tow trucks to tend to car crashes on the highway?"

The words hung in the air for a few moments.

"All you have to do to end our world," she said, "is make people terrified to go to work."

Her expression was bleak.

"And it will take about five days, not five hundred years."

**THEY SAT. TREY** could hear a machine grinding away somewhere down the hall, a phone ringing, cars honking on York Avenue below.

He said, "Where is Clare?"

"Oh, I imagine you've guessed. The government thing." A waggle of her hands to signify meaningless hysteria. "They're working to shut the barn door."

She saw his expression and sighed. "Okay. They enlisted her in some ultra-high-security effort that required her to drop contact with everyone she ever knew. Thereby solving two problems at once: confronting the threat and keeping her from blabbing to the public, which she certainly would have done."

"They did the same with Jack Parker up at the museum," Trey said.

"Yeah?" She flicked a glance at him. "Can't really understand why you and your girlfriend—" Her eyes gleamed. "Why you and your *skinny, gorgeous* new girlfriend are still being allowed to make noise in public. I guess because all you're doing is talking about public health."

"She's not my girlfriend."

"Whatever." Her expression turned serious. "Speaking of which, where is she?"

"Sheila? She's heading down to the Chesapeake Bay to see some friends."

A frown. "Trey," she said, "from now on . . . keep her close."

He looked at her. She was staring at the photograph on her desk.

"Don't be caught too far apart when the end comes," she said.


**THERE DIDN'T SEEM** like much else to say. Trey stood.

Getting to her feet as well, Elena said, "By the way, what did Mariama want?"

Trey wasn't sure he'd heard her correctly. "Who?"

"Mariama. Honso? She said you'd met when you were in Senegal."

"Yes," Trey said. Then, "Elena, I have no idea what you're talking about."

His tone got her attention. She looked into his face, and her eyes went round.

"Mariama called me looking for you," she said. "This was at least two months ago—over the summer. She called from—from Panama, I think it was. Said she'd be arriving in the States in a couple of days and needed to find you. I told her where to look."

She took note of his expression and lifted her hands, an uncharacteristically defensive gesture. "Trey, she asked me not to say she'd called. She wanted to find you herself, show you something in person."

Trey said, "I never heard from her."

Elena's hand went to her mouth. *"Shit."*

He thought about the last time he'd seen Mariama, standing beside the colony of thieves. Saving him. "Did she say anything else? Give any clue at all?"

"No. Nothing." Her mouth twisted. "I'm sorry, Trey."

After a moment, he shook his head. "No. Not your fault. How could you have known back then?"

Still, Elena looked angry at herself. "Damn. I wonder what happened to her."

Trey drew in a deep breath.

"I can guess," he said.

**AT THE DOOR** to her office, she put her arm around his waist. She'd always liked physical contact.

"Listen to what I'm telling you," she said.

"I will." He hesitated. "But I'm beginning to wonder if we've been wrong. Why so few attacks? Everyone's running around, hysterical, but where's the evidence?"

She released him, looked up into his face. "Slave-making ants."

"What?"

"You know, ant species that raid other ants' colonies, bringing back eggs and pupae and making the newly hatched adults into slaves."

Trey said, "I know what they are."

Remembering the raid he'd watched in the Casamance forest, just before that first encounter with the thieves.

"I used to watch them back in Greece when I was a child, and I saw how their strategies worked," Elena went on. "They always attacked the biggest, strongest nearby ant colony, but they never began until they were ready. Until they had enough fighters. Until they *knew* they would win."

Trey nodded.

"Before then?" she said. "When they were preparing? They didn't even allow themselves to cross paths with their chosen victims. They left no sign, no scent, no nothing, until the moment they attacked.

"And by then, the battle was as good as over."

There were sudden tears in her eyes. Trey hugged her, allowing his gaze to stray back to her desk, to the photo with the tall man and the two little girls.

"When it happens," he said, "you can't be here."

Still holding on to him, she laughed. It was a joyless sound.

"Oh! Sweetie," she said. "If I knew of anyplace to go, we'd be long gone already."


*IF I KNEW of any place to go.*

When Trey got back to his apartment, he did something he knew he should have done long ago. He made a series of phone calls.

Getting through in some cases, leaving messages in others.

Starting the process.

The last call was to Kenya. He hadn't even bothered to figure out what time it was there. It didn't matter.

A click on the second ring. "Granger."

Malcolm Granger. They hadn't seen each other since that day in the Casamance when Malcolm had landed the Piper in the field. The day they'd first spotted the thieves' dying forest.

"It's Trey."

"Gilliard!" Malcolm's voice was loud over the line.

"Malcolm," Trey began. "I need—"

"I know exactly what you need," his friend said. "Christ, I've been expecting this call for weeks."

Trey said, "And?"

"What the hell do you think?" Malcolm said.

# FORTY

**"WHAT DO YOU** want from me, Gilliard?" George Summers asked.

Trey looked across the desk at him. "That's easy," he said. "I want you to get out of my way, so I can talk to someone who gets things done."

Being obnoxious on purpose to gauge the depths of Summers's worries, which he assumed were plentiful and multiplying.

Even career bureaucrats with no fear of getting fired didn't like it when their boats got rocked. And nothing rocked the boat like an incumbent president losing his bid for reelection. New department chiefs got named, new patronage posts were handed out, and even those who kept their heads down could find their lives suddenly very unpleasant.

Summers's boat was already rocking. Ever since the revelations that the Chapman administration had known about the thieves for months—but hadn't told anyone—

the possibility of a Harrison victory had grown exponentially. Issues like unemployment, health care, and foreign policy seemed to have been almost forgotten—and when they *were* discussed, it was always in the context of the thieves' impact. That didn't do much for the incumbent's chances, either.

Only the fact that the number of thief attacks had declined nearly to zero gave the president any chance at victory.

A confident Summers, having been insulted, would have tossed Trey out of his office. The Summers who answered, though, merely said, "You have someone specific in mind?"

He was scared.

"Nathan Holland," Trey said. "The president's chief of staff."

Summers gave a bark of a laugh. "Clap harder, Gilliard."

"Here's what you're going to do," Trey said. "You're going to work your way up the food chain until you find someone who has Holland's ear. And then you're going to tell him that if he wants even the slightest chance of saving his man's presidency, and his own butt, he'd better sit down and meet with me. Today."

Summers's mouth hung open.

"I'd ask to see the president himself," Trey said, "but I don't have the time to spell everything out for him."


**TREY HAD ASSUMED** he'd be sent over to the West Wing, but as it turned out the chief of staff came to see him. An hour after Trey made his demand, Nathan Holland was sitting across from him in a room down a long hall on the third floor of the Ag building.

A desk, a few chairs, a dead plant, two lighter-colored squares on the walls where paintings had once hung. Someone's corner office, before all the antigovernment shouters and the bad economy had brought downsizing even to D.C.

Sitting in a chair off to the side of the room was another man, youngish, thick bodied. Trey didn't know whether he was an assistant or some kind of security, or both. Not that it mattered.

The men in the hallway outside were definitely Secret Service.

Holland was wearing a suit that had no doubt cost more than Trey had spent on clothes in the past ten years combined. His gray hair was trimmed into a near buzz cut, and despite the furrows of age, his clean-shaven face had the toned, cared-for look that spoke of expensive skin treatments.

None of it mattered. Nothing could hide the fact that the chief of staff looked old, exhausted.

*Burdened.*

"So here I am," he said. His vowels bore the trace of his Chicago roots. "Now tell me why I should listen to you."

"How's *not* listening to me working out?" Trey asked.

Holland grimaced. "Don't fence with me, Gilliard."

"Okay. No fencing," Trey said. "So tell me: How many reports have you read with my name on them?"

"What?"

"Seems like a simple enough question. I was the first American to see the thieves—or at least the first to live long enough to talk about them. I'm the guy who's been tracking their spread. The guy who's been traveling around the world learning everything I can about them, as I'm sure you already know. So I'm asking you: How often has my name popped up these past months?"

After a few moments, Holland said, "Often enough. Why?"

"Well, shouldn't *that*, by itself, be enough to get you to listen to me?"

The words hung in silence. Holland's steel gray eyes stayed on Trey's face, but it didn't matter. Trey could return gimlet stares all day if he had to.

"And anyway," he added, "you came here today. *Of course* you're going to listen."

Holland's frown deepened, but when he spoke it was to say, "All right. So what do you want to ask?"

Trey laughed, an unexpected sound in the gloomy corner room. "Ask? I'm not here to ask anything."

"Why, then?"

"To tell you what you're going to do for me."

NATHAN HOLLAND SAT across from him, huffing and puffing at his presumption. Apparently Trey had neglected to use the proper tone. Hadn't paid the respect the office of chief of staff was due. Hadn't been a supplicant.

Only . . . Trey didn't do supplication. He never had, and he wasn't about to start now. Human beings were the only species that spent so much time begging, and though this might generally be a successful tactic for an erratic, violent species occupying a crowded world, so far Trey had survived without it.

Often enough, his unwillingness to kowtow had gotten in his way, but it wouldn't this time. Holland would come around. Trey knew it, and he thought the chief of staff knew it, too. They just had to go through this ridiculous little dance first.

Eventually Holland settled back a little and said, "Tell me that name again."

Trey thought Holland remembered it just fine. But he repeated, "Mariama Honso."

"I have no idea who that is," Holland said.

"Sure you do," Trey said. "She was coming to see me back in July, and you stopped her."

"Did we?"

"Yes. You stopped her, arrested her, and stashed her somewhere."

An instant's cloudiness in the chief of staff's eyes was the giveaway. The tell.

"Or maybe you didn't even bother to arrest her," Trey said. "You're still doing that 'indefinite detention' thing, aren't you?"

Holland didn't answer.

"I don't care. We can talk about the morality of that another time. The point is: Mariama's staying somewhere on the government's dime, and I know why."

Holland, his mouth pursed, waited for him to go on.

"Somehow you learned she was coming here," Trey said. "Maybe you'd been tracking her progress all the way from Senegal, or maybe she pinged a watch list when she tried to enter the U.S."

He leaned forward in his chair. "That doesn't matter,

either. What matters is that you put it together—where she was from, what she was going to do. And the last thing you wanted, just a couple of months before the election, was some modern-day Paul Revere stirring up the populace . . . and the media."

Holland looked toward the third man in the room and said, "Kyle, would you please wait outside?"

Without a word, the man got up and joined the agents in the hall, closing the door behind him.

"Go on," Holland said.

"You cared more about shutting her up than learning what she knew. All that mattered was keeping a lid on the story. Making sure it didn't bite your guy until after the election, when you'd have four more years to deal with it."

The chief of staff's eyes were as translucent as old sea glass.

"When you *thought* you'd have four more years," Trey went on. "But now everything's gone to hell anyway, right before the election. Mariama is the least of your worries. She can't possibly have anything to say that will make things worse for you—especially if you make her sign something promising she'll stay quiet or go back to jail. Which I know you'll do."

Holland looked at him, and something changed in his expression. Some life, some spirit, drained away.

"Mariama Honso," he said.

"Where is she?" Trey asked.

"I don't know," Holland said. "But I can find out."

"And bring her here?"

Holland's silence meant, *What do* you *think?*

"Today," Trey said.

Holland's lips twitched.

"You don't ask much, do you?" he said.

**DON'T BE CAUGHT** *too far apart when the end comes,* Elena Stavros had said.

Trey stood outside with the Secret Service while Holland made some phone calls. Leaning against the wall, he thought about Sheila and Kait and Mary Finneran stashed by the Harrison campaign in a safe house on the Chesapeake. Jack and Clare Shapiro. Elena and her family. Mariama.

Christopher.

And about his plan. The one he'd begun to put into place only the day before.

Something moved sluggishly inside of him.

He wondered if he'd have enough time to see it through.

**"WE'VE LOCATED HONSO,"** Nathan Holland said.

His tone struck Trey as odd, but he didn't pursue it. "You'll bring her to me today?" he said.

The chief of staff shook his head. "There are procedures, and she hasn't been staying next door," he said. "Tomorrow."

"Where?"

Holland looked around, gave a tiny shrug. "Here will do."

Trey said, "I'll have to talk directly to her. Just me, at least at first."

The chief of staff sighed. "You'll get to talk." Then his

eyes sharpened. "Anyway, tomorrow we'll be . . . otherwise engaged."

Again there was something in the chief of staff's tone. Trey felt his heart give a single thud in his chest.

"Engaged doing what?" he asked.

The chief regarded him with an unreadable gaze.

"Tonight," he said, "the president will tell you."

# FORTY-ONE

*Higgins Island, Maryland*

**THEIR WOODEN HOUSE**, like most of the others they'd passed on the way, stood on sturdy stilts anchored by solid blocks of concrete. The man who'd brought them had told Kait that, come a flood tide from Chesapeake Bay, you could sit on the front deck and look down at the water flowing harmlessly under the house.

"Sometimes," the man had said, "you can even see schools of bluefish and striped bass swimming past!"

Kait had guessed this was just a story, but she'd liked hearing it anyway. The man and the others with him, who'd been wearing suits but had seemed more like policemen, had been nice enough. At least, they'd tried to be nice. They hadn't ignored her, like so many adults, like so many of the new people, did.

Mr. Axelson, who'd arranged for them to spend a few days here, in this house on the edge of the marsh, didn't ignore her, either. Even when she asked the wrong questions, and she could tell he wished she'd pipe down, he was polite and friendly. Only his eyes gave him away.

Wrong questions, like when the policeman-in-dress-up-clothes told her about watching the bluefish. Kait had said, "Can I ask you something?"

"Of course." He'd smiled at her. "Anything."

"What happens to this house if there's a hurricane?"

That had made his smile go away. His mouth had moved for a second without any sound coming out. What he'd said finally was, "No hurricanes in the forecast, sweetie," which both of them knew wasn't really an answer.

After this conversation, she'd planned to draw a picture of the house being swept away, stilts and concrete moorings and all.

But then, last night, she'd heard something that had made her change her mind. So when she did sit down and draw, the result didn't show them being whisked away by the wind or swamped by a giant wave. No. The house was being borne on the backs of a school of silvery fish. Big, strong fish carrying them to safety.

When she showed her grandmother the drawing, Mary smiled and said, "That's because Sheila's coming for a visit, isn't it?"

No one was smarter than her grandmother.


AND NOW HERE she was. Sheila. Sitting out on the deck under a blue sky, a glass of iced tea "with a kick" in her hand. Her and Mary and Kait, just like the first time back on Marco Island, just after Ma and Da died. The day of the funeral.

It felt like a million years ago to Kait, that day. Though not at night. Not when she dreamed.

She hadn't known she would do it, but the minute she saw Sheila stepping out of her car in the driveway, she'd gone hurtling down the wooden steps and leaped into her arms. She'd heard Sheila gasp, then laugh, and then for a long time they'd just held each other.

But now that she was looking at Sheila from across the deck, Kait could see how skinny she looked. Skinny and sad, and maybe even a little scared. And that made Kait scared, too.

"What have you heard from Trey?" Mary was asking.

"Not much. He's over in D.C., tracking down someone he thinks might be able to help."

"Help how?"

But Sheila just turned her palms up.

Kait said, "You miss him. You wish he was here."

Sheila said, "Stop looking inside my head, Kaitlin Finneran!" Then she smiled. "Yes, of course I do. But if he thinks this is important . . . well, it is."

Her smile vanished. "I also heard from Jack. A text."

"What did it say?" Mary asked.

"'Worst-case scenario. Batten down.'"

Kait wasn't sure she knew what that meant, but this time she didn't ask. Sometimes you could learn more from staying quiet.

"Is it what we guessed?" Mary asked.

Sheila sighed. "I think so, yes."

She was so thin, Kait thought again.

Almost as if hearing her thought, Sheila looked at Kait again. "We think the president is planning to attack the thieves," she said. "He's giving a speech tonight, and we think that's what he'll be announcing."

"I know," Kait said. She looked at her grandmother. "That's why he wanted us to be with him, right?"

Sheila said, "Who did?"

"The president. One of his lackeys called last week." Mary's eyes had that look they got only when she was angry. "I don't know whether he wanted us *there* at the speech—we didn't get into details. They definitely wanted us available to answer questions from the press after he was done. And then—"

She paused. "And then what?" Sheila said.

"And then I think he wanted us to join him while he watched the attack."

Kait could see that her grandmother's lips were almost the same color as the rest of her face and that the wrinkles on her forehead were standing out. This was how she looked when she was *very* angry.

"We said, "No, thank you.' We're not going to be a Ping-Pong ball anymore, are we, Kait? We're tired of bouncing around and being looked at, right?"

Kait nodded. Did anyone like being looked at? Maybe some of the blond girls in her class. But not her.

A shadow passed overhead. She looked up and saw that it was an osprey, almost near enough to touch. When they'd first gotten here, she'd gone down to explore the marsh. There had been deer among the little stands of pine trees and muskrats in the more open water, and gulls and terns. Though no dolphins.

It had all reminded Kait of home, which had made her cry. But she'd been dry-eyed by the time she returned to the house.

Now Mary was saying, "That's when Jeremy Axelson had us brought here. One of Harrison's fund-raisers owns this house, I believe."

Sheila said, "And then, when the president's speech is done, Axelson will announce that you are not available for comment—implying that you disagree with the decision. He'll use your absence to push public opinion."

Mary nodded. "Most likely. We can't stop that." She sighed. "We brought this on ourselves, I'm afraid. But at least we don't have to participate anymore. This Ping-Pong ball is now retired."

Kait stirred in her seat. "I don't understand something."

"What, Bunny?" her grandmother asked.

"The president is going to attack the wasp-things?"

"Yes, that's what we think."

"Where?"

Neither Mary nor Sheila answered. Some bird in the marsh gave a high-pitched, piping call.

"And what will happen . . . after?" Kait said.

When the grown-ups still didn't speak, she stood and walked out to the edge of the deck. Leaning over the railing, she looked out toward the marsh.

Her nose prickled from the faintest taint of a familiar bitter odor. And she thought she could detect, at the very limits of her hearing, the sound of wings.

# FORTY-TWO

*Dry Tortugas, United States*

**MARIAMA'S LAST DAY** in limbo was her sixty-eighth.

She knew this because she asked the guard who brought her breakfast what day it was. The date. Not for Mariama, scratching marks in her cell's stone wall to help her stay sane. She had no fear of losing her sanity.

Nor did she think marking the passage of time was a way to keep in touch with reality. Quite the reverse, in fact.

She supposed that, if you had a cast-in-stone sentence, this many days, weeks, years, watching the marks in the wall multiply might give you hope. You'd be filling in the blanks, knowing that when you got to the last one, you'd walk out.

But for her, scratches in the wall might only mark the last days of her life, whether there were ten thousand of them or only a handful.

Why, then, on this day, her sixty-eighth, did she ask her guard, the yellow-haired Carla, for the date? Why did she expect an answer? She was never quite sure. Maybe on some unconscious level she knew that something had changed. That this day was different.

Anyway: She'd asked. And Carla had glanced back at the second guard, the stoical young man who had never volunteered his name.

Mariama expected him to shake his head. But he shocked her by giving a little shrug.

"Sure," he said. "Go ahead. She'll find out soon enough anyway."

Mariama felt her blood warm, as if she'd been hibernating all these weeks and was now awakening.

"What are you talking about?" she said.

But before either guard could speak, Mariama felt rather than heard the sound. Something new. A vibration, a thrumming in her breastbone before spreading out along the pathways of her skeleton until she could even feel it in her fingers and toes.

"A plane," Mariama said out loud.

Carla was smiling as she put the tray down on the table beside the cot. "It's October fifteenth," she said. Behind her, the other guard allowed himself a small smile as well. He looked like a man who realized that a deadly dull assignment was finally coming to an end.

Mariama counted at last. Sixty-eight days since she'd arrived.

Sixty-eight days lost.

The sound of the plane, props whacking against the trade winds, grew louder. "You have time for breakfast," Carla said. "They won't be ready for you for a couple of hours."

Mariama had no appetite for the eggs and toast congealing on the plate. "Tell me," she said. "Why am I leaving?"

The male guard looked at her with an expression she hadn't seen from him before. Respect?

"All we know," he said, "is somebody told them to jump, and they jumped."

Mariama said, "Who?"

The guard just shrugged. She'd gotten all from him she was going to.

But Mariama didn't care. She knew who it was. Who had told the authorities to jump and set her free.

For the first time in weeks, she felt something that could have been called hope.

## PAPERWORK.

She'd just learned it was the fifteenth of October, and now she had to write it again and again, like a punished student forced to write the same sentence over and over on the blackboard.

Each form had different words, but they all required her to say the same thing. *I will not tell anyone where I've been these past sixty-eight days. I will not tell anyone where I've been . . . I will not . . .*

America was such a strange, schizophrenic mix. It could hide you on a rock for months at a time, not answering or apologizing to anyone. But when it finally let you out, the paperwork still had to be in order.

Maybe that was why scandals like Abu Ghraib made such headlines. Too much evidence left behind. America hadn't yet learned that if you wanted to behave like the rest of the world—most of the rest of the world—you had to jettison your love of record keeping, your need to document all your actions.

Mariama sighed and signed another form.

**SHE WAS SITTING** in an office. A wooden desk held a metal tray, a couple of waterlogged-looking books, and a computer whose background showed a snowy mountain scene. Mariama wondered if this was a joke for whoever usually sat behind the desk, or a dream.

Windows on two sides, the sun spilling in through one, the breezes rattling the blinds in both. Seabirds called somewhere nearby, liquid yelps and shrieks.

All of this a hundred yards from her cell. And now she was free. It was hard to comprehend.

The man in charge was dressed in a military uniform. She couldn't guess at his rank, but she could tell he had some seniority, some power. His close-cropped hair was shot with gray, and in his tanned face his eyes, so dark as to seem black, possessed a kind of canny intelligence that worried her.

Still, she had to speak, had to ask. Looking up from signing the last form, she said, "You will be sending me back to Senegal?"

He looked into her eyes. She found his expression hard to read, another worry. But after a moment he shook his head and said, "No, Miss Honso, you're not going home, not yet."

Relief and worry mixed. "Where, then?"

He didn't reply, looked down at the papers on his desk.

She took a breath. One more question left to ask, the most important one.

"You will give me my possessions back, won't you?" she said.

Instantly he raised his head and fixed her with those knowing eyes. "Why do you care? You had hardly anything with you when you were apprehended."

In that moment, Mariama changed tactics. She had no choice. He was the enemy, and a clever one. Supplication wouldn't work on him. Nor would pretending that she barely spoke English.

Her chin lifted. "I remember exactly what I had with me. A small overnight bag with a change of clothes, a toothbrush, and a tube of toothpaste. A money belt containing more than a thousand U.S. dollars, a paperback book, a bag of pretzels, a watch, two silver bracelets, and a locket I wore on a silver chain around my neck."

He was still staring into her eyes. She knew she couldn't afford to look away. "And you care about which of these things?" he asked.

"The bracelets were made by a friend of mine," she said. "And the locket—that was given to me by my father, whose photo is inside. As I'm sure you know." She kept her eyes on his. "I doubt I will ever see him again, my father, so of course the locket is most important to me."

He stared at her for a little longer. She held his gaze, unwavering. Everything she'd said was the truth.

Finally he nodded. Took the papers she'd been signing and banged them against the desk to make the edges even. Mariama wondered if anyone would ever look at them again.

"You'll receive your personal items when you reach your destination," he said.

Mariama looked down, allowing her immense relief to show as gratitude. "Thank you."

He grunted and got to his feet. "Let's go."

## MARIAMA FLEW.

The little prop plane was a four-seater. The pilot and one guard beside him, Mariama and a second one in the back. The whole flight, she looked at none of them, just down at the ocean below. Staring at the blue-green water, waves looking like ripples, brilliant white flecks showing where the fishing boats and yachts were out.

Blue, green, white.

Freedom.

And more than freedom: a goal, a purpose, renewed.

Mariama flew.

**THEY SWITCHED AIRPLANES** at a small airport in what the guards said was Florida. The new plane was a small jet. It took Mariama and her watchers—ones she hadn't seen before, in suits this time, not uniforms—north.

"Where are we going?" she asked. No one answered.

Down below, the land was gray and green, split by highways and cars that, when they caught the sun, looked like the gleaming carapaces of rain forest beetles. Expanses of savanna and marsh. Lakes that winked in the sun.

Mariama stared at it. All the joy had drained out of her. Already. Her happiness had been so fleeting.

She knew what was down there.

* * *

**WASHINGTON, D.C., THAT** was their destination.

The terminal was huge and cavernous, like the mouth of a whale or a sea monster. No, not a mouth. A stomach. Mariama felt like she'd already been eaten.

She felt dizzy. She'd been alone for so long.

They put her in a big black car and drove her into the city. She was silent, looking out the window at the squadrons of honking taxis and trucks, at the battalions of people going about their business.

In front of an enormous grayish white building with a front lined with columns, within view of the White House, they handed her over to yet another pair of guards. Only then did they give her a manila envelope that contained her belongings.

She looked inside: the belt, the paperback book, the bracelet, and the locket.

She took a deep breath and, with a guard on either side, went into the building.


**TREY WAS THERE.**

She'd thought it must have been him behind her release, but still she'd doubted. All her hopes, all those days of solitude, hanging from such a slender thread.

Yet here he was. Standing in a darkened hallway outside a half-open door. Beyond him, inside the room, she could see the shadowy forms of a crowd, perhaps twenty people, seated before a large, flickering television screen.

"Got your e-mail," he said.

A lifetime ago.

"Sorry it took me so long to figure everything out." He shook his head. "Too long."

She said, "I thought I would be there forever."

They hugged. Stepping back, she looked up into his face and noted how haggard he was. Even in the poor light, she could see that time and worry—and something else—had taken a great toll since they'd last met.

She looked at the silent crowd. "What is this?"

He didn't speak, just gestured toward the television. Mariama followed his gaze. It took her no more than a few seconds to understand what she was seeing.

"Oh, no," she said. "They can't."

"Of course they can."

Mariama put her hands over her mouth.

"I'm sorry," he said.

She couldn't take her eyes off the screen.

"We're too late."

# FORTY-THREE

**THE PRESIDENT OF** the United States, surrounded by a dozen members of the senior staff, military officers in uniform, and other guests, sat in a plastic box.

Trey might have found it funny if his stomach hadn't been clenched in a knot. It was like a gigantic version of one of those cubes that held autographed baseballs, the ones that kept dust and moisture out as your prize sat on your mantelpiece.

"Have you seen my Ted Williams? He hit a home run with this ball in 1941."

"Have you seen my president? He's afraid he might lose the next election."

A box, a chamber. Perhaps seven feet high and as deep, and twenty feet wide, with a door on each end. Perched on a newly poured concrete platform, about ten feet up, connected to the ground by two staircases and two ladders. Set high, Trey guessed, to provide a good view of the action.

Mariama stood still beside him. He could hear her

short, controlled breaths over the muttering of the news-man on the TV and the occasional comment from the subdued group sitting here in the sweaty darkness. He'd expected her to be emaciated, hollow eyed. But she looked the same as she had in Senegal: compact, muscular, her sharp gaze never seeming to miss a thing.

On the screen, Secret Service agents and uniformed personnel arrayed themselves on the concrete platform around the president's enclosure. Then the screen split to show a group of six military helicopters, big Apaches, on a muddy, gray-green field a couple hundred yards away.

Mariama said, "Where is this?"

"South Florida," Trey said. "Old sugarcane land on the edge of the Everglades."

"Why there?"

"Visibility." Trey shrugged. "Doesn't hurt that it's a swing state."

She looked at him.

"One that could go either way in the election next month. At this stage in an election year, it's all political. Beat the thieves in Florida, win Florida."

Mariama opened her mouth to say something, then closed it again.

"Mostly, though," Trey said, "they chose it because thieves are abundant there."

"But aren't they abundant everywhere?" Mariama asked.

**JACK WAS IN** the room, too, leaning against a wall to the side of the television. He'd arrived early that morning, out of sorts and uncharacteristically terse. All he'd said, when Trey asked why his project had been shut down, was, "We didn't give them a magic bullet fast enough."

"So?"

"Any old bullet will do if you're shooting yourself in the foot."

On the screen, Marines and members of the National Guard were hustling around, battling a gusty wind. A reporter leaned against the breeze, his slick shiny hair flying around as he shouted into the camera.

The president, sitting in the box, looked at his watch. The chairman of the Joint Chiefs of Staff, wearing a medal-hung uniform, leaned in close to say something into his ear.

Jack, looking back, saw Trey with Mariama, pushed himself away from the wall, and came over. Trey introduced them, and for the first time since he'd resurfaced, Jack's face showed some animation.

"Took your sweet time getting here," he said to her.

She gave a small smile. "I left Senegal to come here two days after Trey did."

"What did you do, walk?"

"I walked, yes. And rode cars, a fishing boat, a freighter, airplanes. And then I sat."

"Three months to get here," Jack said, shaking his head.

She nodded. "And just in time for this."

**THE HECTIC SCENE** on the television screen stilled. The president, looking stoic and determined, was waiting to give a signal.

The people in the room all leaned forward. Everyone seemed to be holding their breaths.

Except for Mariama. She was full of questions. "Insecticide?" she asked. "Defoliant?"

"From what we heard, both," Jack answered. "And, for all we know, flypaper and bug zappers."

"And when they're done?"

"Declare victory. Go home. Win election."

Mariama looked at Trey. "Did you tell them this is madness?"

"In Senegal," he said, "does your president listen to you?"

She was silent.

"We argued, all the Avengers they'd assembled," Jack said. "No one listened. They just told us they understood what we were saying, but would make the decision they considered 'right for our great nation.'"

"They understand nothing," Mariama said.

**ON THE LEFT** side of the screen, the president and his guests watched the final preparations.

On the right, Marines climbed into the helicopters. Solid metal doors slid shut. Heads topped with helmets appeared in the glass bubbles of the Apaches' cockpits. Support staff hurried away.

One after another, the rotors started to chop, sending dust clouds spiraling into the air.

In that unreachable place deep inside Trey's core, something awoke.

**THE PRESIDENT GAVE** a nod. A moment later, the first of the Apaches lifted into the air, powerful and ponderous. The rest of the squadron followed. Below them, the dust flailed upward like grasping hands, then fell back.

The president was standing, staring through the plastic.

"Those helicopters," Mariama said, her voice a breath. "And that box."

"What about them?" Trey said.

"Are they airtight?"


**IT WAS OVER** sooner than even Trey had expected.

Spread out in formation perhaps two hundred feet above a scrubby marsh, the helicopters released plumes of poison. A strange oily, glittery white, the clouds drifted outward and down.

Trey caught a quick glimmer of movement amid the low underbrush, a gleam of sunlight off dark scales. A big rat snake searching futilely for safety.

He found himself thinking of everything there on the ground, in the water and low bushes, that wasn't a thief. Rare birds. Florida panthers.

The first of the plumes reached the ground. The helicopters flew on.

Trey knew what was coming, knew for sure, before anyone else did. The hive mind told him, spreading the heat of its anger through him in a wave that threatened to stop his heart.

Then everyone knew. Everyone could see. The lead helicopter seemed to stutter in the air, as if it had run into some thicker, denser patch of atmosphere. For a moment it jittered in one place, the two behind it swinging off to the sides to avoid a collision.

And then, as if piloted by intent instead of merely obeying the laws of gravity, it plunged straight downward. In an instant it had passed through the chemical fog and slammed into the ground. The image on the screen shook from the impact. A billow of flame blew upward, white at the center, tongues of green around the edges.

Someone in the room screamed.

Inexplicably—unless you understood what you were seeing—a second Apache flew straight through the fireball. A moment later, it exploded in midair.

In the center of the neon blaze, the helicopter's skeleton showed, laid bare by fire. A human figure twisted like a black wire within it as it, too, fell to earth.

In the room, people sobbed. At a great distance, voices on the television shouted in hysteria.

Trey could not breathe. His mind seemed to blur, then split apart. Part was still here, in the room, but the rest was . . . somewhere else. Among the men dying in the disastrous assault. Among the wasps that were killing them. He was witnessing the destruction as if he were there. And somehow he *was*.

He brought his hands to his face. For an instant it almost seemed as if his alarm, his distress, was being *broadcast* there, to the thieves. He had the fleeting sensation of . . . indecision. Concern.

He felt a touch on his arm. When he lowered his hands, he saw that Mariama was staring up at him. Somehow her gaze seemed to bring him back together again. His muscles quivering, cold sweat drying on his body, but his mind reunited.

For now.

On the screen, a helicopter accelerated and tilted to

the left. It was nearly on its side when its rotor caught the tail of another. Metal flew in strange smoking arcs, one jagged piece hurtling straight toward the camera but falling short, as the remains of the two craft plummeted. Trey never learned whether the pilots of the last two Apaches received an order to return to base. Perhaps they did. Perhaps someone had the presence of mind to order them out of there, back onto the ground.

Or maybe they just followed the most basic animal instinct. Flee. Survive.

But they were far too late. One had completed only half a turn before his craft tilted, righted itself, tilted again, and went down.

The second pilot didn't even make it that far. One last explosion shook the camera and sent a fountain of smoke skyward.

The screen switched back to the president in his box. He was still standing. His eyes were wide, his mouth wrinkled and pursed. He looked dumbstruck. Uncomprehending.

Beside him, the chairman of the Joint Chiefs of Staff was shouting. Others in the group inside the plastic enclosure were staring around, looking as stunned, as lost, as witnesses to calamity always do. The camera zoomed in to focus on a Secret Service agent, sunglasses gone, eyes and mouth stretched wide, yanking on the door from the inside.

"Fucking idiot," Jack said. "Don't open that."

The screen went black.

Someone turned on the light in the room. People scrabbled for their phones, ran for their offices, tapped on their tablets. Desperate for information that would be no different from what they'd just seen for themselves, for reassurance that wouldn't come.

One of Mariama's two guards was turned away, listening over his earpiece. A moment later both turned and, at a run, headed down the hallway, as if she no longer existed.

Trey was calm again. His mind his own. The sweat was drying on the back of his neck. "It's over," he said.

Mariama's eyes were again on his face. She opened her mouth to say something, but before she could speak, his telephone buzzed.

He took it out of his pocket. Saw it was Sheila calling. He hit a button.

"Trey," she said. Her voice a whisper.

His heart thudded. "What?"

*"They're here."*

# FORTY-FOUR

TREY SAID, "WHERE are you?"

"With Kait and Mary. In the safe house."

"I know that," he said. *"Where?"*

"In the bathroom."

"Are there any windows?"

"No." He heard her take a breath. "We jammed a towel under the door. But there are dozens of them inside the house. Hundreds. Kait saw them coming."

A pause. Then, her voice shaking for the first time, "Trey, we don't know what to do."

Trey didn't, either. A call to the police would be sending unprepared cops into an ambush. And how could they make their own rescue attempt into anything more than a suicidal gesture?

Jack had disappeared, but Mariama was standing close, looking up into Trey's face.

"My friends," he said to her. "The thieves have them trapped."

"Yes." She seemed unsurprised. Calm. "Do you have a car?"

Trey said, "No."

At the same moment, Jack came back down the hall. "Sure," he said, spinning a key chain on one finger.

They looked at him. He shrugged. "I called in a favor."

Trey said into the phone, "Sheila, we're on our way. Two hours, tops."

"But—"

"Trust me. We'll figure something out."

"Okay." He could have kissed her for not asking questions. Then she said, "Damn! My phone is almost dead."

By such slender threads our lives hang, Trey thought. "Just hold on, okay?" he said.

"We will." Again her voice caught. "Trey—"

"On our way," he said again and disconnected.


**"WHERE ARE WE** going?" Jack asked, handing Trey the keys as they moved down the hall.

Trey said, "Higgins Island on the Chesapeake."

Jack nodded. "You have the address?"

Trey said yes.

"Good. I'll plug it into my GPS. If you drive fast—"

Trey didn't let him finish his sentence.

"I'll drive fast," he said.


**JACK HAD BORROWED** an Audi A3, which had no problem breaking the speed limit. Driving fast was even easier since Route 50 was nearly deserted. Only a few cars aimed out of town, and almost no one was heading in. The late-afternoon sky was a flat blue-gray and nearly empty as well, though near its apogee a jet caught the sun and seemed to catch fire.

"Humans," Jack said from the backseat, "are so fucking predictable."

Trey knew what he meant. When the world turned upside down, the eternal human tendency was to stay put. Hunker down.

Better to die at home, in your bed, than on unfamiliar turf.

"I'll bet the supermarkets are out of bottled water already," Jack said. "The people who make spring water, they just love catastrophes."

Mariama, sitting in the passenger seat beside Trey, grimaced. "What's the point in buying water in bottles?"

"So you have enough to drink before the water comes back on."

Mariama laughed. "I guess that depends, no? On how long before the water starts to flow again?"

Trey thought about droughts that lasted five hundred years.

But Jack just grunted and said, under his breath, "Talk about your major buzzkill."

**TREY DROVE. THE** D.C. suburbs fell away, and the landscape grew more rural. They passed open fields, farmhouses, interspersed with stretches of minimalls. The color of the light flattened as they drew nearer the coast, and they caught glimpses of rivers and bays, slate gray in the late-afternoon sun.

The few people in sight all seemed to be in a hurry as

well. A hurry to get back home. Trey wondered how many of them would spend their last minutes or hours or—perhaps—few days in the houses they'd retreated to. In their castles. Cowering in windowless bathrooms or broom closets, or stepping forward to fight back, brave, foolhardy, doomed.

"So, when we get there," Jack said, "what's the plan?"

Trey said, "Any ideas?"

"Me?" Jack snorted. "Do I really look like a guy with a plan? You know what I am? I'm a dog chasing cars."

Then, after a pause, "That's a quote. From *The Dark Knight*. The Joker said it first."

"When we get there," Mariama said, "I'll tell you what to do."

THEIR ROUTE TOOK them across the Chesapeake Bay Bridge. There were ducks on the water below and cormorants drying their wings on rocks close to shore.

"Oh." Jack had been looking down at his phone, giving directions when necessary, but now he caught Trey's eye in the rearview mirror. "They rescued the president." He touched the screen. "Our republic is saved."

Trey kept his attention on the road ahead.

"He's in some bunker while the White House and residence are being"—Jack made a sound that was probably a laugh—"bug-proofed."

At another time, Trey would have had plenty to say about this, starting with the impossibility of "bug-proofing" any building. Instead, he just shook his head.

"It wasn't a rescue," he said. "The thieves backed off."

"Trey is right," Mariama said.

Jack made a dissatisfied grunt. "Why? It's their Sabbath? They have a prohibition against eating elected officials?"

"No. They weren't ready for war," Trey said.

Feeling Mariama's gaze on his face.

"They're still . . . building their strength," he said.

Slave-making ants before a raid.


**THEY LEFT THE** highway and followed a series of smaller, winding roads heading south and back west toward the bay.

Approaching dusk, the light was watery, the air still and heavy. They drove through a small town, wooden buildings, empty streets, tourist shops closed for the season. Beyond it, the houses were bigger and set farther from the road, more isolated from each other. Sometimes all that was visible was a gate and a long driveway disappearing into the woods. No sign of the building itself.

"Yeah," Jack said. "Sure. I'd hide people here, too."

He checked his GPS. "Make the next right." Then, "About fifteen more minutes."

Something different in his manner. The ever-present good humor draining away as they drew closer.

Trey said, "Why are they there? Why are they threatening Sheila and the rest now?"

Mariama stirred. "When they're attacked, the thieves grow more . . . brazen."

Jack grunted. "The attack happened in Florida. They'd get brazen a thousand miles away?"

"Everywhere," Mariama said. "At once."

Jack made a sound in his throat.

Trey said, "Sheila killed two larvae. Is that why they came? More revenge?"

"Yes. When they're at sufficient strength, they go after anyone who harms them. You know this."

"And anyone who happens to be in their vicinity."

Mariama didn't seem to think that worthy of an answer.

They drove in silence for a few moments. Then Jack said, his voice very quiet, "The thieves. They're like Horton? They never forget?"

Mariama grunted.

"It's not a matter of forgetting," she said. "It's in their blood. To them, it is always happening right now."

Jack looked out the window. "Hell of a way to live," he said.

**"SHEILA'S PHONE BATTERY** must be dead," Jack said. "But her voice mail sounds cheery."

"She said it was dying," Trey said.

"Doesn't matter. We're almost there." Jack pointed. "Next right. That's it."

They entered a curving gravel driveway. In the encroaching darkness, the trees seemed to huddle over the drive, blocking any view but the one directly ahead.

The two-hour drive from Washington had taken an hour and a half. It felt like they were nearing world's end.

"The house is at the end of this drive," Jack said. "About another third of a mile."

Mariama draw in a deep breath through her nose.

"I hate that smell," she said.

* * *

**THE CHARACTERISTIC BITTER** odor prickled Trey's nostrils.

He could hear them, too. A familiar sound: the hum of wings, so high-pitched it seemed pure vibration, tickling somewhere in the center of his head.

But in this case multiplied a hundred times. A thousand.

The house, wood with weathered shingles, stood in front of them. It had been built on concrete posts and raised on stilts, with a wraparound deck overlooking the water beyond. Eight wooden steps led up to the front door, which hung open.

And then he saw movement on the lawn, on the drive, on the stairs.

A blur in the gloom. Glimpses of crimson. Flashes of black and green.

Jack said, his voice cracking a little at the edges, "Everyone's window closed?"

And, "Would you shut the air vents up there, please?"

Hundreds of thieves, crawling here, flying in short loops there. Dozens whirling into the air like malevolent dust devils as the car crept up the driveway. Others swooping close to the windshield before spinning away again.

Those on the front walk, on the stairs, on the patchy gray lawn, had all turned to watch. A thousand compound eyes staring, or one eye divided into a thousand?

The voice inside Trey awoke. He'd been expecting it to all along the way, but it had waited until now.

He wondered if that had been its intention. To lull him into a trap. Because now, exerting its will, it seemed to drag him toward the car door. His brain seemed to split, half of it here, inside the car, and half outside among the creatures.

He brought the car to a stop beside a gas lamp atop a metal pole, ten feet from where the wooden stairs led up to the open door.

A dozen thieves settled on the hood and stared in at him. Trey shivered, a convulsive movement of his shoulders.

Inside, the voice radiated happiness. Wholeness.

Mariama put her hand on Trey's arm, and after a moment he was able to pull himself back.

Behind them, Jack was staring out the window, his face a pale blotch in the darkness.

"Anybody got a spare Terminator?" he asked.

# FORTY-FIVE

"I'LL GO IN, of course," Mariama said.

Jack leaned forward and stared at her. "What? That's insane. You won't make it three steps across the yard."

Mariama's expression contained a trace of amusement. "They won't attack me," she said.

Jack shifted his gaze to watch thieves moving lightly along the outside of the window. "And why is that?"

"Listen." Mariama's voice hardened. "I have lived among these creatures all my life. I know more about them than you do. They will not sting me."

Jack blinked. "Okay."

Her expression softened a little. "In the Casamance, Trey saw that I was unharmed. I will explain why later, after your friends are safe."

Trey said, "I'm coming with you."

She began to shake her head. Then she stopped and looked up into his eyes. In a sudden, unexpected move, she placed her right palm against his shirt, below his rib cage.

"When did it happen?" she asked.

He knew what she was asking, knew he had to tell the truth.

"In July," he said. "In Australia. Sheila—" He gestured at the house. "That was one of the larvae Sheila took out."

Mariama's eyes were still on his. "Trey," she said. "You feel it, don't you? The . . . consciousness."

After a moment, he nodded.

"That's good." Her eyes brightened. "Right now, that's good. Yes, you can come with me."

"Without, you know, dying?" Jack asked.

Mariama looked back at him. "People like Trey—they confuse the thieves." She switched her gaze to Trey. "It is hard for them to tell what you are—whether you are still a host."

"And how about me?" Trey said. "Will I always be able to tell?"

She grimaced but did not answer.

"STAY WHERE YOU are," Mariama told Jack. "Don't do anything foolhardy, and you shouldn't be in danger. The thieves are much more concerned about Trey and me."

Jack gave a nod, but he didn't seem reassured. He was breathing heavily, and Trey could see sweat on his face.

"The thieves will move away when Trey and I leave the car," she went on. "Then they will come back, but no closer than they are now. Because of me, the inside of this car will seem . . . dangerous to them."

"Okay," Jack said.

"Just don't provoke them."

"Ha!"

She looked at Trey. "I will get out first and walk around to your side. That will give the thieves a chance to understand about me. When I reach you, come out. But do not move too fast."

Trey said, "Got it."

She swung open her door and stepped outside.

**IN THE LIGHT** of the gas lamp, Trey saw a cloud of wasps rise around Mariama. He waited for them to descend again and envelop her. For her to fall, to be dead before she hit the ground.

But it didn't happen. The thieves rose, yes, but to escape. In an instant, the car hood and the windshield were wiped clean.

"Holy shit," Jack said. "She *is* the Terminator."

From his position behind the wheel, Trey caught a glimpse of Mariama's expression. There was relief there, but a kind of fierce joy, too. The joy you take in learning that your power over an enemy is undiminished.

After a moment, she began to walk around the car. The thieves hovering within five feet of her retreated. The ones farther off, either in the air or on the ground, stayed where they were, but there was a tension in their posture that Trey hadn't witnessed before.

He knew that he shouldn't ascribe human emotions to them, but Trey thought he was seeing fear. The thieves were afraid of her.

Mariama reached his side of the car and looked in at him. When he nodded, she swung his door open and took a step back.

Trey breathed in. The voice of the hive mind had receded, and he could hear only his heart thudding and the hum of wings.

Steadily, but not too fast, he stepped out of the car, slammed the door behind him, and straightened.

Beyond Mariama, a cloud of wasps whirled. As Trey watched, one detached itself and flew directly at him. A blur. If it had tried to sting him, he would have had no defense. But it paused, hovering just in front of his face, dipping a little closer, pulling back.

He saw its abdomen pulsing as it spun away.

"We must hurry," Mariama said.

**TO TREY IT** felt like being inside a dome. A shaken globe filled with black and crimson snow. Every step, the cloud whirled around them, up above, to the side, never closer than a half dozen feet. Taking a single glance behind him, he saw that a multitude of thieves had fallen again upon the car.

The sinking sun had disappeared behind a screen of haze near the horizon, turning crimson wings the color of dried blood. Somewhere not far away, a dog gave a sudden series of high-pitched yelps before falling silent.

Trey and Mariama walked. The wasps that had been staking out the pathway to the house and the stairs made way as they approached. Farther away, others rose on their spidery legs, twisting their heads to mark the humans' progress.

The voice inside Trey stayed silent.

Mariama reached the foot of the staircase, Trey a step behind. Most of the stairs were now clear, but at the top a battalion of thieves held their ground. Others moved around the edges of the dark rectangle made by the open door. Farther inside, unseen wings hummed.

A group, five, or maybe ten, came from somewhere off to the side, swooped low over Trey's head, and sped away. The sight of them flickered at the corner of his vision like the aura that precedes a migraine.

"Stay close to me," Mariama breathed into his ear. "You're in danger."

"I had no idea," he said, just as quietly.

Her indrawn breath might have contained a laugh.

"Listen," he said, his eyes on the thieves staring down at him from the top step. "If they decide I'm worth killing, you have to get the others out. You have to save them."

He heard her sigh. "I will do my best," she said. "I promise."

Then she said, "All right. Let's go in."

But even as Trey lifted his right foot onto the first step, he heard a sound that froze him as if he'd been staked to the ground.

A long, drawn-out scream.

He twisted around. The front passenger door of the Audi hung open. Jack lay writhing on the ground beside it, facedown, his arms up near his head, his feet kicking at the grass. Floundering forward in an attempt to escape that he must have known was hopeless.

Nearly every exposed patch of skin—his arms, his hands, his calves where his jeans had hiked up—was covered in wasps.

Especially his face. His eyes. A riot of legs and wings and mandibles.

As Trey watched, pinned in place, Jack's head turned

toward them. His mouth stretched wide open. He gave a wet, choking cry that must have begun as another scream.

Finally Trey awoke from his shock. But before he could move, before he could run back to try to save his friend, Mariama's hands grasped his arms. Her fingers were as strong as manacles.

"No!" Her voice a whip crack, designed to grab his attention. "Trey—it's too late!"

He tried to wrench away from her, but she hung on to him with strength born of desperation. "Trey," she said, each word like a gasp. "Trey! They'll kill you, too. Look at them. Look!"

He pulled his gaze away from Jack's quivering form. All around, the thieves had risen into the air. Their spinning flight, with him and Mariama at the center of the vortex, seemed to Trey to have an edge of hysteria to it. Joy or rage or some alien mixture of both.

Emotions mirrored in the awakening consciousness within him.

"Come on!" Mariama said.

Trey turned his back to the car and, together, he and Mariama ascended the wooden steps.

From behind them came the sound of Jack's last, shuddering breath.

SILENCE INSIDE THE house. Stillness.

Green eyes watched them from the dark corners where the walls met the ceilings. From the shadowy edges of paintings showing sailboats raising colorful spinnakers on bright blue oceans. From behind the DVD player, the rims of vases, and especially amid the leaves of the potted rain forest plants arrayed to catch the sun through a big, cheerful bay window facing south.

Only there was no sun now.

Trey and Mariama stood in the center of the living room. To the right was an open kitchen separated by a granite counter. Sitting on the counter were half-full glasses of what looked like iced tea, a newspaper folded in half, and a plate holding a peanut butter sandwich with one bite taken out of it. A thief stood on top of the sandwich. Not moving, just watching, like the rest of them.

The odor here was very strong, but Trey barely noticed it. He breathed, in and out, until he felt his heart begin to slow, his vision clear.

Then he pointed. "There."

A short hallway led to three doors. Two were open, showing glimpses of bedrooms beyond. The third was closed. Trey could see part of a blue towel jammed in the gap between the bottom of the door and the wooden threshold.

Trey took a step toward the closed door but felt a hand on his arm. Mariama said, "Wait," then gestured toward the kitchen.

They took a detour around the counter. Reaching up into one of the glass-fronted cabinets above the sink, she took down a tall plastic glass. From the counter she grabbed a section of the newspaper.

Turning to look at Trey, she said, "Now we're ready."

# FORTY-SIX

**"SHEILA," TREY CALLED** out.

"Trey!" Disbelieving.

Then Kait's voice. "Are the wasp-things gone?"

Trey's gaze strayed to the end of the corridor. Wings flickered in the shadows.

"No," Mariama said. "But we won't let them hurt you."

A pause. Then Sheila said, "Trey, who is that?"

Trey said, "Mariama." He took a breath. "A friend. Listen to her, and we'll get you out of there."

*Let it be true.*

Mariama seemed to have no doubts. She called, "Unlock the door, then go to the far end of the room."

"It's small," Sheila said.

"As far as you can."

After a moment, they heard the ratchety sound of a bolt sliding. Mariama put a hand on Trey's arm for five seconds, ten, before giving him a nod. He reached out, turned the knob, and, pushing against the jammed towel's resistance, swung the door open.

The three of them stood arrayed against the opposite wall of the small room, where the white and blue tiles met the edge of the glass-walled shower. Mary, pale, exhausted, her arm protectively over Kait's shoulders, Sheila a stride in front of them.

Trey stepped quickly into the room. Behind him, Mariama twisted around in a circle, scanning for thieves—or warning them—then swung the door shut and jammed the towel back in the gap.

Trey let his eyes search the room for any other possible entry point. Someone had covered the vent in the ceiling with a towel, carefully pushing the cloth as deep as she could into each open slot. They'd even thought to jam washcloths into the faucets and drains.

Kait broke from her grandmother's grasp, ran forward, and threw herself into Trey's arms. "I *told* them you would come," she said.

As Trey hugged her, he lifted his gaze and looked at Sheila. Her face was pale, her eyes bloodshot, but she looked focused. Intent. Determined.

She opened her mouth to speak, then saw something in his expression that closed it again.

"Where's Jack?" she asked.

Trey said nothing, just kept his gaze on hers. After a moment her hand went to her mouth. She closed her eyes, and when she opened them again they were red.

"Well, we're certainly glad you're here," Mary said. Trey saw dark circles under her eyes and a crepelike texture to her skin that he hadn't noticed before.

Looking back at him, she seemed to read his thoughts. Her mouth firmed. "Now tell us how we get out of here."

Trey deposited Kait back onto the floor. She looked up at him. "The wasp-things are all over the place," she said. "Why didn't they sting you?"

"Bunny, we'll find out later," Sheila said. She looked from Trey to Mariama. "Yes—what do we do?"

Squatting under the overhead light, Mariama put the plastic glass on the floor and laid the newspaper flat beside it. Then her hands went up and behind her neck. She undid the silver chain and lowered the locket.

But it wasn't the photograph of her father that she was interested in. With quick motions of her nimble fingers, she pressed on the sides of the locket. And it was the back, not the front, that sprang open, revealing a hidden compartment.

Beside her, Trey looked inside and saw three tiny red spheres. Seeds. He'd seen ones like them before. Fitted into the space next to them was a minuscule plastic pouch containing a brown powder.

The hive mind inside released a flash of pure white light inside his head. Some violent sensation ran along his spine and made him shiver.

Mariama pointed at the glass with her chin. "Trey, please fill it. All the way."

When he returned, she was holding the pouch between the thumb and forefinger of her right hand. As he held the glass, she opened it and then, with infinite care, poured the powder in.

A pungent, spicy odor rose from the glass. Like ginger, with a trace of cinnamon mixed in. Trey recognized it, too, although he'd smelled it just once before. Months before, in the Casamance.

It was the smell of the vines, the only healthy plants in the dying forest. And those were the red seeds that the vines produced.

After a moment, Mariama straightened. "All right," she said. "Now the three of you will drink some of this. You first, Sheila. A sip at a time until I tell you to stop."

Sheila was suspicious. "What about Trey?"

Mariama's gaze glimmered in his direction. "There is only enough for the three of you. Anyway, Trey is already protected."

Sheila was unconvinced. "What is it?"

Mariama opened her mouth as if to dismiss the question, then took in a breath. "I'll explain fully later," she said, "when we're—free. We make this powder from a plant, the one Trey saw. It contains a substance that protects us from the thieves, and it will protect you as well."

"What kind of substance?" Sheila said.

Mariama compressed her lips, but again she answered. "An alkaloid. Or a combination of them. We don't know."

Sheila's face darkened. "An alkaloid? You mean a poison."

Mariama just looked at her. It was Kait who spoke. "A poison that makes the thieves sick?" she said. "But not us?"

Mariama smiled. "Yes. That is exactly right. Only it does more than make them sick: It kills them. Then it spreads. They pass it on, one to the next. Maybe through the air, or maybe when they touch each other. We're not certain."

She looked back at the closed door. "What we do know

is that this poison, this alkaloid, can kill entire colonies, whole populations of thieves. They will not expose themselves to it unless they have no choice." Her eyes flashed. "Here, today, they have a choice. They will leave you alone."

Trey said to Kait, "Have you heard of poison dart frogs?"

After a moment, she nodded. "Yes, I saw them on a TV show once. They were beautiful." She paused. "I should draw them."

"Well," Trey said, "alkaloids are the chemicals they keep in their skin."

Mariama nodded. "Plants contain alkaloids. Insects eat the plants. Frogs eat the insects—and end up with the poisons inside them."

"Anything that eats the frogs will die," Trey said. "But the frogs themselves are fine."

"And you will be fine, too," Mariama said.

Sheila was still looking skeptical. "How did you discover this miracle cure?"

"It's not a cure," Mariama said. "It's a protective weapon, just like the frogs have."

"And you came upon it by chance?"

"No." Now Mariama let a flicker of anger show, and Sheila's eyes widened. "Not by chance. The furthest thing from chance."

Mary stirred and spoke. "I don't understand."

Mariama closed her eyes for a moment. When she opened them she was calm again. "Trey knows this: that everything in nature is a battle, a contest."

"Yes," Trey said. "Endless rounds of one-upmanship over the generations."

"Over millions of years." Mariama nodded. "For example: Insects eat plants, so plants evolve poisons to ward off the insects. Then the insects learn how to eat the poisonous plants, and the plants evolve even more poisons."

"Like milkweed, which is as toxic a plant as you can imagine," Trey said. "It's like eating latex. Poison. Yet monarch caterpillars eat it, and wasps and spiders eat monarchs."

Mariama said, "If a plant was ever going to evolve a toxin poisonous to the thieves—and if animals were ever going to discover and utilize that toxin—it would be in the Casamance, where both the wasps and the plants evolved. My homeland."

She turned her palms up, letting her frustration show. "Please, let us talk more later. Now drink."

Sheila said, "One last thing."

Mariama waited.

"There's no way that we can infect—or inoculate—ourselves with this poison immediately. It will take far longer than that."

Mariama said, "That is true."

"But we'll be safe anyway?"

"Yes. The thieves, they can't tell. They can sense, *smell*, when we've been exposed, but not how long the toxin has been inside. Soon after you drink, they will do almost anything to avoid you."

"How do you know all this?" Kait asked.

Mariama's gaze turned toward her. "I told you," she said finally. "My people have lived among the thieves for a long time. They have learned how to kill us, but we have learned how to kill them, too."

Kait nodded. It made sense. She was convinced.

"Sheila," she said. "Grandma Mary. Drink."

**AFTERWARD THEY SAT**, mostly in silence, for about a half hour. Then Mariama said, "All right. It's time."

Kait wriggled her shoulders. "I am *so* ready to get out of here."

"Me, too," Mariama said.

She explained what they were to do. She would lead the way, followed by Kait, Mary, and Trey. Sheila would take the end of the line.

"No," Trey said. "I'll go last."

Mariama's eyes flashed. "You'll do as I say, please."

Then, without waiting, she yanked the towel out and swung the door open.

**SOMEHOW TREY HAD** expected there to be a waiting horde just outside the door, but the house seemed deserted. Nothing left but the thieves' scent.

"The alkaloid," he said.

"They don't like to be in enclosed spaces with it, no," Mariama said. "But they are not gone."

She was right. Even as she stepped out the front door and into the darkness, Trey could hear the sound of movement.

Kait darted back behind Mary and leaned in close to Sheila, who put her arm around the little girl's shoulders. If Mariama noticed the change in order, she made no protest.

Without thinking, Trey turned back and touched Kait's hair. She looked up at him.

"You're an amazing girl," he whispered to her.

And got, from this amazing girl, the ghost of a smile.

**THE NIGHT AIR** was cold and damp. Wisps of fog swirled through the circle of yellow light cast by the streetlamp.

There was no sign of anything living—no birdsong, no dogs barking, no human conversation or laughter— except the relentless presence of the thieves that still besieged the house.

The five humans stood atop the stairs that led down to the lawn, to the pathway, to the car. Trey could tell that the effect darkness has on the deepest roots of the human nervous system was spreading its tendrils even into this intrepid crew.

Kait's smile had long since vanished, and her short breaths were almost gasps. Mary was leaning heavily on the railing. Sheila's head was turning this way and that, as if she were trying to see through the darkness, as if seeing the thieves coming would protect her.

Only Mariama seemed unmoved. "All right," she said. "Trey, give me your car keys."

She put them in her pocket and then took a step forward, her head tilted. They all listened to the responding whirl and hum of the invisible horde.

For an instant, the hum grew louder, broke apart. Trey felt something ripple through his hair—the current of air created by unseen wings.

Mariama felt it, too. "All right," she said again, her

tone a degree grimmer than it had been. "Let's try something else. Trey, you carry Kait."

"I don't need to be carried," Kait said at once.

"I know." Mariama's voice was firm. "I know you don't. This isn't to protect you, but him."

"Forget it," Trey said. "I'm not using her as a human shield."

For a moment Mariama didn't reply. Then she said, "Trey, they are beginning to understand what you are. If you refuse, I think you won't reach the bottom of the stairs."

Kait pulled away from Sheila and stepped over to him. Like a little girl, she raised her arms.

"Up I go," she said.

After a moment, Trey hoisted her up onto his right hip. He felt one of her arms drape along his shoulder, her other hand touch his shirt just above his heart.

He said, "Thank you."

"It's okay." Then, "Sorry I'm so heavy."

He looked into her face, just a blur in the shadows close to his, and hoped she could see or hear his smile. "Are you kidding?" he said. "I could carry you for miles."

She shifted a little on his hip and said, "Just to the car, please."

Mariama led them down the stairs.

**MARIAMA, MARY, TREY** and Kait, Sheila.

Eight steps to the ground, ten down the path. Unseen multitudes of thieves watched them from the darkness. The occasional green-ice gleam when multifaceted eyes caught the light.

An overwhelming *awareness* all around them.

As they drew closer to the car, Trey could see the humped shape lying near it. Eyes that were holes of infinite blackness, bared teeth gleaming in the light.

At the same moment, he heard Sheila draw in a breath, understanding what she was seeing.

Trey shifted his grip on Kait, who had stiffened. With his left hand, he turned her head so that she was facing in toward his shoulder.

"Sweetie, don't look," he said. "Just . . . don't."

She put both arms around his neck and buried her face against his collarbone.

Trey saw that Mariama had taken Mary's arm. They walked the last few steps to the car. Mariama, keys in her hand, said, "Kait, get down now. But stay close to Trey."

When Kait was standing beside him, her arm around his waist, Mariama said, "I'll go in first. The rest of you wait until I tell you."

She swung open the back door, then the driver's one, and slid in behind the wheel with an eel-like quickness. A moment later, the engine roared and the headlights went on. Trey saw moving shadows, harsh in the brilliant light, recede from the beams into the more impregnable darkness behind.

But Mariama wasn't concerned with anything outside the car. Trey saw her turn on the overhead lights, saw her twist around in her seat. Wasps rose from all around her, fleeing through the open doors.

She climbed into the back, checking under the seats, in the storage compartments and seatback pockets and cup holders. Trey could see she'd done this before.

Once, then a second time, she paused. Her hand darted with the speed of a snake striking, and a moment later the smell of the thieves rose more strongly.

"Next time," Mariama said, "leave when your friends do."

She turned her head. "It's clear."

Kait scrambled into the backseat beside her. Trey helped Mary in as well and slammed the door. Once the two of them were inside, Sheila climbed quickly through the driver's side into the passenger seat. As Trey got behind the wheel, he saw her look down at the ground, at Jack. She took a deep breath but said nothing.

Trey closed his door, put the car into reverse, and sped down the driveway, the tires kicking up gravel. Looking back one last time at the house, he saw movement at the edges of the headlights' beam, a last huge swirl in the darkness as the thieves rose to leave the abandoned building.

Pulling out into the quiet street, he aimed them back toward the mainland. A quarter of a mile ahead, at the intersection with a bigger road, he could see traffic. It seemed surreal, that people were still living their lives out here.

"Where to?" he asked.

"Someplace to eat," Mariama said. "We all need some food. We have to be able to think."

"I couldn't eat," Mary said.

"You must."

Kait was twisted around in her seat, looking back the way they'd come. "But won't they be following us?"

"No, I don't think so. Not as we are now."

"Then we're safe?"

When no one answered, she frowned and shook her head, as if disappointed in herself.

"I won't ask that again," she said.

# FORTY-SEVEN

**THE FIRST PLACE** they found was a diner, with harsh fluorescent lighting, Formica tabletops, a white caddy containing little plastic containers of jams and jellies, paper placemats adorned with ads from local businesses, and a little can of worn crayons that Kait immediately reached for.

Even as she drew, her face turned away, Trey could tell that she was alert to every word they spoke.

The rest of them were quiet, numb, as they studied the menu, merely mentioning out loud what they might order. Yet even through his haze of shock and sorrow, Trey realized he was hungry. Mariama had been right: They were running on empty. They needed fuel.

Jack would have ordered half the dishes on the menu. He also would have filled the quiet with jokes, observations, *words*. He'd hated quiet above all else.

Sheila had been dead-silent throughout, her face clenched, her eyes dark. After they'd ordered, she looked up and said to Mariama, "I don't care how much of that potion you had. You should have saved some for Jack."

Mariama, calm as always, returned the fierce gaze. But she seemed troubled as well.

"Jack shouldn't have mattered to them," she said.

"But he did."

"Yes, and I don't understand it." She paused. "The last place the thieves would have wanted to be was in the car—not after I'd been there. The smell should have terrified them. Since he was just another human to them—of no special concern—he should have been safe."

At that moment, Trey realized the truth. Understood it and felt a deep swerve toward sorrow.

"Oh, God," he said. "It's my fault."

Everyone looked at him. Taking a deep breath, he said, "Jack was of 'special concern.' Mariama, he killed one, too. An adult. Back in July."

He saw Mariama's face set.

"The one that came back with me from Australia, when I was infected."

"I see," she said.

Trey's voice sounded harsh in his own ears. "That means Jack was doomed, wasn't he? The moment we left the car, he was doomed."

Mariama did not reply.

He looked down at the tabletop, at the pattern in the brown Formica, designed to mimic wood. Somewhere, most likely in China, there was a factory built to fabricate fabricated wood. Was it still open? Or were the workers hiding at home, and were the plastic molds crawling with wasps?

"I always thought when Jack went, he'd go down fighting," he said. "With some grand, noble gesture, something brave and stupid. Not . . . this."

"Trey," Mariama said, "you're missing something."

Sheila said, "Yes, you are."

Trey raised his eyes.

"*You* might not have realized that the thieves would target Jack, but I am sure that *he* did," Mariama said.

Trey was silent.

"And I think he knew what might happen to him." She leaned toward him. "He knew that some thieves might get in when we opened the car door, or through the vents. He knew that it's nearly impossible to keep them out if they want to get in.

"He knew, but he kept quiet, because he wanted you to save the others. Because he understood that there was no other way: We couldn't bring him with us, we couldn't protect him when we went into the house, and you wouldn't have been willing to leave him to die. So he did what he had to do."

Very softly from beside him, Sheila said, "She's right, Trey. That was Jack."

She leaned closer. "A grand, noble gesture," she said. "Something incredibly brave . . . but not stupid."

Mariama nodded. "We should each have such an honorable death."

THEY ATE IN near silence. Burgers for Trey and Mary, gumbo for Mariama ("It reminds me of some of the soups we have at home," she said), Caesar salad for Sheila, and chicken fingers with honey mustard for Kait. "I eat it everywhere," she told them, "and compare."

There was a television on the wall in the corner, but it was shut off. When they asked the waitress what news they had missed, she shrugged.

"The president will be back in the White House tomorrow," she said. "He's gonna speak again then, but it'll just be words. And what good do words do?"

Besides that, she said, the news was filled with reported sightings of the wasps in places they hadn't been seen before. Only a few reports of attacks, virtually none confirmed, but people were staying inside, stores and schools were closed, businesses were shuttered.

The waitress looked around the diner. Only about a half dozen seats were occupied in a space that could have fit eighty.

"Some of us have to work, though," she said. "What choice do I have? Bugs or no bugs, I bet the government is still planning to take its chunk out of my paycheck."

When she was gone, Trey said, "All these reports. Are people just noticing them now, or are the thieves really showing up in new places?"

"The latter," Mariama said without hesitation. "I told you they'd become more brazen, and that's what they're doing. They're testing us."

"And next?" Sheila asked.

"Next? They're in no hurry. They'll wait to see how we respond."

"CAN I ASK you something?" Kait said to Mariama near the end of the meal. She had folded up her drawing and stowed it in a pocket and was now looking down on a huge piece of red velvet cake with gloppy icing and a scoop of melted ice cream.

The rest of them were drinking coffee.

"Of course," Mariama said.

"How do you know that the poison is going to protect you?"

Mariama looked thoughtful. "As I told you, back in Senegal we have lived with these creatures for a long time. We could hardly help but learn something about them."

Kait put her fork down with a little clatter and sat up straight in her chair.

"No," she said. "That's not what I mean. I mean, *every time* you go where the thieves are, how do you know it will save you? How can you be sure it will work?"

Again a pause. Then Mariama said, "I can never be sure."

"The wasp-things must hate you," Kait said.

Mary said, "Kaitlin!"

"It's all right." Mariama paused. "I don't know if they feel 'hate,' but they definitely know who I am—and that I have killed many of them."

Kait thought about this. "So you are being brave, too, whenever you go outside." Her eyes widened. "Whenever you go *anywhere*."

Mariama just smiled at her and didn't reply.

Mary stirred cream into her coffee. After saying little through the meal, she seemed to be regaining some focus.

"So, inside that locket of yours," she said.

Mariama tilted her head. "Yes, what about it?"

"You brought the powder from Africa. Did you come all this way to save us? To save the world?"

Mariama's smile turned rueful. "I suppose," she said. "I suppose that was what I was hoping to do—bring the sample to Trey, have him take it to the Centers for Disease Control. I thought they'd listen to him, the way they wouldn't to some unknown lady from Senegal. I dreamed they'd synthesize it, produce it in large quantities, and— yes—save the world."

The amusement had left her face. "But it was a hopeless dream. Even if I hadn't been imprisoned, I would have been far too late. Bureaucracies don't work fast enough."

She shrugged. "And now it doesn't matter anyway."

Trey said, "Were the seeds going to save us, too?"

"Yes." She reached up and took off the locket. Popped open the false back and carefully dropped the three red seeds onto the table. One of them rolled a few inches away, but Kait corralled it with two fingers and pushed it close to the others.

"You harvest the alkaloid from these seeds?" Sheila asked.

"It is also found in the leaves, but, yes, it's most con- centrated in the fruit and the seed coverings."

Trey thought it over. "So some mammals eat the fruit. The alkaloid doesn't harm them, and they absorb enough of it to protect them while they disperse the vine's seeds."

Mariama nodded.

"I saw squirrels in those vines," Trey said.

"Yes. They eat the fruit, are unharmed, and disperse the seeds. All a balance, with everyone getting what they need."

"Except the wasps," Sheila said.

Mariama shook her head. "It worked for them as well,

historically. In a forest with so many mammals, so many primates, there've always been enough that didn't carry the poison. And the vine only grows in light gaps, so there were vast stretches of forest without it." She grimaced. "Until about twenty years ago."

"When logging arrived," Trey said. "And hunting for bushmeat."

"Yes. Fewer mammals and more light gaps. More vines. The balance was destroyed."

Sheila said, "And presto, the thieves need to move to more hospitable turf. So they start to search."

Mariama nodded.

"Only to find a world filled with hosts—and no vines. No alkaloids. No defense."

Mariama said, "That's right."

Trey looked down again at the seeds. "You brought the seeds so we could grow the plants here."

"Yes, that was my plan. To help people grow their own protection."

"Mariama Appleseed."

Her smile turned into a sigh. "Now we must depend on our other plan."

Trey thought: Yes.

The only one left that made any sense.


**HE WAS WAITING** for the waitress to bring his credit card back, imagining the worldwide chaos that would ensue in the first ten minutes after the computers that approved credit-card transactions crashed, when Sheila said to Mariama, "There's one thing we're still not sure about. The 'summoning.'"

A spasm of something that looked like disgust crossed Mariama's face. "You haven't encountered that?"

"No, not yet."

Trey said, "Jack thought it might be a fungus."

Mariama gave him a curious look.

"Like the fungi that infect the brains of ants and other insects—make them crawl to the top of bushes before dying. You must have seen them."

"Of course." Mariama's expression was bleak. "No, it's not a fungus. You will see."

That was all she would say.

IT WAS KAIT who broke the silence that followed. Her eyes on Mariama, she said, "You're a butterfly."

Mariama smiled at her and said, "Thank you."

The corners of Kait's mouth turned downward. "No. Listen. I read a story this year. What was it called, Grandma?"

"Which story?" Mary rolled her eyes. "You read so many."

"The one about the dinosaurs. And the big gun."

Trey said, " 'A Sound of Thunder,' by Ray Bradbury?"

"Right!" Kait looked back at Mariama. "Have you read it?"

Mariama shook her head.

"This man travels back in time to hunt dinosaurs. It's like a safari. You have to stay on a boardwalk and you're not allowed to kill anything there except a dinosaur, because all dinosaurs went extinct anyway. You understand? If you killed something else, it might change the future."

Mariama, a little wide-eyed, said, "Yes?"

"Well, this man, he gets scared and runs off the boardwalk. When they get back to the future—" Her hands grasped at air. "I mean, their *present*, they find everything's different. The world is different. The man looks at his shoe and sees that when he went off the boardwalk, he'd stepped on a butterfly. That's all it took to change the future—one butterfly!"

After a moment, Mariama said, "Why is the story called 'A Sound of Thunder'?"

"Because at the end this other man, the one who took him to hunt dinosaurs, he shoots him." Again Kait frowned. "But that's not the point. I was talking about the story with my—"

She took in a quick breath, almost a gasp, and her eyes filled with sudden tears. Scowling, wiping the back of her hand across her face, she went on.

"I was talking with Ma about the story, and she said that with most things, it doesn't matter whether they live or die, it doesn't change anything." Her chin lifted. "They matter to the people who love them, Ma said, but not to the future. Not like the butterfly in the story did."

"I think I agree with your mother," Trey said. "We're like—" He hesitated. "Like molecules of water in the ocean. Individually, we're just not that important."

"Oh, but you are," Kait said.

Everyone looked at her. Red spots appeared on her fair cheeks, but she went on.

"People like me and Grandma, we might only be important to each other—"

"And to us," Sheila said.

Kait shook her head. "But you—" She pointed at Mariama. "You." Sheila. "And you." Trey.

"You three," she said. "You're the butterflies."

None of them knew what to say.

"So don't die," Kait said. "Okay?"

# FORTY-EIGHT

*BRAZEN.*

That was the word Mariama had used, and that was what the thieves had become. Brave. Fearless. Brazen.

It had begun immediately after the failed helicopter assault in Florida. ("A disastrously ill-conceived October Surprise whose only lasting impact may be the end of a presidency," as one prestigious newspaper put it.)

Now, less than two weeks later, it seemed like they were everywhere. Spreading through nature preserves and city parks. Occupying rent-controlled apartment blocks and expensive suburban developments. Establishing colonies in beachside dunes and golf resort sand traps.

Far more visible than ever before. And why not? Why should they worry about being seen? People were terrified of them. No one would go near an adult thief, much less try to kill it. Everyone knew you couldn't fight them without risking an overwhelming attack in response.

The media, as always, stoked terror in the guise of

providing information. You couldn't watch the cable news networks without seeing endless replays of the Florida catastrophe, along with footage of several other large attacks in different parts of the world.

Trey had seen one filmed in Russia. The screams had echoed in his head all day. After that, he stayed away from the coverage. It had nothing to teach him.

He did see one newspaper chart that was updated each day. With colorful graphics, it tracked the thieves' progress across the world.

"Just like our old map," Sheila said.

She was right. The chart showed how the wasps had followed trade and travel routes, radiating outward from Africa to ports, canals, and big cities around the world. From there, blessed with abundant food supplies and hosts for their offspring, they'd undergone an enormous population explosion, colonizing new territory in all directions and at breakneck speed.

By now, they'd established themselves on six continents. Only Antarctica had remained untouched, though one thief, dead of some unknown cause, had been found aboard a supply ship heading to McMurdo Station.

Mariama had shrugged at this news. "I do not think they'll try to populate Antarctica."

"Too cold?" Trey had asked.

She'd sighed. "I used to dream of living in a cold climate, because it would make me free of them at last. Now I think no place is safe. The thieves are opportunistic and hardy. If they have to live inside in the coldest regions, in corners, in attics and storerooms, they will."

"Then why is Antarctica exempt?"

"I didn't say it was." Mariama had looked directly into

his eyes. "The thieves won't bother with it because it is doomed. Those few humans at McMurdo pose no threat, and they will die off on their own soon enough after the end comes."

That was what conversations with Mariama were always like. Not if. Not even when.

After.

**AFTERNOON SHADING INTO** dusk in Central Park. Some late-season softball players were trying to get a game together on the Great Lawn, but there weren't enough of them to make two teams. The thieves had been staying away from the park's big open expanses, so far, but so were most people. Coming out here, as these young men and women were doing, was itself an act of defiance.

"This feels strange," Sheila said.

Trey said, "Well, yeah."

She gave him a sideways look. They were sitting on a splintery bench under the cold autumn sun, side by side, facing the empty gray grass.

"I mean," Sheila said, "where's Jack?"

"I knew what you meant." Trey sighed. They were here in the park because they'd gone to the museum to clear out what they'd left in Jack's office. Books, mostly. And memories.

Sheila slid down on the bench a little, leaning her head against the back, stretching her long legs out in the dirt. Her eyes were closed.

Trey thought she looked like she was made of some pure, icy substance: porcelain, maybe. Or unforged silver. Incomparably beautiful but untouchable as well.

"My mother's mother was one of twelve children," she said. "Nine of them died before they reached their sixth birthday."

She opened her eyes and stared down at her hands. "Can you imagine losing a brother or sister every year or two? Or burying your own children?"

Trey said, "We're the first generation to think we have the right to live forever."

The small group of softball players left the empty field and trailed past them.

"We were," Sheila said. "But that's finished."

Trey looked at her. After a moment, she sensed it and turned her head. Then, in an instant, her arms were around his neck and she was kissing him. Her lips were warm and soft, not porcelain, but there was something hungry, even desperate, about her grasp.

She broke away, loosened her grip, but kept her face close to his. "You," she said.

"What about me?"

"What Kait said: *Don't die.*"


**THEY WALKED PAST** Turtle Pond, its fringing brown cattails rattling in the breeze, to the area called the Ramble.

This hilly, densely wooded expanse had once been popular with two groups: gay men seeking rendezvous out of the public eye and birders seeking rarities. Today, though, it was the sort of place where only the insane would willingly venture.

The insane or the protected. Sheila had nothing to fear from the thieves. And Trey, though his safety was more equivocal, had decided not to hide, especially when he was in the company of one of the immunes.

They left the quiet park road, ghostly without its usual myriad of cyclists and joggers, and headed into the woods. Neither of them spoke, but they both knew what they were looking for.

It took only a few minutes. As always, the smell alerted them, at first just a harsh whiff carried away by the chilly breeze. Then stronger. A smell so omnipresent now, so familiar, that if they weren't searching they sometimes didn't even notice it.

The man lay on his back at the bottom of a small gully overgrown with bittersweet, mile-a-minute, and other invasive vines. He was wearing black pants, the right leg ripped to the knee, a Hannah Montana T-shirt, and an unzipped down jacket that had once been cream colored but was now caked with dirt.

He looked like he'd been homeless long before the thieves summoned him.

It took Trey a minute to find the wasp guarding its larva. The creature gave itself away with movement among the vines, a quick, agitated back-and-forth. As thieves always were, it was disturbed to be close to the poison and, perhaps, to Trey as well. To the corrupt, half-finished remnant of the hive mind he contained.

The wasp's head twisted as it kept them in view. There was likely another one or more somewhere in the vicinity. Staying hidden, watching, waiting to see if they presented a threat.

Sheila was looking at the man. No one would try to help him, they both knew. No one would go near.

And his death would make as little impact as the deaths of the homeless men who perished out in the streets whenever the city was gripped by a deep freeze.

Beside Trey, Sheila shuddered. They'd made it a practice to stop, pause, wherever they found a human host, to seek them out in parks and vacant lots and beneath underpasses and abandoned piers.

It had been Sheila's idea, her insistence, to seek out the infected. "Someone has to acknowledge them," she'd said. "Someone has to remember that they were once human."

Though each time she saw one, each time she witnessed the inevitable, she seemed sadder, more haunted.

"Let's go," Trey said and took her arm.

But at that moment they heard a rustling in the brush beside the trail. A man emerged, another host. Walking with purpose, his head turning this way and that. Trey wondered what he was seeing through that silvery gaze.

"Trey," Sheila said in a sudden, tortured whisper. *"Look."*

Trey had already seen it: a thief clinging to the back of the man's neck. Its slender abdomen was arched, and as the man passed they could see that it had plunged its needlelike stinger deep into his flesh, just between the second and third cervical vertebrae. Its head turned to watch Trey and Sheila, twisting to stay on them as the man moved down the trail.

Trey and Sheila both understood what they were seeing. The summoning.

He should have guessed. He'd seen wasps do this before, riding their victims, guiding them to their doom with chemicals administered directly to their brains. Only their victims had been cockroaches and spiders and other wasps, not primates. Not human beings.

That colobus monkey he'd seen in the Casamance, staggering into the thief colony's clearing, it must have had a rider as well. Trey had missed it. He hadn't known what to look for.

The man followed a curve in the path and moved out of sight. Again Trey said, "Let's go," and this time Sheila didn't resist.

**THEY WALKED EAST** and then up to Eighty-sixth Street and met Mariama at a Starbucks. She was staying with some old acquaintances in a Senegalese neighborhood in Brooklyn, but every day she and Trey talked, made plans, prepared.

Got ready for *after*.

The Starbucks was reasonably crowded. Logically or not, people felt more secure indoors, especially in crowds. Anyway, no matter what, they still needed their coffee. The last human force in the final battle would be fueled by Starbucks.

Sheila's mind was still on the latest victims she and Trey had seen. "Nobody was looking for them," she said. "They had no one."

Mariama shrugged. "That's how predators hunt. You know that. They choose the weak. The vulnerable."

"They cull the herd," Sheila said.

Trey breathed in. Someone had left a newspaper on their table, the *Times*. The headlines were all about the ongoing plunge in the stock market, factories closing because not enough workers were showing up, oil prices skyrocketing.

The president counseled patience. But Anthony Harrison promised that, when *he* was elected, things would change, and fast.

"This herd won't put up with being culled," Trey said.

Mariama gave another shrug. "Then they'll be overwhelmed."

**"WHY DO I** have it inside me?" Trey asked. "The . . . mind?"

Mariama had hinted around, but until now he'd refused to talk about it. Suddenly, sitting here, he knew he was being ridiculous. After, there would be no room for anything but complete honesty.

She gave him a considering look, as if debating with herself how to answer.

"You saw," he went on. "You knew right away."

She nodded.

"That means you've seen it before."

After another moment, another nod. "Of course I have. There is nothing about the thieves that we haven't seen." She widened her eyes. "Except for their poison, they're not very complex."

"Complex enough to bring down a civilization," Sheila said.

Mariama shrugged. "A one-celled organism could do that."

She turned back to Trey. "How long had you been infected when Sheila removed the larva?"

"Two days, I think." He hesitated. "More. Closer to three."

She raised her hand and touched the side of his head. "And how did you feel . . . in here? Before the worm was removed?"

"Like my mind was being eaten from the inside."

"Yes." She dropped her hand. "Yes. Others have used similar words."

Sheila moved in her chair. "How much longer before he would have died from the surgery?"

"A few hours. Perhaps less. It is . . . not predictable."

"So that's what happens even if you live?" Trey found this hard to say. "Some of it gets left behind?"

"Or it causes some kind of permanent changes in the chemistry of the brain." Mariama frowned. "We do not know. In the Casamance, our scientists have not had the tools to study such things."

Sheila's gaze had turned inward. "I should have noticed sooner," she said. "And when I did, I shouldn't have hesitated."

"No." Mariama reached across the table and touched her gently on the arm. "You were brave. Even in the Casamance, many would not have been as brave as you."

Sheila didn't reply, but Trey thought she looked a little calmer within herself.

"And by waiting, we've gained something, too," Mariama went on.

Trey thought of the white light that had filled his brain as the Florida assault had begun, as the helicopters had burst into flames.

"Awareness," he said. "Knowledge."

Mariama nodded.

"But what has Trey lost?" Sheila said.

Mariama didn't reply at once. Trey glanced over at the

table next to theirs. A woman was huddled over her laptop with the news on the screen. She was watching a clip of Anthony Harrison giving a speech in front of a huge crowd. He was gesturing as he talked, pointing, his face alight with anger.

Trey looked back at Mariama. "What's inside me . . . it's never going away, is it?"

She tilted her head as she looked at him, her silence an answer.

"This—illness." He struggled to find the right word. "This condition. Does it get worse over time?"

After a moment, she said, "Yes. Most often . . . quite slowly. But, yes, it's progressive."

Sheila made an impatient movement. "Progressive," she said, spitting out the word. "I guess that leaves me only one option."

Trey said, "Which is?"

"To be the doctor who develops the cure."


**THEY STOOD OUTSIDE** the subway station. Eighty-sixth Street had always been a little shabby, but now it was virtually abandoned. Small groups of people, in threes and fours, headed into one or another of the electronics stores or fast-food restaurants, but the street had none of the market-day bustle it had once possessed.

"Five days till the election," Mariama said.

Sheila wrapped her coat closer. "What will happen?"

Trey said, "Harrison's going to win."

Mariama said, "And then—"

And then.

"Mary and Kait and I are seeing Jeremy Axelson and the Harrison campaign team tomorrow," Trey said.

"Will they listen?" Sheila asked.

"I doubt it."

Sheila said, "Is it worth it? Mary's worn out. I don't know how much help she'll be."

Trey said, "I don't think the greatest orator on earth could change their minds. And I'm no orator."

The wind gusted, blowing some old papers down the street and up into a brief messy whirlwind.

"But I have to try," he said.

# FORTY-NINE

**TWO CONVERSATIONS.**

The first took place in a hotel on Fifty-fourth Street between Madison and Fifth. Trey had never noticed it before: the Gaumont, a redbrick, five-story town house surrounded by restaurants and boutiques, with only a single modest sign hanging in front to announce its presence.

Inside, it was opulent but tasteful, all burnished oak and brocaded walls and oil paintings of handsome ladies and gentlemen in ornate gilt frames. As Trey and Mary and Kait waited outside the conference room door on the top floor, a man wearing livery pushed a wooden cart carrying silver-topped dishes down the hall.

Trey watched him go past and thought about the *Titanic*. Its maiden voyage had lasted—what?—four days and ended in two hours. Who was to say that the voyage of the human race couldn't last for millennia and end just as suddenly?

Kait said, "I didn't think Mr. Axelson would like a place like this."

Mary, who had been paging through a glossy magazine she'd found on a side table inlaid with mother-of-pearl, looked up. "I doubt he picked it."

"Then why is he here?"

"To celebrate," Trey said.

"But—"

"To celebrate quietly," he said, "since he has to pretend he doesn't know what will happen on Election Day."

He looked at Kait. She was wearing Uggs, purple tights, a red skirt, and a white sweater, all obviously new.

"You look nice," Trey said. Then, surprising himself, "Actually, make that *beautiful.*"

She stared down into her lap and blushed.

Mary managed a smile. "A Fifth Avenue shopping spree," she said and shrugged. "Heck, it's only money."

Trey nodded.

"Meaningless slips of paper," she said.

**THE HEAVY DOOR** to the conference room swung open, reflecting the shaded light cast by sconces set along the walls. A young woman in a business suit stood there. Her expression revealed a certain measure of curiosity, carefully masked.

"Please come in," she said.

She led them through the door into a lush, dim, red-carpeted room scattered with small desks, sideboards, gleaming tables, and soft-cushioned chairs. Two Secret Service men stood in the center of the room. At the far end, close to where the curtained windows let in some light from outside, sat Jeremy Axelson and a scowling man Trey recognized as Ron Stanhouse, Anthony Harrison's campaign manager. Two younger men wearing identical impatient expressions sat a little farther off.

Axelson stood, shook Mary's hand, and then bent over to get closer to Kait's level. "How are you doing, sweetie?" he said.

She looked into his face. "I'm fine." Then, "Are you going to listen to what Trey tells you?"

He blinked, then laughed as he straightened. "Of course we will."

"I mean it. *Listen*."

Some of the humor drained from his expression, and he raised his eyes to look at Trey. "I guess we'll have to see what Mr. Gilliard says, won't we?"

Whatever Mr. Gilliard was going to say, he had no intention of addressing it to Jeremy Axelson. Stepping past, he walked over and stood above Ron Stanhouse, who had not gotten to his feet or even rearranged his slouch.

Stanhouse leaned his head against the back of his shiny, brown-leather-and-gold-button chair. There was amusement tinged with malice in his expression.

"Behold," he said. "The man who won us an election."

Trey was silent.

"Without all your work—and that of your friends—we would never have connected the dots," Stanhouse went on, his lips twitching behind his beard. "You couldn't have helped us more if you'd been on the payroll."

"Well, that's what I live for, helping you." Trey kept his voice calm, but there was something in his expression that made Stanhouse's eyes widen. Trey felt the brief, light touch of Kait's hand on his arm.

"What I live for," he said again. "Yeah. I get it. It's victory lap time—or it will be in a few days. Well, go ahead, pat yourselves on the back and keep all the credit. I don't want it."

He took a step closer. Stanhouse, looking uncomfortable, stiffened a little in his chair.

"The question is," Trey went on, "what happens then?"

Stanhouse's lips twitched again. "Well, he'll work with Congress on a jobs package, and—"

Trey just looked at him, and after a moment Stanhouse wriggled his shoulders. "Why are you here, Gilliard?"

"To tell you: Back your guy off."

Stanhouse knew exactly what he was saying. The malice in his eyes rose to the surface. "Now? Why should we do that? Pre- or postelection, it's a winning issue."

"And a losing battle," Trey said.

Stanhouse looked disgusted. "Come on, Gilliard. Stop being such a pansy. They're just *bugs*."

Beside Trey, Kait made a small sound.

Trey felt his hands form fists. He thought of Agiru, the old Huli warrior, who'd said the same thing. But Agiru had understood the *binatang*. These men didn't.

"And how many lives," Trey said, "will you be willing to sacrifice to these bugs?"

Before Stanhouse could answer, Jeremy Axelson stepped between them. "Look, Trey," he said, "Governor Harrison has run on a platform of strength, of determination, and he won't back away from that now, no matter what your fears may be."

"He has a choice," Trey said.

Stanhouse said, in a tone of complete disgust, "Like what? What Chapman tried? Stashing a bunch of scientists in a lab somewhere, then waiting around for them to come up with a solution? Sure."

Again, it was Axelson who played the good cop. "You must understand that showing weakness now—or early in the first term—would send just the wrong message to the American people, to our allies, and to our enemies themselves."

"You saw what happened in Florida," Mary said to him.

"The president's mistake in Florida was in thinking too small," Stanhouse said. "I can promise you, we won't make the same mistake."

But Trey was barely listening to him. He'd heard this boilerplate before.

Instead, he was thinking about what Axelson had said. *Our allies.*

With a growing sense of horror, he said, "You're co-ordinating an attack on the thieves with other countries."

Stanhouse smiled at him. "You know only the president is allowed to do that . . . and our man isn't president. Yet."

Trey ignored this. "When is it going to happen, then? The attack. On Inauguration Day?"

Stanhouse didn't answer directly, but he didn't need to. Inauguration Day or soon thereafter, it didn't matter.

"Listen to me," Trey said. "*Listen.* It won't work. You'll lose."

We'll lose.

But Stanhouse was flapping a hand in dismissal.

"Those creatures," he said, "will not be allowed to rule our lives."

The meeting was over.

**THE SECOND CONVERSATION,** via telephone, was much shorter.

"Mr. Gilliard," Nathan Holland, the president's chief of staff, said. "What can I do for you?"

His voice, as gravelly as ever, echoed with exhaustion. He sounded a hundred years old.

Trey took a breath. "You need to tell President Chapman—"

"I have a better idea," Holland said. "Tell him yourself."

Trey said, "What?"

"Please hold," Holland said, bitter amusement in his voice, "for the president of the United States."

Waiting, Trey was struck by a vivid memory: sitting in various hotel rooms on his journeys into and out of the wilderness and watching repeats of *The West Wing* on television. How strange it always felt when the president talked to regular people.

There was a crackling over the receiver, and then a new voice, deeper than Holland's and more polished. Familiar.

"This is Sam Chapman," the voice said.

Trey plunged ahead. "Mr. President, you were on the right track. Your approach was on target, and it has to go on even if you lose. Somehow you need to convince Harrison of this."

"My approach?" There was an edge of amusement in the president's tone. "Which one?"

"The smart one. Calling together a team of scientists. Jack Parker from the American Museum, Clare Shapiro from Rockefeller—"

"I shut that effort down," the president said.

"Yes, I know, but you shouldn't have."

There was a pause, and then the president said, "You're right. It was a terrible mistake."

Trey was silent.

Chapman's voice was quiet. "You're far from the first to tell me this, of course. I should have had the will to see that effort through and not worried so much about losing the election."

His laugh was quieter than Holland's, but just as mirthless. "The election! I couldn't have done more to guarantee my defeat if I'd been working for the Harrison campaign myself."

Still Trey didn't speak.

"Be honest with me, though, Mr. Gilliard," Chapman went on. "Would it have made a difference, leaving that initiative in place? Would all my experts have figured out a way to defeat these creatures?"

"Defeat them?" Trey said. "No. Live with them? Coexist?" He took in a breath. "Maybe not. But it was the best of a bad set of options."

Now it was Chapman's turn to be silent for a few moments. When he finally spoke again, his voice was very quiet. "As you may have noticed, we're not much for 'living with' in this country. We don't do coexistence well. I'm also afraid—"

He fell silent.

Trey finished the sentence. "That the next administration won't do 'coexistence' at all."

Chapman sighed. "Nor will they listen to a word I—or anyone in my administration—says. Reinventing the wheel is a longtime tradition in our political system."

"I know," Trey said. "But I had to call."

To try.

The president cleared his throat. "I told Nathan I wanted to speak with you," he said. "To thank you for everything you've done since this all started."

Trey said, "Done?"

"You and Dr. Connelly. Going on television, talking to magazines. Providing real information. Trying to help people stay calm."

Trey said, "For all the good it did."

"Trying to do good counts."

"Thank you." Trey took a breath. "Mr. President?"

"Yes?"

"That secure location where you went after . . . Florida."

"You mean where they bundled me off to after the disaster. What about it?"

"Just . . . keep it handy."

Again the president laughed. "Thank you, Mr. Gilliard. But I'm not going to hide behind locked doors while my countrymen die around me. Not this time. Not again."

Trey was silent.

"I'm still the captain. Win or lose, that's how I'll always think of myself. If the ship goes down, I'm going down with it."

# FIFTY

Trey woke up pouring with sweat. Sheila, beside him in the bed, held him as he fought. "Trey—" she said. Then, when he focused on her, still half trapped by his dreams, she said, "What's it . . . saying?"

*It.*

Trey heard nothing but silence. It didn't matter. He was filled with cold certainty.

"It happens today," he said. "Not Inauguration Day. Today."

Her hand covered her mouth. "How can you be sure?"

Trey was quiet. How to explain the voice inside?

There was no explaining it. To understand you'd have to be like him. Not completely human anymore.

Sheila, watching, believing, took a deep breath and let her hand drop back to the sheets. Her chin lifted.

"If we have time," she said, "I still want to vote."

\* \* \*

**THE SILENCE ECHOING** inside him, Trey made a series of telephone calls.

Everyone was ready. They'd all been ready for days.

Except one. The one who mattered most.

"Still waiting on that part," Malcolm Granger said, his voice over the phone as cheerful and easygoing as always. "You told me we had days. Weeks."

"I was wrong. Can you get it today?"

Malcolm laughed. "Okay. Gonna take some hours, though. We got hours?"

The hive mind was as quiet as if it had fled forever, though he knew it hadn't. Trey knew it was there, though. Hiding.

No, not hiding. Waiting.

"I don't know," he said.

"No worries." Malcolm's tone was light. "Doesn't matter."

Trey didn't say anything.

"Listen," Malcolm said. "Whatever it's like when the time comes, we've flown through worse, you and me."

**SHEILA WANTED TO** watch the news. The reporters said that voting was light across the country. This was especially true in rural areas, places that required long drives, long walks, visibility, in order to cast your vote. But in cities, too.

During these last few days, the thieves had nearly disappeared. Only a scattering of reports of new attacks had come in, and many of those were late accounts of incidents that had taken place days earlier.

An unusual number of absentee ballots had been requested and filled out, yet overall voting numbers were way down. Only a small fraction of the typical turnout for a presidential election was making it to the polls.

"Low turnout favors the challenger," Sheila said. "It's the people who want change who go to the polling place no matter what."

"America, you have a choice to make," Anthony Harrison had said in his speech on Election Eve. "A life lived in fear . . . or one filled with hope?"

Words. They were just words.

There was no longer any choice at all.

**"LET'S GO."**

Trey looked at her. She returned his gaze, and color rose to her pale cheeks. Without speaking, she got to her feet and picked up her fleece jacket from the back of a chair.

"No matter where I've been living, I've stayed a citizen of this country, and I've always voted," she said, slipping her arms into it. "I even changed my registration to be able to vote here. I'm not going to miss this one."

Trey didn't argue, just walked to the door and waited as she found her shoulder bag.

*Don't be caught too far apart when the end comes,* Elena Stavros had said.

He wasn't going to convince her to stay in the apartment.

And he wasn't going to let her out of his sight.

* * *

**A BUS WENT** by down on Seventh Avenue, a flash of blue-white light, a squeal of brakes that sounded like a distress call. Trey could see a couple of dark figures inside. A few cars, windows rolled tightly up against the chill—or in a hopeless gesture at safety—followed. Other than that, the avenue was empty.

Nearly empty.

Sheila said, *"Damn."*

The man walked past without seeing them. He was wearing suit pants, black socks but no shoes. No jacket or dress shirt, just a sleeveless undershirt.

His eyes gleamed silver in the streetlight.

As he passed, they could see the thief on the back of his neck, its stinger buried deep. A summoning, out in the open.

Trey caught a glimpse of the nightmare that had woken him that morning: Hundreds, thousands of people with their thief riders. Filling the streets. Filling the city.

The doomed man walked into a trash-strewn alley between a closed flower shop and an empty storefront that had once housed a pet store. Trey began to follow.

"Forget it," Sheila said. "Let's go."

Then, uncharacteristically, she added, "Trey, I've seen enough."

But he hadn't. He took a few steps into the mouth of the alley. "Come here," he said.

Still she hung back.

"Sheila."

She came up beside him. The man they'd followed had slumped back against the flower shop's crumbling brick wall.

A few feet farther down the alley lay a second man, and at their feet a woman was flat on her back. She looked as if she were staring up through the gap between the buildings, trying to see the stars.

"Three . . ." Sheila's voice was just a breath. "Together."

But this was only part of it. "Look," Trey said.

Sheila saw. These were no homeless people, no pierside prostitutes, no runaways. Not the ones so easily sacrificed while the rest stayed safe.

The second man's coat was open, revealing a dark suit, white shirt, a tie that might have been red but looked black in the faint light. The skirt of the woman's expensive suit was hiked up, revealing sheer hose that had run and legs bluish from the cold.

Trey raised his gaze, peering into the shadows. He knew what he was looking for, and in a few moments he found it. Two pairs of eyes. No, three, faceted gleams like green diamonds reflecting moonlight.

Darker than the shadows, the thieves moved forward to the mouth of the alley. Then stopped there, a half dozen feet from where Trey and Sheila stood. Staying far enough away to be safe from Sheila, but still sending a message as comprehensible as if they'd used words.

*Don't come any closer. We'll sacrifice ourselves to save our young, but we'll kill you first.*

"Let's go," Trey said. Sheila nodded.

But then a sobbing woman pushed past them.

**SHE WAS BEYOND** reach and down the alley before Trey or Sheila could do a thing to stop her. He took a step to follow, but Sheila grabbed his arm, hard, and yanked him back.

"No!" she said. Then, more quietly, "Trey, it's too late."

She was right. He took a breath and steeled himself to watch what happened next. The inevitable.

Only it wasn't what he expected.

He'd been sure that the thieves would make short work of the woman, but that was not what took place. Although they all rose high on their legs in the alarm posture, the wasps stayed where they were. Eyes on Trey, on Sheila, on the street beyond, as if expecting—guarding against— a further attack.

Leaving the woman down the alley . . . to what?

Half lost in the shadows, she knelt over the man Trey and Sheila had seen entering. Pulling on his arms, trying to get him to his feet, calling out to him, her voice almost drowned by her tears.

He lay there, dead weight, unresponsive. Lost to her, and even she must have known it.

But as Trey and Sheila watched, the other two hosts stirred. Stirred as if awakening, rose to their knees, and reached for the woman.

She screamed.

Even with his sharp vision, Trey could make out only a shifting in the darkness, a tangle of limbs. The blur of her face as she fell back, the white of her stretched-wide eyes. Her hands reaching up, grasping at air.

He heard a loud, dull impact, the crack of something— her skull—breaking. The woman's second scream turned into deep-throated moans, and then silence. Yet still the two hosts worked at her body.

Trey thought about the ravening prisoner Thomas Nyramba had taken him to see in Uganda. About what that man, his brain controlled as these ones were, would have done if he'd been able to break his bonds.

"Let's go," Sheila said. Her voice was harsh in the silence.

Trey looked at her, and though he didn't speak, she understood his question.

"Home," she said.

Still he didn't move.

She made a sound that might have been a laugh. "Voting!" she said. "Now? What a ridiculous dream."

**TREY'S CELL PHONE** sounded just as they walked through the apartment door. "Granger," the caller ID read.

"We'll be ready in an hour," Malcolm said. "Get your butts over here."

Trey opened his mouth to say okay, they were on their way, but he never spoke the words. At that instant, his brain filled, overflowed, burst with white light, and then the phone had fallen from his hand and he was lying on his back on the floor.

Sheila knelt over him, her eyes full of panic, but he could barely see her. Her mouth was moving, but he couldn't hear anything but the sound of wings.

Information poured into him. Messages from the hive mind, a torrent of them, like frames spliced together from a thousand, a million, different movies. Overwhelming him, drowning him, even as he understood what he was seeing, what was happening right now, at this moment, all over the world.

There was just enough of his mind left to understand that he and Sheila had waited too long.

# FIFTY-ONE

**TREY ZOOMED ABOVE** a blood-tainted river, looking down at a mass of floating bodies. Every moment there were more, arms drooping and flapping in the current. Not waving, drowning. Drowned.

He flew amid a huge crowd, thousands of people, fleeing from a stadium. He saw them crushing, trampling, each other, witnessed those who escaped being picked off by the whirling cloud he was part of. One falling, then twenty, then a hundred. Clutching at their eyes, rolling on the ground, jerking and twitching.

He spun away from an oil tanker just as it broadsided a cruise ship. The resulting explosion caught him, killed him—he could feel his body shrivel in a wave of fire—but it didn't matter. He was instantly somewhere else, still alive, still part of the greater whole.

Such scenes and a thousand more, a million, flooding his brain. His human brain, not designed or equipped to contain, to survive this flood.

His human brain. He grabbed hold of that sense of recognition and used it to unite the shattered pieces that were still him.

*I'm Trey Gilliard. I exist—*

His vision cleared a little. He heard screams and shouts and knew they were coming not from within him but from the street outside the apartment. Sirens blared, then were cut off by the shriek of rending metal and a shattering crash. Another scream, a high-pitched sound of despair that seemed to go on and on.

Black smoke came around the door and through the windows into the apartment.

Sheila, still kneeling above Trey, was listening on his phone. She said, "Okay," snapped it shut, and bent close to him. Her face was bone white, but her expression was determined. Composed. Sheila the doctor, doing what had to be done.

"We have to go," she said.

Trey said, "No."

Or maybe he just mouthed the word. It didn't matter. Sheila understood it. "That's not a request," she said. "Come on."

Then, as his head spun from the immense keening hum, she got her shoulder under his arm and hoisted him up.

He worked, tried, to help. Somehow he got his feet under him. Not quite dead weight, though he would have fallen again if she'd let go of him.

"Where?" he managed to ask.

Sheila grimaced. He could see the tendons standing out in her neck, along her jaw, but she didn't waver.

"The park," she said.

Prospect Park. A block and a half away.

"Long Meadow."

Even farther. He shook his head. It was impossible.

Another siren blared in the distance and was cut off. He heard shouts, a loud rushing noise, what sounded like gunshots, and, farther off, an explosion. The apartment was filled with smoke.

Trey swayed on his feet, the images racing through his head joining with his own visions, his own memories. Every place he'd ever visited spun in the kaleidoscope. He could feel them being sucked out of his shattered brain and into the vast processor that was the hive mind.

The campsite where he'd lived for four months in the thorn forests of Peru, undiscovered temples rising out of jungles in Cambodia, the lion that had stood nose to nose with him at the mouth of a tent in Botswana. The grizzly bear in Montana.

His mother. His father. Christopher when he was a child. Past, present, real, or imagined, all part of the maelstrom.

It was as if time had no meaning, as if there was no place—no living thing—beyond the thieves' grasp.

Trey finally saw exactly how the hive functioned. The kaleidoscope shaking his mind free from its moorings functioned perfectly for them. They didn't need to ponder, to remember, to analyze. The wasps just saw everything at the same instant, saw and processed and acted.

It was his weakness, his humanity, that was driving him mad.

Sheila shook him. Coming back, he heard more crashes, three distant explosions in quick succession, and—most of all—the sound of wings. Not inside his head. Out there.

"We're going," she said. *"Now."*

They went, his legs maddeningly weak beneath him. Inside his head he was flying, but here he could barely walk. Yet somehow they made it across the floor to the front door and out onto the stoop.

The outside world was wreathed with black smoke billowing from the brownstone across the street. Red flames licked the sky, while white ones ate the building's heart. Already the inferno had spread to the buildings on either side.

Three fire engines, two pump trucks and one hook-and-ladder, blocked the street, engines on and lights spinning. Trey could see the bodies of three firefighters sprawled on the asphalt and one slumped behind the wheel of the hook-and-ladder. No one was left alive to hold the hoses, which writhed and danced like giant worms, vomiting streams of water first toward the sky and then in racing rivers down the street.

As they watched, the brownstone collapsed in on itself. A column of flame rose in the air. A landslide of rubble slid forward and, with a sound that shook the street, entombed everything beneath it: bodies, trucks, spewing hoses.

A blast of hot air blew past them. Thieves died in the collapse and in the burst of flames that followed. Trey saw them, felt them, *was* them. Again and again he died, but still he stood there, still he lived.

Trey saw how foolish, how weak, it was to be human. To care about something so inconsequential as a single life, when all that mattered was the whole.

Sheila pulled him forward, got him moving again.

Together they made it down the steps to the street. Then half ran, half stumbled toward the row of leafless trees that marked the edge of the park. Thieves flew freely all around them, buzzing in for the kill, peeling away when they sensed what Trey—and especially Sheila—carried.

Traffic was stopped at every corner, cars entangled like sculptures, like works of kinetic art. Stopped forever. The arteries of a city could be so easily blocked. A vast infarction, a heart attack New York could not survive.

Malcolm was just thirty miles away, but it might as well have been a thousand.

The contents of breached gas tanks spread across the streets. New fires were already erupting here and there, spreading, licking at the bases of the nearby buildings. Smoke came billowing upward from a subway entrance, carrying with it hopeless cries of terror and agony.

Trey knew that no one would be coming to fight any of these fires. By morning much of the city would be aflame.

How many other cities around the world as well?

Bodies lay here and there, but not as many as he had expected. The electricity was still on, and he could see faces in many of the windows. The horror-struck expressions of people who were terrified to stay where they were, but more terrified to go out.

He thought of the great tsunami that had struck Japan in 2011. Some people tried to flee and were swept away. Others chose to hunker down . . . and were swept away. Condemned to death, no matter which choice they made.

It went against the human belief system. There was always supposed to be an alternative. Survival was always assumed to be an option.

It was the same here. Some humans—the ones who fought back, who seemed like a threat—were being killed now, while others would be left alive to carry the thieves' young within them. Left alive for days, even weeks. But doomed nonetheless.

It was simple: Slave-makers never let anyone go free. One way or another, the only purpose in a slave's life was to serve.

# FIFTY-TWO

**THEY MADE IT** to the park. The branches above their heads stretched like skeletal white fingers into a reddish sky filled with flowing flags of smoke. In the darkness ahead, footsteps thudded, people screamed and wailed, a dog barked hysterically, and ten thousand wings whirred.

Behind them, the staccato thud of explosions and the roar of another falling building.

A half dozen steps down the path, Trey broke away from Sheila, stopped, and bent over. The crescendo inside his head raged, a battle, a war between the dictates of the hive and his desperate attempts to keep himself from being conquered.

Sheila squatted beside him.

"Why are we here?" he said.

She didn't answer. Just reached for him, helped him straighten. Through the onslaught, he could see the mix of emotions in her expression. Compassion. Understanding. Love.

"Not much farther," she said.

They moved on down the trail, but Trey knew it was hopeless. Wherever they were going, whatever Sheila's plan, it was too late. He was losing the battle, becoming unmoored. Only Sheila, her strong body holding him up, kept him standing on the earth.

"You can do this," she said into his ear.

He thought, *Maybe this form can. This . . . shell.*

But not me.

**BODIES LAY SPRAWLED** across the path, cut down as they ran. Eyeless faces turned toward the sky.

The living cowered in the shadows, their gazes following Trey and Sheila's progress.

Others were here, too. Neither dead nor alive. As Trey and Sheila stepped onto the expanse of Long Meadow, they saw a dozen shadowy forms moving across the grass. Hosts in their final rabid stage.

Roused by the frenzy of the thieves' final assault, the hosts moved among the living. Killing those who fought back, holding down those who did not resist. Thieves arched their backs and plunged their ovipositors into the flesh of people who lay on the ground, unprotesting, paralyzed with fear.

Moving fast, three of the late-stage hosts came across the night-gray grass. A middle-aged man, a young woman, and a girl in a bloodstained white dress. Trey, barely able to move, merely watched as their hands reached toward him. But Sheila stepped forward, put herself between them.

Then a nearby thief relayed a warning to the hive mind,

which immediately assessed it and sent it back out again. *Beware!* It was like a shout inside Trey's head, and he knew that the jumbled remnants of the human hosts' dying minds heard it, too. The three of them hesitated, staring at Trey and Sheila through silvery eyes before turning away.

Sheila was scanning the sky. Then, making a sound in her throat, she pulled out her cell phone. Glanced at the screen, shook her head, and dropped the phone to the ground. Turned her eyes to the sky again.

And put her hands over her ears.

At first Trey didn't understand why. Then he did.

The sound, unrecognizable, penetrated his shattered brain. A horrendous clattering roar growing louder and louder, causing even the hive mind to give off a signal of distress. Something was coming, a light and commotion in the sky above the trees to the north.

It came into view: a huge passenger jet passing overhead, perhaps fifty feet above the ground. Upside down, its windows lit, figures glimpsed in the light. Flames spat from the engine in its tail.

Trey was inside the cockpit, looking through the eyes of the single wasp within. The pilots were dead, he could see that, lying facedown over the cockpit controls.

The screaming hulk disappeared from view. An instant later, there was a tremendous blast that turned the sky a brilliant white. The trees at the far end of Long Meadow ignited, casting dancing black shadows that stretched across the grass.

The hive-mind fragment aboard the plane died and was instantly sloughed off, as meaningless as a flake of skin.

Trey lay sprawled on the ground, Sheila beside him. He rolled onto his back, staring upward.

At first he didn't see the lights above him in the flickering sky. Lights that moved, seemed to stand still, and grew brighter again.

Sheila got to her feet. She pulled off her sweater and waved it in the air.

**"TREY," SHE SAID** to him, "get up." A catch in her voice. *"Please."*

Amid the rushing of wings, the shocks that made the ground beneath him twitch and spasm, the smoke that carried the smells of burning rubber, plastic, wood, flesh, Trey saw a small two-passenger helicopter land on the meadow just twenty feet from where he lay.

Malcolm sat behind the stick inside the plastic bubble.

"If we don't get over there," Sheila said, "they'll kill him."

Trey knew she was right. The thieves would soon investigate this new arrival, judge it a threat, eliminate it.

Even now, he was with the half dozen closest ones, all turning their attention to the helicopter and the enemy within.

Sheila was running across the meadow, but Trey knew that she was going to be too late. Feet could never compete with wings. Already the wasps were finding their way through the air vents and the gap beneath the rotor and roof. Only a few seconds remained before they fulfilled their assignment: to end one more human life.

Malcolm's life.

Trey never knew how he had the thought, or whether it was a thought at all. Maybe it was just another step in being absorbed by the hive mind. Maybe it was just part of the process of abandoning who he was, who he'd been.

But somehow at that instant, Trey understood something. Something he had only guessed at when his mind blurred, split in two as he watched the attack in Florida.

He was not just a witness to the hive mind. He was a participant. He, too, was part of the whole, adding his own shard of information to the vast data trove that forged a single organism from an entire species.

He didn't have to just watch as his friend died.

Lying on the ground, unmoving, he cast his own consciousness free. He was no longer trapped in the husk of his body. He was there, in the helicopter, alongside the wasps who had come to kill Malcolm.

He was there, sounding an alarm.

*Danger.*

*Infection.*

*Death.*

Adding his voice to the constant stream of warnings that ruled the organism's actions. The same warnings that sent a flock of pigeons hurtling away from the falcon's talons, a school of fish flashing away from the marlin's sword. A burst of information designed to be instantly processed and obeyed, not questioned.

You need intelligence to question.

The thieves inside the bubble hesitated for an instant. Then, as one, they pulled back, turned their entry points into exits, and were gone. Leaving Malcolm alone, still alive.

Trey saw Sheila reach the helicopter, saw Malcolm open the hatch, saw—and heard—her shout something. But he couldn't understand what she said. Human language no longer made sense.

A moment later Sheila and Malcolm were both running across the grass toward him. Toward his body. Then Malcolm had him in an embrace, a fireman's carry, and they were heading back toward the helicopter.

When they reached it, Sheila climbed through the hatch and then reached back for Trey as Malcolm clambered over them and sat behind the controls. As she hoisted him up, and he struggled to help, the helicopter lifted from the ground.

His legs were still dangling from the open hatch. He could hear Sheila's tortured breaths as he began to slip from her grasp. But then, with one last convulsive effort, she pulled him to her. Trey's head banged against the edge of the passenger seat, something whacked him in the stomach, stealing his breath, but he was on board, the hatch door slamming shut behind him.

On their knees, they clung to each other as the helicopter rose through skeins of smoke, wallowing in the heavy, wet autumn air. Malcolm, grim faced, fought with the controls, swinging the wavering craft around to face north. The engine groaned and complained, the rotors stuttered, but their tiny lifeboat stayed aloft.

Through a thousand eyes, Trey looked out over New York. Below, the city was going dark. One block, another, and then more, more, a cascade of failures of the grid that would never be reversed.

Going dark, but for the flames.

As they flew up the East River, the hive mind's ultimate triumph rose in a wave, a climax, inside him once again. The scene overlain with a hundred others, the effortless worldwide destruction of the most powerful species on earth. Its hugest metal and stone towers crumbling like a termite mound under an anteater's claws, leaving the people hiding within as soft and vulnerable as the white ants.

Seemingly impregnable species with no defense against such an attack.

The images spewing through Trey's brain were so horrific he would have done anything to avoid seeing them. But he had no choice. They were inside him. They *were* him.

As the helicopter flew past an Empire State Building lit only by fire, he gave up at last, let the remnants of his consciousness go. Surrendered and was at peace.

# FIFTY-THREE

**HE AWOKE TO** a quiet, steady humming noise.

Not wings, neither inside nor outside his head. And not the frantic chop of a helicopter fighting its way through treacherous air. A steady, even sound, felt as much as heard.

He opened his eyes, tried to orient himself. First understanding nothing, but eventually attaining some kind of awareness. This strange shape was a body. His body, lying on its back.

His conscious mind still somewhere else. It was a tapestry so tattered you could see the light gleaming through it. A frayed flag hanging from a pole, pieces of it missing, gone forever.

He stared upward as his consciousness gathered itself. Above him was a curved surface, rows of yellow-green lights. He watched them for a while and then suddenly understood what he was looking at: the ceiling of an airplane. He was lying in the center aisle of a small jet. The hum was the sound of engines cruising through still, thin air.

His awareness sharpened. The shapes around him were faces. Sheila's face, upside down because his head was resting on her lap.

Then Kait's. Kait was squatting next to him, half in the aisle, half between two rows of seats. She had a white towel in her hand, an ice bucket at her feet, and as he shifted his eyes to look at her, she placed the cool, wet cloth against his forehead.

She saw him looking at her. Her expression was calm, only her bloodshot eyes showing any signs of emotion. "Hey," she said.

He moved his mouth, but no sound came out. Even that effort made her face blur, and he closed his eyes again.

Lying there in the dark, he thought: *At least the hive mind is quiet.*

He had that thought and realized at the same instant that he was capable of thought. That brought him part of the way back.

Listening inside, he heard only the most distant sound of wings, of screams. The thieves were still at work, but not here, and not with the intensity he'd witnessed— participated in—before unconsciousness had taken him.

For now, at least, he had been released.

He opened his eyes. Focused and tried again and managed to say, "Hey, you."

The corners of Kait's mouth turned upward. Before she could speak, though, Sheila tilted Trey's head and held a plastic cup before his mouth.

"Drink," she said.

He drank the cool water and felt his mind knit together

a little more. Taking a deep breath, he struggled to get up. At first, Sheila protested and tried to keep him where he was, but eventually she sighed and helped him sit.

He'd been lying near the back of the Citation X corporate jet that Malcolm had spent weeks refitting for long-distance travel. In preparation for this one-way journey that Trey and Sheila had almost missed.

Among the passengers, about a dozen in total, he recognized a handful. But he knew who—and what—they all were: Doctors. Scientists. Architects. Carpenters. Brilliant researchers and people who knew how to fix anything that broke.

More empty seats than had been intended, though. Trey and Sheila clearly hadn't been the only ones trapped by the thieves' sudden attack. They were just the only ones who'd been rescued.

He looked at Sheila. She was wearing the same clothes she'd had on in Brooklyn. She hadn't even washed her face, which was smudged with soot and streaked with old tears.

"That's twice now," he said, and he took in a long, ragged breath. "That you've saved me."

She tilted her head and looked into his eyes. "Just give me a chance to take a breath before you make me do it again."

Then she leaned forward and hugged him.

When they pulled apart, he said, "Where are we?"

She glanced at her watch. "About three hours out, four to go."

Trey had no memory of it, but he knew they'd left from Westchester County Airport. Now they were heading east over the Atlantic.

He looked around again, and his heart gave a sudden thump. "Where's Mariama?"

Sheila made a calming gesture with her hands. "Don't worry. She's here." A gesture toward the front of the plane. "In the cockpit."

"Help me up," he said.

"Trey . . ."

But already he was pulling himself to his feet. She helped him, and after a moment he stood, each hand on the back of a seat, propping himself up. All around, people were watching, but no one said anything.

Looking at him as if he were a walking corpse. Like he was still . . . the *other*.

He made his way forward. The cockpit door was ajar, the compartment beyond lit only with green and blue instrument lights.

With care, he pushed the door open, his eyes taking in the three figures within. Malcolm and a solidly built, blond-haired young man in khakis and a short-sleeved shirt sat at the controls. Both of them glanced back at him, then returned their attention to the black night that the jet was arrowing through.

Standing between them was Mariama, who turned. Her eyes widened and her mouth opened. Then she stepped forward and gave Trey a fierce hug.

"Don't break me, please," he managed to gasp.

She released him, stared up into his face. "You're very strong," she said.

"I don't feel strong."

Her eyes were still wide. "I didn't expect you ever to awaken."

Trey didn't reply. He looked out the cockpit window

at an icy half-moon hanging in the darkness, and then down at Malcolm sitting in the copilot's seat.

"You know," he said, "thanks."

Malcolm glanced back. "One-time offer, mate."

Trey said, "Deal."

"And if Nick here wasn't staying behind, ready to fly this bird without me, I would've left you and that brave girlfriend of yours to fate."

Trey, knowing it was the truth, shifted his gaze. "You, too, Nick. I owe you."

Nick said, "No worries."

"Christ," Malcolm said, a rough edge to his voice that Trey hadn't heard before. "Have to tell you, when those bugs were coming for me, I worried plenty."

Mariama said, "How did you protect yourself?"

"Protect myself?" Malcolm gave a laugh. "I 'protected myself' by sitting there and waiting for them to bite me." He shook his head. "Didn't do a thing. They just, like . . . disappeared on their own. Like they suddenly decided I wouldn't taste good. It must've been my lucky day."

Again Mariama turned to look at Trey. He returned her gaze but didn't say anything.

"Strong," she said again.

He was silent.

**A FEW MINUTES** later another piece of the fragile quilt of Trey's mind knitted itself back together. He remembered something new: a glimpse he'd gotten of LaGuardia Airport in the distance as they passed nearby in the helicopter. The runways blocked by abandoned airplanes and emergency vehicles. A jumbo jet broken nearly in half, flames belching from the passenger windows.

Trey said, "Your runway was clear?"

Nick said, "Clear enough."

"Man's being modest." Malcolm's voice held echoes of what Trey guessed had been a terrifying experience, even for him. "He got us off the ground with about three feet of clearance."

"I closed my eyes," Mariama said.

There was silence for a while. Then Trey asked, "Is air-traffic control still broadcasting?"

"What? Wake up, pal." Now Malcolm sounded uncharacteristically angry. "The last controller went off-air about fifteen minutes after we were airborne. You know the last thing he said before he started screaming?"

Trey waited.

" 'Don't land. Whatever you do, *don't land.*' "

The words hung in the quiet cockpit as the jet flew on, alone in the empty black sky.


**A PALE SMEAR** on the horizon ahead. Emerging from the smear, a darker line. The west coast of Africa.

The plane banked and headed south, staying over the water, skirting the coast.

"Is it over?" Mariama asked.

They were sitting in the back, where six seats faced each other. Trey, Mariama, Sheila, Mary, and Kait.

The core group, missing only one.

Trey went deep inside himself to seek an answer. "No," he said at last. Then, ". . . and yes. I think—" He struggled with the words. "I think it will take weeks or months before it's really over."

Weeks or months of unimaginable deprivation, of agony, for those humans who were still alive.

"But if you're asking whether the war is over, then I think the answer is yes. Over and lost."

"To the thieves, it's not a war," Mariama said, sounding like Jack. "They don't know the meaning of the word 'war.' To them, this was just another raid."

Trey thought about what New York City—what other cities—must look like now. "Whatever you choose to call it," he said, "we made it too damn easy for them."

"Yes."

Then Mariama's mouth firmed and her chin lifted.

"But never again," she said.


**THE PLANE BEGAN** a long, slow descent. Trey, sitting beside the window, looked out and watched as the land approached. Along the coast, a strip of white sand stretched out of sight in both directions, blue waves rolling to the shore. Beyond lay gray-green savanna, red earth, and the glistening silver stripe of a river. And, beyond that, the vast, rumpled green of the unbroken rain forest canopy stretching to the horizon.

Morning in the Casamance. Birds of prey—honey buzzards and black kites and a martial eagle—had already risen on the air currents and hung still, unmoving, as if pinned to the sky.

Beside him, Kait gazed at the forest and said, "It looks like broccoli."

Trey remembered that Malcolm had said the same thing. All those months ago, on the day they'd first glimpsed the thieves' homeland.

"One advantage to the rain forest," Sheila said from across the aisle. "You'll never run out of things to draw."

Below, a lighter streak at the edge of the forest resolved itself into a long paved airstrip. Trey recognized the field where he and Malcolm had almost crashed their plane, but it had been transformed.

Beside the airstrip stood a wooden hangar with a tin roof, a limp wind sock drooping from a pole, and, pulled out of the way, a two-seater Piper like the ones Trey and Malcolm had flown so often. Around the hangar stood a small cluster of figures.

The jet took a long swing over the forest, bumping a little on the air currents, and then aimed its nose at the runway. As they swung around, Trey caught a glimpse of buildings below. Wood and stone dormitories, storage facilities, a medical clinic, a bigger tin-roofed structure that he knew was a laboratory. People moved between the buildings or stood looking up at the approaching jet.

They'd made remarkable progress, but the hard work was just beginning. The work of keeping the human species from going extinct.

The jet made its final descent, touched the ground, bounced along, and pulled to a stop.


MARIAMA LED THE way down the stairs. Sheila and Kait helped Trey follow.

About a dozen people were there to greet them. Trey

recognized only two. One was Seydou Honso, who wrapped his arms around his daughter like he would never let go of her again.

Honso and others here in the Casamance had understood what was happening. Months before, they'd looked into the future, known what it meant, and begun to prepare.

The other familiar face belonged to Clare Shapiro, tanned and fit. She'd been one of the first foreigners to join the Senegalese.

The team she'd gathered—scientists from a dozen disciplines and as many nations—was already studying the alkaloid that provided the "vaccine" against the thieves. Unlocking its secrets. Looking toward the day when it could be synthesized, mass-produced, used to save whatever was left of the world.

Somewhere in the compound, Trey knew, he'd find Elena Stavros, a member of Clare's team. She was here with her husband and the two girls whose photo Trey had spotted on her desk. He was looking forward to seeing them.

If Elena hadn't told him about Mariama's phone call, none of them would be here today.

"You look like something the cat drug in, Gilliard," Clare said.

He summoned a smile. "And you look revoltingly healthy, Shapiro."

"I know. It doesn't suit me." She grinned, then stepped forward and, wonder of wonders, hugged him.

When she stepped back again, though, her expression was somber. "Once you're settled," she said, "come see me. We'll figure out what we can do for you."

He nodded.

She looked up into his face. "We've lost all contact with the outside. Did you see what happened?"

"I saw enough." He closed his eyes for a moment. "I'll tell you more later."

"But we're on our own now."

"Yes."

Clare drew in a long breath. "Then I'd better get back to work."

As she walked away, Trey felt someone nudge him. It was Kait, pointing over his shoulder.

"Look," she said.

Trey looked, noticing for the first time the wooden sign nailed to the side of the hangar.

*Refugia*, it read in drippy black letters. *Welcome!*

"*Refugia*," Kait said, sounding out the unfamiliar word. "What does that mean?"

Sheila came up to stand beside them. She linked one arm with Trey's, draped her other over Kait's shoulder. Her face was gaunt, pale, filled with sorrow but also fierce determination.

"It means home," she said.

# EPILOGUE
*Refugia*

**MY FATHER USED** to talk about a book, a novel, he'd read when he was a teenager. It was about a society that had survived an apocalypse, but all they had left to remind them of what came before was . . . a to-do list.

With items on it like, "Drop clothes at laundry." Things meant to be forgotten ten minutes after they were written down.

But they weren't forgotten. Not by the survivors, who were so desperate to have something, *anything*, to remind them of the past, that they began to worship the list.

Dad said that the story didn't seem very believable to him even when he was a kid. But something about it must have stuck in his head. Because soon after we arrived here, he started to insist that those of us who had been there, in the Last World, had a responsibility to write down what we remembered. To leave a record for those who were too young back then, or who were born here, or who just chose to forget.

He said we had to make sure we never get stuck with shopping lists for memories.

So here I am, sitting inside and writing, even though I'd rather be doing almost anything else. But no one gets to opt out. We all take turns, writing down our memories and telling about the lives we live now.

So future archaeologists will know we were here, we were human, and we helped build the Next World out of the ashes of the last one.

YOU'RE SUPPOSED TO write an entry every six months. I confess: It's been more like two years. One of the reasons I get away with this is because I'm the colony's resident illustrator/art teacher. I usually tell Refugia's story the best way I can—through pictures.

Back at the very beginning, on the morning after the Last World ended, Mom told me I'd never run out of things to draw. She was right, of course.

Though all I had back then was the single pad and plastic bag of colored pencils I'd brought with me. As if, when I used them up, I'd only have to visit the local art supply store to get new ones. Sure. Uh-huh.

But I was lucky. During the early years, when Malcolm and Nick were heading out on their foraging expeditions, somehow they found me a huge supply in a warehouse in what used to be the Gambia: cases of pencils, reams of paper.

But still, it wasn't enough. Not to last forever. So one of the things my students and I do now is make our own paper, paints, and inks.

That's how our world works. For as long as they last,

you use the things mass-produced in the last one— whether they're colored pencils or internal combustion engines—and then you either do without or come up with replacements.

It's amazing how little we miss the things we used to take for granted. And how much we're capable of, as a species, when we use our hands and our minds.

**BEFORE WE CAME** to Refugia, I used to draw the thieves again and again. I can't really remember why.

I don't draw them anymore. There's no need. Anyway, it would be a waste of paper.

The wasp-things. *Philanthus parkeri*.

The first species to be given a scientific name in the Next World.

**OTHER PEOPLE, THE** ones who were alive a lot longer in the Last World than I was, have told its story much better than I ever could. I was only ten when it ended, and even though I have a good memory, most of that time seems fragmentary to me now. Surreal. A dream.

It's funny talking to those who were born here. It's hard enough to describe long-distance telephone calls, the idea that we could talk with someone on the other side of the world over wires. And when you try to describe how cell phones worked, they look at you like you're insane.

It seems pretty crazy now to me, too, actually. I mean, imagine it: To send a text message to someone in the next room, you needed the help of a satellite orbiting the earth.

Who ever thought *that* was a good idea? Who ever imagined that system would last?

I remember begging for a cell phone and being told I had to wait until I was thirteen. Of course, by the time I was thirteen, no one had them. They had become part of the dream. The dream of the Last World.

You know what satellites are to us now? A show. You lie on the beach at night, looking west over the ocean, watching for meteors, and every once in a while there's this huge one, a fireball tumbling across the sky. Those are satellites falling back to earth because no one is tending to them anymore.

When he was little, my brother, Jack, asked if anyone was ever hit by a falling satellite. Mom kind of laughed and said that, even in the Last World, sometimes satellites would fall. And, yes, people would worry, but she didn't think anyone was ever actually hit by one.

"Even then, it was a pretty empty world," she said.

"But emptier now?" Jack asked.

She said, "Yes, honey. Emptier now."

And the skies are so much clearer than they used to be.


**SATELLITES. SPACESHIPS THAT** went to the moon. Airplanes flying people every which way around the earth. The world is a whole lot quieter these days, especially since the last airplane, Malcolm's baby, broke for good. How long ago was that? About ten years, I guess.

Everyone was sure its final flight would end in a crash, and Malcolm would have to walk home. But the truth was, one day it just didn't work anymore. Some part he'd been patching with bubble gum finally gave up the ghost.

That was when he began to follow his next obsession. The one that's about to take flight tomorrow.

If I can be poetic for a second.

**THE LAST TIME** I wrote here, I talked a lot about my grandma Mary. I won't go over it again, but I wanted to make sure I mentioned her. She is not forgotten.

I visit her grave sometimes, but not so often as I once did. I've decided I want to remember her alive, protecting me, bringing Mom and Dad to me.

Mom agrees. "The world is full of memorials," she says. "Memories are more important."

Mom says things like that.

Mom, Sheila Connelly, is not my birth mother. You need to know that, and also that I do remember my real ma and da. They're in all the histories people have written about the Last World. Their part was important, even though they never knew it, because it brought Grandma and me together with Mom, and then with everyone else.

Everyone else: the names in every history of Refugia. Grandma Mary's, Mom's and Dad's, Mariama's. And Jack Parker, who died rescuing us from the thieves.

The graveyard here gets steadily bigger, of course. People die . . . but not as fast as babies are born. That's how it has to be, if we're going to survive.

The first step, at least.

It's been years since the thieves killed any of us. Clare Shapiro, Elena Stavros, and their group have made the vaccine work so well that the wasps don't dare come near.

Why should they? It's still a big world out there, and they don't like the way we taste.

I wish they had stayed here in the Casamance to begin with. I wish they had never figured out that humans made good hosts. I wish they had gone extinct without ever being discovered and named.

I wish I wish I wish. But here's the truth: I'm selfish. Because I would have accepted all the lives lost to spare just one. . . .

**AS YOU ALL** know, the last person killed by the thieves was my father. Trey Gilliard.

He was never stung. Once we came here, he was protected by the vaccine, just as the rest of us are. It just came . . . too late for him. Back in the Last World, the thieves poisoned him, and despite everyone's best efforts to find a treatment—Mom's and Clare Shapiro's most of all—there was nothing that could be done.

What you also need to know is that he wasn't in pain, those last years. His mind was quiet, and that was all that mattered. That and seeing us, Jack and me and the rest of Refugia, grow up. Thrive.

Near the end, he liked most to sit on the beach and watch Malcolm, Nick, and their team at work. To sit and dream of what was to come, even if he knew he wouldn't be part of it.

The next New World.

At his funeral, everyone cried. Even Clare, though she didn't want anyone to notice.

Me? I thought I'd never stop crying. I hadn't felt like

a little girl for a long time, maybe not ever, but I did then. When I think of it, I still do.

**AS I SAID**, the thieves have the run of a big world these days, but maybe it's not as comfortable for them as it used to be. When his airplane was still working, Malcolm reported that he saw fewer and fewer every trip. They'd killed or used up too many hosts in their last great raid, and too many possible other hosts (people, dogs, horses, cattle, even rats) had died off in the chaos that followed.

The thief population had to crash, and it did. That's how things work in nature. No one escapes unscathed.

They'll never go extinct, of course. They're here to stay. We're always going to have to live alongside them.

Dad said that the human race once believed it owned the world. No one thinks that way anymore. Now we consider ourselves lucky just to get to live on it for a while.

**I MIGHT NOT** be related to Dad by blood, but I seem to have inherited his love of exploration. (He called it his itchy feet.) So when Malcolm's baby, the obsession that kept him—and whoever else he could dragoon into helping—busy every waking hour for a decade, was finally done, I was the first to sign up.

Malcolm's baby: a gorgeous square-rigged sailing ship built from tropical hardwood and equipped for ocean travel. Modeled after the great expeditionary craft that crossed the seas in the Last World, before the steam engine and the silicon chip and nuclear power and satellites took over.

After Dad died, Malcolm named it the *Trey Gilliard*. I painted the letters on the bow.

We cast off tomorrow morning. As many as Refugia can spare are going: doctors and scientists and those who, like me, just want to see what lies on the other side of the horizon.

I'm bringing a pad and a bag of colored pencils along, so when we come back I can show you all what the New World looks like.

**WE'RE PLANNING TO** find out who else is out there. Because there *must* be others, somewhere, living in their own Refugias. Everyone is sure of it, even Clare Shapiro. We have to believe we're not alone.

Dad often spoke of one Refugia he was positive still survived in the highlands of the island of New Guinea.

"You have an uncle and aunt there," he told me and Jack, right near the end. "And cousins, too. I want you to meet them."

We will, Dad. I promise.

*—Kaitlin Finneran Gilliard,*
*Founder and Citizen of Refugia*

The novel of the fantastic unknown
by the Nebula Award–winning author
of *Time Travelers Never Die*

# Jack McDevitt

# ECHO

AN ALEX BENEDICT NOVEL

Eccentric Sunset Tuttle spent a lifetime searching in vain for forms of alien life. Twenty-five years after his death, a stone tablet inscribed with cryptic symbols is revealed to be in the possession of Tuttle's onetime lover, and antiques dealer Alex Benedict is anxious to determine what secrets the tablet holds. It could be proof that Tuttle discovered what he was looking for.

To find out, Benedict and his assistant embark on their own voyage of discovery—one that will lead them directly into the path of a very determined assassin who doesn't want those secrets revealed.

M725T0712